BLOODSHOT

BLOODSHOT

CHERIE
PRIEST

SPECTRA

BALLANTINE BOOKS | NEW YORK

A Spectra Trade Paperback Original

Copyright © 2011 by Cherie Priest

All rights reserved.

Published in the United States by Spectra, an imprint of The Random House Publishing Group, a division of Random House, Inc., New York.

SPECTRA and the portrayal of a boxed "s" are trademarks of Random House, Inc.

Library of Congress Cataloging-in-Publication Data
Priest, Cherie.
Bloodshot / Cherie Priest.
p. cm.
ISBN 978-0-345-52060-9 (pbk.) — ISBN 978-0-345-52061-6 (ebook)
1. Private investigators—Fiction. 2. Vampires—Fiction. 3. Thieves—Fiction.
I. Title.
PS3616.R537B58 2011
813'.6—dc22
2010040168

Printed in the United States of America

www.ballantinebooks.com

2 4 6 8 9 7 5 3 1

Book design by Susan Turner

ACKNOWLEDGMENTS

Like most books, *Bloodshot* wouldn't have happened without the assistance, time, and input of a small army of exceedingly awesome folks. Therefore, it's only appropriate to give some shout-outs and pass along my undying (or undead?) thanks to all of the following: my amazing new editor, Anne Groell, for her outstanding patience and remarkable insight; her assistant, David Pomerico, who has kindly answered many a wacked-out question without complaint; my marvelous agent, Jennifer Jackson, for brokering the whole thing in the first place; and to my husband, Aric, who is probably sick to death of hearing about vampires.

Perpetual thanks also go to my awesome-sauce day-job boss at Subterranean (Hi, Bill and Yanni!), for helping me keep the lights on between writing gigs; to Team Seattle, scattered to the four winds though it may be; to the Seattle-area booksellers who have been so outrageously kind to me, including Steven and Vlad at Third Place Books and Duane at the University Book Store—plus the Barnes & Noble crew at Northgate, in particular Covahgin and John B.; to my webmaster Greg the Mighty, who hasn't pushed me off a cliff yet, despite what must be overwhelming temptation to do so; and as always, to everyone in the secret clubhouse that serves the world, for always believing that I can do it, even when I don't agree.

BLOODSHOT

1

You wouldn't believe some of the weird shit people pay me to steal.

Old things, new things. Expensive things, rare things, gross things.

Lately it's been naughty things.

We've all heard stories about people who regret their tattoos. But I'd rather spend eternity with Tweety Bird inked on my ass than knowing there's a hide-the-cucumber short film out there with my name on it, and my bank account tells me I'm not alone. I've done three pilfer-the-porno cases in the last eight months, and I've got another one on deck.

But I think I'm going to tell that fourth case to go to hell. Maybe I'll quit doing them altogether. They make me feel like an ambulance chaser, or one of those private dicks who earns a living by spying on cheating spouses, and that's no fun. Profitable, yes, but there's no dignity in it, and I don't need the money that badly.

In fact, I don't need the money at all. I've been at this gig for nearly a century, and in that time I've stored up quite a healthy little nest egg.

I suppose this begs the question of why I'd even bother with loathsome cases, if all I'm going to do is bitch about them. It can't be mere boredom, can it? Mere boredom cannot explain why I willingly breached the bedroom of a fifty-year-old man with a penchant for stuffed animals in *Star Trek* uniforms.

Perhaps I need to do some soul searching on this one.

But I say all that to simply say this: I was ready for a different kind of case. I would even go so far as to say I was *eager* for a different kind of case, but if you haven't heard the old adage about being careful what you wish for, and you'd like a cautionary fable based upon that finger-wagging premise, well then. Keep reading.

Have I got a doozy for *you*.

It began with a card I received in the mail. A simple card doesn't sound so strange, but the extenuating circumstances were these: (1) The card arrived at my home address; (2) it was addressed to me, personally, by name; and (3) I didn't recognize the handwriting. I can count on one hand the number of people who might send me a note at home, and I've known each of those folks for decades. This was somebody new. And instinct and experience told me that this was Not A Good Thing.

The envelope also lacked a postmark, which was a neat trick considering the locked residential boxes downstairs. So it wasn't marked in any way, and it didn't smell like anything, either. I held it under my nose and closed my eyes, and I caught a whiff of leather—from a glove? the mail carrier's bag?—and printer ink, and the rubbery taste of a moistening sponge.

What kind of prissy bitch won't lick an envelope?

That's easy. Another vampire.

Under the filthiest, most nonbathing of circumstances we don't leave much body odor, and what we do manufacture we prefer to minimize.

That extra bit of precaution told me plenty, even before I read the card. It told me that this came from someone who didn't want to be chased or traced. Somebody was trying to keep all the balls in his court, or all the cards in his hand—however you preferred to look at it.

I wasn't sure how I knew my mystery correspondent was a man, but I was right. The message within was typed in italics, as if I ought to whisper should I read it aloud. It said,

Dear Ms. Pendle,

I wish to speak with you about a business matter of utmost confidentiality and great personal significance. I have very deep pockets and I require complete discretion. Please contact me at the phone number below.

Thank you for your time,
Ian Stott

And he signed it with a drop of blood, just in case I was too dense to gather the nature of my potential client. The blood smelled sweet and a smidgen sour—not like the Asian sauce, but more like the candy. It's subtly different from the blood of a living person—both more appealing and less so. It's tough to describe.

We're dead, sort of. Everything smells and tastes different.

A few things look different, too. My pupils are permanently dilated, so although my eyes once were brown, now they're black.

I'm as white as a compact fluorescent bulb, which you might expect from a woman who avoids the sun to the best of her ability, and my teeth . . . well, I try not to show them when I smile.

They're not all incriminatingly pointy, don't get me wrong. When I yawn I'm not flashing a row of shark's choppers, but my canines are decidedly pokey. Thank God they don't hang down as long as they once did. (I know a guy. He filed them for me.) These days they may be short, but they're still sharp enough to puncture an oilcan, and that's how I like it.

My hair is more or less the same as it always was, a shade of black that doesn't require any further descriptors. It's short because—and I tell you this at the risk of dating myself—it was cut in a flapper style when I was still alive. It used to bother me that it won't grow any longer now that I'm post-viable, but I've convinced myself that it's just as well. It helps reinforce that whole "sexual ambiguity" thing.

Did I mention that already?

No? Well, it's easy to sum up. I'm on three Most Wanted lists internationally . . . and on every single one I'm listed as a man known only as "Cheshire Red." I'm not sure how this happened, or why.

I'm tallish for a woman, or shortish for a man. I'm slender, with breasts that are small enough to go unremarked. In the dark, at a glance, on a grainy security camera, I could pass for a young man. And far be it from *me* to argue with the feebs. If they want to keep on the lookout for a dude, so much the better for my career path and continued operation.

But anyway.

Ian Stott.

The number at the bottom of his summons wasn't local, and I didn't recognize the area code. Call me paranoid, but I had some reservations about dialing it up. I considered jaunting down to the nearest gas station and using the pay phone. Then I remembered that the bastard already knew where I lived, and I'd just be closing the barn door after the horse had run off. Hell, I was lucky he hadn't shown up on my doorstep.

Come to think of it, I wondered why he hadn't.

I wondered if he was watching me. I wondered if . . .

Okay. You would be right to call me paranoid, obviously, yes. But you don't survive as long as I have by being sloppy and easily accessible. That's a recipe for disaster. I'm much happier when I feel invisible.

I fondled the card between two fingers and tried to talk myself out of my phobic spiral.

He'd given me a name. Was it his real name? There was no telling. But he'd signed it properly, although I noted after looking again at the envelope, the signature didn't match the chicken-scratch scrawl of the address. The signature was large and smooth, and easy to read. My address would've been more legible if it'd been composed in pickup sticks.

Okay, so he knew where I lived, but he was respecting my space. Apparently. Again I had an irritating flash of nervousness, wondering if he was right outside—or across the street, or downstairs, or hiding in a closet.

Because I couldn't stop myself, I rushed to the hall closet and flung it open to make sure. Packed with shades of brown, black, and gray as usual, it was devoid of any two-legged lurkers. For about five seconds, I was relieved. Then I scanned the rest of the room with renewed frantic suspicion.

I grabbed a big black knife—my personal favorite, a carbon steel jobbie nearly a foot long—and I kicked in my own bathroom door. Empty. And now it also had a cracked tile on the wall where the knob had knocked it. Fantastic.

Too crazy to stop once I got myself started, I ran to the bedroom and checked that closet as well. More brown, black, and gray. No intruders.

Into the kitchen I burst. The walk-in pantry was secure.

The spare bedroom, of course! But it was likewise bereft of uninvited guests, as a mad crashing investigation shortly revealed.

Having exhausted my innate store of neurotic lunacy, I felt like an idiot. I really should've just called the number in the first place. I sat down on the arm of the couch, fished my phone out of my bag, took a deep breath, and dialed.

The phone at the other end only rang once before it was answered.

"Hello, Ms. Pendle," said a smooth, low voice.

"Hello, Mr. Stott." I tried to keep it dry and droll. No sense in letting him know he'd rattled me.

"Please, call me Ian. I thank you for responding to my message. I realize you're a busy woman, and I am certain that your time is valuable, but I wish to state up front that I'm prepared to pay you handsomely for it."

I listened hard and tried to get a good handle on the speaker. Another vampire, definitely. I'd known that much already, but hearing the preternatural, almost musical timbre in his words would've cinched it, regardless. He was well educated and calm, and American.

"That's what you implied in your note, yes," I said. "But as much as I love the money-is-no-object school of business, I still need to know what you're after before I can name a price."

"That's quite reasonable, and I'm happy to accommodate you. However, I am reluctant to discuss such a thing over the phone." Hmm. A dash of technophobia? He might be older than he sounded.

"Okay. You want to meet up? I can make that happen."

"You'll want someplace public, I expect. Bright lights, people milling about." He didn't have much of an accent, and I couldn't place what I detected. Not southern, not urban northern, not midwestern. He could've been a TV anchor if he hadn't been speaking so softly.

"This isn't a blind date, Ian. I don't need a room full of witnesses and a girlfriend who knows the get-me-outta-here safe word. There's a wine bar down on Third Street called Vina. It's dark and quiet, and it's often busy but it's never conspicuously crowded. Two primary entrances, easy to escape if necessary, easy to hide out in the open. Will that work for you?"

I heard a smile in his voice when he echoed, "A blind date. Funny you should put it that way." Then he said, "Yes, that's fine with me. Is tonight too soon?"

"Tonight is never too soon. Can you meet me there in an hour?" I checked my watch and noted that it wasn't quite eight PM. "Wait. Let's make it two hours. The bar doesn't close until two in the morning, so we'll have plenty of time to chat."

"Very well," he said. "I'll see you then, Ms. Pendle." And he hung up.

I hadn't bothered to tell him he could call me Raylene. As a freelance contractor I like to keep things stuffy on my end. I get little enough respect as it is, since I'm not affiliated with any of the major Houses—either here in town, or anywhere else.

Vampires tend to be pack animals out of social convenience. They coagulate around one particularly old, strong, or charismatic figure and entrench themselves in legitimate enterprises in much the same way the Mafia does. More often than not, this works for them. They mostly get left alone, and when they don't, they're tough enough as a group to smack down any external threats.

But external threats are few and far between, and usually they come from other vampires. Did I say that we were social creatures? I might have misspoken. It's a love–hate thing, the way we get along with one another. It's just as well there are so few of us anymore.

I could've made it down to Vina in an hour, but I didn't feel like rushing.

I felt like changing clothes, freshening up, checking my email, maybe playing a game of Internet Scrabble, and then wandering down to Third Street at my leisure.

There was method to my madness.

For one thing, it's important to always project the appearance of control. We would operate on my terms—when I want, where I want. I always try to establish this right out of the gate, because it gets clients accustomed to the idea that I'll be calling the shots. They pay me to achieve an objective. How I achieve that objective is up to my own discretion and no one else's, and I will accept no restrictions. This is not to say that I'm a rabid berserker off the leash or anything. That's bad for business and bad for the low-key, invisible vibe I struggle to maintain.

But I *am* the queen of situational ethics.

And for another thing, Stott had thrown me more than I would've cared to admit, and I needed to calm myself down. I wanted to meet him after a bath and maybe an adult beverage.

I'm not Dracula and I do drink . . . *wine.* In fact I rather enjoy it, though more than a glass at a time makes me woozy. Blame it on a semi-dead metabolism or anything else you like, but I don't process alcohol well or quickly. I've never met a vampire who does. Therefore, I kept it light—just a few sips of something out of a box. It was enough to settle my nerves, but not enough to slow me down.

I dressed, but I didn't dress up. It attracts too much attention.

I wore three shades of gray with black accents—boots, bag, et cetera. I ran a hand through my hair and called it "done." I closed my wee, lightweight laptop and stuck it into my bag. I picked up my keys and stuffed them into my pocket. And I left the condo, locking it behind me. The locking part took a full minute. I like locks, and I have some good ones.

Down in the parking garage under the building I keep a blue-gray Thunderbird. It's not the newest model, but it's not old enough to count as a classic—and it's got more miles on it than you'd guess. I could afford a better car, sure, but I like the way this one drives and no one ever looks at it twice. Only this time I left it in its assigned space. Traffic would be a bitch, parking would be worse, and I could make it to my destination in thirty minutes if I kept up a steady pace. It was all downhill, anyway.

I'm not a rooftop-to-rooftop kind of woman. Not unless I'm really desperate.

By ten o'clock I was standing outside *Vina*. I did a last-minute check of my messages, my bag, my hair, and I steeled myself. I hate meeting new people, even new clients who intend to give me money. I try to be pleasant, but I'm not very good at it. The best I can usually pull off is "professional if somewhat chilly." It's not ideal, no. But it beats "awkward and bitchy."

On the phone, I hadn't asked how I'd know Ian when I saw him, but I was willing to bet he'd be the only vampire on the premises; and if he wasn't, then I had bigger problems than his anonymity.

But no. There he was.

I saw him through the window, and knew him even before I could hear him or smell him.

It could've been his exquisite sense of posture—something you don't often see in men these days—or it could've been the way his long silver hair lay perfectly flat against his shoulders. His candle-white hands curled around the underside of a wineglass, holding it in the gentle way we vampires sometimes affect when we're holding something fragile.

Sometimes we don't know our own strength.

I let myself inside, nudging my way past a hostess and giving her a nod that told her I'd found my party. Or maybe it just told her I was a pushy, impatient cunt. Regardless, I didn't need her help to find my table.

My business date was wearing glasses. They weren't sunglasses, exactly, but they were tinted blue. The lenses didn't hide his eyes or mask them, so I wondered why he bothered.

"Ms. Pendle?" He added an unnecessary question mark to the end of my name as he rose from his chair to greet me. He extended his hand, and I took it to shake it.

"Mr. Stott. Or Ian, as you prefer."

He gestured at the seat opposite his. While I made myself comfortable, he said, "You're right on time. It's good of you to meet me so soon."

"I'm always on time," I understated. I'm usually early. "And it was good of you to stay out of my apartment."

His eyebrows knitted softly behind the wire frames. "I beg your pardon?"

"You obviously know where I live, but you went to the trouble of being polite about it. To tell you the truth, I'm still not sure how I feel about that. People usually contact me through a third party." I let my jacket dangle from the edge of my chair's back, and set my bag down on the floor next to my feet.

"Ah." He took a sip of wine, and a waitress noticed that I was drinkless.

I put in an order for something white and devoid of sparkles, and when our server had toddled off, I said, "Ah? Is that all you've got to say about it? If I were a different kind of woman, I might have perceived your invitation as a threat."

"I can assure you, I meant no such thing. I only wished to snare your attention in a way you would not ignore. I understand you make a habit of avoiding . . ." He didn't lower his voice, which was good. Other people's conversations are never so interesting as when they're whispered. "People like us."

"That's true," I confirmed. "You're my first potential client of this sort since . . . in a long time. But I'm not working for you yet, so I can't really accuse you of breaking my streak."

"I can hardly blame you for your caution. I understand that you have few family affiliations, so staying away from us is probably your wisest course. This is one reason I've gone to such lengths to seek you out."

"Is it?" I asked.

"Oh *yes*."

The server returned with a lovely crystal glass filled with shimmering liquid the color of quartz. We paused in our repartee while she set it down and asked if we needed further attentions. We told her no and sent her away.

I picked up the thread. "You're not trying to recruit me, are you? Because I know all about Japalito's drive to flesh out his organization, and I've already told him where he can stick it. Likewise, Marianne knows that she can go jump in a lake. If I wanted to be part of a House, I'd have joined up a long time ago. So if that's what you're here for, you're out of luck."

"Then let me set your mind at ease: I, too, lack any House affiliations. Anymore," he added after a pause.

I almost scooted my chair back on the spot. Instead I held my wineglass and took a hard sip. "You're an outcast?"

"Not exactly."

"What's that supposed to mean?"

He matched my sips, but he had a head start and his glass was already half empty. "Precisely what it sounds like. I'm not an outcast. There is no bounty on my head, and no allegiance you might offend if you opt to assist me. But there's a chance you might draw fire from . . . another quarter."

"Hard to believe," I grumbled.

Ian Stott pressed his lips together and squeezed out a thin smile. "I trust you're comfortable with dangerous cases. I can't imagine you charge exorbitant rates for mere cakewalks."

"I'm not afraid of a little dirty work and, generally speaking, I'm not afraid of pissing people off. But there are circles whose notice I'd prefer to escape. If there's no House hunting for you, then why set yourself apart? Who are you afraid of?"

"In my state? Almost everyone. Even you. *Especially* you."

I didn't get it, and I told him so. "Your state? What's wrong with your state?"

"You can't tell?" He seemed a bit surprised, and cautiously happy about it. "My . . . *state*." He set his wine aside and removed his wire-frame glasses, giving me a good look at his eyes.

They were as light as his hair, a silver-gray color that was part David Bowie and, I realized as they failed to focus, part Ray Charles.

He was undead. His pupils should've been like mine, big as nickels. He should've been the most striking fellow I'd ever seen, with that shocking light hair and the youthful face. All it would take to round out the package would be a set of ink-black eyes.

"You're blind? But you can't be! I've never heard of a blind . . . one of us." I was stunned, and I've got to tell you, that doesn't happen very often. All the vampires I've ever known—myself included—heal up fast and thoroughly. We're tough to knock down, and even harder to keep down because we recover so well from injury. I've always liked to consider it a trade-off for our inability to tan.

I flipped through my mental Rolodex of kindred. I could recall a guy who was missing some fingers, and I knew of one old ruffian who had lost an ear. We're not starfish; we can't regenerate lost parts. But except for the occasional old-timer with a peg leg or one-armed goon, I'd never heard of a vampire with a permanent disability. Unless . . .

"Wait. Were you blind already when you were turned?" I asked. But even as I said it, I knew it was a bad guess. It happens, sure. Mostly permanent disabilities are served up as a punishment for bad behavior. Probably not this guy, though. When folks get worked over and "turned," vampires don't just take their eyes. And they certainly aren't allowed to remain beautiful.

He shook his head. "I'm afraid not."

"And it hasn't repaired itself? How long have you been like this?" It was hard to keep the creeping horror out of my voice. I did my best to sound like I didn't want to run screaming away from him, but I *did*. It scared me in a primal way, in a way that made me sick to my stomach.

"No," he said. "It's repaired itself to the fullest extent that I can reasonably expect. And it might surprise you to know that it's much, much better now than it was ten years ago."

"Really?"

"Yes." He reapplied his glasses and took another drink. "At first there was nothing. It was as if I were wearing a blindfold. Over the years I've regained some of my vision—just bits and pieces, but it's better than before. I can track light and motion, and I can see colors if they're large and bright enough."

Something dawned on me about his initial summons. "The handwriting," I said out loud.

"Excuse me?"

"The handwriting, on the envelope. It didn't match your signature. You had someone else address it for you."

He nodded. "I have an assistant." The emphasis he placed on the word told me I wasn't supposed to worry, but it only made me worry more. His assistant was a ghoul, and bound by blood-sharing or kinship to serve him faithfully. It's rather like having a pet person. I've never gotten into that kind of thing, myself. It leaves a bad taste in my mouth. And anyway, it's dangerous.

I scanned the room and picked his "assistant" out of the crowd with ease. I'd have noticed him sooner if I'd thought to be on the lookout. He was a blond man, perhaps thirty-five years old. An aging hipster, all decked out in artfully slouched clothes that were so expensive they should've fit him better. I got the feeling he'd only recently put away his faux-hawk in favor of something looser and chunky.

I knew his type. He was maybe an asshole, and maybe just a guy who never had any direction. Well. Apprenticing yourself to a vampire—*that'll* give you direction.

"What's his name, this assistant of yours?" I asked.

"Cal. You see him over there, I assume?"

"Like for Calvin?" I still hadn't taken my eyes off him. "Yes, I see him. He's watching your back, like a good boy."

I've never trusted ghouls. There's supposedly a soul-bond that occurs when you give an ordinary mortal just enough of your blood to leave them wanting more, but not enough to change them. And it's *bullshit*. Everyone knows it. All you're doing is creating someone who's addicted to your bodily fluids—somebody who assumes that one of these days, you're going to go whole-hog and turn him (or her) into a vampire. A few decades of service (or however long) in exchange for a steady supply of your favorite drug and eventually . . . eternal life. Yeah. I can see what's in it for the ghouls.

But like any addict of any stripe, sometimes they get greedy. Or they get angry, or they fall in unrequited love with their boss, or any number of other monkey wrenches that can trash your arrangement. It doesn't happen often, but every now and again a ghoul will snap and rebel.

Those folks I mentioned before that vampires worked over? Mostly unruly ghouls. Besides, when you let somebody get that close to your affairs, he or she can do real damage when going rogue. No thanks.

In Ian's case, though, it was different. I could see how a reliable assistant could mean the difference between independence and living isolated and in fear.

"He's more than a good boy," he admonished me. "He's been my lifeline for the last six years. Please don't assume the worst. Without him, I would lead a much more limited existence."

"So he's a Seeing Eye ghoul," I said before I could stop myself. I felt stupid for having aired the observation and I cringed. I do that a lot. My mouth operates in a higher gear than my brain.

Ian didn't take it too badly. He said, "Something like that, only much more useful. And he's genuinely good company, I might add. Don't judge him by the hair gel, and try not to worry."

"Try not to worry? Your buddy over there knows where I live, and he knows a whole lot about me. I don't like any of that."

"Don't let it alarm you. You have other 'homes,' do you not? You keep a condo in Atlanta, and a house in Tampa. You have a loft in Louisville, and—"

"Knock it off," I said sharply. He was dancing on my tenderest sore spot, and it was almost enough to make me walk out. "I get it. You and your ghoul can find me. *Bravo.* But if you think you can blackmail me into taking the case by threatening my safe houses, you've got another think coming," I lied. I was keeping my voice steady, but I feared for my body chemistry. The anxiousness was rising up and it'd be welling out of my pores before long, and that wasn't good. He'd smell it and know he had the advantage.

I used to think that not much scared me. But the older I get, the longer the list of exceptions grows—and that list definitely includes Other People's Ghouls being all up in my business.

"I'm not trying to blackmail you," he insisted. "I'm trying to impress upon you how very hard I've worked to find you, and how serious I am about the importance of my case—and the discretion with which it must be handled. I told you I wasn't an outcast, but I've confessed that I've lost my sight. Can't you gather the rest?"

I said, "Don't make me."

With a sigh he said, "There is a large House in Southern California, and I was once a powerful member of it."

Ah, I got it. So I interjected, in time to look like I was paying attention, "Powerful enough that you had challengers?"

He nodded. "After *this* happened, I stayed away as a matter of necessity. I wouldn't survive until midnight if word got out that I was vulnerable . . . not even that long, if the reason for my infirmity were known."

"All right, but blind or no, you tracked me down—and that's something several international agencies have been working on for years, so don't expect me to believe you're harmless."

"I never said I was."

"Then are you going to beat around the bush all night, or are you going to explain the purpose of your business call?"

"I'm going to explain it to you," he said grouchily. "I have to. I know *what* happened to my eyes, but I need to know *how* it happened. I need to get my hands on the paperwork that documented the destruction. There's a doctor in Canada named David Keene who's trying to help me. He's sensitive to the particulars of my needs, and he's performing some research that might give me much better vision. But he's made it very clear that my chances of success depend on getting that paperwork."

"And if you give it to him, he can fix your eyes?"

He polished off the last of his wine with one more sip and waved the server away when she noticed the empty glass. "Probably not, though he thinks the improvement could be significant. It would be wonderful to read again," he said, and it was wistful and sorry. It made me feel like a heel for being hard on him.

But only for a minute.

I said, "Look, it sounds like you don't need *me*. You need a good PI, somebody who specializes in problems that afflict people like us. Not to put too fine a point on it, but tracking down paperwork isn't my specialty."

"You don't need to track it down. You only have to go and get it from a storage facility, where it's been sitting for years."

I shook my head and copied him by downing the last of my wine. "I'm missing something here. How about you start at the top and work your way down? Stop talking your way past the problem."

I smelled fear, and I was a little shocked to realize it wasn't my own. He lifted his empty glass as if to take another swig, then put it down again with a sigh. "I don't mean to beat around the bush. It's only . . . if you knew what a chance I was taking, telling you the tale—"

"Yeah, yeah. You're going out on a limb here." And all of a sudden, I understood—he'd learned so much about me in advance just in case he needed it later. If he was really this nervous about opening up, his request must be a real corker. "Keep talking, I'm listening. But find your way around to the point while the moon's still up, if you please."

He was impatient with my impatience. "Very well, the *point* is this: Ten years ago I was captured by the government. I was held for approximately six months in a maximum-security base that is so virtually unknown, I doubt even the president is aware of it. They performed experiments on me, focusing on my eyes. I escaped. And now I'm blind. I need to know what they did. And I want to know why."

Twice in one night, he'd shocked the hell out of me. I hardly knew what to say, but that didn't keep my jaws from flapping. "Wow," I said. "I did *not* see that coming. I thought maybe you'd been in some kind of duel, or you'd lost a bargain with a demon from the wrong side of the tracks. But *that*? The government? Wait—*this* government, Uncle Sam?"

If I hadn't annoyed him enough already, I was hopping up and down on his last nerve by now. "I hate to destroy any illusions you may have about the forthrightness and fairness of this nation's governing elements, but yes. It was the government, and it was *this* government, and I *still* don't know what they wanted from me."

"Who on earth—or who in the military hierarchy, as the case may be—even *believes* in vam—" I almost said it, but caught myself because my voice was getting too loud. "In this day and age, I mean. I didn't know anyone believed in us anymore, not really. Especially not anyone in the military. They seem like such a . . ." I started to say *rational bunch*, then became spontaneously aware of how idiotic it sounded.

"I didn't know either," he said, and the words were miserable.

I said, "Christ, man. I'm sorry. I didn't mean to yank your chain, but that's the craziest thing I've heard all week. Well, I don't mean you're crazy, obviously—I mean the situation is crazy—"

"I know what you mean, and I appreciate the sentiment. The situation *is* crazy, yes, and bizarre, and difficult to understand. God knows, I've spent years trying. I've played the game of *Why Me?* until I could hardly live with myself anymore, and I've gone digging around in every way I possibly can, trying to figure out why it happened." This time, when the server came by with a helpful look on her face, he agreed to another glass.

I did not.

"So you want me to get my hands on these records—your medical records," I amended. It sounded so strange, a vampire's medical records. There couldn't be many of *those* lying around.

"Yes. If Dr. Keene can see what procedures precisely were conducted, he might be able to reverse-engineer the process and restore some of my vision." He added, "He's been very kind and fair, and he urges me to keep my expectations reasonable."

"Reasonable. That must be tough."

"I'll take what I can get."

I heard a small sizzle in the air. Or I didn't *hear* it exactly, but that's the closest word I can grab for the experience. I caught a humming sound that wasn't quite a sound—it was the buzz of Ian Stott communicating with the Seeing Eye ghoul. There was nothing urgent or rushed about it. I have to assume he was telling him everything was fine, and that I wasn't going to whip out a sword and slice anyone in two right on the spot.

Cal gave a little nod and gathered his things. He paid his bill and left without so much as a wink or a smile in our direction.

"He's very discreet," Ian told me. "I found him as a graduate student out at the university, and I rather like him. He knows how to keep his head down and his mouth shut. He's told me before that it's his secret power, the ability to go unnoticed."

I shrugged and said, "He's pretty nondescript, and he certainly dresses to fit with the locals. All he needs is a band T-shirt and more facial hair, and I couldn't pick him out of a crowd."

"Like I said, he's very discreet." Ian was warming up as he was drinking down. It happens to the best of us, but I didn't want it to happen to me, so I sent the somewhat pushy, somewhat hovering server away again when she tried to foist another glass onto our tab.

No false sense of security for me. For all I knew, Ian had also been the recipient of strange metabolic experiments that let him drink like an Irish sailor.

But just in case I was holding an actual advantage, I pushed the conversation back to business. "So tell me, Ian. What do I need to know in order to get started with this case?"

"We're not going to talk money first?"

"No. Money will depend on the circumstances. And I hate to make the comparison here, but think of me as one of those expensive boutiques. If you have to ask about the cost, you probably can't afford me."

He grinned, almost exactly the same way I do—no teeth showing, just a tight pinch of the cheeks. Oh yes. The wine was relaxing him. "I can afford you. I asked as a matter of curiosity, not concern."

From underneath the table he produced a sealed manila envelope. He slid it across the table, and I took it with a question-lifted eyebrow.

"Do I open this now?"

"You can if you like. Or save it for later, whichever you prefer."

I picked at the metal tabs and squeezed the envelope to make its opening gape. Within, there were smaller envelopes, documents with black bars all over them, and something with a CONFIDENTIAL stamp that had been stamped over yet again with a mark that read DECLASSIFIED. I didn't pull any of it out to examine it then and there. He might have been comfortable with it, but I wasn't.

He told me, "That's everything I have, and it ought to be everything you need. The short version is this: A group of animal rights activists used the Freedom of Information Act to release a pile of paperwork that had nothing to do with animal experimentation." He set his wine off to the left side and started using his hands to gesture in time with his statements. I thought it was kind of cute. He'd been so uptight and controlled when I first arrived, and here he was wiggling his fingers over the table.

Ian continued, "The military had been deliberately tweaking the documents to indicate that the subjects were apes and chimpanzees, though they had an internal shorthand that designates the falsehood."

"What's this shorthand look like?"

"For vampires?" He said the word in a normal speaking voice; I doubted we were overheard, but it still made me itchy. "It's a nine-digit serial number that begins with six-three-six."

"Okay." I made a mental note of it and continued to gaze down into the shadow of the envelope. "That's easy enough to remember."

"And keep your eyes open for anything relating to Project Bloodshot," he said.

"Keep my eyes open. Very funny."

The look on his face told me he hadn't noticed he'd made a joke, but when he caught up to me he laughed, giving me a flash of teeth. They were nice teeth—picket-fence-straight with good, uniform shapes and a milky blue-white color. I'm something of a connoisseur of teeth, I suppose. You can learn a lot about someone by his teeth. Or her teeth. Especially vampires. For some of us, hygiene goes out the window when our body temperature drops. We might not need much in the way of deodorant, but I swear—a little Listerine never hurt anybody.

I could appreciate the fact that he couldn't see for shit, but he cared enough to keep himself presentable. That's dedication, right there. Or maybe it's vanity. I didn't know him well enough to say.

"Project Bloodshot," I mused as his wine-fueled mirth ran its course. "Tacky."

"I couldn't agree more."

"So they pretended on paper that you were a chimp and tinkered with your eyes, and the animal rights people got hold of the news, and they were incensed on your behalf. Or they would've been, if you'd been a monkey. Do they know you're not a monkey?"

"I hope not. I certainly don't intend to set them straight. It horrifies me enough that the government knows we're not a bedtime story; the last thing we need is for well-meaning hippies to declare us an endangered species."

He was being funny. I liked it. The red wine brought a little color to his face and made him look softer, warmer, and more like an ordinary guy instead of a powerful creature who had been crippled.

"Good point," I said. "We're close enough to extinction as it is. But far be it from me to try and bring us back from the brink."

"Oh, I don't know about that. Once in a while I get the feeling that I'm the last of my kind, alone in a godless universe. And then I . . . " He was hunting for a word. "*Detect* someone. Or I learn of someone, like you. And I find myself speculating about mysterious characters in the news, thinking that perhaps I'm less alone than I think."

He said it like it was a pleasant thing to consider. But then again, he was a little drunk.

We chatted that way for the better part of an hour while I waited for him to sober up, or for Cal to return. I didn't know which would happen first and I didn't want to leave him to his own devices. Ian Stott might not have been helpless by any stretch of the imagination, but it unsettled me, the way his eyes wouldn't focus behind those lenses, and I worried for him.

My distress over his condition could've been as simple as plain old empathy. It wasn't fair. It wasn't his fault he couldn't see. It wasn't his fault that he made me feel vulnerable, like if his sight could be taken from him, then mine could be stripped from me, too.

It wasn't fair, but life isn't fair—and as far as I know, neither is anyone's afterlife. I hope I'm wrong and there's a heaven or a hell, and that in the long run, everyone gets what's coming. Then again, if we all get what's coming to us, there won't be anybody left to see the flash of light and the puff of smoke. So I guess I don't really want to know. Sometimes I think I don't want to live forever, or live however long a vampire can make it last, but then I wonder what happens next and I'm too chicken to die.

And then I see someone like Ian.

"Forever" loses a lot of its shine when you can't see a damn thing.

At half past one, Cal returned. He didn't come inside to interrupt; I saw him through the window, milling around in the cold. He stomped his feet and tugged an oversized scarf tighter around his neck, and I would've felt sorry for him if he hadn't been too hip to wear a coat.

I could hear him, too—or sense him, or feel him, or whatever. He was sending out a psychic inquiry, the details of which I couldn't discern. But I got the gist. He was asking if all was well and if it was time for him to escort his boss home. I don't know if it was a school night or what, but Ian took the hint and signaled for the check.

I let him get it. He'd done most of the drinking, anyway.

2

Ian and I said our good-byes, and I said I'd give him a status update and a cost estimate within a few days. He agreed to this because—as he'd made clear—he was a man with reasonable expectations.

He knew better than to think I could fix his problem tonight. I'd need to pin down locations, study security systems, confirm specifics, and decide what equipment I might need to acquire. I own quite a selection of useful devices and helpful tools, but sometimes I have to order online just like everybody else.

There are faster ways to steal things, but none of those ways are very conducive to flying under any mortal radars.

Sloppy thieving leads to broken or damaged loot. Broken or damaged loot leads to a poor reputation; a poor reputation leads to fewer jobs; fewer jobs lead to lower rates; and lower rates lead to less money and eventual home-lessness, starvation, et cetera.

Sure, I'm enlarging the problem to show detail, but you see how I think.

I could sit here and complain about it—the way I live in per-manent consideration of how every slight slipup could set into mo-tion a chain of events that will lead to my death, disrepute, and ruin—but I'll restrain myself. I can't really complain about it, since that obsessive instinct has kept me alive and fed for all these years.

It's all my father's fault, anyway. Isn't that how it goes? We get to blame the things we don't like on our parents?

My dad's been dead now for longer than he was alive, but he taught me how successful being crazy can make you. He was a detective, see. He worked with the Pinkerton agency in California, back when I was a kid, and he was one of the best damn detectives you ever heard of. They still talk about him out there, and there are still pictures of him on the walls, in the boardrooms, and in the offices. I've always had it in the back of my head someplace that Dash Hammett based Sam Spade on my dad, Larry Pendle, but that's probably wishful thinking on my part.

I met Dash once or twice when I was little. He was a thin, handsome guy who was probably too smart for the room, but he didn't try to lord it over anybody. I don't remember much about him, except for him telling me once that my daddy was a great gumshoe, and I didn't know what a gumshoe was. I wound up with a weird and deeply incorrect idea of what my father did for a living.

Anyway, I liked Dash. And when I sneak myself one of his books, every now and again, before bedtime at sunrise, I hear my fa-ther's voice when I read along to Spade.

If it sounds like I'm digressing, that's probably fair; but it's not a pure digression, I assure you. I'm wending my way around to the fact that it was more than plain old money that made me take Ian's case.

It was the mystery.

He'd told me that he needed to know the *how*, and that was fine. But I wanted to know the *why*. I wanted an answer at least as badly as Ian did, and I wasn't even the victim of anything. It could be that's half of what motivated me: the thought that if I didn't understand it, I could fall prey to it, too.

But the other half of my motivation came from farther back in my brain, in the curious part that I inherited. It came from the spot in my skull that feels the burning need to unravel puzzles, finish crosswords, indulge in Internet games, and read all the mystery books I can get my grubby little paws on.

Like it or not, need it or not, and want it or not, I can't leave a good mystery alone.

And Ian's case was a mighty good mystery. There were so many questions lurking under the crust of that pie. How did Uncle Sam find out about us? What did the military want with Ian? Now that the army knows we're a fact, what do they intend to do about us?

I had other questions, too, but they had the kinds of answers I could probably pry out of Ian if I really felt the need. Among other things, I wondered how he'd gotten caught in the first place, and how he'd escaped. The longer I thought about it, the more I felt like I'd let him out of the wine bar too full of unshared information.

It might be useful to me, knowing how he was captured and what happened to him while he was in custody. Then again, it might not.

I stuffed the envelope into my bag and began the walk back home.

All of it was uphill, but that wasn't the worst thing in the world. And it was cold, but it wasn't wet outside. I was feeling pretty spry about the whole thing. I had an interesting case—

Well, no I didn't. Not really. I'm not in the business of solving mysteries. I'm in the business of *making* mysteries. But something must be hard-coded into my genes because I really loved the idea of solving *this* one. Or maybe I loved the idea of solving Ian Stott.

It'd been a long time since I'd hung around any vampires (by my own choice), and I didn't miss them much. Even so, once in a while it's nice to sit down for a beverage with someone who doesn't require any explanations. I could've said things like, "Christ, the other night I came *this close* to snacking on a trust-fund gothling, just because I loved what she was wearing. That's wrong of me, isn't it?" And then my vampire friend could say, "Oh *no*, sweetheart, I've been there!"

Granted, Ian couldn't have said any such thing. And this thought led directly into another, more personal one: How on earth did he feed? Did he operate by smell, or by hearing, or did the lovely and talented Cal bring him bags of O-negative on a platter? Come to think of it, Cal himself might make a friendly meat-sack. Did they even have that kind of relationship?

I know, I know. None of my business. But you can't blame a girl for wondering.

At the bottom of my bag, my cell phone buzzed and tooted. I paused in front of a darkened shop window and retrieved it, saw the number, and answered it fast.

Without any fanfare I demanded, "What?"

A thin, whispery voice on the other end said, "I think someone's trying to get inside." The voice sounded scared and girlish, because let's be fair—it came from a frightened little girl.

"Son of a bitch," I swore. "Listen, I'm out and about, and I don't have my car with me. I'll be there as soon as I can."

"What do I *do*?"

"Where's your brother?"

"I don't know," she breathed. "He went out. What do I do?"

"Hide," I told her. "Stay put. I'm on my way."

I flipped the phone shut, threw it back into my bag, and started to run.

I suppose I should make a few things clear before I tell too much of this part. First of all, I wasn't running out to save some scared little girl. I'd be lying if I said I didn't *like* the little girl in question; she's a perfectly nice little girl, so far as small people go. Her big brother is a bit of a dick, but he's fourteen, so that's to be expected.

I admit, to the casual observer it might appear that I'm a touch fond of them. But what I said earlier, about no pet people? That goes for kids, too. No pet kids. They're not my ghouls. They're my security system.

See, I own this old building down on the fringes of Pioneer Square. I think it used to be a factory that manufactured rubber products a century or two ago, but I'm not sure and I don't really care. At present, this building's job is to store my stuff.

Okay, so *most* of it's my stuff.

Or at least *some* of it's my stuff, and the things that aren't my personal stuff are things that I personally have stolen, and that counts, right? Sometimes it takes a while for payment and paperwork to go through over some items. And every now and again a client will die or go to jail—leaving me holding the bag, or the diamonds, or the family heirloom, or the absurdly valuable painting, or whatever.

Anyway, this old factory serves as my personal, private storage unit for all the in-transit or in-process items that I would prefer not to keep around the house. Sure, it's a bit of overkill. The place has four floors and eighteen-foot ceilings, and it occupies about a third of a city block in an old industrial neighborhood.

But nobody wants the old place, and as long as I don't try to fix it up too nice, no one will even wonder about it. It looks abandoned, and I like it that way.

Hell, it *is* abandoned. Mostly.

Except for the kids.

And now one of them had called the number that she damn well knew was *only* for emergencies, and someone was trying to get inside.

If it'd been the police, Pepper would've said so. She fears and loathes the police like only a child who's been minced through bad social service programs can. I've tried to explain to her that, at least hypothetically, the police are there to help—unless they're looking too closely at my building. She's tried to explain to *me* how she only ever sees cops when things are really terrible, and they only make things louder and scarier or worse. I maintain that we both have a point, but there's only so much arguing you can do with a second-grader whose arm is covered in cigarette burn scars.

Her brother Domino is even worse. If I don't keep an eye on him, he'll deliberately antagonize the cops. One of these days that poor little asshole is going to end up dead or in jail for life.

And then who'll look after his sister?

Not me.

No pet people. Even if they're cute and slightly fey, and smart and somewhat needy. Absolutely not. It's the cute ones you can't get rid of. Just ask anyone who's ever "kept an eye on" a stray puppy for a couple of days. You know what I'm talking about.

Also, forget everything I said before about not being a rooftop-to-rooftop kind of jogger, because I needed to get some real speed going—and I couldn't do it there on the street, in front of God and everybody. The best way to preserve my anonymity was to take to the higher path, and I don't mean Zen. I grabbed a fire escape and climbed that sucker like a scratching post.

Once I made it to the roof I was home free, for all practical values of the expression.

From my starting point I was maybe a mile from the factory

building. For the millionth time I wished that everything you hear about vampires is true. I wished I could fly, or turn into a bat, or do any one of a hundred useful things that would move me faster through space.

But I had to settle for the old-fashioned Run Like Hell.

Above the crowds, or at least the trickling late-night party-goers, I could go as fast as I'm capable—which, if I do say so my-self, is pretty damn fast. I can manage a really good clip if the cityscape is even enough.

In the old part of town, most of the roofs are more or less the same height, give or take a story or two.

I took the longest strides I could, and I made the farthest, stretching leaps that I dared manage. I pitied anyone who might've been indoors. All the grace in the world isn't church-mouse-quiet when it's flinging itself fifteen or twenty yards at a time. I'm not very heavy—though I'm not sure how much I weigh, but let's say 140 pounds. Still, drop something that weighs 140 pounds onto your roof from a great height and terrific speed, and you can bet it's going to make an impact.

It was even colder on the rooftops than it was down on the street, though that might've been my imagination, or the fact that I was moving much faster. Above me, the moon spun low across the sky and a few watery clouds hung from the stars like cobwebs. In my ears there was only the rush of the frigid air, and the pumping and thudding of my feet and my heart.

I slowed down a block away from my destination.

No sense in announcing myself.

I scanned the area with every jump, straining to see the streets and sidewalks that surrounded my building. They were empty as far as I could tell, but that didn't necessarily mean anything.

I might have a transient, or I might have something weirder and worse on my hands. I hauled myself to a stop on the edge of the roof next door. I stalked as far as I could around its perimeter, and I thought that the side door might be open a crack.

It shouldn't be.

I launched myself over the side and landed more carefully, almost silently, in the alley beside the door.

A bending on the frame and a crease in the metal showed where it'd been jimmied, and I was not reassured to note that the jimmying job appeared to have gone quite smoothly. Someone had popped it fast, and without a lot of struggle.

My stomach tightened with irritation and outright anger. Another pro?

The thought made me want to bite something until it stopped twitching. If I found another thief inside, he'd suffice.

(Yeah, or "she." I'm not trying to be a hideous sexist with my presumption of a male pronoun. I'm a lady in a tramp's game, that's all, and no one's more aware of it than me.)

I pushed my fingers lightly against the door, and it opened inward on hinges that gave only the faintest squeak. I didn't move. I waited for the squeaked alert to settle into the silence, and I listened around it.

Upstairs at least a floor—maybe even two floors—I heard footsteps that were far too dense to come from an eight-year-old girl or her teenage brother. Upstairs, a man was moving with the kind of careful precision that thinks it's being sneaky, but I heard it anyway. My ears are just like the rest of my sensory organs—exceptional, courtesy of supernatural enhancement—and Mr. Sneaky Feet did not fool *me*.

I closed the door behind myself and didn't mind the creak so much since I was alone on that floor.

I figured I was alone, anyway. I extended my mind just a tad, listening with my piddly-but-occasionally-useful psychic senses for the heartbeat of something small, crouched, and concealed. No,

Pepper wasn't down here. She was upstairs someplace. At the very fringe of my perception, I sensed her heart fluttering like a canary in a coal-mine cage.

She was terrified, and becoming more so with every passing second. Wherever she was hiding, I hoped she was fully concealed.

I crossed the room lightly, dodging between the boxes and ducking past the crates stored on shelves overhead. I reached the stairwell door and gave it a swift but controlled yank, pulling it away from the frame and slipping through the opening. It shut itself behind me, tugged back into place by a set of fat iron coils that passed for springs.

It didn't make enough noise to give me away, not to an intruder a full floor above.

Or so I thought—until he quit moving.

He froze and I froze, because I knew good and well that I'd been quiet even in my haste. So either he'd heard me, or he'd found something he wanted. But I didn't get the feeling, from the eager silence that smothered the whole building, that he was examining anything. I got the feeling that he was waiting to hear that sound again.

If he'd found Pepper, everyone within a mile would've known it. That child can scream like no mere mortal I've ever met. I tell her that she must be part banshee, and I'm only half teasing.

Wherever she was stashed, her presence had gone undetected.

Mine, on the other hand, might have been blown.

I waited for him to make the next move. He didn't. He was patient, the son of a bitch. I had to give him credit.

All right. That was fine. I had worn my comfy boots—chosen partly because they look good with everything, and partly because they have soft leather soles that don't make a peep when I walk in them. Yes, I am *always* prepared for action. Trust me when I say it *seriously* beats the alternative.

My initial guess had been that this was another professional creeping in on my turf—trying to steal my rightfully ill-gotten gains. But a second possibility dawned on me. Could it be another vampire?

What were the odds? Prior to Ian Stott, I hadn't seen or spoken with another one of my kind in . . . I had to think about it . . . the better part of five years. And then two in one night? Surely not.

But I didn't believe he was holding still up there. I didn't believe he was that patient, or that stupid. It's one thing to hold your ground and wait out a threat—but this guy was out in the open on the floor above me. From his last foothold I'd guessed his location, and there was no way he was just camping there, waiting for me to come smack him around.

That's what I told myself. My ears argued. They couldn't hear a thing. Not a scraping boot or an accidentally brushed box. Nothing.

I wasn't armed with much.

When I left the condo, I'd been heading out to meet a potential client in a public place; there was no sense in dragging a big blade or a big gun along. And it's not like I live in fear of being mugged or anything.

However, I *do* live in semi-nervousness (if not fear) of having my storage facility breached, so there was a stash of weaponry on the premises. I don't leave the stuff out in the open—not least of all because I don't want Pepper or Domino to get hold of it—but behind a pair of loose boards under the stairwell I keep some sharp things, some loud things, and some heavy things.

"Fuck it," I said under my breath. He knew I was there, and I knew he was there, and he was either sneaking up on me or sneaking away. I threw my quest for absolute silence out the window and made a headlong charge for my cache of deadly items. I didn't feel like I had time to make a cautious prying of the boards, so I punched my fist through the top one and grabbed whatever my hand found first.

The Glock subcompact. Noisy, but effective. I crammed it down the back of my waistband and made a little squeak. That thing was *cold* against my spine. But I'd rather not shoot if I don't have to; why call more attention to a tense situation? Let's not wake the neighbors.

I threw my purse into the hole. There was nothing useful inside it except the laptop, which wasn't much of a melee weapon.

I took another split second to fish around and pulled out a reverse-blade katana that I almost never use, but in which I place a great deal of faith. I love a good sword. In this day and age, it's so damn *unexpected*.

There was more inside the cubbyhole, but I was in a hurry.

With the gun in the back of my pants and the sword held in the ready position, I bounded up the stairs with more speed and light-footedness than anyone should've been prepared to expect. At the second-floor landing I made a fast ninety-degree turn and broke for the main room.

Its floor plan was open in order to accommodate machines and workstations; it wasn't created to be a maze. But fifty years' worth of accumulated junk can turn almost anyplace into a labyrinth, and for a brief second I thanked heaven that I hadn't owned the building any longer than that. It was hard enough to navigate around the boxes, crates, slabs, and refurbish-ready sheets of drywall as it was.

I whipped my way around the corner and stopped, then jerked myself back into the hallway. The asshole had turned the light on. The lone bulb swung dimly from a contractor's-style wire frame, which had been draped over a high beam.

On the floor beside me I saw a large black bolt, covered in dust. I picked it up and flung it into the light, which shattered, and the whole room fell into darkness.

Good.

The advantage was once again mine. If he'd had any special night-vision glasses, my intruder wouldn't have turned the bulb on in the first place. So now he was blind, and I was in my element. We were on my turf, surrounded by my belongings. The setting was homey to me, and unfamiliar to him. It was only a matter of time before he blew it and I turned him inside out.

So why the hell couldn't I find him?

Back in sneak mode, I crouched down low and went tiptoeing across the slightly cleared expanse between two rows of shelving units.

I saw boxes and books, and open crates with files, and old pieces of manufacturing equipment that had come with the building. I'd left them, because they were too heavy to move without assistance, and I didn't want any assistance. Let 'em sit there and rust, that's what I figured. They weren't hurting anything.

Except now they were providing cover to my intruder.

I sniffed the air like a dog—which is not a comparison I'm fond of, but it's accurate. I can't smell as effectively as a dog can, but my nose is comparable to a cat's, and I can learn a lot about a room by tipping my nostrils into the air.

For example, even though I couldn't see her, I knew that Pepper was off to my left—burrowed back inside the old air system. I can't always be so specific, but the scent of freshly disturbed aluminum and stale air gave away her hiding place. I felt a twinge of admiration for her. She'd found a good spot, and she was following directions. Hold still. Stay quiet. *Done.*

And I knew that there had been a man paused roughly beneath the now-broken lightbulb not thirty seconds earlier.

I couldn't tell much about him, though. No after-odor of shampoo or cologne lingering in his wake. No *eau de guy* funk. All he left was a trace of minty-smelling astringent.

My nervousness was climbing to new heights.

A professional jimmy-job. Super-quiet movement. Prepared for the prospect of a superhuman nose, or at least a propensity toward mouthwash. This was Not Good.

And I still hadn't gotten a good look at him yet. I didn't even know where he was, but I didn't think he'd left.

Pepper was still hiding, and even if she didn't have my hearing or eyesight, she had exceptional instincts. I hunkered myself against a wall, taking preemptive cover between an old rubber-cutting device the size of a compact car and a set of steel shelves that reached halfway to the ceiling. There was nothing behind me but a brick wall. I was as safe as I was going to get.

But I felt like I was wide open, standing in a clearing, holding up a sign that said, COME AND GET ME.

I was straining for all I was worth—to hear something, or smell something, or see something. *It's not another vampire,* I thought. He wouldn't have turned on the lights. Whoever he was, he was mortal enough to die. And I was immortal enough to take quite a beating before going down, so what exactly was I so afraid of?

Again I tried to run a scan with my mind. My psychic powers aren't profound, and I'm lucky I have any at all. Some vampires don't, and those who do tend to be women—though nobody knows why. It's kind of like how men are more likely to be left-handed or color-blind; it's not a hard, fast rule, but a generality. My abilities aren't very good, but they give me a slight leg up.

I can usually scope a room and pinpoint the places where everyone was standing. Or sitting.

Or . . .

I looked up.

There he was, doing his best bat impression—hanging from a square iron beam that used to be part of a ceiling track for machinery. He was clinging to the support at the other end of the room like a baby monkey on its mama's back.

And he saw me.

He'd probably seen me come bursting in, smashing up the light, and squatting behind my inherited machinery. He'd been watching the whole time, and now he could see me, seeing him.

I did not wait for him to make the first move. He'd already made the first move by breaking into my building. If that isn't a grievous act of aggression, then I just don't know what is.

With a scramble worthy of the aforementioned monkey, he righted himself on the beam and scurried along it. He was running toward me, and I was running toward him, but he was about twelve feet above me and I was on the floor.

As soon as I realized what he was up to, I hit my metaphoric brakes and doubled back to the door. He was trying to zip past me and get out behind me. No way, José. Whoever he was, he wasn't going anywhere until I'd gotten some answers or some blood. I'd settle for either one, but I'd shoot for both.

I reached the door about half a second before he could. I kicked it shut and whirled on my heels, katana poised, as I faced him.

He did a backward shuffle-hop on the beam and I was certain he was going to fall, but he didn't. Instead he did a quick gaze-around-the-room, then bolted down a side beam toward a small square window at the far end of the premises.

Never at any point did he appear properly on the verge of panic. And never at any point did I get the impression that the darkness was inhibiting his flight.

I didn't see any goggles or glasses but he wasn't missing a step, and that beam wasn't more than eight inches wide. Great. I had a night-spying ninja on my hands. Was he armed? I couldn't tell. He wasn't trying to fight back yet; he was intent on getting away—which was a good move on his part because when I caught him, I intended to hurt him. A lot.

I chased him from the floor level, tagging along underneath him as he bolted for the nearest promising exit, and while we raced, my hopeful guess that he wasn't a vampire was borne out. I outpaced him easily—skipping up a stack of crates and vaulting up onto the beam between him and the window without even breaking a sweat.

Yes, I know. I already told you that we don't sweat. But you get the idea.

Now he was nervous. He'd kept his cool nicely until we were eye-to-eye and he was empty-handed against my sword and my terrifically bad attitude.

In the fraction of a moment between me startling him into immobility and his fight-or-flight mechanism kicking in again, I sized him up.

He was taller than me by a fair measure, probably a whole head taller, but it was hard to tell with both of us crouching to keep from knocking our heads on the ceiling. Wearing black from head to toe, he might've stood out on any street except for one in downtown Seattle. Even his hat was black, and fitted close against his head. Around his eyes and across his cheeks he'd smudged black greasepaint, which I thought was overkill. How much difference did he think the guyliner would make?

Not enough to save his ass, I could promise him that.

I don't know what the track used to carry, but it must've been heavy, because it didn't creak at all beneath our weight—not even when I bounced on it just a touch to see how stable it was. I'd never fought anybody Errol-Flynn-style before, up on some high ballast. I wasn't really looking forward to it, but if I was going to cut the shit out of some guy while trying to hold my balance, I wanted to be sure that the surface would hold us both.

He beat a retreat, backward, not very well this time.

His right foot missed, almost, he slipped, and I'll be damned—he caught himself, just in time to sling out an arm and snag the beam. He lowered himself in a hasty drop that was impressively smooth and painless.

I jumped down after him, and it was equally smooth and painless. Probably more so, since I'd made my descent on purpose. I was almost disappointed that he hadn't seen me do it, but he'd turned tail and was running like the wind again, back to the door, betting that I'd only kicked it shut and that I hadn't broken it. He was willing to give it another shot, since he didn't have much of a choice.

"Oh no you don't," I told him, and before he'd gotten another two steps I was in front of him. He tried another direction, but I was in front of him that way, too. And there it was, the fear, wafting up off his skin. His eyes, too. Smudged with the greasepaint for added invisibility (or something), they were on fire with the realization that he had not been busted by some half-asleep rent-a-cop.

As for my eyes, they were probably on fire, too. I could smell him and it turned me on, for lack of a better way to put it. I was hungry; I hadn't eaten in the better part of a month, and look. Delivery.

I grabbed him by the throat and I would've killed him on the spot but I felt like someone was watching me and I hesitated.

Oh yeah. Pepper. She'd crawled out of her hidey-hole and she was staring, blank-faced, at our little tussle.

The guy in my grasp twisted and managed to kick me hard in the gut. It hurt, yes. I made the appropriate "oof" noise and almost let go, but didn't. He kicked again, but I dodged that one. With the momentum of my dodge, I pulled him after me, yanking him off his feet and dragging him over to the door. Hey, he'd wanted to go there, right? I was only helping.

I knocked the door open with my shoulder, even though it was supposed to open in, and not out. So I'd have to replace the hinges later. No big deal. But I was angry, and wound up, and trying to blow off enough steam to keep from sucking him dry in front of a little girl.

He fought like a wolf, though. He wrestled and contorted himself, and it was hard for me to drag him along by the throat or anything else, but I did it. I hauled him a few feet at a time, letting him use his weight to play a futile game of tug-of-war. Back and forth we went, me gaining ground, and him losing it.

Out to the stairs we bumbled, and I threw him down them, which took the edge right off him. After that, he was slower and easier to haul. We had one more flight of stairs to the basement, and he took them the hard way, too. At the bottom I half dragged, half kicked him around the nearest corner with a door so I could close it and make sure we were alone.

It's more than being a secretive eater. It's a matter of practicality (easier to force him down than up), and consideration for others (Pepper, who frankly did *not* need to see it), and ease of cleanup (concrete floor with a slightly sinking foundation).

Down in the basement it was so dark that even I could barely see, but I didn't mind so I didn't do anything to correct the situation.

My quarry was starting to babble. I don't usually like to start up conversations with people I intend to nosh on, but I wanted to know what this paramilitary freak was doing on my premises, and it was either ask him now or figure it out later.

I planted my boot in his back somewhere near his kidney.

He groaned, and I demanded, "What are you doing here?"

He groaned some more, so I swung my foot into his ribs some more until he answered, "Looking around. Just looking around."

I could smell blood when he talked. His face must've met the corner of a stair. Good. Or rather, good for me. Bad for him. Between the salt-and-vinegar tang of his sweat and the rich, metallic scent of bleeding, he needed to talk fast. He had less time left in this world than he knew.

"Bullshit," I told him. The word came out funny. I was salivating to a degree that could best be described as embarrassing.

He fumbled around, reaching for something. I didn't want him to retrieve any weapons or get a good handle on anything potentially defensive that might be lying around on the floor, so I pounced down on him, rolled him over, and pinned him spread-eagle. I tried not to drool all over him when I said, "Tell me what you're doing here, or you're never leaving this room alive."

"Just looking!" he almost wailed. "And climbing . . . climbing around," he added.

I didn't believe him.

Nobody dresses so thoroughly in special-ops garb just to take a stroll through an old building. But he didn't sound like he was ready to spill any good beans, and the smell of him had me so starved that before I could even make the conscious decision to bite, my hand was over his mouth and my teeth were in his throat.

He struggled and whimpered, but not for long. Going head-first down the stairs had really softened him up, and I filed the information away for future reference. Violent trip down the stairs equals bruised-up victim who doesn't fight hard and doesn't lose too much extra blood ahead of time.

My dad once told me that the old mob boys used bags of oranges to beat the snot out of people. I'd always thought it was strange before. Now it made a little more sense, at least from a vampiric standpoint.

I took my time feeding on the trespasser.

It's rare that I take human meals—or any meals at all, anymore. Mostly I do what other vampires do and settle for whatever I can nab from a sympathetic butcher's shop—or else bribe a blood-bank worker to slip you a little on the side (my personal preference, in a pinch). Only sometimes do I ever pick off a real, live person. I don't need to feed like I once did. When I was first turned I needed it every night—or else. But the older I get, the less necessary it is. I suppose it's like newlywed sex. The first few years, you get busy anytime, anywhere, baby. But after a few anniversaries, you'd rather stay up and watch Leno.

Still, every time I'm facedown in a gushing artery, I swear to God it feels like the first time all over again—and I wonder how on earth I've gone so long without it. The hot, sticky taste of rust and salt goes down so smoothly, if not tidily. I've read that the average human body holds about six quarts of blood, and that sounds about right. Depending on how hungry I am, I can hold maybe three of those quarts. In leaner times, or in more convenient times if I had a lot of equipment, I might try to pound, squeeze, or suck the last drops out and store them. But this wasn't one of those times.

This was a dine-and-dash of a whole different sort.

He was malleable and unconscious in under a minute. He was dead in twice that long.

When I finished I sat back and panted, because it's exhausting and exhilarating, taking a meal like that after it's been a while. It's also a bit disorienting—like afterglow, and there I go again with the sexual metaphors. Am I being too obvious? Well then, fine. It *is* sort of like sex. The biting, the fluids, the sucking, the feelings of bliss and elation (for me, if not the victim) . . . it's such an easy comparison to make that naughty-minded writers have been doing it for hundreds of years.

So I was down there still, catching my breath, and up above I heard the pattering steps of little girl feet, joined by older boy feet. Domino. I hadn't heard him come inside and up the stairs, but that's no surprise. I wouldn't have heard an air horn up my ass while I was feeding.

Their voices hummed quietly. She was explaining, he was listening, then he was swearing, and she was trying to calm him down. He was getting mad, and she was getting patient; he was talking about all the things he would've done if he'd been there, and she was telling him that it was okay because I'd taken care of it.

I didn't need to hear the exact words. I could infer.

Guilt followed. He never should've left her here alone—no, sometimes he had to, and that was okay, and he shouldn't feel bad about it, blah blah blah. Pepper's got far more patience than I do. If I'd been up there, I would've popped him in the mouth.

But I wasn't up there, I was down in the basement with the slowly cooling husk of my latest meal. It was like a bad one-night stand. I was finished with him, and I didn't want anything more to do with him. Ten minutes before he'd been irresistible. Now he was a mess that needed cleaning up.

I stood and my legs were shaky, but my buzz was losing the worst of its befuddling powers and I found the light switch by the door without any trouble. I can see all right in the dark, yes, but like everybody else I see better with a little illumination. One bald lightbulb like the one upstairs gave me plenty of glow to see by; in fact, for a moment it was almost too much. I let my eyes adjust and then came back over to the battered fellow who was lying on my floor, mucking up the dust with his excess seepage.

I sat on my heels down beside him and began to poke my fingers around in his clothes.

Most of what he was wearing came from Banana Republic. Odd. I'd figured it for military surplus.

I lifted his shirt and found a cheesy tribal tattoo across his belly. Unimpressed by this show of flash-art individuality, I went digging through his pants and remained unimpressed by what I found there, too. By which I mean I found his wallet, and there wasn't much in it—thirty-four bucks and a condom, with a driver's license that identified him as Trevor Graham.

I immediately felt better about killing him. I've never known a Trevor who wasn't a total douchebag. It's just one of those names that goes so nicely with selfish, arrogant, malicious behavior—and really, what did I know about this guy? Nothing, except that his name was Trevor and he'd been nabbed in the midst of breaking-and-entering. That was plenty.

The score was Raylene: 1/Trevors of the world: 0.

This is not to say that I feel the need to justify my choices in victims—far from it. No, I'm only being practical. Here in the real world, where I do my best to remain unnoticed, it's simply illogical to run around killing small children on their way to school, or old ladies who bake cookies for all their neighbors, or upstanding medical professionals and charity workers.

Because those people are missed, that's why.

They're missed promptly, and they're missed badly, and they're avenged by the media or the cops. And I really don't need that kind of attention.

From Trevor's wallet a couple slips of paper floated leaf-like onto the floor. The first one was a business card for a group professing that "anyone can learn *parcours*, and reap the benefits of high-energy, high-interest exercise that doubles as a defensive art."

Sounded like bullshit to me.

The other piece of paper had a phone number on it, next to a scrawl that read "Major" something-or-another, and the note, "about the website." I hung on to the note and the business card, took the money out of his wallet—because hey, why not?—and crammed it back into his pocket.

It was cold down there in the basement, and Trevor's spilled blood was already turning black.

I listened to the kids upstairs, and this time the talk was all about how they ought to go down and see if I was all right, no because I could take care of myself (she was right, obviously) and maybe I'd gotten hurt and that's why it was so quiet, or maybe I'd just left and hadn't told them, and so forth, and so on.

Over by the wall the building's foundation is starting to drop away from the supports, which makes my building in no way unique in the city of Seattle. Many of the older structures are suffering similar fates, due to the fact that they're built on tons upon tons of sawdust. It's a long, stupid story. The highlights version is this: The old parts of the city are sinking, and no one knows how low they'll go because no one knows how much sawdust is underneath it. It's a thrilling place to live, I tell you.

One of these days, my poor factory is either going to need serious remodeling or it's going to get torn down—and my money's on demolition.

But back to Trevor.

Over by the wall where the foundation is peeling away, the earth under the city is exposed and there's a great wealth of mold, mud, moss, and general dampness. If it were warm, it'd be an absolutely God-given place to dispose of bodies *au naturel;* but since it's cold under there, it's not quite perfect. The process of decay takes a little longer when it's chilly, but since it rarely freezes and there are fugitive wharf rats under the place by the score, I could safely bet that Trevor would be reduced to bones within a few weeks at most, a few days at best.

I took a box lid and broke it in two, then used one side to dig the wall away a little more. Was I unbalancing the precarious stability of the factory's structural integrity? I doubted it. It'd remained upright this long; it could remain upright with a little less footing just a little longer.

I folded Trevor like a clean shirt and inserted him into the muddy slot like a pizza going into an oven. Then I scraped down enough dirt to cover him up good and keep the stink down.

Small feet scampered up to the edge of the stairs out in the hall. Pepper asked, "Raylene? You okay down there?" She's such a smart kid. She said it in a normal speaking voice, not in a grade-school holler that could shatter the ears of coal miners in West Virginia.

I heard her, even through the door I'd closed between us. I didn't holler back. I dusted my hands off on my pants and opened the door. I told her, "Yes, baby, I'm fine. Everything's fine, and you can quit worrying. I'm just cleaning up down here, all right?"

"Okay," she said, and it was as simple as that. She said in a whisper to Domino, "I told you she was fine. Leave her alone. She's cleaning up."

Her big brother kept his mouth shut for once. Both of them retreated from the edge of the stairs. I'd forgotten how they both hated the basement, but I was glad to remember it, even if I didn't understand it. I don't think it's haunted or anything, though I could be wrong, and no, there aren't any windows—but most of the windows upstairs are boarded up anyway, so it's not very different from any other floor.

Whatever the reason, I was glad they avoided it, and I was doubly glad now that I was hiding bodies down there. The odds were low that either child would take a spade and investigate a mushy spot in the wall even if they did find such a hole.

By the time I'd concealed Trevor as well as he was going to get concealed, the kids were getting impatient and I wasn't getting any cleaner. I shuddered to wonder what I looked like. I could take a guess, and that guess was gruesome.

At least my hair was dark enough not to show any splatter—and that was one more advantage to having it short: It stayed out of tasty open wounds.

There was no working washroom down in the basement, but there was one on the first floor, and that was where my purse was still located, anyway. I wiped my face on the back of my sleeve, hoped I wasn't leaving some ghastly clot sitting on my cheek, and took the stairs back up to the cubbyhole where I'd tossed my personal effects.

Pepper was there, solemn and silent, with her hands folded behind her back. She could be a creepy thing sometimes. That's probably why I like her so much.

"Hey." I gave her an awkward greeting. I didn't try to hide the cubbyhole, since it was busted wide open and the kids had surely seen it already. I reached inside and retrieved my bag, then told her, "I'm going to hit the ladies' room. Give me a second, huh?"

Inside the narrow water closet the kids had stuck a piece of broken mirror up over the sink. The mirror told me I'd seen better days, but I wasn't about to instigate widespread panic with my appearance, either. I made a show of washing up and pretending that I was an ordinary, civilized woman who was, perhaps, recovering from a bad date—and who had most certainly *not* been hiding bodies in anybody's basement.

My hands had gotten the worst of it. I scrubbed as much of the muck out from under my nails as I could, splashed a little water on my face, and left the restroom with what I hoped was a friendly smile.

"Hey guys," I said to the pair of them, since they were both hanging out right on the other side of the bathroom door like a couple of cats. "You two, uh. Are you all right?"

Domino answered with another question. "What the hell happened?" he demanded, his scruffy little almost-gonna-be-facial-hair swirling around on his chin.

My smile dissolved, to be replaced by an eye roll. "Ask your sister," I said.

"I did. She said some guy broke in here. Guys aren't supposed to break in here," he informed me, as if it were a news flash. "Who was he?"

I said, "Trevor. He was just looking around. It's taken care of, and I'd like to consider the subject dropped."

"Where is he?"

"Didn't I just say something about a dropped subject? He left."

The boy fired off a frown that called me a liar. "He left?"

"Yes. I threw him out. He won't be coming back."

"You threw him out from the basement?"

"No," I lied. "I threw him out through the first floor, before you got here. I went down in the basement because I was looking for something. I figured, since Pepper had called me here with an alarm, I might as well be productive."

Domino was not convinced. He folded his arms and acted like he wasn't going to let me past him until I gave him some answers, but I don't take orders from teenage boys, and I moved him aside by twisting his shoulder like it was the hot-water knob in the shower. He squealed a protest and said to my back as I walked away, "What was it?"

"What?"

"What did you get from downstairs?"

Damn him for being so sharp. "Nothing." And that was the truth, wasn't it? "I couldn't find it. That's what took me so long. I was . . . digging around." More truth. I was practically telling the truth! Look at me, a veritable choir girl.

"What were you *looking for*?" He tagged along behind me, and Pepper tagged along behind him.

I led them Pied-Piper-style into the stairwell and up to the second floor, where they live. I said, "That's none of your goddamn business, and you know it. What are the rules? Do I need to make a list of rules again? I know you thought they were insulting, but you're almost a man now. It's about time you learned how to take an insult from a woman."

I was mostly being flippant, but I got a bit mean because if I could piss him off, I could distract him from the original subject.

"You're a bitch," he spit. I told you he was obnoxious.

"So go find another landlord, you little shit. Speaking of which, how are the accommodations holding up, my darling illegal tenants?"

"They suck," he complained.

"They don't suck," Pepper argued. "They're fine. Everything's fine, like you said."

"Good to hear, baby. Heat's still running all right?"

"No," Domino groused. "It's freezing downstairs."

"But it's warm enough on *this* floor, right?" I asked.

"Yeah, it's okay," he sullenly confessed.

"Then I don't care about the rest of the place. I can see that the power's still working, though I owe you a new lightbulb," I noted. The heat didn't work anywhere else in the building, by my own design. For one thing, heating that monster of a place was fucking expensive. For another, I kept my least interesting stuff on the second floor, so the less time they spent wandering the other levels, the better. If there weren't so much of it, I'd just haul it all down to the basement and trust that they wouldn't touch it, but it's so hideously damp that nothing will keep. I already have to run half a dozen dehumidifiers upstairs to keep the contents from moldering into oblivion. That's where the rest of the power bill goes.

I put my hands on my hips and looked around, trying to see what—if anything—Trevor had disturbed. I didn't see anything opened or tampered with, and then I remembered that there was a short, beady-eyed witness standing right behind me.

"Peps, what did our uninvited guest seem most interested in?"

She shrugged and said, "I don't know. He was just looking around. And climbing around. He could climb real good."

"Yes he could," I agreed. I hadn't seen him do anything special, but he hadn't made it to the machinery rail by teleporting. "I wonder what he wanted."

"You didn't ask him?" Domino said, naked skepticism dripping off his words.

"He wasn't very forthcoming," I murmured.

Pepper asked, "What does that mean?"

"It means I asked, but he wouldn't tell me. Listen, hang on, would you? Let me go get another lightbulb. I'll swipe one from downstairs." I trotted back down there, removed the bulb, then returned, pushing a crate underneath the contractor's cage with the long orange cord. I crawled on top of the crate and screwed the bulb into the groove. It came on, searing my eyes with the suddenness of its glare.

I looked away, and then back at the room underneath me.

Off in the corner, a mattress was lying on the floor, covered with a gorgeous silk and feather-down duvet that was intended for use on my bed, only it never made it there. I'd bought it in India a couple of years before; I'd been indulging in some retail therapy in an attempt to unwind from a difficult case when I spied the blood-red bedding with pretty, understated swaths of gold threadwork. I bought it, boxed it up with some other goodies for yours truly, and shipped it back to the States to the storage facility via a museum contact of mine.

That museum contact is another story. I'll get around to telling it later; I'm wandering far enough off topic as it is.

Anyway, I got home to Seattle and went looking for my box of goodies, and when I found it, it had been opened. It had been raided. And the culprits were still in the building. I rounded up Domino and interrogated him, because I couldn't find Pepper—who back then was just plain *tiny*, and who has always had a gift for hidihg in unlikely and inaccessible places.

Domino clearly didn't know shit. I figured out he was only

squatting so I made plans for better locks and prepared to evict him . . . but I couldn't. He wouldn't let me, and he had a good excuse. His little sister was somewhere in the building and he couldn't find her. He couldn't leave without her, could he? No, no of course not.

I gave him twenty-four hours to shoehorn the kid out of her hiding spot and told him that when I came back, they'd both better be gone.

But when I came back, she was still hiding—or she'd gone into hiding again, whichever. Domino begged another twenty-four hours off me, and when I came back yet again, I couldn't find either one of them. To this very day I don't know where they were hiding. They won't tell me, in case I get a wild hare up my ass and decide to throw them out again.

How did they know I wouldn't call the cops and force an eviction? My guess is that they'd done enough exploring and/or opening of boxes to gather that I wasn't exactly jonesing for civic scrutiny. Or maybe they were just stubborn enough not to care, I don't know.

From then on out I started treating them—to abuse the comparison again—like stray cats. I tried to coax them out of hiding with food, and that didn't work. So I tried to coax them out with money, and that didn't work either. Then I tore the place apart trying to find them and fling them out onto the streets with my bare hands, if necessary, and I failed royally at this attempt also.

It took me more than a year to figure out that I was taking care of them. All that time, I thought I'd been trying to eliminate some pests. But no. I'd been feeding the strays, and now they belonged to me.

The more I thought about it, the more accustomed to the idea I became. After all, if homeless people were going to make themselves comfortable on my property, they might as well be homeless people who answered to *me*. Eventually I gave them a prepaid cell phone (for emergency use only, thank you, Pepper, good girl) and turned the power on so they wouldn't freeze to death during the winter. Could I do more for them? Probably. But remember what I said about not keeping pet people? This factory isn't my doll-house, and those kids aren't my Barbies.

But I let them keep the duvet. They'd already been sleeping all over it anyway; I'd have had to dry-clean it, and I hate the smell of dry-cleaning chemicals. So it was just as well.

I asked Pepper, since she was more pleasant to talk to, "You guys still doing all right for food?"

She nodded. Domino answered. "*Duh*. Yes, we're fine for food. I bring in plenty."

He meant he stole plenty, but what was I going to do, lecture him about it? "Okay," I said instead. "As long as you're covered, I won't worry about you. Good job on the lookout, Peps. Keep up the good work."

She beamed up at me, and I gave her a wink.

I told the pair of them to keep their eyes peeled in case Trevor had any friends, and I barred the place up behind me as I left. I wasn't worried about locking the siblings inside. They'd get out if they wanted to. They always did.

I finally convinced myself that future intruders would have a tougher time gaining entry, and that the kids would hardly sleep the rest of the night anyway, for all the excitement.

I pinched my purse and felt Ian Stott's envelope distorting the bag's shape from within. Morning was coming in another couple of hours, and I had some reading to do.

3

Back at the homestead, I was too wound up to settle in for the day—even though the first light streaks of dawn were working their way up over the mountains. I shut all the blinds and drew down the curtains, closing myself up in my little cave. I flipped on a couple of lights for the sake of ambience and booted my laptop.

It was too late in the evening (or too close to morning, however you look at it) for me to get much work done, but thanks to the wonders of the Internet I could still get prepped and ready for the next night's business.

Ian Stott's envelope sat on the desk beside the computer. The blind vampire was a paying client and I should've started with his case, but floating somewhere in my purse were two scraps of paper relevant to Trevor, and they were fresher in my memory.

I retrieved the business card and the torn sheet of notepaper. The card had a handy-dandy URL listed on it: www.northwest parcoursaddicts.com. Sounded manly. I plugged it in and let it load, and yes, the testosterone reeked out from the digital window.

The home page looked like a high-school boy's idea of a good time on the weekend. Lots of black, lots of bulky guys wearing gray-scale camo, lots of gear, lots of posing in an adventuresome fashion. Up top there was a link "About *Parcours*," and on that page I learned that my idiot trespasser might well have been telling the truth after all.

If I was feeling uncharitable, I might call *parcours* a French martial art designed around the skill of running away. But I was forced to admit, some of the videos looked pretty cool. It consisted mostly of running, jumping, and climbing around on stuff in odd places.

And oh, look. Another link.

"Two great tastes that taste great together: Urban Exploration and *Parcours*."

Oh *dear*. The more I read, the more it appeared that the dumb-ass had been on the up-and-up. He belonged to a club of people who liked to (a) poke around in abandoned buildings, and (b) climb around on stuff while dressed like commandos from a video game.

Even so, I couldn't beat myself up about it too much. After all, he wasn't just unlucky to pick my building—he was stupid, too. As I understood the rules on the website, you don't explore any-place that people routinely visit, occupy, or presently utilize. My old factory may look like a dump from the outside, but once he got in, he should've known he'd blown it. He should've turned around on the heels of his faux army boots and left the way he'd arrived.

It was his own fault that he was dead.

Something still felt "off" about it, though. The rules on the website were clear, and when I clicked through the image galleries, all the posted pictures depicted places that had been visibly empty for decades. All the other boys were playing by the rules. So why not my supper?

The other piece of paper drew my eye. *Major*, said the one legible word. *Major* as in "British slang for important"? Or *major* as in "ranking military official"? I didn't imagine that a five AM phone call would please anyone waiting at the other end of the line, so I didn't do any dialing yet, but on the off chance it might tell me something, I plugged the digits into a search engine and came up with nothing.

Que sera.

Oh well. I could sit and obsess about the intruder all day, or I could use the residual energy from feeding on him to be productive.

I reached for Ian's envelope.

It'd become battered while riding in my purse, but everything inside was intact. There wasn't much to mess up—mostly just some photos and negatives, and some documents that had been declassified, though only in the loosest sense. Long black bars blocked out huge chunks of text for the sake of national security, ass-covering, or God knew what else.

The photos were grainy black-and-whites, with coordinates listed on the back and time/date stamps in yellow. The dates roughly matched Ian's incarceration ten years previously. At the center of each picture was one building in particular—amid several others, with what appeared to be a wall around the whole compound. It could certainly be a small military base.

What I could see of the surrounding terrain wasn't very helpful. There were trees, some of them quite bushy and dark, as if the base was smack in the middle of a jungle. Had Ian mentioned from whence he'd escaped? I was a moron for not asking, but I had his number. I'd call him come evening and clear up a few things.

Beside my laptop I kept a pad of paper, and in a drawer underneath the desk I store enough pens and pencils to last an inner-
city school for months, but it took me a couple of minutes to find
a functional writing implement. Everything was broken or dried
up, and I don't own a pencil sharpener, which is ludicrous, I know.
You'd think I could throw some of that old junk away, but perhaps
by now you've realized that I'm a bit of a hoarder at heart.

So. I found a pen that didn't tear up the paper with its spinster-
dryness, and I made a little list:

1. Ian escaped from base; he must know where it is. Find out.
2. How did he escape?
3. What does he remember from the procedures?

That was all I could think of for the moment. I took the paper
and working pen with me into the bedroom and left them on the
nightstand while I washed my face and stripped for bed.

Finally I slipped in between the sheets and pulled my (sadly,
not red silk) duvet up across my chest. I leaned over and turned on
the electric blanket because I don't care that I'm not technically so
much alive anymore—that's no excuse to be cold all the time. Then
I turned on the tiny bedside lamp, put my pen in my mouth, and
began to read between the black bars.

It was an eyelid-punishing task. Every time the content was
about to get good, some asshole would black it out with a Sharpie
and I'd spend a few ridiculous seconds squinting madly at the black
boxes, trying to make them tell me something.

No such luck.

But this is the condensed version of what I was able to ascer-
tain about Ian Stott's mysterious capture and incarceration:

In the mid-nineties, the army instituted Project Bloodshot. At
least four subjects (and maybe as many as seven) were acquired and

relocated to a base that was so small and so secret that there was, in effect, no record of it at all. One of the subjects died within the first week; another one died some months later, both of unspecified causes. Of the remaining two subjects, one ceased to be mentioned in the documentation—but whether he (or she) had died or gone missing, the black lines refused to divulge. And as for the final subject—Ian, I assumed—he broke out of the facility and disappeared, doing some damage on the way out. After his flight, the documentation abruptly ended and there was a final note saying that the program had been scrapped by the higher-ups.

I picked up my pad of paper again and added more questioning notes:

4. Were the other subjects vampires?
5. What other experiments were being performed? If Ian only went blind but a couple of the subjects died, something else must've been going on, too.
6. What did Ian do to the compound when he left?

Inside the folder I only had one more stapled clump of papers to read, and even though the sun was fully up outside—gold and runny like a frying egg—I was still riding high from my first meal in ages so I kept on reading. This last batch of paperwork had fewer strokes of the obfuscating marker.

It was a letter from one blacked-out name to another, discussing Project Bloodshot as an expensive failure and a potential PR nightmare. This letter urged discretion. It suggested in no uncertain wording that the recipient of the missive should shut up about the project, already, and turn his (her?) attention to a different line of scientific inquiry, because Uncle Sam wasn't going to pony up the bill for any more of this nonsense—especially not after what happened at Jordan Roe. Furthermore, the note's author made abundantly clear that he (she?) expected all paperwork on the matter to be shipped to the facility at St. Paul.

Cal's exquisitely bad handwriting coiled sharply in the margin. If I read it right, his addendum said, "Stored at Holtzer Point, St. Paul. Mr. Stott's serial number: 63-6-44-895."

"Okay," I said out loud.

Tomorrow night, I'd look into the security system at Holtzer Point and see about letting myself inside.

I set the aggravatingly and minimally declassified documents aside and turned in for the day.

The phone woke me up a little after five PM. The sun was still up but it was on its way down; I could feel it immediately, without bothering to futz with the curtains. I hated that stupid phone. It jangled away in my purse, in the other room, nowhere near my bed, which was where I wished to remain.

It wound through its cycle and I lay there, expecting the electronic blip that warns of incoming voice mail, but no. It began to ring again with an immediacy that implied the caller was prepared to go on doing this all night, if necessary.

So it must be Horace.

I mentioned earlier, when I was trying to contain my natural tendency to digress, that I have a contact at a museum. He's a crooked little motherfucker who used to work as an acquisitions manager at a big NYC auction house, retired, and took a leisurely sort of job as a collections assessor at a museum. If ever there was a corollary to the old adage about the fox guarding the henhouse, this is *it*.

I'm not going to lie and say it hasn't been good for me. I get most of my best cases from Horace, so he's a handy fellow to know. He's mercenary to the core, with no regard whatsoever for art, history, or sentimentality. His whole business model could best be described as, "I know a guy who wants a thing. Raylene, I'll pay you fat sacks of cash to go and get it."

Usually I say yes. Sometimes I say no.

I hauled myself into the living room and answered the cell phone before he'd finished his third round of persistent redial. He didn't wait for me to say anything like "Hello," "Raylene here," or "Damn you, you bastard, you woke me up." He just dove right into his sales pitch.

"This will be an easy one, if you're game," his nasally voice wheedled. "It's just a little box, somewhere in the basement of the Smithsonian. I've got a collector who thinks there's an Aztec relic inside. I've emailed you the details, the deadline, and the budget."

"Tell me . . ." I cleared my throat and tried again. I tasted clotted O-positive in the back of my throat, which was not nearly so nice as the fresh stuff. "Tell me what the deadline is."

"Why? Do you have a hot date or something?"

"I have another client," I told him.

"You're shitting me!"

"I shit thee *not.*"

He paused, and if I knew him, he was chewing on the end of his glasses while he thought about it. "Another client. But I'm your favorite, right?"

"Favorite?"

"Most reliable. Highest paying. Most flattering, oh my beautiful, sticky-fingered queen of the night?"

I yawned. "You're pushing your luck."

"Then let me give it another little shove. This woman I'm talking to, she's got a wish list as long as your arm and more money than God. You'll love her."

"I don't want to love her if she wants her goodies anytime in the next couple of weeks." I guessed at how long I'd need for Ian's assignment. It might go as quickly as forty-eight hours, or it might take me a month. A couple of weeks was a good middle-of-the-road estimate, and one that was flexible.

"We're talking next month. Is next month too soon? She wants it in time for some weird calendar event; I think she's one of those multicultural hippie pagans who's trying to get in touch with someone else's tradition."

"What's that mean?" I asked.

"She's a white woman who's inordinately fond of indigenous religious artifacts." He stopped, as if he was finished with the thought. Then he added, "If you want my opinion, she's a little creepy about it."

"Next month," I echoed his earlier statement, since that was the one I found important. "Next month might be doable."

"Is that a yes?"

"It's a maybe. It's a *probably* yes, but it isn't a yes."

Not everyone can sulk out loud without saying a word. Horace has elevated it to an art form. "What are you, a Magic Eight Ball?" he finally demanded. "Ask again later? Is that how it's going to be?"

"Ask again later, yes. That's an excellent idea. It's a perfect idea, in fact, and it's one I plan to insist upon. Let me get a bit deeper into this current case, and I'll get back to you."

"You will? You promise? You're not just trying to get rid of me?"

"Oh, I'm trying to get rid of you, yes," I assured him. "I just woke up. I need a shower. It's kind of cold in here, and I'm in my underwear. So make no mistake about it—I *am* trying to get rid of you. But I'll also make a point to call you in another week or so. Deal?"

The pretty-pretty princess sighed and said, "Fine. I suppose I'll have to take it."

"I suppose you will," I said, and I hung up without any more salutation than he'd offered at the start of the conversation. It's okay. He knows me. I know him. We never take it personally . . . or at least I don't. Maybe he takes it personally sometimes, but as long as he continues to throw work my way once in a while, I don't give a damn.

But I didn't really need the work right at that moment, and if he was going to get pissy about it, he could kiss my ass. Sometimes I swear he thinks I'm on call for him, 24/7. Well, I'm not. And he could learn it the hard way, if he had to.

Besides, I had to assume he had other, um, "acquisitions specialists" on the payroll somewhere. If he wasn't willing to wait a few weeks, he could field the job out to a member of the B-team—if it was such an easy job as all that.

Of course, this made me think that it wasn't such an easy job after all. Otherwise he would've been happy to pay someone else a lot less money to take care of it. Even more reason to put him off.

I wandered back into the bedroom, gathered a few clothes, and took a nice, hot shower—during which I mentally sorted through the things I'd need for the evening. I could start on the Internet, and why wouldn't I? The information was easy, free, and even if it wasn't accurate (which was always a risk), it usually gave me a good starting point for finding better facts elsewhere.

Within about half an hour, I'd learned that Holtzer Point was a top secret facility in St. Paul, Minnesota. I'd gathered that much already, but it was nice to have it confirmed by a series of websites that appeared to have been composed by middle-school-aged conspiracy theorists with a passion for stupid-looking animated graphics.

Depending on which frothy-mouthed Internet pulpit-beater I chose to believe, Holtzer Point might conceal anything from alien artifacts to Bigfoot's sperm samples, plus a few pickled flipper babies from Three Mile Island and Jimmy Hoffa's stomach contents.

I'd like to make fun of those guys, but I had information from a blind vampire that the storage facility held details of medical experiments conducted by the military on the unwilling undead.

So far be it from me to call anyone nuts.

I composed an email to a mortal colleague of mine, a guy whom I jokingly call the Bad Hatter. Hey, if I'm Cheshire Red, we might as well run with the Wonderland theme, right? We also have a Red Queen and a White Rabbit. Someone get us a White Queen and a set of flamingo croquet mallets and we'll be in business.

Though when I talk about Duncan being my colleague, I only mean it in jest. At best he and I (and those other couple of specialists) are a loose network of freelancers. You see, sometimes when you work by yourself in a field such as ours, it helps to share knowledge among professionals. I'm not saying that we watch one another's backs or anything, because we don't. It's more of a back-scratching than a back-watching affair, as in, "You scratch my back, and I'll scratch yours."

Officially, none of us has ever heard of any of us.

In real life, I've got a few email addresses and a phone number or two. I don't use them often, and the freelancers don't often use mine. But if I can help a brother out, it's often worth the trouble of doing so. A year or two previously, the Hatter needed some specs to help him pilfer on-site from a marine recovery operation. I gave him the hookup, and now I needed a hookup in return.

I didn't know much about Duncan. I might've been able to find out more with a little digging, but as a matter of professional courtesy I never tried. I'd inferred that he'd been part of some special forces branch, and he'd demonstrated before that he was savvy about military affairs and locales.

So when I wanted a few preliminary observations about Holtzer Point, he was the man to ask. While I was at it, I double-checked the envelope and added a query about "Jordan Roe," whatever *that* was. As far as the Internet was concerned, it didn't exist. And in this day and age, if the Internet says it doesn't exist, it's either dead boring or totally fascinating in a top secret men-in-black kind of way.

After hitting SEND, I leaned back and pondered my next move. The scrap of paper beside my laptop was still staring at me, with that one word "Major" snagging my eyeball every time it rolled past.

I picked it up again, made an educated guess as to whether the first number was a five or a six, and plugged the sequence into my cell phone. Someone else's phone rang twice, and was answered by a scowl I could hear all the way over on my end of the line.

"Who is this?"

I don't want to sound like one of those bitchy old ladies who fusses all the time about how kids these days have no manners at all, but just once I'd like to hear someone answer a phone with "hello."

I said, "Hello?" And maybe it was just because I'd had army-on-the-brain all evening, but I went ahead and guessed, "Major?"

"Who is this? How did you get this number?"

He didn't answer my question. This called for multitasking. While I laid out the fresh-from-my-ass story, I went into the kitchen and opened a drawer. "I got the number from Trevor," I said. I pulled out a cheap prepaid cell phone. (I keep a small stash. I'm paranoid, remember?) "He said you wanted to talk about the website?" I put a Valley girl question mark at the end of the sentence because I had now officially exhausted every ounce of information I possessed.

"The website? Trevor?" he grumbled, sounding confused. For a minute, I was afraid I'd blown it.

"For Northwest *Parcours* Addicts?" While I fumbled with the conversation I fumbled with the extra cell phone, too. I dialed in the digits of the number I'd just called. "You know. *Trevor.* From the website. I think you talked to him already, and he said I should talk to you, too."

I was repeating myself, trying to keep him on the line—even if I sounded like a moron.

I guessed lucky and he ignored the in-beeping of my other call. He said, "Oh yeah. Him. I didn't tell him he could pass this number along to anybody!"

"But I'm . . . special," I said lamely. I totally winged the rest. "Trevor said you were looking for the best, but he wouldn't say what you wanted. He said I'd have to talk to you myself if I wanted in."

"Did he, now?"

"Yes sir," I said, and right at that moment the voice-mail system picked up on the other phone. I struggled to listen to both devices at once.

He replied, "If you're looking to pick up some extra cash, we might be able to talk, but I don't need any weekend tea parties, honey. You said Trevor pointed you my way?"

Great. A terrible phone persona, and a sexist pig to boot. "Yes, and I don't do tea parties but I'm a world-class trespasser."

I would've said more, but the voice mail was prattling in my other ear. It said, "You've reached the desk of Major Ed Bruner, I'm unavailable right now . . . ," and the rest was typical phone etiquette denouement. But I had a name. Major Bruner. Aka Ed. I snapped the other phone shut and gave the living, breathing major my full attention.

"Trespasser, eh?" he said. "I thought you kids didn't like that word."

"Some kids don't, but I like to call a spade a spade," I told him. I don't really sound like a kid on the phone. If anything, I have a somewhat low-pitched voice for a woman, but I got the impression it didn't matter. I had tits, so I was going to get talked down to. I played along for expediency's sake.

"That's good, that's fine," he said. "All right, then. What's your specialty?"

"My . . . my specialty?" He had me there. I was all out of bull-shit, and I needed a prompt.

"Yeah. Specialty. Trevor has some martial arts training, doesn't he?"

"Oh yeah, he's a ninja all right. But I don't have any training like that," I admitted, once again trying to stick to the truth in order to make better lies. "Look, why don't you just tell me what you're looking for, and I'll tell you if I think I can be of any service, eh?"

"Pushy little thing, aren't you?"

"Sometimes, very. Now are we just wasting each other's time here, or what?"

He was quiet so long that I thought maybe he'd hung up. Then he said, "You must understand, I can't ask you to do anything, and I can't publicly pay you to do anything. There would never be any transaction between us."

Translation: Say anything to anyone, and I'll deny the hell out of it. This whole operation is under the table.

"I can live with that," I said. "If Trevor says it's okay with him, then it's okay with me."

Someone interrupted him, and he put his hand over the re-ceiver so I couldn't hear the chatter. I did hear it, but it wasn't very interesting—just somebody telling him that an appointment had canceled.

When he returned his attention to me, he said, "Do you have an email address?"

"Of course I do."

"Give it to me, and I'll send you some information. We can talk more later, maybe."

I pretended to balk. "Not so fast, buddy. I want to know what I'm getting myself into. Can't you just give me a hint?"

"Give me your address and I'll give you a hint."

"Fine," I fussed, and then I gave him a Hotmail account I keep under a phony name. "Now, please. Hint."

Before abruptly hanging up, he said one word: "Reconnaissance."

I hated to admit that it chilled me. It was the worst possible word he could've uttered for the sake of a hint, because it told me just enough to get me good and worried. Someone was doing reconnaissance in my building? Why?

I tried to convince myself that it was just another stupid homeland security initiative, but I kept thinking about Ian, and what happened to him, and I couldn't distract myself from the fact that I'd kept the factory for fifty years and really, I knew better. That was too long, and I was getting soft. The longer I held still, the better chance I had of being caught. That was old-school criminal wisdom, right there, and I hadn't been taking my own advice.

I slammed my laptop shut and disconnected it in an irrational fit. I stuffed it down into my purse, which was easily big enough to function as a laptop bag, and it very often did. I often called it my "go-bag" or sometimes my Useful Things Bag, because it had everything I needed in order to *go*. And all of it's useful. The computer knocked against the Glock. I'd forgotten I'd brought it with me, but I was glad to have it. I might need it.

I was working my way up to a panic attack, but I couldn't figure out how to stop it. I frantically flailed for something else to think about, and I settled on Ian Stott. I could call *him*, couldn't I? And I could talk to him, and it would make me feel better all around. It was business, yes, but he was personable.

Cal answered the phone, which surprised me more than it ought to have.

To his credit, he didn't ask any questions when I asked for Stott; he just handed off the phone to his master like a good little ghoul. Ian must've been somewhere else in the house. It took a minute or two for the phone to find him.

"Hello?" he said, and ah, yes. I'd finally gotten my phone hello.

"Hello," I said back, trying not to sound too relieved. "Listen, I've got some questions I want to run past you, is that all right?" Simply the act of speaking normally was deflating my fear, which only meant that I kept on speaking well past the point where I should've let Ian have a turn. "If you don't want to chat on the phone—you said that before, didn't you? That you didn't like to talk on the phone?—then we could meet again someplace. I don't mind if you don't mind."

He took a few seconds to answer me. I think he was making sure I'd finished babbling. "That would be fine. Is your preference still public but reserved? Or could I persuade you to join me at my suite?"

"You have a suite?"

"Well, I don't live here in Seattle. I've made arrangements for myself and Cal downtown." He named a high-end, high-rise establishment, and I complimented him on his taste. He said, "Thank you. Yes, it's quite nice. You can find me in room number twenty-one sixty-seven."

"I'll be there in an hour," I told him.

I was there in forty-five minutes.

By then, I wasn't quite such a wreck. I let the thought of seeing him again serve as distraction and comfort. I know, I know. He wasn't good "friend" material just because he was pretty and he couldn't see me very well. I'd learned the hard way, through the trial and error of almost a century, that other vampires and I are simply not meant to hang out.

So what was I doing knocking on his door, feigning a business call, using him as a safe zone to bail myself out of a psychic meltdown?

I have no excuse except for my own weaknesses, though when he opened the door, I was prepared to amend that list of excuses to include Ian's cheekbones.

He was wearing black slacks, soft leather slip-on shoes, and a fitted shirt with three-quarter sleeves. The effect was rich-guy casual, and it did a beautiful job of showcasing the long, lean lines of his torso.

"Please, come in," he said—and I was glad someone had said something, because I'd just been standing there with my mouth hanging open. As a second thought, I was also glad that he couldn't see his hand in front of his face, because that meant he hadn't seen me standing there with my mouth hanging open.

Selfish? Yes, very. But also practical. Silver lining, and all that.

"Thank you," I said as I slipped in past him, because all this politeness was cheering me up and I felt like participating. I thought about my list of questions and how I'd left them at home beside my bed, but that was all right. I remembered what I wanted to know.

Inside the suite the décor was exactly what you'd expect from accommodations that cost a few thousand dollars a night—understated luxury on a taupe palette with maroon and silver accents. The bed was offset by a pair of folding double doors, and a lovely sitting room ensemble was parked off to the side of a full kitchen. A fruit-filled gift basket sat ignored on the granite counter.

"Could I offer you some wine? You preferred white last night, is that correct?"

"That's correct, and thanks for the offer, but no. I've still got a long night ahead of me." And I didn't add that I was feeling kind of stupid about coming down to see him in the first place. You'd think I'd learn, eventually—panic attacks pass. They pass, and I always feel ridiculous for whatever escape measures I took while attempting to rid myself of them.

"Then I hope you don't mind if I indulge," he said, retrieving a crystal goblet from a track above the sink.

"By all means."

"And won't you have a seat?" He waved a lovely hand at the settee, and I gratefully—but gracefully—dropped myself into it. The brocade cover was posh and lumpy. I settled against it while he poured himself a glass. He took the seat across from me, where I noticed a slim white cane had been left propped against the arm. He must've gotten to know his temporary quarters exceedingly well for how easily he navigated them. If I hadn't known, I would've never guessed that he was blind.

He said, "You had some questions for me?"

"I did, yes. I mean, I *do*. I've gone through the information in the packet. I'm still in the process of tracking down a few of the finer points of this project, but I think it might help if you could tell me a bit about what happened to you—and where you were."

He didn't exactly frown, and he wasn't exactly upset with me. But he didn't want to talk about it, that much was apparent. "As I understand it," he said, "the documents are not housed at the place where I was . . . kept."

"That's true, or it looks like it's true. But in case Cal didn't fill you in on the blocking out, more than half of the info in that paperwork has been declared 'sensitive' by the feds, so any scrap of fact you can throw my way will be helpful."

Ian took a hard swallow and reached for his cane. He fiddled with the end of it while he spoke. "I was kept on a base in Florida called Jordan Roe, on a small island off the west coast. But the base is no longer operational, or so I am led to believe."

"That letter you included certainly implied as much. Speaking of which, where's Cal? Is he lurking around here someplace, listening in?"

Translation: *Does he sleep in here with you? Just curious.*

"Cal is in his room next door." Ah. So that's why it took him so long to deliver the phone call.

"Sorry, I don't mean to pry. I'm just—" I was going to say "paranoid" as a plausible excuse, but he cut me off by saying, "Careful."

"Careful, sure. I like that word better."

"You can hardly be blamed. It's a dangerous line of work you're in. I suppose it must be very exciting."

I saw what he was trying to do, divert the subject from my line of questioning, but I wouldn't have it. I said, "Sometimes. Sometimes it's disgusting, and sometimes it's boring. But sometimes, yes. Exciting. Now tell me, Ian, if you would please. You weren't alone on this island, were you? There were other vampires there, according to what you gave me—or at the very least, there were other subjects present."

"There were . . . other subjects, yes."

I noted his failure to use the word *vampires*, and I hoped he'd take another drink or two to loosen himself up, or we'd never get anywhere.

I was about to ask in a more pointed fashion when he sensed my impatience and added, "I can't tell you anything about them. I couldn't see them. One of them was a vampire, yes, but the other two—I'm not sure. And there were new additions by the time I escaped—one more vampire, but I didn't recognize anyone else's scents. They could've been anything, or something altogether outside my experience."

"Ooh," I said, not for being impressed, but for being distressed. "Wow. The implications of that. Huh." If the military knew about vampires, and it knew about a few of the other less conventional brands of humanity, too, then what was the big plot? They obviously weren't trying to recruit us, which was sort of a shame. I imagined a full unit of vampire soldiers and I got a little giddy, and distracted.

Bad idea, maybe. But it'd be epic, wouldn't it?

"Yes, the implications. They're quite alarming, if you ask me."

"But I *am* asking you, Ian. I'm asking you to tell me what you know, and what you learned about the project, and how you left it. I'm sorry if you feel like I'm prying, but I think it's important that I know how you escaped."

"I can't imagine what that has to do with anything," he said, but I could tell I'd worn him down. His words said "No, and go away." But his tone said, "If it'll get you off my back, *fine.*"

He sighed and folded his hands in his lap, though he twisted them together as the story began to unspool.

"It was summer and quite warm, I remember that much. And I could smell the ocean, but then again I always could. The island was scarcely three miles long and a mile wide; regardless of how deeply they kept us underground and isolated, the smell of salt and seabirds always wafted down. They opened doors, they closed doors. The breeze came and went, even in the filtered air down below. After a while it was something I lived for, small and sad as that may sound. I lived to hear the slide of the glass and the peep of the electronic lock, because when the doors opened, I could smell the night outside.

"In time, I could tell when the tide was high or low, just by the scent. I cannot explain how, not in a thousand years. But that *awareness,* for lack of a better way of putting it . . . that awareness was the first sign that something was changing."

"In the laboratory?" I asked, not sure where he was headed with this.

"No. In *me.* And I'm sorry, but I can't be more precise. I can't give words to something like this. I can only describe what happened, I can't tell you *how* it happened. And what happened was that, at first, I could sense the tides outside—just by the smell of the air the workers brought downstairs with them when the shifts changed."

"All right, I'm trying to follow you."

"Good." He nodded. "So first I knew about the tides changing, and before long I could tell things about the weather, too. I could smell rain, and dampness. I knew when it was storming, and when it was about to storm. Write it off to barometric pressure if you like, but I could feel the air above and the water outside, working together, pushing against each other. Let me ask you something, Ms. Pendle."

"Go for it," I urged. I seriously had no clue where he was going with this, but I was willing to grasp at whatever straws he offered.

"When you were still alive," he broached, "did you ever have migraines?"

"Migraines? I don't know. I had headaches sometimes, sure. It's been a long time."

"I'm not speaking of ordinary headaches. Migraines are different, from a neurological standpoint, or so I have been told. I had them, and I sought treatment for them for years before I was turned. And I can only compare my new forms of awareness to the sensation of having a migraine. There was pressure across my forehead, and a light, tingling feeling at the base of my skull, where it meets my neck. I saw lights, too—bright swirls that dipped and rolled across my right eye's field of vision. These things, these sensations. My knowledge of the weather and the water . . . it came from the same place."

"So . . . having a built-in meteorologist is kind of like a really bad headache?"

He appeared to struggle with his words—wanting at first to argue, then changing his mind. "It is not altogether different. But it's as if the pull goes both ways. I . . ." He untucked his hands from each other and used them to gesture again, drawing the words in the air in front of him—trying to force this odd communication. "I could feel the ocean and the clouds pulling at me. And one day, it occurred to me that I might be able to pull . . . back."

I frowned without meaning to. "Are you trying to tell me you can control the weather?"

He unleashed a nervous laugh and said, "No, no. Nothing like that. Not anything as huge as the weather . . . but perhaps something that drives the weather. Pressure changes, electromagnetic fields, the earth's rotation, the persistent motion of gravity . . . I don't know. Something, though. Something large called to me, and I called in return."

Pausing then, he reached out for the glass of wine he'd nearly forgotten. He tapped it gently with the back of his knuckles to locate it. Another swallow or two, and he was ready to continue talking.

"I experimented at first, and in the process I wondered if I hadn't completely gone crazy. But I used my mind to pull it, to nudge it. To push it around. And in the beginning, I couldn't tell if it was working or not. It was a process, you understand—learning my way around this new thing. We were so far underground, after all—"

"Wait," I interrupted. "You said 'we.' How many people were down there by the time you left?"

"Oh, let me see." He narrowed his eyes from some long-ago habit of thoughtfulness and then, after a few seconds, said, "Not many. Of the half dozen or so cells . . . only mine and two others remained occupied. One was a young man, another vampire who sounded like he might've been from Texas. The other was something else, a were . . . wolf or something else. She was female, at any rate. I could smell that much. And she never made a sound."

"But there'd been others, like us, in the cells before?"

"Several. They came and went. But something was changing down there; people were packing up equipment and moving it out, and moving in larger pieces. The personnel shifted. Two men left, and were replaced by a different man and a woman. The routine of the place had been disrupted, and it worried me—for all that I sometimes thought I had nothing left to worry about anymore. After all, it seemed like the worst had happened, hadn't it? How much worse could it get? But I didn't want to find out."

I sat back in the chair, both chilled and intrigued. "Can't say as I blame you. So you started playing with this new . . . power? Whatever it was?"

"You could call it a power, I suppose, though I don't think it was new. Nothing they did to me produced this. I think it was in my head all the time, perhaps as a result of the faulty wiring that made me prone to headaches. Or maybe it's similar to the mortal phenomenon, where people who lose one sense gain sensitivity in the others. There's no way of knowing now. Privately," he confessed, lowering his voice and holding tight to the wineglass, "I think it might be a combination of the two. My strangely functioning brain, struggling to compensate for the loss of my sight . . . that's how I like to think of it, anyway."

I understood. It was another mortal phenomenon, after all— the desire to understand something by retroactively assigning it a myth. I told him, "Sure. But you still haven't told me exactly how you escaped. You're avoiding that part."

"Am I?" He sounded surprised. "I don't mean to. It's just that what I've told you so far is so difficult to discuss. The rest can be summed up quickly, if you like."

"Tell it however you want," I said. I liked to hear him talk, and now that I knew I could drag the whole story out of him, I didn't mean to rush him.

"Hm. Well, as I said, I tried out this power in small ways at first, trying to find a rhythm for it. Imagine, if you will, pushing a merry-go-round. At first it's difficult; it's heavy, and slow. But soon you find the weight of it, and you learn how to keep it moving—and then all it takes is the occasional shove to keep it going at full tilt. That's what this was like. At first, I was trying to move something huge and impossibly heavy, trying to make it spin."

"Spin?"

"Yes. I wanted the world to turn, or at least the Gulf of Mexico."

"So you . . . *made* a hurricane?"

"No." He stopped me quickly with a wave of his free hand. "Nothing like that. More like a tornado, yet nothing like a tornado at all. Believe me, I was as shocked as you are."

"How do you know how shocked I am? You can't *see* me."

"No, but I can imagine the look on your face," he said with a smile. "My initial attempts yielded no definitive results, but then I was making the windows rattle, and shaking the doors, and I could hear the fencing outside uprooting itself." He sat forward on the edge of his seat now, closing the space between us. "They didn't know it was me. Even if I'd told them it was me, they wouldn't have believed it. But one night I heard them coming. I heard the doors opening and smelled the tide, and I couldn't bear the thought of them even one more hour. I called down the vortex—if I must call it anything, then that word will suffice—and the building . . ." He shook his hands, almost spilling a little of the wine. "It came apart."

"That's it? It came apart?"

He shrugged. "Blew apart. Exploded apart. I felt my way out of the rubble, and I went blindly into the woods where I hid for several nights, feeding on whatever I found or could coax into my hands."

"Then what?" I asked.

"Then . . ." More hand-waving. "I was found by the captain of a shrimp trawler who had ventured close to the island. I persuaded him to assist me. He took me off the island and over to St. Petersburg, where I threw myself upon the mercy of the Broad House."

I couldn't believe he'd taken the chance. "Seriously? And they didn't kill you on the spot?"

"No. They're ostracists," he said, which meant that the House members were the equivalent of anarchists. They didn't play nice with other Houses, and they tended to take in the freaks, geeks, and weirdos—the undead dregs. Few ostracist Houses (if they can loosely be called such) are very powerful, and they live on the fringes like the Hollywood stereotype of Gypsies.

"Still. Ballsy move, mister."

"Thank you. Eh . . . Ms. Pendle, is your phone ringing?"

"What?" I didn't hear it until he said it. "Oh. Well, it's buzzing at me." But I'd missed the call, and had to wait until the little blip told me I had a message. I pried it out of my purse and checked the number. It looked familiar but I didn't recognize it outright. I sighed and said, "I'm sorry, I don't mean to be rude, but so few people have this number that I need to check it as a matter of professional duty."

"There's nothing rude about it. You're here on business, and more business has come calling." I thought it sounded even more rude when he put it that way, but I didn't argue with him. He downed the last of his wine and rose, going in search of a refill.

I flipped the phone open and realized that my caller hadn't left a voice-mail message, but rather had sent a follow-up text. It said, "Call BH ASAP re: HP and JR." The sign-off was a callback number unrelated to the text's origin.

I unpacked the message to read, "Call Bad Hatter as soon as possible about the Holtzer Point and Jordan Roe information." But

I'd never actually spoken to Duncan in person before, and the prospect weirded me out. We'd exchanged emails, and a couple of text messages here and there, but never when it wasn't of the utmost importance.

I cursed the other thief's sense of timing, and when Ian returned to his seat with a fresh glass of wine, I said, "I'm awfully sorry. I mean, I'm even more sorry now than I was before, because I think I have to call this guy. It's about your case, if that makes any difference."

"My case? It makes all the difference in the world. Make yourself at home in the bedroom, there, if you'd like a bit of privacy." I liked the sound of that—even though I knew I was only being dirty-minded and that anyway, he could probably hear every word without even trying. But I accepted his offer and closed myself behind the double doors, into a large space dominated by a frothily overstuffed king-sized bed. I dialed the number that was included at the end of the text message, and it was answered on the first ring by a man who sounded too old to be in this business.

"Cheshire," he said.

"Yes," I admitted. "And before you go all strange about it, I'm a woman."

"I know."

"You know?"

"I guessed. But that might not hide you."

"What are you talking about?" I demanded.

"We have problems."

I said, "*We* have problems?"

"That PDF I sent you was flagged."

"Wait. What? You sent me a PDF?"

He said, "I didn't know until after I sent it. There are . . ." I could almost hear the gears in his head turning, tumbling, trying to think of the easiest way to explain it to me. I'm tech-savvy for an old lady, but I don't know all the ins and outs of the Web. He went on, speaking very fast. "Uncle Sam's keeping a lookout for key-words related to the info you wanted, presumably because it was a classified program—a *very* classified program. When the keywords are tripped—like when I nab a file that's loaded with them—a quiet little note goes back to an administrator someplace, and then the tracing begins. I'm a lucky fucker; I know what to look for. Other-wise I would've never seen it coming. I figured it out in time to move, and now I'm telling you, because it's my fault the thing's been sent your way."

"Sent my way . . . ," I repeated, only barely following what he was telling me.

"Yeah, like a hot potato. Someone's going to follow it, you can bet on that. They're already all over my IP and breathing down my network's neck. I'm sure you've got your ass covered in all the usual ways, but this is not a usual situation. I don't know how they found me so fast, but Jesus, they found me *fast*."

"Found you—are you all right?"

"I got out in time. I may be old, but I'm not slow," he said, re-inforcing my impression that he sounded like someone's grand-father. "Are you at home?" he asked. "That place of yours on Seventeenth Street in Seattle?"

"What? No. Why do you know that address?" I demanded.

"Same reason you probably know mine. Insurance."

Damn him, he was right. I'd dug up a general location on him years ago. "Fine. But no, I'm not home."

"Good. And if you want to play it one hundred percent safe, don't *go* home. I had to leave without destroying everything I wanted destroyed, including some personal info on some of my fel-low freelancers—I'm telling you, kid, they were on me like *light-ning*. I can't promise they won't come after you, too. Don't check anything, just check the fuck out. You've got safe places. Pick one and camp there for a few weeks, lie low, and keep an eye on what happens." It wasn't a question. You didn't get to our tier in the game without a backup plan.

"Yeah, I do," I said, and the panic was coming back, right up into my throat. I chewed it back down and said, "Thanks for the warning."

"You understand though, don't you? This wasn't deliberate. I wasn't trying to junk you." And now we were at the crux of the matter. His call wasn't just a guilty heads-up; it was a double check that I wasn't planning to rat him out as a traitor to the industry, via network gossip.

"I get it," I said. I tried to make it cool, but I was shaking inside. "Duncan, what do I do?"

"Anyplace where you access those files from the Internet is a potential ground zero. If you think you can get them fast enough from some remote location, have them printed out and mailed to you, that's your best bet. Carry them far away and as fast as you can. And destroy your phone. Don't throw it away, *destroy it*. I had your number listed in some of the stuff those assholes seized."

"Uh, okay. Okay. And I guess we'd both better run."

"Damn right. I've got some more phone calls to make."

"More warnings to hand out?"

"You got it," he responded and the connection went dead.

I shoved the doors open. Ian was still sitting in the overstuffed brocade chair, looking confused. "Is something wrong?"

"Yes. I've got to run."

"Is this anything to do with—"

"You? Yes. Quite a lot to do with you, actually." I grabbed my purse. "I think someone is still looking for you. Someone's keeping an eye out for your files, anyway. I have to run, and I might not be back."

"But we haven't even talked about—"

"I know. And we will one day, I promise. And the price is rising by the nanosecond, because I'm probably going to have to move away from here when all is said and done."

"I don't understand . . ."

"Me either. Get rid of your phone, get Cal, and get out of here. We need to treat this like an outbreak of a disease. Everything that's had any contact with me, or with that PDF, has to *go*."

He was standing, and then in the blink of an eye he was between me and the door—wearing an expression that was half earnest, half frustrated. "I don't understand."

I took him by the shoulders, gently—lest he think I was trying to play rough. I said, "I have some info about your situation, but I can't get to it yet—and the man who sent it to me has been outed. Whoever else tries to get those files will be likewise chased, harried, and hounded, and the time frame for this event is absolutely unknown. I might have five minutes or I might have weeks, but if you want to know what I've got, you need to let me run, and run like hell. I need to get home, print your shit, and get out of Dodge before they descend on my place, and it might already be too late."

I hoped to God that I was overstating the urgency, but my internal Panic O'Matic assured me that heavily armed commandos were already rifling through my underwear drawer.

I let go of him and he got out of my way. "You shouldn't stay here," I added as I reached for the door. "You could go, you could . . . I know. Go out to Ballard and get a boat. Stay out at the marina and I'll find you when I can."

He was on the verge of saying something but I was already out the door, and it was already shutting behind me.

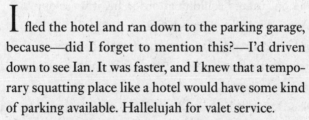

4

I fled the hotel and ran down to the parking garage, because—did I forget to mention this?—I'd driven down to see Ian. It was faster, and I knew that a temporary squatting place like a hotel would have some kind of parking available. Hallelujah for valet service.

As I got my car and got out of the covered garage area, my mind was doing a hamster-wheel of the damned trying to figure out exactly what the trouble was and exactly what I was going to do about it. So Duncan had sent me an email with some juicy gossip. I wished he'd been more specific about . . . well . . . about any of it.

Note to self: Cultivate more demanding interview persona. I need to learn how to get more details before letting people get away from me.

It wasn't far back to my place, but Seattle traffic is

not to be believed sometimes—and oh, *fantastic*. One of the electric buses had blown a fuse, or busted a wire, or stopped in the middle of the road for some other equally aggravating reason.

The detours were killing me, but they were giving me time to think.

Flagged information had been sent to me. I hadn't opened it. How could anyone possibly know where the Hatter had kicked it off to? In my wholly uneducated estimation, it wasn't possible to pinpoint the info while it was in transit. Until I downloaded and moved the content, there'd be nowhere to trace it to. Right?

The thought didn't calm me much, and the traffic was only fueling my horror. I'd been doing so much so *wrong* lately. Keeping that awful factory for storage, staying in my pretty little condo for too long, meeting up with vampires when I damn well ought to know better . . . I must've been getting sloppy in my old age, and if there's one thing I couldn't afford to be, it was sloppy.

What I needed to do was *think*.

So I sat at a red light for its third cycle (what were those people *doing* up there, knitting a sweater?) and I forced myself to breathe.

Okay. Duncan had said I shouldn't go home, and he was the expert—so maybe I shouldn't go home.

He'd also said I could print the information out somewhere and have it mailed to myself. But I didn't know anyone I could trust with the task. Conversely, I didn't know anyone I disliked enough to foist a federal smackdown upon him. Or her. And surely that's what would follow.

The light turned green. Behind me, a car honked and I realized that I was sitting there, learning to knit or whatever, and on this occasion *I* was the asshole. I hit the gas and dragged my car up the hill, and then took it in circles around the block while I plotted my next move.

I passed an Internet café on my left.

I'd been there before. They had printers. I could download the files and print them on someone else's public location—or better yet, I had a thumb drive in my purse, and it might be big enough to simply download the files and abscond with them to a computer without an Internet connection. But this one was within a few blocks of my own abode, and that wouldn't do.

I racked my brain for somewhere farther away. I couldn't think of anyplace, but hell, if there's one thing other than traffic in Seattle, it's coffee. You can't swing a dead squirrel without hitting a Starbucks, or failing that particular evil empire, an indie establishment.

Upon completing my loop of the neighborhood, I got back onto the interstate with a very good idea—or it seemed like a very good idea at the time: I'd go out to the airport. It's fifteen miles outside of town, and it's a huge international hub. For all the feds might know, I could be someone who flew into town and then flew out again—poof! Just like that.

Once I made it to the interstate, the drive took less than half an hour.

I pulled over at a gas station and hauled an overnight case out of my trunk. In the filthy, dimly lit ladies' room of the Chevron I donned a shaggy red wig (not too flashy, not too trashy) and changed into a bright red jacket and a black pencil skirt with fuck-me kitten pumps. Not how I usually dress, but that's the point.

I didn't have time to gussy up as a boy, though I've done it once or twice before. I don't think I make a very convincing dude. I think I look more like a lumberjack lesbian with an eating disorder than a kick-ass drag king.

I emerged from the restroom and slipped straight into my car. I didn't notice anyone noticing, which was good.

Down the street and around the block was a spot called Mean

Bean. It advertised gourmet coffee drinks and pay-to-play WiFi, plus printing services at a quarter a page. A quarter a page? Jesus. For that kind of money I could buy my own printer and throw it away when I was finished.

Well, I didn't know that yet—not for sure. But if Duncan had sent me sensitive government property of the variety likely to get me exposed or killed if caught, I damn well expected that property to have some heft.

So screw it. I had that flash drive in my bag. I'd download it and scoot.

Inside the Mean Bean, a heavily tattooed forty-something worked behind the counter, wielding the barista wand like an orchestra conductor's device. The line was short and moving none too fast, but that was okay because I didn't want to look like I was in a hurry. Best-case scenario, I wouldn't stand out in any way except for the "hey, hot redhead" kind of way, and that would be all right.

In the corner behind the cash register a camera was mounted near the ceiling and aiming my way. I'd anticipated as much, and I was prepared for it. I knew from the get-go that I was bound to pass at least one camera (and maybe more) on my way to get my goodies.

Thus my cunning disguise.

I waited patiently, using a recent edition of *The Stranger* as an excuse to duck my head at an inconspicuous angle, pretending to read the local free mag. They'd never get any good footage of me; I'd see to *that*.

When it was my turn I asked after a computer and got talked into a tall, sugary, chocolatey drink since they wouldn't let me use anything without buying a beverage, which conflicted with my personal idea of "pay to play" with regards to the Internet, but whatever.

I paid for the drink and an hour of Internet time, took my receipt, and sat down at a terminal that backed up to a wall. It had no near neighbors, and there was no one to look over my shoulder. Behind me and to the left was an emergency exit. Hopefully, I wouldn't need it. But I liked knowing it was there.

I set the frosty iced drink down beside the keyboard, gave the room one more suspicious overview, and then logged into my email account.

It took forever. Whatever the Hatter had sent me, it was reassuringly big and fat. It turned out to be a PDF with the file name Holtzer, which was promising. I thought about opening it on the spot, but then I figured that it might only make my chances of getting busted better. Every moment I sat in that chair connected to the Internet was a moment that the feds could be tracking me, pinpointing my location and preparing to deploy violent, armed maniacs with badges.

I dug out my thumb drive and shoved it into the USB port, then ordered the system to shoot the document my way. I waited while the little task bar filled up (oh, so slowly). When it finally chimed "Done!" I whipped that drive out, snapped its little lid on top, and retrieved a small spray can of nonstick cooking spray from the depths of my purse. Making sure no one was looking, I lightly spritzed the keyboard. Generally speaking, I don't leave fingerprints. My body doesn't make much oil anymore, but I'd fed recently.

A fresh influx of blood always makes my body a little more human. I'm not sure what that says about me, or my undead condition, or the state of the universe, but there you go. Filling up with blood is a surefire way to make sure I start oozing and stinking again.

Once I was satisfied that I'd left no identifying trace, I bolted—

or, well, I bolted as smoothly and nonchalantly as I could manage. I slipped my arm up under my purse strap, pushed my chair up under the table, and made my way to the door.

· My car was right where I'd left it, and not boxed in by cops or feds, thank heaven. I crawled inside, dropped my purse on the passenger seat, and did my best not to peel out of the parking lot. It's great, feeling like you've gotten away with something.

It's less great being afraid that you *haven't*.

A few blocks away I made a sharp turn and hid my car behind a strip mall. It was well after hours by this point, and there weren't even any streetlights to illuminate the loading docks. It was perfect.

I changed back into my original clothes, then took the wig and the jacket and threw them in a dumpster marked RECYCLING. I debated the wisdom of starting a fire, but then figured that it'd draw more attention than it was worth, so I covered up the discarded finery with cardboard and hoped for the best.

I kept the skirt and the shoes. They're nondescript enough, and they're sexy. Back into the trunk they went.

Back into the driver's seat I went, and then I drove back toward town.

On the way, I passed the Mean Bean and my stomach sank to see three very shiny black cars with government plates now gracing the parking lot. I tried not to kick the gas and make a scene, but I couldn't get away from there fast enough.

Look, for all I know, even the feebs need their coffee every now and again, at oh, say, ten o'clock at night. Out near the airport. About twenty minutes after I'd used the coffeehouse to download and effectively steal sensitive government documents.

But I wasn't willing to bet my life and freedom on it.

I turned my cell phone over while I was driving, ripped the battery out of its back, and threw the battery out the window. I smashed the phone itself against the dashboard, and once it was in a satisfactory pile of inert pieces, I threw them out the window, too.

My heart was throbbing a magnificent Thrill Kill Kult tune by the time I was back on the interstate, and no amount of mental down-talking could cool me back to mellow sanity. I thought—and I assured myself—that I'd thrown them off the trail. Hadn't I? Now they'd go combing SeaTac and they wouldn't be camping out at my own homestead.

I wanted to go home—I wanted *badly* to go home—but I was too damn scared. And let's be serious for a minute: There was nothing in that condo that I couldn't afford to lose. I'd made it that way by design. All my safe houses were similarly equipped with all the comforts of a long-term residence, but all the personal effects of a Motel 6.

I thanked God—or anyone else who might be listening—that I'd grabbed my laptop on the way out the door. I keep it pretty well locked, but that's no guarantee against anything and we all know it.

It was the only thing I owned that I truly feared losing.

It wasn't particularly valuable; I could buy another one at the drop of a hat. But I hadn't wiped my email logs or erased my contacts lists—and now I didn't really want to. They were all I had. Well, that . . . and a little thumb drive with something very important on it.

I needed to find out more. I needed to get a look at whatever I was risking life and limb for.

Ian and Cal wouldn't be the best people to contact. If they knew what was good for them they were already in transit. A boat in Ballard. Was I a genius, or what? It was perfect, and mobile, and tougher to track than a stationary listing.

I hoped.

So where could I go to take a moment and look at the files?

There was always the factory.

Hmm. Was that a good idea or not? I couldn't make up my mind. The factory had power, but it also had a recent break-in and a couple of nosy kids trunked up in there.

Reconnaissance, Major Bruner had said.

The word clicked back in my brain and stung me. But if I were to examine that word, it didn't imply anything but curiosity, did it? Reconnaissance meant that they didn't know anything and they were just taking a look. And with Trevor stashed in the basement, there hadn't been anyone to make any reports . . . though his absence in and of itself might be construed as suspicious.

Then again, I'd called Bruner and talked about Trevor as if he were alive. So there probably wasn't *too* much suspicion. Not yet.

I was making myself crazy, thinking myself in circles, trying to justify a course of action that was likely not the wisest or safest one to pursue, but in times of crisis I'm pathetically human. I didn't want to go hop a flight for a distant locale and set up someplace new. I wanted to go somewhere familiar and feel safe.

I was still talking to myself in those same pretty pirouettes when I pulled up to the block beside the factory.

Since the factory wasn't owned in my name—or any name that could be traced back to me—I told myself that I was doing something smart after all, and if nothing else, I was warning the young 'uns inside that trouble might be coming. Did I owe them that? No, I didn't. But I'd feel like a douche if I didn't pass them a heads-up, and it was extra fodder for my resolve to visit.

I let myself inside through a back door. This door was usually covered by a pair of shipping pallets, but since it was my building I knew where to look. The kids knew that if anyone noodled with that door that it was almost certainly me, so it didn't set off any of their little alarms, either.

Inside, everything was quiet. Everything was always quiet for the first few minutes, while the kids worked out that there wasn't any trouble.

I sensed them, both on the second floor where it was warmest. They weren't upset or stressed, though their ears perked up and I received a twinge of cautious alert when they realized someone was inside. I stretched my psychic side and felt my way around the premises; I didn't detect anybody else, so I announced, "It's me, guys."

From upstairs, Domino said, "Again already? Fucking-*A*, lady, leave us alone."

I climbed the stairs and found Pepper at the top. "Hi," she said.

"Hi," I said back. "And tell your idiot brother that I'm not here to bother you. I'm here to leech the power supply, and since I pay for it, I am fully entitled to do so."

"My brother *is* an idiot," she said, but there was no malice in it—just agreeable acquiescence.

I was already extricating my laptop from the bag. "See? I knew you were smarter than him," I told her. "Tell me, short-stuff—where's the nearest power outlet in this joint?"

I so rarely needed them that I didn't know where they were located.

"By the light, I guess." She pointed at the contraption whose lightbulb I'd broken, then replaced, on my last visit. It was plugged into a raised spot on the floor.

"Right. Dumb question." I pulled up an elderly dining room chair to the crate I'd stood on the night before, and voilà—makeshift work space. "Don't mind me. I'm having a scatter-brained kind of night here."

"It happens to the best of us," she said.

My God, how the hell did that poor kid end up so much older

than her years? Half the time when I talk to her, I feel like I'm addressing a forty-year-old woman.

I checked the laptop to make sure that the wireless card was disabled. So far as I knew, there wasn't any free WiFi in the area, but I wasn't taking any chances. Not anymore. No more sloppy operations for *me*. I wiggled the safety prong into the power outlet and let my machine boot.

"Hey guys, gather 'round, would you? We need to have a little talk," I said as I waited for the screen to come alive.

"Screw you," Domino said. He didn't move away, and he didn't come any closer.

Pepper came to sit at my feet. "What's the matter?" she asked.

I smiled down at her because it was hard not to. "What are you, my therapist now?" Everything restarted on cue, bringing my screen back up to full function with a grouchy little window at the bottom complaining about the lack of an Internet connection. I closed it away.

"What's a therapist?"

"It's . . ." I reached into my purse and pulled out the thumb drive. "A doctor who makes you talk about your problems. But that's not the point. The point is, I need for you two to go on *serious* lookout duty over the next few days. Or maybe even few weeks."

"*Serious* lookout duty?" The boy was mocking my tone, but he was also interested in what I was saying. He liked a challenge, and I liked that about him. It made him easy to manipulate.

"That's right, bucko." I clicked while I talked, prompting the machine and telling it to open the PDF in whatever program it liked best, but for chrissake *open it already.* "I might've gotten myself into a little bit of trouble with the government."

"Is that why the man in black came inside?" Pepper asked.

I didn't like the way she put it. "Man in black." Men in black are always trouble, without a doubt. I said, "No, I don't think so.

I think he was more of a random intruder, though I can't be sure. But be on the lookout for more guys like him, just in case. And there might be other people, too—real official-looking people who have badges and guns." The fear level in the room rose a notch. It radiated from both young parties.

The PDF took forever and a day to sort itself out through Adobe. This no doubt had something to do with the fact that it was more than six hundred pages long (score!) and chock-full of images.

"But don't get too worked up about it," I added. "I don't think the government knows about this place—"

"You don't?" Domino interrupted.

"I don't," I confirmed. "Otherwise I wouldn't be here right now, doing this. As I was saying, I don't think they know about the factory, and I'm damn sure they don't know anything about you guys. So if people do come poking around, the odds are very, very good that they aren't looking for *you*." I found that it was easier to keep cool when I was forced to keep cool so other people wouldn't panic.

Pepper said softly, "They'll be looking for *you*."

"Sort of. They'll be looking for *this*." I pointed at the screen. Then a miserable thought broke through the surface and whispered nastily, *They might be looking for this, but they might be looking for me, too. Just like Ian. And just like those other chimps, whoever they were.*

But I didn't spill that part. Instead, I said, "Someone sent me some information that's very important. He didn't know it, but he accidentally alerted some very nasty people to the fact that I wanted it. Let me be clear," I said, tearing my eyes away from the screen. "It's got nothing to do with you. But that doesn't mean you won't get caught in the middle if you're not careful. I don't want you caught in the middle, okay? I want you to keep your heads down and stay out of sight, and if that means leaving, then you have to go find someplace else for a while. And by the way, that cell phone number I gave you doesn't work anymore."

"It doesn't?" Pepper sounded worried.

"It doesn't, but I'll get you a new one as soon as I can, okay?" I reached for my purse again and pulled out my wallet. Inside, I had more than two thousand dollars in cash. I handed the whole wad to Pepper. I've got half a dozen bank accounts under that many identities. One or two, the government flunkies might catch, but I wasn't worried about every single one of them getting frozen, and these kids might need to be mobile.

"You're just giving us . . . that's a lot of money."

"Not as much as it looks like," I said. "And yes, I'm giving it to you—on one condition. If you *do* get caught, you've never heard of me. I don't know you're staying here, and you've never seen me before, and you didn't even know anyone owned this building, got it?"

She nodded with all the gravity of a black hole, but I wasn't finished yet.

I said, "I'm not fooling around with you here—or you, either, Domino. These people who are looking for me, if they get hold of you, you *have* to convince them that you've never heard of me. If they don't believe you, they're going to fuck you up *bad*. Do I make myself understood?"

"Yeah," he said, still playing it cool and bored.

I restated, "I'm serious!" because I didn't think he grasped exactly how serious I was. "If you tell these guys the truth, you're fucked *way* worse than I am. If they think you know anything at all, they'll never let you go. Total ignorance is your only recourse, dude."

"I said, I *got* it."

"Good. Now shut up, and both of you leave me alone for a few minutes, all right? I need to concentrate, and you don't need to see any of this."

"Is it porn?" Domino asked.

"No, it isn't *porn,*" I told him, and shooed at him with my left hand. "It's way more boring than porn, I promise. Go out and get yourselves some hot chocolate or something. The joint around the corner is still open. Will you do that for me, please? I'm only try-ing to look out for you here." I wished it hadn't sounded so much like I was pleading with him, but it did sound that way, and it worked.

The two of them trotted back downstairs, stuffing their pock-ets with cash that would surely be gone by sunrise. I wished I could put them up someplace, but they wouldn't let me. I know. I've tried it before.

The little shits had decided they were home, and they weren't going anywhere.

Fine. They could stay here and get interrogated, then.

I didn't like it, but I didn't know what to do. I could've killed them, I guess. I won't say the thought didn't cross my mind, be-cause it did, and it wouldn't have been any skin off my nose to plunge a tooth or two into Domino's greasy little neck. But I couldn't do that to Pepper. Her powers of cute were too strong, and she relied on her brother too much for me to take him away from her—though for a second, I considered it. I could leave him behind and travel with this kid, and . . .

And then I came to my senses, and I started reading as fast as my comprehension would allow.

Coincidentally enough, I was reading about a break-in.

My Bad Hatter buddy had sent me an inventory of Holtzer Point's contents, following a breach of security some years previously.

I didn't see anything about Bigfoot sperm or Jimmy Hoffa; in fact, most of it looked dull as hell. This is no doubt due to the fact that I didn't have a secret decoder ring. There were code words for people, and projects, and subjects, and expeditions, and . . . and I had no idea what else. To tell you the truth, most of the time I couldn't even infer whether or not I was reading about a person, or a place, or a mission, or whatever.

To save time, I ran a keyword search. "Jordan Roe" turned up nothing. Neither did Ian's serial number, at first. Then I got crafty. I tried "JR" since the army loves abbreviations so much, and I landed a hit.

My first two matches were abbreviations for other things, but the third had potential. I scrolled back, and up, and around until I found the section that was being discussed. Wouldn't you know it—I'd landed in the chapter wherein missing items were cataloged.

To sum it up more concisely than the government did . . . someone had beaten me to the punch. Files pertaining to "JR" had been among those stolen by the intruder. I brainstormed my way around the facts and kept on scrolling, hoping to stumble on something useful. Hell, I would've settled for some kind of confirmation that "JR" was in fact "Jordan Roe."

And then I found it. A different abbreviation, one I hadn't thought to scan for: "J. Roe." A joke about a Japanese pop singer sprang immediately to mind, but I was a good girl and didn't say it out loud—even though there was no one to hear me.

I just kept on reading, and collecting more questions than answers.

A few pages down I found some more serial numbers, and I felt like a real boob. Ian's was right there, hyphenated a little differently, but still in sequence. It was odd to see it—proof of everything he'd told me, and proof that yes, the government was quite certain that vampires exist. Of course, this was also proof that we could be captured, and that we were flesh and blood. We could be altered, and hurt.

I ran my finger over the screen and touched the other serial numbers that didn't match Ian's.

We could be killed.

Sure, I knew that part already. And I knew it had nothing to do with garlic, or crosses, or sunlight. We don't die easily; it takes a lot of fire or firepower, or a lot of cutting. But without our heads, we're the same goners as everyone else.

And then there's the sun. That's one legend with some truth to it. More than a few seconds of direct sunlight and our skin begins to blister. More than a few minutes and we're a bubbling, vampire-shaped blob that's too far gone to save.

When I was a young fledgling of a night-stalker, I accidently got myself a smidge of sun poisoning, and I don't mind telling you, it was completely fucking miserable. If there are worse ways to shuffle off this mortal coil, I don't want to know about them.

I shuddered with the memory of it and returned my attention to the PDF.

Again, I wished I'd had more time to talk to Ian, and I resolved to make more time when the danger was somewhat past. Even if the case ended, and even if I gave him everything he wanted, I wanted more from him than money. I wanted to know what had happened, and why.

Farther down the endless document with its tiny font I found more of what I was looking for—an admission that Jordan Roe had been decommissioned. As I was already aware, its top secret stash had been sent to Holtzer Point. But according to the PDF, it wasn't there anymore. It hadn't been there for years.

"Goddamn," I said.

Some other thief had stolen the stuff I wanted to steal.

I tried to tell myself that this was a lucky break—because now,

I did not have to break into a high-security facility and sift through boxes upon boxes of stale old paperwork. Now, all I had to do was find the thief and wrestle it away from him.

It might not be that difficult. The feds already had a suspect.

I didn't have a name for him, but I jotted down his serial number. Mr. 887-32-5561.

I noted from the lack of a 636 that he wasn't part of the super-secret program. Good. Then he wasn't a vampire, or anything else interesting enough to warrant supernatural caution on my part.

This was not the world's safest assumption. So, I vowed to re-visit it later.

I scanned the document for more clues. Mr. 887-32-5561 was a military man (woman? Oh, screw it—masculine pronoun for convenience), but I had no idea which branch of service he'd been a part of. He'd gone AWOL shortly before the burglary and was presently wanted by the military police. He'd been on the lam for nearly eight years by now, and as an internal memo noted, it was as if he'd "stopped the planet and got off."

I liked him already, and I psyched myself up for the prospect of tracking him down. I had every advantage, after all. I was not a bulky, cumbersome government agency without a clue in the dark. I was a thief—the very best of my kind—and I was slumming down the food chain after a man who might be a professional soldier, but was surely only an amateur stealer.

I said to myself, "Self, this is going to be a piece of cake."

And I tried to make myself believe it.

5

Yes, yes. I should've known better than to say something like that out loud, in front of God and everybody. And sure enough, it eventually came back to bite me in the ass.

I clapped the laptop shut and, since the kids weren't back yet from whatever errand they were running with their fresh influx of cash, I left them a note saying that I might be gone for a while. I tried not to make it sound like too much of a formal good-bye, because I sincerely hoped I wasn't abandoning them (and all my stuff) once and for all; and besides, I didn't want them to freak out when they discovered I'd left. I needed them nice and calm, not wondering if they ought to report me as a missing person—especially since I'd just wound them up with a whole slew of warnings before ushering them out.

I closed the place up behind me—not so tight that they couldn't find their way in, but tight enough to deter any casual trespassers—and then I struck out for home.

Home was a calculated risk. I figured I'd scope the place out, and if I spied even the faintest hint of security breach or goggle-eyed operatives, then I'd hightail it elsewhere. But I didn't yet have any good idea where Elsewhere might turn out to be, and there were a handful of things I'd prefer to destroy or collect from the old homestead if it were at all possible.

I parked my car on the edge of my neighborhood, at an easily accessible spot that would also make a straight shot of a getaway point. There's nary a convenient parking space on any curbside of Capitol Hill, so I had to leave the Thunderbird parked entirely too close to a stop sign. But seriously, if the city meant for drivers to keep their cars thirty feet away from the corners, they'd mark the damn corners with paint or something. I'm convinced that it's a conspiracy to write more tickets and bring in more revenue—so if I looked at it that way, then really, I was just doing my part to support Seattle's public servants.

I mean, if they caught me.

And if I felt like paying the ticket, depending on where my Elsewhere turned out to be.

I took to the rooftops, even though I've already made a disclaimer on the subject. But it's not every twenty-four hours that I pick up a vampire client, end up on the receiving end of a break-in, and inadvertently tangle with Uncle Sam. So really, it's a wonder I managed to keep it to such a minimum.

I wasn't sure what time it was, but it was pretty late and pretty cold. Tar paper under my feet gave way to expensive shingles and slanted roofs that were tougher to cling to than the open, flat spaces of downtown's old industrial district. I slipped, caught myself with less silence than I would've preferred, and regained enough footing to leap over to a freakishly large evergreen of some sort, where I crouched and hovered and hoped for the best while I got a whole row of stink-eye from a family of crows that had been happily sleeping there.

I could see my condo, and see my bedroom windows. Without blinking, I watched those windows, wondering how well my tracks had been covered and how long I had before my safe house was outted, gutted, and sifted for evidence of . . . crimes?

But what crimes? I was a professional criminal, yes—but Uncle Sam's sudden interest in me did not, hypothetically, have anything to do with any of my previous felonies. They were looking for me because I was looking for Ian's past. I was running because they were chasing me. I was smack in the middle of all these causal relationships that made precious little sense, but might mean the difference between my continued freedom and a fate like Ian's.

Or worse.

I didn't want to think about that. The prospect of spending eternity blind, or deaf, or hideously scarred, or mentally impaired . . . none of it made me want to do anything but run screaming into the night.

My windows were blank and black. No matter how hard I strained I couldn't see any hint of anything moving within, and I was patient enough to wait a full five minutes before scooting past the crows and praying they wouldn't fly off, alerting the whole world to my position.

They didn't. The crows and seagulls in Seattle are as unflappable as the kind they carve on totem poles. They live in the middle of a city, surrounded by people. We don't impress them.

I quietly thanked them for their apathy and bounced over onto my own roof. I skidded to a halt and held my breath, hoping and praying that no one had seen me or heard me, and that I hadn't kicked anything important that would need repairing.

Nothing in the world moved, and the neighborhood stayed quiet.

I was alone on the roof, except for the ruffling, mumbled protests of sleeping pigeons who were every bit as unimpressed by my presence as the crows had been in the tree. I held up a finger and said, "Shh!" as if it meant a damn to them.

But surely if armed men in commando uniforms had stormed the condo, even such blasé birds as these would've scattered, wouldn't they? I told myself it was a good sign and that I may as well let myself down into my place, just one last time—long enough to cover my tracks.

For a moment I considered firebombing the condo behind me, but that would mean even more civic scrutiny, and I'd learned the hard way over the years that fire destroys pretty much everything, but not always everything. No, I'd be better off doing a hasty Houdini than trying to scorch the earth in my wake. And anyway, my neighbors were perfectly nice, and some of them owned pets.

The thought of cooking anyone's dogs, cats, birds, or aquariums bothered me more than the thought of torching those animals' owners. Call me strange if you want, but I've been known to feed animals, and I've likewise been known to kill and eat people. So I guess the math isn't that tough after all.

In the bottom depths of my bag I keep an assortment of useful tools that I can't take through an airport screening, including a glass cutter. I leaned down over the edge of my (luckily, top-floor) condo, and dragged my little tool along my bedroom window in a small circle, popped the resulting bit of glass inside, and reached around to unlatch it from within.

Still, I didn't hear a sound.

Good.

I let myself in, moving about in full-on sneak mode—not turning on any lights, but letting my undead eyes do the grunt work on the shadows. Everything looked exactly as I'd left it, down to the unmade bed with the covers straggling about on the floor. Room to room I wandered, collecting small items and stuffing them into my bag. I picked up a notebook here, and a ring of extra keys there; I lifted a book I hadn't finished reading yet and a necklace that once belonged to my grandmother, who died before I was born.

Then I went to my drawer full of cell phones and other useful things. I picked up three or four at random and took the remaining half dozen into the kitchen, where I jammed them into the microwave and pressed the three-minute button. Immediately sparks began to fly and the microwave hummed a distress signal, like I'd given it indigestion. But I wanted the phones good and dead, even though I wasn't strictly certain I'd ever used any of them.

The sputtering wail of melting plastic and cooking circuitry made my ears hurt, but I ignored it and went back to my bedroom while the phones turned to mush and, very likely, destroyed the microwave. A very loud *pop* reinforced this suspicion, so I ran back to the kitchen and hit the CANCEL button, since I'd resolved not to burn the place down.

On the turntable behind the glass door I saw a lumpy cluster of smoking, sparking phones, and it occurred to me that I'd better not open that door lest I set off the smoke alarm, which would not be good for my full-on sneak mode.

Back in the bedroom I lingered against my better judgment. I stood beside my bed, staring around the room and fretting, wondering what else I should take. It shouldn't have been such a major crisis; I've abandoned living spaces before, more than once, without any heartbreak or waffling. But most of those abandonings took place at my own whim, at my own instigation—or at the very least, they happened as a result of my own criminal activities.

Maybe that was the problem.

I didn't feel like I was leaving. I felt like I was being unjustly pursued.

I wanted to muster some righteous indignation, but I was too hyped up on my own fear to manage it. I'm not often driven to tears by such things, but as I stood there, hunting desperately for something to gather—or maybe just dithering in my confusion—I almost wanted to cry.

But after a minute or two of hand-fluttering, I pulled myself together and grabbed a duffel out of the closet. I crammed it full of my most worn clothes and a pair of beloved boots that Fluevog doesn't make anymore, and I left everything else. I went out the way I came in, for whatever silly reason I couldn't tell you. But back out in the night, on the roof, beside the mildly irritated pigeons and the occasional rat that ran along the power lines, I jumped back down to the ground and walked the rest of the way back to my car.

I didn't have a parking ticket.

I didn't really expect one.

I threw the duffel bag and my purse onto the passenger seat, leaned my forehead against the steering wheel, and forced myself to think.

What now? Where should I go? What should I do?

I'd sent Ian and Cal off to Ballard, and I'd left the kids as secure as I could leave them, so I was faced with a handful of options—none of which seemed strictly ideal. I could officially and completely leave the city, pretending that I'd never heard of any of them and that I didn't owe any of them anything. But while I was prepared to insist that I owed my feral squatters nothing, I was harder-pressed to conclude that I didn't owe Ian the time of day.

True, he was the one who'd gotten me into this mess, but he *did* warn me. And I didn't believe (then, or now) that he'd deliberately put me on a federal watch list and sent the men in black after me. At this point, I was already eyeballs-deep in his problem anyway. There was an excellent chance that if I couldn't solve Ian's problems, I might never untangle myself from Official Interest. And God help me if whoever was after me put two and two together, realizing that the woman in the condo was in fact the thief known as Cheshire Red to all those international agencies.

But I was getting ahead of myself. I was doing it again, assuming the worst and doing my best to plot against it, even though the worst-case scenario is often either incorrect or vastly under-calculated.

None of this changed anything. I was mired in Ian's situation whether I liked it or not, and if I'd had the option of declining his case before, that option had gone out the window when I'd taken that PDF from the Bad Hatter. Logic dictated that I needed to see this through, and sort it out at the source if I ever hoped to resume my wholly understated existence.

Merely coming to this decision bolstered me a bit, and made the world look a little less overwhelming. I could do it! All I needed to do was track down the missing paperwork, hand it over to Ian, perhaps flee the country with him and Cal (hey, why not?), and start over Elsewhere, as I've done a dozen times before.

Plan: Achieved.

I reached for my car keys and slipped the right one into the ignition. The moment before I turned it, a sleek black car with government plates went sliding around the corner with all the perfect quietness and glide of a UFO. If that thing had an engine in it, I couldn't hear it—but there's always the possibility that I'd become totally unhinged with fear.

I backpedaled for a second, trying to rationalize and justify a means whereby that car was absolutely *not* cruising my neighborhood because its driver knew where I lived, but within moments that car was joined by a second vehicle, rolling smoothly down the perpendicular road and vanishing around the side of an Indian restaurant that had been closed for hours. The sneaky black sedans moved with preternatural slickness, like they were touring the town on frictionless tires.

I sank down low in the driver's seat until, it was to be fervently prayed, anyone driving past couldn't see me. Carefully but quickly, I fired my hand up to the rearview mirror—tilting it so that I could see the street outside without revealing my oh-so-clever hiding place . . . in the front seat of my car.

The first car oozed past and turned down the street I'd walked along mere minutes earlier; the second car was out of sight. Both of them had government plates, which I noted with a god-awful sinking feeling. I didn't see anything else and I didn't hear anything else, but once I couldn't see either one of them anymore, I took a chance and started the Thunderbird. It came to life almost cheerfully, and far too loudly for my comfort—but at least it started. I'd been half afraid that the engine would pull a horror-movie cliché on me and refuse to turn over.

I eased the car forward toward the stop sign and pretended to mind my own business all the way into the main drag, where I took excellent care to obey every damn traffic law I could think of, to such maniacal excess that it no doubt looked far more suspicious than if I'd just gunned the car and shot down the hill.

Nobody stopped me. No flashing red lights or crow-black cars with tinted windows came stalking up to my bumper. And eventually I was away. I was out of my neighborhood and instinctively heading toward the interstate again, but I stopped myself downtown, pulling into an all-night parking garage to regroup and make some more distinct plans than "solve Ian's problem and bill him an arm and a leg."

I parked in a back corner of the bottom floor, in a half-empty row of other vehicles that had been abandoned over the evening by third-shift workers or drunks. I pulled Ian's file out of my bag and examined it again, hunting for direction or inspiration under the lemon-yellow and sickly orange security lights of the garage.

Cal's atrocious handwriting stood out from the margins of the first thing I grabbed.

"Holtzer Point, St. Paul."

But whatever Holtzer Point had once held, it was long gone—stolen by Mr. 887-something-or-another, and relocated to parts unknown.

I reached up to click on the car's dome light so I could read a little better, then turned it off again when I realized it made me more visible. Such indecision. I was plagued with it.

This guy. Mr. 887 . . . forget it. In my head I nicknamed him The Other Thief.

Whoever he was, I needed him.

And I had no idea where to find him, but it didn't sound like Uncle Sam knew, either. This was a problem. I couldn't just poke my way into government files and turn up his name and address.

However . . .

I tapped my knuckles against the steering wheel. I always fidget when I'm thinking. Can't help it.

However, Uncle Sam knew The Other Thief's identity. The serial number told me that much, and I wondered if there was some good way to take that number and turn it into a name. It'd be nice to know who I was looking for.

If I could pin down his identity, I could pin down other things. Family members, friends. Former service buddies. Co-workers.

I might even be able to get my hands on his old phone records or credit card statements; it's amazing what you can find with the right phone calls and law enforcement clearance . . . not that I have law enforcement clearance. I don't. But my fellow freelancer the Red Queen does, or if she doesn't, she knows how to fake it.

Bad Hatter's info might have burned me, but I believed him when he said it wasn't deliberate. And even if Red Queen knew about my personal meltdown over here, it likely wouldn't mean anything to her. She owes me one. About three years ago she needed architectural schematics for a large, unmarked building belonging to some Italian cardinal . . . but located in St. Petersburg, Florida. I got them for her. And no, I never asked what she needed them for.

At any rate, my number one priority was to track down The Other Thief's name and then backtrack him clear to the cradle. The more I could learn about him, the better my chances of predicting where he'd run and hide. The fact is, very few people actually disappear with the kind of thoroughness required to stay disappeared. The odds were strong that someone, somewhere, knew where he'd gone.

But first things first. How to pry his personal information away from the government? I glared back down at Ian's folder and I wondered: Could I find it at Holtzer Point?

Maybe. After all, one unauthorized downloading of the Bloodshot PDF had been serious enough to warrant a platoon of Men in Black. Surely the government hadn't just let hard copies detailing the nitty-gritty details vanish—not without looking into it? There would've been an investigation. There would've been sensitive paperwork. And where did sensitive paperwork of this stripe wind up?

Holtzer Point.

But if the military or the feds were looking for me, did I really want to run straight into one of their most private facilities? For the moment, I'd given them the slip. A very narrow, very uncertain slip—but my fragile liberty was liberty nonetheless, and they hadn't caught me yet.

At best, it wasn't exactly a cunning strategy to impress the ages and achieve the status of tactical legend, but it was better than nothing. And otherwise, all I had was nothing apart from "run that guy's serial number through the Internet and hope to strike gold."

I had every intention of doing that, by the way. I'm not an idiot.

But since I'm not an idiot—and knowing what had happened when Duncan had nabbed that PDF—I decided to do it on the way out of town.

And I definitely needed to get out of town. I wanted to put as much distance between me and Seattle as possible, in order to re-group and see if I couldn't brainstorm my way to some better idea once I achieved some breathing room and could calm the fuck back down.

With luck, I might even cough up some less stupid plan.

I squeezed the brittle old papers and made my resolution. Then I stuffed them back into the envelope, took a deep breath, and started my car again.

I'd never been to Minnesota before. But there's a first time for everything.

So I'd begin my withdrawal and regrouping at St. Paul, but I wouldn't leave from SeaTac—the Seattle-Tacoma airport. It was probably crawling with leftover feds from the Mean Bean, if my ruse had worked. The only way to find out was to try and fly out, and I couldn't see taking that kind of risk. It wasn't like me, and it wasn't healthy, and I wasn't in the mood for one of those plans where you let yourself get captured in order to escape with infor-mation.

No, the Thunderbird's tank was full and I was feeling like a road trip instead.

About three hours to the south, Portland, Oregon, has an airport, too—and by sunrise I was nervously ensconced in a Marriott hotel immediately outside it. I closed all the curtains, plugged all the cracks, and turned off all the cell phones. I rigged the door with a cheap alarm that would give me time to . . . I don't know, panic and cry, if anyone tried to bust in.

And shortly after sundown the next day, I had a plane ticket that would bring me to the Minneapolis–St. Paul International Airport. I also had the entire contents of my Thunderbird packed into the suitcase from the trunk, which I checked in order to keep my very sharp little tools and whatnot. I left the car in long-term parking. Maybe I'd be back for it, maybe I wouldn't. For all I knew, it might sit there for weeks before anyone thought to tow it. There was always the chance this would blow over and I could just go back home, picking up where I'd left off.

Optimism! Okay, forced optimism. But it was all I had.

I checked the Internet to see if The Other Thief's serial number turned up anything via Google magic, but no. Nothing.

And then I ran, not even sticking around to see if anyone was going to chase me down for running that search. Call me a coward if you like, but it didn't really matter if they were following me or not.

I was headed to the airport.

I don't typically enjoy flying. There are too many variables, and I'm on a narrow kind of time frame—I simply *must* be indoors in the dark when the sun rises, unless I want to wind up a steaming, wibbling pulp—so the red-eye is fine by me. But any delays or reroutes can be downright deadly.

I made my connection in Denver and skidded into Minnesota with an hour or two to spare before morning.

I won't bore you with the particulars of what came next, except to say that I found another hotel (a Hyatt, this time), burrowed in for the day, and then went looking for some slightly more solid accommodations downtown. I wasn't 100 percent certain of where Holtzer Point was located, and I'd need some time to lie low and do some research. This sort of research is hard to accomplish when you're stuck in an airport hotel, and much easier (and less eyebrow-raising) to manage when you're in a very posh establishment nearer to the center of everything.

Eventually I paid up for a full week at a four-star establishment on the other side of the river, hunkered down, and spent a couple of days scavenging for paperwork, rumors, and hints. It was mostly boring—which is to say, I didn't learn anything new or exciting about Ian's incarceration and nobody kicked down my door. But I did eventually locate the storage facility and learn a bit about its security protocols.

At a glance they were pretty pathetic, but that might be meaningless. Even the shittiest schematics can be made troublesome by enough manpower on guard duty.

I inferred from the diagrams that Uncle Sam simply didn't believe there was any good reason that anyone, anywhere, would want inside . . . even if anyone could find it. (Conspiracy nuts on the Internet be damned.) And yet a token effort at security was undertaken as a matter of general principle.

It reminded me of a story I'd stumbled across years ago about a bank vault full of Susan B. Anthony and Sacagawea dollars that nobody wanted. Thousands and thousands of dollars, just sitting there—and the bank couldn't give them away, not for trying. But out of a sense of duty or whatever, they kept the coins locked up in the basement behind a barred cage frame.

At the time, I wondered why anyone would bother.

But as I sat in my very posh hotel, wearing a fluffy white robe with the hotel logo on the right breast, staring down at a bedspread sprinkled with marginally informative files stamped CONFIDEN-TIAL, I concluded that guarding Holtzer Point was even sillier. The only people who wanted to get inside it were sitting at home eating Cheetos from their beanbags, filing Freedom of Information Act petitions and coding way-too-much Flash into their alarmist webpages. They were armchair wingnuts. They weren't nosy vampires with a skill set like mine, and nothing better to do than go check the place out.

Then a lightbulb popped brightly over my head. Metaphorically, you know.

The only people who knew about Holzter Point were the folks involved in the military projects that were documented and destroyed there. *Somebody* has to sign off on all that stuff, and the military is nothing if not fond of its paper trails. It might shred all the paper in the end, but everything gets written down *someplace*.

By someone.

Therefore it struck me as a strong chance that The Other Thief was someone who'd been party to the experiments at Jordan Roe in Florida.

I jotted this thought down in my trusty notebook, reminding myself that I was looking for a wayward military man . . . but military men come in many flavors. Maybe he wasn't a soldier. Call it a hunch, but something told me I was looking for a former researcher or scientist collaborator—maybe someone with a conscience, or someone with an ax to grind.

The prospect of a grinding ax gave me another option that hadn't dawned on me yet: The Other Thief could have a connection to a victim of the program, maybe one of the other vampires (or other creatures) who were held and tested. I already knew that the military's suspect wasn't a victim of the program because of his serial number. But he could've been a friend or lover.

Lots of possibilities there.

I gathered the paperwork together. There wasn't much to hold, and there was even less to call important or helpful. But I had enough to find my way inside a place that was every bit as secretive as the spot where Top Government Officials told Indiana Jones they were "examining" the Ark of the Covenant.

I didn't know what I'd find when I got inside—maybe nothing—but I didn't have any better ideas and I didn't dare try to contact Ian for further brainstorming. Not yet.

I checked my email, though, on the off chance he might've sent me something. I didn't recall having ever sent him my digital address, but then again I never sent him my bricks-and-mortar address either, and he'd turned that up no problem. A girl can dream, can't she?

A girl can be disappointed, too. Nothing new or important.

Then I remembered I had a Hotmail address, and I'd even handed it out recently. I hopped online and went to my inbox, where lo and behold I had an email from EABruner via gmail. That struck me as funny. I had to assume the guy had an official email through a work account, but he shoots me a note from something as fake as the addy I'd given him. Nice.

It read:

All right, kid. You want to come out and play? Let's talk. You've caught me at a disadvantage here since you know my name and I don't know yours, but Trevor said he had friends who might be interested, so here's how it works.

This is not a military operation. It's a civilian operation operated and financed by civilians, which I can say with a straight face because I'm no longer on active duty. So don't get any big commando ideas in your head. This isn't like that, and if it was, I sure as hell wouldn't bother to write a girl about it.

We're looking into some properties around the country, including Seattle. We want people who can get inside, maybe take some pictures, maybe just report back about what's inside. We need people who aren't afraid of a little trouble. If you get picked up by the cops you're on your own. We aren't bailing you out. But I've attached a document to this email. Look it over. It'll tell you about King County's laws with regards to trespassing and breaking-and-entering. You'd be surprised what you can get away with when you know your rights.

Just so we're clear, not everyplace we want investigated is abandoned. You might run into people, guard dogs, surveillance systems . . . God knows what. If you're not afraid of spending a night in the clink, or if you think you're good enough that you won't get caught, read over that document and write me back.

~EB

PS: How well do you know Trevor? I haven't heard a goddamn thing from him in several days. Tell that asshole to call me, if you see him.

Boy. The charm just never stopped with that guy, but I couldn't pretend the email wasn't useful. It didn't tell me much, but I'm good at reading between the lines, and what I saw between the lines told me I really, really didn't like this douchebag.

It also told me that "Major" was more of a nickname than a title, if he was retired. I wasn't sure what to make of that, except that plenty of people retire from the military and go on to other careers—and just because my new client had been a victim of military manipulation and mutilation, that didn't mean anything. Could be a perfectly meaningless coincidence.

Only I hate coincidences. So I wrote him back:

My name is Abigail, in case you care. I don't have a problem poking around in other people's stuff, believe me. I'm not really worried about this danger of which you speak, but I'd like a little more info. Are we talking crazed drug dealers here? Because if you want me to spy on the Mafia or organized meth-heads or anything, you're out of your fucking mind.

Other than that, I might be interested. Should I meet you someplace? Do you have an office in Seattle, or are you somewhere else? Trevor didn't say. And I haven't seen that asshole either, or I'd just ask him. I'll call his roommate and leave him a message that way. Maybe he'll get back to one of us, one of these days.

Abbie

My mother's name was Abigail. Perhaps I'm desecrating her memory or something, but I doubt she would've cared.

If I was lucky, he'd respond in an open, honest fashion—informing me of what his precise plans were, where exactly he was located, and freely volunteering the identity of his financial backers. I didn't ask any of this stuff because I couldn't think of a credible way to work it in without giving myself away as someone with a way-too-personal interest.

I closed the laptop and settled in for the evening.

The next night was supposed to be clear and cold and moonless, so that made it as good a night as any to take my life and sanity into my own hands. And God help me, but they weren't kidding about the cold. What amounted to a chilly, damp mid-fall in Seattle was more like a deep freeze in Minnesota. Maybe I ought to have expected it, but I'd never been there before and the shock of the air outside was enough to stun me. It was like breathing liquid nitrogen; it went straight down my throat and chilled me from the inside out.

I shook it off as I kept moving, down to the car I'd bought off a used lot an afternoon or two previously. Yes, I can go out in the afternoons, if I stay in the northern latitudes. I love it when the sun sets at three thirty—everything is still open for a while after I wake up, and I can go shopping for anything I need. Summers are more of a trick, I admit. But most of the year the night is long, and it belongs to *me*.

My new vehicle was a very shiny Nissan with fully a hundred thousand miles on it, but somebody loved it once, and it was in good shape. I think its original color was white, but it'd been painted over with a dark green that looked like pond slime at midnight, so I liked it, and I bought it, and voilà. New wheels.

I rolled these new wheels out through the maze of neighborhoods and across roads that had been scraped so clean of ice, they couldn't have chilled a can of Diet Coke.

I gave three quiet cheers for Minnesota. In Seattle a dusty inch of anything white and chilly means the city lapses into full-on panic mode, as if each falling flake crashes to earth with its own individual baggie of used hypodermic needles. It's ridiculous.

But the city before me was shiny and dark, hard-frozen around its edges and glinting from the ice that coated the corners of buildings like cake frosting made of crushed glass. The streets were empty since the wee hours were approaching and hey, for all that I'd cheered, St. Paul was no Seattle, and there didn't appear to be much in the way of nightlife—at least not through the places where I was driving.

I had a printout of directions from the Internet sitting on the passenger seat beside me. They weren't directions to Holtzer Point exactly, but they were maps of the rough location where I figured Holtzer Point could be found. I already knew I was going to be relegated to foot patrol at some point, so I didn't mind playing it a little fuzzy.

Soon the bare but civilized streets of St. Paul gave way to emptier places with shorter buildings and fewer streetlights . . . and then no buildings, and no streetlights, and after a few turns I was urging the Nissan along a two-lane road in the middle of what could best be described as the geographic center of Godforsaken, Bumblefuck. The roads out there in Bumblefuck weren't quite as pristine as the ones in town, and the Nissan struggled with the curves. I should've put new tires on it before taking it out. I'm sure I had some good reason for not doing so at the time, but I kicked myself about it as the back wheels spun and I clenched my teeth. I wasn't desperately worried about getting stuck; I'm strong enough to shove my own car out of a mushy ditch. I just didn't want to do it if I didn't have to.

At the tail end of my flippant prayer to the gods of winter, the car lurched forward and carried me another mile before any farther distance would be an ill-advised pressing of luck. I pulled the car as far off the road as I dared and backed into an improvised spot between two trees. Then I took all my paperwork pertaining to Holtzer Point and stuck it into my Useful Things Bag, which I slung over my shoulder. There was no sense in leaving a treasure map to my intended location lying out in the open, in case anyone *did* find the car and deem it suspicious enough to open.

I got out, wished that the car had still been painted white so it'd be harder to see, and made sure my boots were laced tightly. I didn't want any snow down my ankles and I didn't want to stop and tie anything at a crucial moment of reconnaissance.

As I stood there, already half frozen solid and breathing pale puffs of air across the hood of my car, I hated myself for thinking of that word again.

Reconnaissance. Then I thought of the major and his audible sneer, and I told myself that turnabout was fair play.

I stomped off alongside the two-lane road, following it rather than walking it because I didn't know if it was being watched—but I might as well assume the worst. The snow made progress an exhausting sort of slog, and no amount of lacing could keep all the icy slush out of my socks. I wished for rooftops to jump between, but didn't get anything for my wishing except for a knee-deep drop through a crackling crust. I hoisted my legs up, one after another, and forced myself to remember that I was making noise, and that I was on dangerous ground. But it was a hard job to convince myself, out there in the astonishing no-place-ness of the frigid forest.

Until I hit the fence.

Chain link all around with razor wire at the top, the fence was maybe nine feet high. I didn't see any signs right away, but as I trudged along its length I eventually encountered an admonition to KEEP OUT. PROPERTY MONITORED AND MAINTAINED BY THE UNITED STATES ARMED FORCES. TRESPASSERS WILL BE SHOT.

It might as well have said, WELCOME, RAYLENE. LET YOURSELF INSIDE, BUT KEEP YOUR HEAD DOWN, M'KAY?

That's how I read it anyway, and that's what I did. I figured if the military really wanted to keep people out, it could spring for something more off-putting than a chain-link fence because, seriously—any idiot with a bolt cutter could slink on through in under a minute. I'm no idiot, and I had a bolt cutter. I made myself a pet door, bent the clipped oval up, and slid underneath. Then I drew it down behind me for appearance's sake, on the off chance that the property really *was* being monitored.

Again I found it peculiar how little security had been detailed or visible. I'd made my excuses, but surely following a break-in tighter measures might be instituted? Or was I just overestimating the commitment of the armed forces to keeping its secrets?

I didn't have a map of Holtzer Point because the place practically doesn't exist, except in tinfoil-hat-land. Even my handy-dandy PDF of useful stuff didn't give me any good idea about the joint's layout, so I was going to have to wing it.

I was wearing white, of course. I even had a white hat to cover my dark hair. No sense in taking chances. And while the fence's perimeter was handy, it probably wasn't the best thing to follow in the long term. People don't put buildings on fences. They put fences around buildings, and often they aim cameras at fences. Ergo, I'd have to venture out into the semi-open.

Inside the fence there were still plenty of trees, and inside those trees I could not spy any hint of hardware. If I was being watched, I was being watched discreetly. No matter how hard I sniffed, I couldn't pick up even the faintest traces of warmth from small lights or the funny ozone and metal stink of electronics.

I kept low and kept to the largest trunks I could find, and trusted them to hide me. And eventually, after an ass-numbing hour of swearing my way through the snow, I found five buildings clustered together, as if for warmth. One was quite large—easily the size of a big barn—and the others were much smaller. In the tiniest of the five, an ill yellow light was burning within, and the one lone window marked a pitiful square of occupancy.

I felt sorry for whoever was home. I'd been in cemeteries that saw more action.

By my best guess, the tiny shack with the square yellow window was a guard's hut or something. One of the other small buildings looked like a storage shed, perhaps, and the big barn must be where pay dirt was housed. The other two structures were inscrutable. If there were windows, I couldn't see them, and if there was any sign of life inside, it didn't leak out into the open where I could detect it.

I could've just bopped into the guard's hut and cold-cocked the occupant, sure; but if I could possibly manage it, I wanted to get in and out without anyone knowing I'd ever been there.

I sidled around to the back of the nearest building first, just trying to get the lay of the land. And anyway, it was less visible from the guard's hut. While I was there, I may as well be thorough, and may as well tackle the easiest targets first.

On the side opposite the guard's hut I found a row of windows that were small enough to be merely ornamental—if the military ever did anything for the sake of aesthetics. They latched from within, of course, but a quick zip of my glass cutter gave me enough access to open them. I replaced the cork of glass when I was finished. It wasn't perfect, but unless you were looking for signs of an entry—I mean *seriously* looking—you'd never notice I'd done anything.

I took a deep breath. Since this inflated my chest and made it bigger, I let the breath out again and then, with my temporarily leaner physique, wormed my way through the ridiculously narrow slot. I nearly lost a boot on my way inside, and if my pants had been even half a size bigger I would've gotten stuck. But all went well and I slipped on through, slicker than whale shit through an ice floe.

I caught myself with my hands, and landed with nothing more noteworthy than a muffled *thud*.

As I'd originally suspected, I'd deposited myself into a garden toolshed, though it was almost too big to call a shed. If I'd been bold enough to shine a light in first I'd have known that for certain. But if the place was occupied at all—even if it was by a slumbering old coot with a Barney Fife complex—then discretion must remain the better part of valor.

I tiptoed around the riding lawn mower and perused the shelves as a matter of principle, but I found only bug spray, WD-40, paint thinner, and bundles of greasy rags. It could've been anybody's dad's garage. And if being undead hadn't taken care of my allergies, I would've been sneezing my brains out. A thick coat of dust covered everything, and I'd disturbed it, which disturbed me. But spring was months away and maybe whatever I'd kicked up would settle back down before anything needed mowing or weeding, or that's what I told myself as I squirmed my way back out into the open air.

The big barn, then. That's where I'd try next.

I poked my head out of the window, looked both ways like a first-grader crossing the street, and started wiggling back outside again. I was about two-thirds out—hanging at my hips, working up the momentum to flip myself forward with enough leverage for a smooth landing—when I heard it.

Somewhere nearby.

The *crunch-crunch, crunch-crunch,* of someone walking briskly through the snow. Nay, not walking briskly. More like . . . sneaking. Or marching. Sneak-marching. And absolutely nothing about that sound warmed my heart in any fashion whatsoever.

I didn't quite manage the landing I'd wanted—I toppled forward out the window and fell with more of a "splat" than with tidy cat feet *en pointe*—but it got me to the ground. Funny, I didn't remember the snow under the window being quite so deep on the way in. I sank into snow that came up over my knees, and I tramped around in it, both trying to be quiet and trying to figure out which direction to run, if any.

I held still for a few seconds and listened hard, hoping to better pinpoint the noise, which had now been joined by more *crunch-crunch*es and seemed to be coming from everywhere at once.

Stupid woods. Stupid snow. Stupid silent night.

It was coming from the left—no, the right. No, both.

Shit.

I didn't panic. Yet.

Perhaps forty yards of open snow stood between me and the big barn, and the side I faced, but I didn't see any easy point of entry. I could make a run for it, but I'd only be running straight at a blank wall—with no way up it, through it, or inside it. Obviously the thing had to have a door somewhere. I fought to remember: When I'd approached under the fence, down into the main compound . . . had I seen it?

Yes. It was around on the left side, I remembered now.

But someone was closing in on me by the moment. The *crunch-crunch* was close enough that I could hear the faint, low buzz of electronic communication. It was probably moving through ear-buds or very small radios; the sound wasn't perfectly clear, but it was distinct.

I'd been spotted. And I had nowhere to go.

Across the yard—around the right side of the barn—something glinted quickly and vanished. It could've been anything. Probably moonlight off a button, or a pair of glasses.

I was not frozen, not paralyzed. Just pinned by indecision. I looked up and saw the shed's gutter above me, and I thought: *What the hell? Might as well try going up.* They already knew where I was; I could sense that much from the way they were closing in. They weren't hunting, they were coming right for me.

I didn't see them yet, so they had a leg up on me. They'd see me if I jumped up on top of the shed, maybe; and more likely than not, they'd hear me regardless.

I stretched to reach the overhang, but couldn't quite make it. The snow felt like quicksand, and even though it wasn't, I couldn't help but feel that it was holding me down. I picked up my left leg, covered in snow as it was, and braced it against the side of the building, using it to give myself a boost. I hoisted myself up out of the snow and latched both hands around the gutter. The damn thing squealed as if it'd been shot.

Too late to double-think. With a pop of my arms and a fling to toss my weight up onto the gently peaked surface, I was up.

No time for a false sense of security, either. As I scrambled to find a good foothold that wouldn't leave me sliding right back into the snowdrifts, somebody below opened fire.

Bullets sprayed toward me and I ducked, flattening myself on the roof—which had a good foot of snow on it, thank you very much. I wondered if they could see me, if I just went facedown in it, wearing my white suit and everything. It would've been nice if

I could hide there, smushed into the snow. I'd freeze my tits off, but if they couldn't see me, they couldn't shoot at me, right?

Boy, howdy. The bullshit I'll tell myself when I'm completely out of ideas.

Then somebody below barked an order and all bets were off. Two more people were shooting from the other side of the shed. They didn't know exactly where I was, thank God, so the snow was good for something after all, and the peaked roof threw off their angles. It's hard to shoot something that's above you, and reclined on a plane.

But it wouldn't stop them for long.

I blew a frantic second or two wondering how many bullets I could take before going down. In a moment of crisis? I mean, absolute and pure desperation—still having the stamina to run like hell? Maybe three or four to the torso, more if they just winged me. But man, that kind of worst-case-scenario thinking wasn't going to help me. Not then. Not when it was far too late for any preventive measures.

Right. No time to wish for what I didn't have (solitude) and think instead about what I did have (a .38 Special inside my Useful Things Bag).

I didn't want to open fire back. Not immediately. Not while they still were foggy on precisely where I was, apart from "up there someplace." Any gunfire would tell them my exact location immediately and with great clarity.

So I left it stashed for the moment, and writhed around in the snow until I had my bag slung across my chest, leaving both hands fully free and maneuverable. I tightened its strap to keep it close—I didn't want it flopping around during any of the acrobatics I was about to try—and I kept my head low while the bullets clipped shingles closer and closer to where I was hunkering.

This *sucked*. How had they found me? Had I missed a camera? Had they found my car? What easy fuckup had I committed this time? Jesus.

I guess they could've been expecting me. After all, someone, somewhere knew what was in that PDF and knew what it'd tell me. All I could do was hope they didn't know *what*, exactly, they were dealing with.

Me.

I couldn't make a forty-yard hop to the barn. It wasn't going to happen. But I could make it in three or four good hops, especially if the first hop came from an elevated position—or that was my reasoning, anyway. Maybe starting from a rooftop only made me feel better. I couldn't say, and it didn't matter, because I was going to have to make a run for it.

And people were still shooting at me.

They weren't shooting a lot, at least. Nobody was wasting much ammo. Mostly they were taking potshots. I could hear them below, splitting up and surrounding my hiding spot—at least it was a *big* little building—and closing off my avenues of escape. Or so they thought.

I rolled over flat, facedown in the snow, and lifted my head enough to peer out over the compound. The crew that'd surrounded the shed . . . I couldn't see those guys. They were too close, and I'd earn myself a bullet up the nose if I looked over the edge to get a gander at them.

Pulling myself up to the lowest of all possible crouches, I took a deep breath. I braced myself. I dug my boots deep into the packed snow and ice, and I jammed my knees down into it, and my hands as well. I needed traction. I needed to jump.

Shit, what I really needed was to leap a tall building in a single bound. But since we all knew that wasn't in the cards, I'd settle for a good launch and a mad dash. If I moved fast enough, and if they didn't know to expect a vampire, I might surprise the hell out of them.

They might not even see me. I might appear as nothing more than a streak, and those very far-spaced footprints over there someplace.

Below I heard them talking into tiny microphones, and receiving instruction through their tiny earbuds. They were close enough that I could hear whoever the honcho was. He was giving hand signals, and I could hear the rustle of his clothes as he fired them off.

Someone was forcing the shed door.

They were going to come inside and shoot through the ceiling to get me if they had to, and that meant I'd officially hit the "now or never" moment.

One more deep breath. I tensed. I held my head low, checked my bag one more time, then shoved myself off with such force that half the snow slid off the roof . . . collapsing onto the guys who'd been lurking underneath it.

I'm going to go ahead and pretend I knew that would happen, and I totally meant to do it.

The victims of the impromptu avalanche cried out in surprise, but it was muffled by a few hundred pounds of snow. And then it was far behind me.

The frigid air stung my ears as I ran, leaping so fast and so far that I might as well have been flying for all any of the mere mortals could have seen. I hoped.

The largest building, the one I'd mentally denoted as a "barn," was close enough that I reached it in the span of a couple of leaps and a couple of seconds. I skidded around its side, clamoring up to the door. It was locked, no big surprise there. It only took one hard shove for me to figure out that I could open it, yes—but it'd take more time than I wanted to invest in the endeavor. More time than I could *afford* to invest.

My pursuers were running in circles, shouting and trying to reorganize. And I guess someone might've gotten busy trying to dig those poor bastards out from under all the snow I'd kicked off the roof. But they'd be on my tail again before long.

How long did I have? Maybe seconds. Maybe minutes. No longer than that—no way, no how.

Like the storage shed, the barn's only windows were high up and designed for passage by few things larger than a leprechaun— which is not to say that they thwarted me, but I'll confess to being inconvenienced. But while I still had the benefit of uncertainty on my side, I jumped, hopped, and scrambled into position, popped out some glass, and skooched my way into the interior.

My shoulders and hip bones ached from the scraping press of forcing my body into what was, essentially, a ventilation portal, but my first glance around the interior suggested it might have been worth it.

It'd better be. And it'd better be worth it *fast*.

I knew this, because my first glance also told me that there were cameras inside this big-ass information dump. If they didn't know where I'd gone yet, they'd figure it out before long.

And to think, I'd been fantasizing about taking a leisurely poke around the place, maybe having a nice picnic lunch and a nap before heading on my way. If there has been any doubt in your mind about the state of my sanity, I hope this revelation cinches that up for you.

Anyway, I dropped down onto a level that was something like a hayloft, loaded up in rows and stacks of crates and boxes, stamped from various facilities around the world and around the country, too. I saw FORT SAM HOUSTON as a return address on one package, and FORT KNOX on another one. I had no earthly idea where info on The Other Thief might have hailed from. I'd never find anything about him by sifting through postmarks, but it gave me an idea. I wondered if anything might've been shipped from Jordan Roe, in Florida—but that seemed unlikely, if it was only a facility and not a town.

I shimmied between the rows of stacked containers and let my eyes dilate as widely as they could. My one slight advantage—and the one thing that might buy me extra snooping seconds—was that there weren't any windows low enough for the exterior commandos to actually watch me do my investigating. But boy, I could hear them outside, buzzing like a hornet's nest.

The darkness opened enough that I could see piles and rows of discarded secrets, unlabeled and unorganized as far as I could tell. And there I was, standing in the shadow of a towering stack of sawdust-covered crates, with no earthly idea of what I was looking for. And I could've hung around and looked in that barn-sized depository for days.

Not an option.

Frantic and serious, I set to work flinging open drawers, smashing open crates, whipping open filing cabinets, and bashing in boxes.

Outside, someone practically shouted into his tiny microphone, relating a string of military abbreviations and acronyms I didn't understand, but I got the thrust of "Subject in Alpha Building Four. Copy."

Ah. So I was in Alpha Building Four. For all the good knowing it did me.

"Roger," the same shouter replied.

And then they surprised me. They didn't come bursting in—which I'd expected, and begun to prepare for. I was just thinking that the loft where I'd first entered would be a fairly easy place to defend, or at least exit. All I had to do was get the hell away from them, after all. I didn't have to fight them all to the death in a cage match.

But they didn't storm the premise of Alpha Building Four. They locked it.

The motherfuckers locked me in and surrounded the place with firearms readied and aimed at every visible in-and-out of the joint. Whether or not they'd be able to shoot me upon exit I couldn't say, but I didn't like the prospect. Did they know how I'd gotten inside? Were they watching the ventilation windows upstairs?

I would've had to climb back up there to find out, and I didn't, because the clock was ticking and I was a little worried. I don't like it when people get unpredictable on me. Not at all.

I distracted myself from my worry by ratcheting up my search. While the men outside chatted back and forth in barked commands and responses, I found a set of crates that were approximately the size of a pair of high-school lockers side by side, and both of these crates had return addresses stamped ST. PETERSBURG, FLORIDA. Close enough, right? There were more islands in Florida than just the ones dangling off Miami, I knew that much, and Ian had said it was on the west coast.

Besides, out of all this crap, it was the first sign of "Florida" I'd found so far.

When I ripped the crates open I found whole filing cabinets nestled within. In a stunning display of laziness, haste, or apathy, the cabinets had been duct-taped shut and shipped that way.

I pulled my flat, fixed-blade knife out of my Useful Things Bag and started cutting the tape for the same reason the bear went over the mountain: to see what I could see. Also, because someone didn't want me to see it. So let this be a lesson to you—about 80 percent of all research is boring as hell. Legwork sucks, but it's necessary, and if I didn't do it, nobody else was going to do it for me.

I spied the word JORDAN and almost choked with surprise. I seized the folder and everything inside it. It wasn't the prayed-for lead on The Other Thief, but I didn't have time to pick and choose my clues.

"On my command!" ordered somebody new. Without taking a breath he hollered, "Now!"

But I didn't hear anything new or exciting, so I kept on flipping through those files. My fingers moved in a blur as I shuffled the contents, dumping everything pointless right onto the floor. PBS declared one folder's label, and BSHOT said another. I grabbed those, and added them to my stash, looking up just long enough to wonder exactly what order had been given, and why no exciting action had followed.

Then I smelled it.

Gasoline. And moments after the gasoline, I heard that *whoof* sound of something flammable meeting an open flame. A warm, orange glow came peeking in through what precious little exterior glass was available to let it inside.

"Awesome," I declared. Then I saw JROE and said with more enthusiasm, "Awesome!" I swiped that file, too, and stuffed my collection deep into my Useful Things Bag. I zipped up the thing and strapped it down across my back, in case it might stop a bullet or something. Because baby, I was ready to dash—and I had no intention of letting them catch anything but my figurative taillights on the way out the door.

Or out the window.

The stink of smoke was wafting inside now. The warmth of the orange light was growing ever brighter as I stood there, collecting my loot and my wits as I prepared to bolt. I felt like I had little choice but to take the same way out. I didn't see any other promising options, and I'd already popped the glass. Even if they were watching it, if I could move fast enough—if I could fire myself out of that thing like a goddamn bullet—they'd never hit me.

Right?

I monkeyed myself back up to the loft and pushed a couple of crates under the window—which was far enough off the ground that I couldn't just flop myself out. They'd see me doing that worm-wiggle of escape and open fire on the spot, I was sure of it.

I was even more sure of it when I peeked out from a distant corner window and saw that the commando dudes had encircled Alpha Building Four, and I was pretty much screwed coming and going unless I could get some major hang time out of this exit.

Deep breath.

Double-check the gear.

I climbed atop the crate, keeping my head low until the last possible second.

And I dove.

I flew out hands-first, with as much kick as I could manage. They saw me. They *had* to have seen me—my feet weren't quite as slick as the rest of me, and I splintered the frame on the way out. It sounded like a gunshot, or maybe it's only that gunshots followed my exit. It took them a minute to track me, to find my trail, to even figure out which direction I'd run . . . but they did, and they began to chase me.

I assume they saw the hole I left in their chain-link fence when I shot through it like a Japanese bullet train.

I didn't care. I was so freaking elated that I'd done it—I'd gotten away with it! Fuck those men in black and everything they stand for!—that I didn't care I was trudging at light speed through snow deep enough to drown in. I didn't care that my thighs ached, and my chest hurt from sucking down the icy night in fits and gasps. I didn't care that they were coming right for me, and that behind me I could hear the guttural cough of snowmobiles being cranked into duty.

I was almost back at my car.

And they hadn't found it yet.

After the preternaturally speedy run through the forest, the mundane task of retrieving my keys and forcing them to navigate the half-frozen car door lock seemed impossibly slow. But I did it. And when I started the car and started driving, I'd left the snowmobiles far enough behind me that even if they knew where I was, they wouldn't have been able to catch me.

All the way back to the hotel, I breathed so hard I coughed fog onto the rearview mirror, and even though I was so cold I could barely move, I didn't think to turn on the car's heater until I'd already gotten the thing into the parking garage.

You could make an argument for the fact that I'd been lucky.

I'd argue with you, though. I scarcely think one can call an outing "lucky" when it involves being shot at by commandos, locked in a barn, and set on fire.

Gotta admit, I didn't see that coming.

I didn't honestly think they'd sacrifice the whole joint just to nab me. Even if it was the kind of place where information went to fossilize, it blew my mind that someone had issued that order and told someone to pull the trigger on it.

So to speak.

This only served to underscore, reinforce, and otherwise buttress my neurotic insecurity and all-out paranoia with regard to this case. Whatever I was chasing was serious. And someone out there was serious about keeping me away from it.

Sadly for that mystery someone, I had actually scored some pretty useful loot . . . or loot that had the potential to be useful. And unlike the PDF that started this whole mess, the feebs, the feds, the whoevers . . . they had no idea what I'd gotten my grubby little hands on. For all they knew, I might've found nothing at all— or Bigfoot's DNA profile, or Batman's birth certificate.

Good. Let 'em sweat. The assholes had burned the place down behind me, so now they'd never know, either.

And what did I find?

Oh yes. That's the part where you could make a case for "lucky."

Buried at the bottom of some files that had otherwise been coded and classified into near uselessness, I found a lead on one of the experimental subjects. I'd have been happier with details on my burgling competition, but it'd have to suffice—and hey, it was one more lead than I'd had earlier that evening.

So I ran with it. And less than twenty-four hours later, I was on a plane to Atlanta.

6

I've never cared much for Atlanta.

It's crowded and hot, and even in the dead of winter it doesn't get dark as fast as it does up in the northern hinterlands where I usually hang out. This means I have less people-interaction business time, and less running-around time in general. Yes, I keep a safe house there, and yes, I was happy to find myself back in a cushy spot instead of a hotel room, but I wasn't so charmed to be back in the Southeast.

My condo was a wreck, which is to say, it was as pristine as my place back in Seattle except that everything was coated in dust. I've never trusted housekeepers enough to pay one to visit during my absence.

The bathtub had a spider in it.

But it could've been worse. It could've been hot, and it wasn't. It was merely muggy and kind of cold, which wasn't vastly different from Seattle, but was vastly better than the bone-gnawing freeze of Minnesota.

The city of Atlanta sprawls like hell because there are no natural boundaries to stop it, and its neighborhoods are practically their own individual nations. I don't mean the blocks are broken down by ethnicity per se, though in some of the zip codes you could certainly make a case for it. I mean you've got your hipster sections, your New Money strips, your Southern Hollywood club ghettos, and the relics of the Olympic Village, plus a dozen other subdivisions of subdivided class, type, and preference.

There's even a gayborhood—sort of. It would probably be more accurate to say that Atlanta is the gayborhood of Georgia, but there are parts of town that are more rainbow-friendly than others, and the spot I wanted was right on the edge of a gaudy strip filled with drag bars and bathhouses.

Why did I want this spot? Well, I didn't find a Holy Grail at Holtzer Point, but in my hard-earned score I nabbed a small lead on another member of Project Bloodshot in a fat stack of material that was otherwise kind of useless to me. The rest of what I'd stolen hadn't amounted to much, though I now was the proud owner of Ian's paperwork without all the aggravating black bars. Unfortunately, the lack of bars didn't tell me much. They might tell him more, I didn't know, but I resolved to pass it along to him and Cal next time I saw them.

Mostly the net gain was a collection of serial numbers.

Much to my personal queasiness, the other three personnel dossiers (which including Ian's, made the sum total of my loot) all appeared to detail subjects who'd died while part of the program. But although two of the deceased were listed without next of kin or any other personal contacts . . . subject number three actually came with a name and a hometown.

She was easily the best documented, with all her physical stats like hair and eye color, height and weight, as well as the results from some series of tests she'd taken. But I didn't know what those tests were, or what they meant.

All the attention to detail had me thinking that she might've been a special case. Maybe they had bigger and better things in mind for her at Jordan Roe, or maybe she was only more cooperative than the others. I had no way of knowing.

Anyway, I had a woman's name—Isabelle deJesus—and I had a place of birth, Atlanta, Georgia. And from what was left of her processing sheets, I was almost 100 percent certain she'd been a vampire.

She had the correct 636 serial number starter, and I noted a few other telltale marks that bolstered my suspicion. She'd been kept in an underground bunk like Ian (no windows), and the lone fragment of her chart mentioned a required dietary supplement that was provided twice a week. Gosh. I wonder what *that* could have been.

I ran her name through a phone book and my Internet sources, and turned up a big fat nothing . . . short of the fact that "deJesus" is not a hugely uncommon Spanish name and I could spend the next fifteen years interviewing every "deJesus" in Fulton, Cobb, and DeKalb counties.

Then—on a hunch—I ran the scarce facts through a missing persons list. After all, Ian hadn't gone along willingly; maybe Isabelle hadn't, either.

And then I understood that I'd gotten things wrong.

Isabelle hadn't been a woman. She'd been a girl.

I found a listing for her as a teenage runaway, gone missing about ten years ago. Someone had been looking for her. Looking long and hard. The case had been pushed to the media every couple of years, and ads had run in *The Atlanta Journal-Constitution*. Someone hadn't wanted to let her go.

That put a damper on my glee. I know it happens—hell, everybody knows it happens—that teenagers sometimes fall into bad times and bad habits, and I even had insider knowledge that some of the skankier vampire families will go out of their way to recruit kids like Isabelle when they want disposable foot soldiers. If you forced me to speculate about their rationale, I'd have to say that it probably has something to do with strays. If you take care of strays, the strays will take care of you, later on. And besides, if you get them young enough, they're easy to control.

That transition point sometime in the late teens, from homeless kid to homeless person, that's a real bitch. That's when they get you—or so I hear.

Ironically, ghouls tend to come from a higher social tier than young vampire soldiers. They're people who have something professional to offer a vampire House or family. They have accounting skills or computer skills; they have law degrees or other certifications. They're white-collar and ambitious, hoping to upgrade to a cape.

With a little digging, I turned up an address for Isabelle's parents. It turned out to be a modest beige house with red shutters and a pair of tall, gangly roses growing up around an arch in front of the porch.

I parked my car across the street from it and stared down at a picture I'd taken from the Center for Missing and Exploited Children: Isabelle's sophomore-year high-school photo. She looked thin and pretty, with hair she hadn't yet figured out how to tame and lip gloss that was a little too bright for her coloring. But she had nice eyes and good bone structure. Her Hispanic ancestry stood out in the width of her cheeks and the set of her mouth.

I'd spent some time working out what I might say to her parents. I hadn't been able to scare up too many details of the kid's case, except that she'd either run off or been kidnapped sometime in the middle of summer break before her senior year and she'd never returned home, but her case had been closed with the missing persons bureau.

I suspected government intervention on that point. Of course, by then I was seeing government intervention under every rock and in every corner.

Man. I thought I'd been paranoid before I took Ian's case; now I was downright *deranged*.

I wondered when she'd become a vampire and who had done it to her, but I doubted her parents would know. I didn't even know how I'd go about asking, but I figured that pretending to be a concerned cold-case detective might work. I have a badge I bought off eBay a couple of years ago. I think the cop who originally wore it is dead. Regardless, it's never gotten me double-checked or refused before.

Before I'd made the drive down to the quiet little inner-city suburb, I'd nabbed some new clothes at a high-end mall and I'd utterly failed to find a new car I wanted to buy on the spot. Something innocuously authoritative—like a dark blue Crown Victoria or something—would have been ideal, but I couldn't find one for sale that suited my fancy so I'd been forced to rent one.

My rented pseudo-cop-car did a good job of completing my Professional Law-Enforcement-Type-Person package. I was wearing a gray pantsuit and black ankle boots, with a button-up long-sleeved shirt that was white and crisp. I almost felt like a gangster from the forties, but I told myself it all worked fine and I walked up to the house, pretending like I belonged there.

I knocked, and I heard a flurry of activity inside before someone came to the door. The peephole went dark for a moment, then a series of locks worthy of my abode in Seattle went clicking and retreating, until only a chain remained. The door opened as far as the chain would let it, and a man's voice asked, "Who's there?"

An eyeball followed the voice into the narrow crack permitted by the chain; it belonged to someone middle-aged, and suspicious.

I held up the badge for the eyeball's perusal and said, "I'm Raylene Jones, a cold-case detective with the Atlanta Police Department. I was hoping I could talk to you about your daughter."

The door closed, and a second voice came to confer with the man. They spoke in rapid Spanish that was too muffled for me to follow. I understand it a little but not much, and not very fast. But through the solid old door I couldn't pick up anything but a spare syllable or two.

After almost a full minute, the chain slid back on the other side and dropped swinging against the door with a clatter. The knob turned and the door opened, revealing a matched set of fifty-something Latinos who'd begun to look alike, as long-married couples sometimes do.

"Mr. and Mrs. deJesus?" I guessed.

They nodded. The mister was half a head taller than the missus, with a balding pate and a badly matched shirt and pants off the JCPenney specials rack orbiting his waistline. The missus was wearing a plain blue dress and flat shoes. The missus said, "Please come inside. You can sit down."

"Thank you," I said, and followed her. The mister stayed behind me and rebolted the locks. I liked him already, even if I wasn't wholly keen on the idea of being secured within the smallish home with the Catholic-ish décor and worn green shag carpeting.

I followed them to a terrifying gold-and-cream couch and sat down on the end, on the edge. They sat across from me, interrogation-style, like they'd be the ones asking the questions.

"Our daughter has been missing for years," the missus said flatly. "Why you here, now?"

I dug deep and called up every episode of relevant television I could recall and said, "I'm from a cold-case unit. It's my job to take a second look at cases that were closed, or went . . . erm . . . cold. And I understand that your daughter's case—"

"Our daughter's case was closed." The missus cut me off. There was no eagerness in her face, not like her husband's. He wanted to talk, he wanted to ask questions. I could see it in the perk of his eyebrows. But she wasn't going to let him. She'd run out of hope, and she refused to borrow any of his.

I told her, "I realize this. We think it might have been a clerical error. And I'd like to ask you about Isabelle. According to our records, police believed she ran away. They didn't believe she'd been abducted. Do you think she left on her own?"

The mister shrugged quickly and said, "She left. We don't know why."

"But were you surprised?" I pressed.

Even the mister, the almost-optimist of the pair, was forced to admit, "No. She was unhappy. Her brother—"

At this, the missus seized hold of his arm and mumbled something accusatory in Spanish and, when the mister dug in his heels for a moment of back talk, they excused themselves to the kitchen, where they argued some more in that speedy clip of chatter.

Their behavior told me plenty, of course. The missus didn't want to admit domestic disharmony, and since she didn't believe Isabelle was coming home anyway, she didn't see the point in being helpful. And the mister was daring to hope that maybe the APD was back and something new might come of his daughter's case. It made me feel a little like a heel, that I was taking advantage of these people's confidence. But the truth was, I *did* intend to do their daughter a favor if I could—and if I couldn't, I'd use her experience to help other people.

Or other vampires. Whatever.

While the couple argued quietly in the other room, I scanned the living area and saw no pictures of Isabelle or her all-too-briefly mentioned brother. If I didn't know better, I would've sworn that these two somber, matching older folks had never procreated. There were no awards, no family photos, no trophies or tokens of anybody's childhood. Not even the ghosts of little pitter-pattering feet that once made the parents proud.

Somewhere off in the kitchen, the mister put his foot down long enough to come back into the living room and ask me, "Do you really mean to help? Are you really with the police?"

"Yes," I said, my eyes as innocent and sincere as I could force them to look. "Absolutely. Look, sir, I can't make you any promises, except that I promise to try. I know that the situation wasn't handled very well the first time around; I know there were screwups and gaffes." It was an easy guess. He didn't contradict me. "But my job is to help find your daughter."

He swallowed, and cleared his throat. "And if she isn't alive anymore?"

"If she isn't, then maybe I can give you closure. Even if I can't give her back." I knew I couldn't give her back. Not even if I found her, and she'd escaped, and all was well and she was happily sipping a too-true-to-description Bloody Mary in a nightclub, and sleeping with the drummer of the skeezy house band. But *I* needed to know, and I swore to myself, if not out loud to the trembling mister, that if I learned anything benignly useful or helpful, I'd hold up my end of the charade and pass the information along.

Since he seemed disinclined to keep talking, I tried nudging him again. "Please, if there's anything at all you can tell me about what happened to her, or—"

"Her brother," he whispered.

"I beg your pardon?"

He glanced over into the kitchen, where the missus was loudly banging glasses and pans around, pretending to do something.

Maybe she was angrily making coffee. I don't know. But he said again in that lowered, soft-shoe voice, "Her brother. Adrian. He went looking for her."

The brother again. I seized on it, and asked, "Did he have any luck?"

The mister stiffened. He said, "I could not say. I do not know. But I think he might have."

"What does that mean?" I asked too fast, almost dropping my Cool-Professional-Cop-Voice. "Your son went looking for your daughter and you what . . . you just didn't ask about it?"

"He is no longer part of this family!" he said almost loud enough to halt the banging in the kitchen, but not quite.

"How does that work?"

"He isn't . . . He's *not like us*. He never has been like us," the mister said, leaning on his words for some emphasis that I was just too thick to parse. Did he sprout antlers? Take up cannibalism?

"Not like you . . . how?"

The mister was getting frustrated with me, but that only made the feeling mutual. He grabbed for a phone stand and seized a piece of paper from it, then scrabbled around until he'd found a pen. "You don't understand," he mumbled, writing quickly.

The noise in the kitchen stopped and he froze, as if he'd been caught doing something naughty. Then he wrote faster, wrapped up his brief message, and shoved it into my hand.

The missus emerged from the kitchen with a Crock-Pot inexplicably in hand. She grumbled in top volume and rapid-fire Spanish and the mister whined back, denying something. I squeezed my fist around the scrap of paper and could guess exactly what she suspected.

They argued for another few seconds, and I rose from my seat, stuffing the note into my pocket and announcing that I was going to leave before the missus had a chance to throw me out. I barely made it; she was ushering me to the door before I could even reach the hall to make my big exit.

I felt bad for the mister, standing behind her as she herded me out. His head was bowed and he was still holding the pen he'd used to tell me something—something important, but unspeakable. He didn't look up as I left; he turned his back and stood in his living room, or that was the last I saw of him as the missus shut the door with a slap, a click, and then the subsequent sound of locks being reset.

I wanted to yank the paper out of my pocket, uncrumple it, and read it on the spot, but I waited until I got back to my car. I wanted to be out of that woman's reach. She scared me. Sort of. Her *type* scared me, anyway. I half expected her to reach out through the living room window and snatch it out of my hands.

I locked my car doors because, well, I lock everything. And I was sitting in the dark, parked on a street in a Not-the-Best-But-Not-the-Worst part of town. I wasn't really worried about being mugged, but I didn't want to be interrupted. Maybe if I'd been hungrier I might've welcomed a bit of thuggish attention, but I wasn't hungry and I didn't want it.

I stuck my feet down past my car's gas and brake pedals and straightened my body enough to reach into my pocket for the paper. The car's overhead lamp was yellow and feeble, but with eyes like mine it was enough to read by. The note said "2512 W. Peachtree Circuit. Sister Rose."

Or at least that's what I thought it said. The mister's handwriting was bad, and rushed. I scanned it again, concluded that I'd been right the first time, and wondered exactly which "Peachtree" street "Peachtree Circuit" might be. If you've never been to Atlanta, then let me save you a bit of grief. If someone tells you something's on "Peachtree," you must demand that they get more specific. There are probably a dozen incarnations of Peachtree, going in at least that many directions through every part of town.

In short, even though I'm fairly familiar with the city, I'd need to find a phone book or an Internet connection before I could draw any conclusions about where this place was located.

All the way back to my condo I wondered what the address was, and what it signified. Sister Rose. I could've gathered by the deJesus home décor that they were Catholic, but were we talking a convent? Did they even have convents in downtown Atlanta? Upon reflection, I was forced to admit that I didn't see why not, but that didn't make it feel any less weird to me.

And if Sister Rose was a contact for Adrian deJesus, I'd have to do my best to look her up. Thank God (or whoever) that lore about the crucifixes isn't true.

I made a mental note that I shouldn't assume Adrian shared his family's last name. For whatever reason, he obviously wasn't considered part of the family anymore, so he might've renamed himself.

Back at the homestead, I ran a search through Google Maps and was a bit surprised (and aggravated) to learn that the address was less than five miles from the deJesus home. In fact, the longer I stared back and forth between the helpful little map and the squished piece of paper, the more I suspected that I'd drawn some incorrect conclusions about Sister Rose and the nature of the location. Another quick Internet search confirmed my new suspicions.

This was the address of a drag bar called "the Poppycock Review."

Sister Rose in*deed*. No wonder the mister didn't want to talk about what junior was up to in his spare time. Or, erm, her (?) spare time. I've never been very clear about how the pronouns were supposed to work in such circumstances as these. I decided to err on the side of caution and assume that, just in case . . . Sister Rose might be a woman who knew Adrian deJesus. And I'd sort out the particulars later.

I would've gone out that same night, except that I didn't want to drive all the way back out to the heart of the gayborhood when I'd practically been right there not an hour before. Atlanta traffic is not the sort of stuff that inspires a body to commute, even in the evenings.

Especially in the evenings, in that part of the city. It's a popular destination.

Instead, I settled in with a long hot bath and the television remote, or that was the plan until I figured out I hadn't paid my cable bill in a couple of years. Therefore, confronted with the wasteland of network television—until I realized that my TV wasn't even compatible with the "digital revolution"—I closed up all my windows, locked everything lockable, and called it a day.

When the sun set and I woke up the next evening, it was far too early to approach any self-respecting drag bar. Instead, I made a point to pick up a new stash of disposable cell phones—buying one each from three different drugstores. I memorized the numbers and stuck the phones in a drawer, just like I kept them in Seattle. And after I'd done a ritual Checking of the Living Space, I concluded that no one was listening and no one was watching, because if I didn't, I couldn't make the necessary phone calls with any peace of mind.

I didn't call the Bad Hatter. I didn't have anything new or important things to say to him, and it would only piss him off if he thought I was wasting his time just to tell him I was alive. I couldn't call the stray kids because—if they'd followed directions—they didn't have a phone anymore. So I sealed one of the new phones into a padded envelope and express-mailed it to a post office box a few blocks away from my old warehouse. Pepper had a key to it. She knew to check it. She'd probably already done so.

No, my first call was to Pacific Northwest Information, and then to a handful of other out-of-the-way reference-type institutions, none of which were very well known and two of which were not strictly legal. Then I spent another few minutes on the Internet, and before long, I had the Minion Cal's real name and a potential phone number.

It was risky, yes. But I needed to talk to Ian.

The digits I dialed didn't look familiar, and I didn't recognize the area code. I could feel myself flushing as the line rang, rang, and wasn't answered. I was nervous—intensely nervous—about trying to contact Ian. There was always the hypothetical possibility that I was putting him in danger, and I didn't like the thought of that even slightly.

But I needed to ask him about Isabelle deJesus. And by God, I was *gonna*.

Voice mail picked up, without a personalized message—only the electronic robot-woman informing me that customer number 8862 was not available right now, and I was welcome to leave a message.

I did. I said, "Cal, I'm looking for my client. Have him call me at this number." And then I hung up. I knew I was leaving my call-back digits in the other phone's memory, so now it was only a matter of time and luck.

Then, on a different phone—just in case the message to Cal didn't work out and I had to junk it—I called Horace.

He answered on the first ring, with his typical flair.

"I don't know this number," he began, and without taking a breath he added, "and if I don't know you, you shouldn't know mine, either—so I'm going to assume this is someone entitled to the information. Now speak up fast and prove me right, or this conversation is over."

"Jesus, Horace. Lighten up."

"Raylene!" I heard an honest element of glee. "It's you! Jesus, woman. I was starting to wonder."

"Wonder what?"

"Where you were. What you were up to. Did you know your voice-mail inbox is full? Well, it *is*."

I tried not to smile too big, lest he hear it and infer that I was happy to talk to him. I said, "Since you're one of the only people who ever calls me, I'm going to go out on a limb and guess that you've had something to tell me."

"I might've made a call or two. Haven't you been checking it?"

"No," I admitted. "And you may as well trash that number. I don't expect to be using it again anytime soon . . . or . . . well . . . ever. Just pretend it never happened. For the time being, you can reach me through this phone—as long as you don't abuse the privilege."

"Darling, is something wrong?" I heard real concern, but I knew better than to assume it was concern for me, personally. It was concern for how he was going to get his crazy white woman in touch with whatever property she wanted stolen.

"I've had to relocate somewhat unexpectedly."

"Relocate?"

"Think of it as a reboot. I needed to get out of town for a bit. I might've attracted a little attention of the most unwanted variety." I was taking a chance telling him that much, but I told myself that I wasn't sharing anything he couldn't guess.

He proved me right by making another logical leap. "That client. You put me off because you said you had a new client. Did he get you into trouble? If he did, you just let me know right now, and I personally will pay some very burly people to kick his ass."

"It's not his fault, Horace. It's got something to do with his case, yeah, but he didn't do anything, and if I thought for a moment that you could track him down or wound him, I'd have my hands on your throat within an hour," I lied. Horace was in New York City. It'd take me at least four or five hours.

"Be that as it may, I don't like this. You never accepted my new case—the rich white weirdo with indigenous myth-envy."

"And I still can't make you any promises, not right now. This case, from this guy," I said, and only then did I realize I'd revealed Ian's correct pronoun. Horace had assumed it, but I'd confirmed it. I wanted to kick myself, but there wasn't time. "I can't explain without giving you more information than I'm prepared to share, but I need for you to understand—this guy's case, it has something to do with me, too. His mystery and his mission have gotten personal."

"Okay . . ."

"And I'm only telling you this much because I don't want you to think I'm bailing on you to chase down cash from another source. I'm not putting this client's needs above yours, my felonious pimp. I'm simply trying to sort out something that affects him quite deeply, yes—but it affects me, too. In a very concrete and unpleasant way," I added under my breath, but not so quietly that he didn't hear me.

"Old boyfriend?"

"What?"

"Is your client an old—"

"No, no. Christ, no. It's not like that."

"Then what's it like?"

"It's like . . ." He wasn't going to let it go. I knew he wasn't going to let it go, so I fished for something to throw him off the track, but meaty enough to keep him from digging further. "It's . . . we have something in common," I said. "A medical condition." Which was sort of true, wasn't it?

"A *medical* condition?"

"Yes, a *medical* condition. It's rather personal and I don't care to explain, but suffice it to say, my client and I share a medical condition and his . . . erm . . . health is, in its way, related to mine."

In more ways than one, I nearly added.

"Okay, fine. You're both sick, you're both—"

"I didn't say we were *sick.* I only said we shared a medical condition. For all you know, we both have green eyes, or we both pee a little when we cough."

"And you're the one who didn't want to share!"

"Oh shut up, Horace." I shifted my grip on the phone and settled down into my couch. I'd be lying if I'd said I wasn't enjoying the conversation. I only just then realized that it'd been days since I'd simply talked to anyone apart from a salesclerk or a tollbooth operator. "The thing is, I can't drop this guy's case—not even if I wanted to. So your weirdo will have to take a backseat."

"When do you think you'll be back on the pony?" he asked, every vowel oozing impatience.

"Later," I said with more confidence than I felt. "Give me another couple of weeks here, and then you can start bothering me."

"I don't know if she'll wait a couple of weeks."

"Then go find someone else to put a smile on her face, because I won't make bargains any sooner than that." I'd be lucky to take a new gig even that soon, all things considered.

"A couple of weeks," he said, but he said it funny, like he was only repeating what I'd said—and like he had a pen in his mouth. He was probably looking for a calendar, circling the day on which he could begin to harass me without fear of reprisal. "All right, a couple of weeks. You're a hard negotiator, Ray-Baby."

"I'm going to get a lot harder if you call me that again."

"Give me a minute. Less than a minute. I'm almost certain I can make a filthy joke in response to that."

"No," I told him. "No, for the love of God, *don't.*"

"Oh fine. But I've got you down for two more weeks of peace

and quiet, and then . . . then I'll come calling again. I recognize this area code, don't I? Where's it from . . . ," he asked, not really asking me, but asking his memory.

"Don't do that, Horace. I'll come to you, or I'll call you." He'd figure it out soon enough, but let him. Atlanta's a huge place, filled with millions of people spread out over dozens of square miles. If he could track me down by an area code, I deserved to be tracked down and berated by a fierce and pissy little man who wanted me to steal things.

An awkward silence passed between us before he broke it by saying, "So everything's all right, then?" He wasn't accustomed to pretending to care, and it came out stilted.

"Everything's all right," I said, whether it was true or not. "I'm going to go ahead and hang up, but if something crazy or pressing comes across your plate, go ahead and give me a call."

"Works for me," he said, and closed his cell phone before I could close mine.

I stared at the other phone for a few seconds, willing it to ring in the wake of Horace's forced interest, but Cal didn't reply and neither did Ian. I considered trying to give the major another call, but thought better of it. It might be tempting fate, considering that I'd been all but chased from my home by some form of organized long black car brigade, and I'd freshly broken into a military storage facility.

But it might be worth checking to see if he'd responded to my previous email.

Sure enough.

Abigail,

Still no word from Trevor on my end. I don't know what's up with that guy, but I might have to write him off. On the upshot (for you) it means I might have an assignment or two you could take. We have places that need exploring, and now I'm short a guy. If I have to settle for a girl, I'll settle for a girl. You think you can handle it?

So if you're a friend of Trevor's, I don't suppose there's any chance you could handle his last assignment, could you? Since you got my info from him, and all. You must've talked about what he was working on.

Christ on a cracker, I hated that guy. But that didn't stop me from writing him back, since I had the laptop open and everything. I did a lot of self-editing, believe you me. And this is what I sent back.

Major,

Can I handle it? I could handle it in my sleep. And no, I haven't heard from Trevor either. His roommate said he skipped out on rent and he's thinking about filing a missing persons report. I don't know what to think.

I knew he'd been inside some building downtown, because yeah, we talked about it. But are you saying he never reported back at all? I don't know what he was looking for or anything. What do you want to know about the place? Maybe I could go there and check it out.

Anyway, yeah. Hit me with what you've got. Give me an address, and I'll get inside. Should I assume you're based in the Seattle area? If not, where's your office? Would I need to come in and sign some kind of release or something?

That wasn't too much, right? I was trying to walk a line between credibly curious and not overly snoopy. Didn't want him to get the idea I was prying, or otherwise behaving suspiciously. As if emailing some dude about breaking into abandoned buildings in order to perform "reconnaissance" wasn't amazingly suspicious already.

Was it ballsy to ask about my own building? Perhaps. But it was also well within the realm of possible questions a prospective employee might ask. And since I'd gotten "lucky" with my find in Alpha Building Four, I might as well see if lightning would strike twice and I'd learn something good.

I hit SEND and hung around on the Internet for a bit, leeching off some neighbor who didn't know any better than to leave his WiFi connection unsecured. I visited a few blogs, read some Hollywood gossip, and generally pissed away thirty minutes doing not much of anything.

When much to my surprise, the major wrote back.

I checked my watch. It was pretty damn late for business.

Abigail,

Trevor was looking at an old factory down on Pioneer Square. It wasn't technically abandoned, but the owner was a real pain in the ass to locate—and might be involved in some illegal activities. But we're pretty certain no one comes or goes from the place, with the exception of a teenage squatter or two.

So Trevor didn't say anything about it? Did he tell you he'd run into any trouble, or that everything had gone smoothly? I want to know what he saw in there.

To answer your other question, no, I'm not based in Seattle. I pass through every now and again. I do a lot of traveling. My office is in D.C., so you can't just swing by and sign anything. And it's like I said on the phone, there won't be anything to sign. There won't be any evidence whatsoever that you and I ever talked, much less any evidence if I opt to send you out on an errand.

These emails don't mean anything. No one will ever trace the address back to me. I trust my tech.

Let me know if you're still game. Here's the joint. Case it, break it, and let me know what you find inside.

Then he'd cut-and-pasted a link to a Google Map pointing directly to my warehouse.

His email gave me chills. Such chills that I sat there and stared at it, rereading it for a few minutes, trying to milk every last drop of information from it. I unpacked it until my eyes crossed.

Then I fired off one more quick email, in case he was still online—and in order to feel like I'd gotten the last word in.

Major,

You sure know how to reassure a girl, don't you? But I'm hard to scare. So count me in. And hey, D.C.? I'm actually headed that way next weekend. Me and some friends are crashing town for a convention. Maybe if I can prove I know my shit, you'll invite me to tour the facilities or whatever.

Anyway, I know that neighborhood. I'll check out your mystery building and report back within twenty-four hours.

~Abigail

The line about the convention might come back to haunt me, but I was willing to bet it wouldn't. It's Washington, D.C., and I defy you to find a single weekend wherein not one single convention is being held there. For all he knew, I was scooting into the District for a *Star Trek* event or a gun enthusiast show. I just hoped he wouldn't call me on it.

I wanted to dwell on this, to fester over it and try to paste together some psychic defense against it, but it was coming up on nine o'clock at night.

This meant it was still entirely too early to check out the Poppycock Review (a name I loved, by the way) . . . or so I'd assumed, until I managed to convince myself otherwise. The night may be too young for me to show up as a customer, but the time was damn near perfect if I wanted to get in and out in a sneakier fashion without battling the disco-darlings and their tribe.

Who was I kidding? I was bored, and out of ideas, and only trying to justify getting out of the condo when I was almost too frightened to do so. A little fresh air would help calm me down. Probably.

I skipped the MARTA and drove myself back down toward the deJesus residence, then took a handful of turns that led me deeper into the frat-boy-and-bachlorette-party-plagued blocks where the bitch-techno blared and the locals complained about all the slumming straights. The pure agony of finding a place to park made me almost reconsider my loathing of the public transportation system, but eventually I found a narrow slot in which to leave my vehicle. I had to bash the bumper of an SUV to squeeze into the nook, but I didn't exactly shed a tear over the event and no, I didn't leave a note. That's what they get for parking too close to a fire hydrant, with one wheel on the curb. An asshole who leaves his (or her) vehicle in such a fashion deserves whatever automotive detailing inconvenience comes his (or her) way.

(I do have auto insurance, believe it or not. Over the years I've stolen the identities of a few people—none of my victims, that's too close for comfort, but I've got paper trails leading back to tombstones here and there. My insurance is listed under one of those identities, and it all looks legit. But that doesn't mean I jump at the chance to hand it out.)

The Poppycock Review was a two-story building that somehow managed to look short and squat, regardless of its peaked red-and-white roof. The wall that faced the main street was painted 1983 Prince-Purple, and the side wall where the front door was located was bright yellow, with giant rhinestone sparklies rimming the door frame like salt on a margarita glass. Curtains were artfully draped, covering the window and obscuring the interior view. These curtains were rainbow-themed, with gold and silver threading giving them a touch of added shimmer.

Here's to truth in advertising.

But all its aggressively bad trappings aside, the Review looked like an aging hooker—tarted up real pretty, but starting to break down beneath the cosmetics. The windowsills had all been painted over recently, but that didn't hide the fact that they were warped and splitting with age, and the glass in the window was clean but scratched all to hell. I got it. The place had seen better days, and this wasn't the top-of-the-line destination it might've been thirty years ago.

But if the warm-up music inside was any indication, the joint was still ready to hop. I heard a house-style remix of something funky from the late seventies kicking inside, though when I tried the front door it was locked. A tiny, peeling sticker on the inside of the window to my right said that things got started around ten o'clock, so yes, I was plenty early despite the traffic.

But I wasn't the kind of girl to be deterred by a locked door, so I pulled out my kit, took two of my most basic tools to the ancient and wobbly lock, and had the door open in ten seconds or less. I shoved the tools back into the little roll and jammed them back into my purse, in case anyone saw me stroll inside. If they saw me with lock-pick tools, they'd know I was up to know good. If I turned the knob and acted like I owned the place, I could always swear it'd been unlocked when I got there.

I didn't see anyone in the foyer area, so I shut the door behind me and made a point to leave it unfastened, to bolster my story.

The carpet under my heels was worn but not sticky, so I thanked heaven for small blessings. I wasn't really dressed for clubbing, but I wasn't really visiting the Poppycock Review to see the show, so that was fine. I'd gone with something understated and gray, with ankle boots that had a low heel for easy running away, should the situation call for it. I'd stuck to maroon accents for a little color, but I hadn't gone nuts with it or anything—just a leather bag and a belt. I've never been one of those women to coordinate everything from my lips to my toenails. It's just too time-intensive, and it gives you more goop to smear on a crime scene. Forget it.

The lights were all dimmed except for the dance floor, which I could see on the other side of a big beaded curtain that looked like a varsity cheerleader's chest at Mardi Gras. Someone was in the DJ booth, tweaking settings and laying out a playlist, I guess. I couldn't really see what was going on back there, just that there was a person-shaped shadow behind the Plexiglas.

I stood away from the curtain, so that I couldn't be seen any better than I could see.

The light from the dance floor augmented the low-lit party lights in the foyer, so there was plenty to see by. Costume masks and rainbow schwag was posted up on the walls, over the windows, and all across the wood paneling that no doubt originally came with the building. It was awful, but it was being handled cheerfully, to the good-natured credit of whoever was in charge of the decorating.

I didn't take too many pains to be super-quiet as I wandered down first the right corridor (where I found a glass-and-neon bar) and down the left, where I found a series of doors that were mostly shut and often locked—except for the unisex restrooms all lined up in a little row.

One of the shut doors that wasn't locked revealed a dressing room stacked from floor to ceiling with large and glittery high-heeled shoes, tackle boxes overflowing with makeup, halters, corsets, feather boas, and the occasional pink sheer dressing gown. I admired the dressing room owner's commitment to fabulousness and kept on snooping.

Down at the end of the corridor I heard voices, low and male, but with a flourish. I considered how best to play the situation—

should I walk up, introduce myself, and ask questions, or finish my reconnaissance?—but the deliberation took too long and a leggy blonde stepped into the corridor.

Bouffant B-52s hair was fluffed and cascaded to such a size that it could've stuffed a couch cushion, and beneath an orange terry-cloth robe a pair of crimson stilettos peeked. The wearer was probably not six feet tall in bare feet, and had both suspicious shoulders and a far finer grasp of cheekbone shading than I, personally, have ever possessed.

She came up short and startled. "Well pardon me, Sunshine," she said, and I'm going to go ahead and use the feminine designation here for convenience—the Adam's apple be damned. If she was going to go through all that trouble to look like a lady, I was not going to disrespect her by insisting on my own pronouns. Also, I kind of liked being called "Sunshine," and I decided on the spot that I was going to steal it.

I stood up straighter and forced an injection of confidence and total I'm Supposed to Be Here into my voice. "Hello. My name is Raylene Jones, and I'm looking for Sister Rose."

"Raylene Jones, looking for Sister Rose. Is this some official business? Because sister, it is *too soon* to party."

"Official business, yes." Because it's always better to let them think you've got some kind of authority backing up your right to be present. "But not," I hastily clarified, "the strictly bad kind. Rose isn't in any kind of trouble."

"You look like a cop," declared a second girl, from around the corner of the door they'd been chatting behind a moment earlier. The newcomer was going for an Elvira thing, and it was comical, but I couldn't say it didn't look good on her.

I nodded and pulled out my badge. "I *am* a cop. I'm a cold-case detective from the APD, and I'm looking into the disappearance of a teenage girl a few years ago. Rose might have a little information for me. Or then again, she might not. But I'm low on leads, so here I am. Can you point me in the right direction?"

"The right direction's right around the corner, baby," the blonde said. "First door on the left. She shares it with a couple of other girls, like we all do—you know how it goes. But she's working tonight and her shift starts in half an hour. She's in there."

"Thanks," I said, and did a stiff little half bow that implied I was finished here. I navigated the narrow, claustrophobic corridor with all its dense, dark wood and deeply piled but matted carpet until I'd passed both of the ladies and reached the indicated door around the corner.

I planted myself in front of it, feet splayed and ready for action, and I knocked. Twice. Real loud, very authoritative, if I don't mind saying so myself. "Sister Rose?" I called, hoping I came off as less Itchy Trigger-Fingered SWAT Team than Concerned Authority.

"What?" came the answer from inside. It sounded irritable, impatient, and somewhat aggravated—at the world in general, or maybe at me in particular. "What do you want?"

"I'm looking to have a word with Sister Rose. My name is Raylene Jones; I'm a cold-case detective working for the Atlanta Police Department," I said, laying out my story and my pseudonym, since it'd served me well so far. "You're not in any trouble, I only want to ask you a few questions about someone else."

The door opened swiftly and violently, before I'd heard anyone within make a peep or a step toward the knob. Inside the room, with one rather intimidatingly beefy arm slung lazily over the door's latch, stood the most insistently innocent drag queen I'd ever set eyes upon.

She was tall—taller than me by nearly a foot, which would put her around six-four or six-five—and she was wearing a mermaid-inspired blue-sequined dress that left little to the imagination, and much to the imagination's Department of WTF? I knew she was packing under that bikini bottom with the dangled sparkles, but I'd be damned if I could tell you where she'd put it. On her head sat a black Amy Winehouse wig that was just as tall as the British singer's do, but less cracked-out and more tidy. Around her neck was a flamboyant fake necklace that would've been worth seven figures if it'd been real.

With a diva voice that neither matched nor contradicted her appearance, she asked, "Someone else?"

I was so taken aback I only stared for a second before asking, like an idiot, "What?"

"Someone else. You said you were here asking about someone else. Not me?"

"Not you. No. But . . ." I looked over my shoulder and saw nothing, but I didn't trust that the walls had no ears. "Could we have a moment in private? Is it private in there?"

"As private as anywhere." She shrugged. "Come on inside, if you're gonna."

I let her hold the door ajar while I passed into the inner sanctum, where it smelled like talcum powder, wax, and hair spray. I waded through knee-deep piles of stockings and playbills before excavating a seat in front of the largest mirror with the smaller set of lights. The smaller mirror had brighter lights, and Sister Rose took the seat there.

She took a moment to glance at herself, pick at a stray false eyelash, and pretend I wasn't present, then she eyed me with an eyebrow lifted in an arch that Wolverine would've died for. Then she said, "Who are you looking for again? I don't think you ever said."

I ducked the question by asking another one. "You're Adrian deJesus, aren't you?"

Sister Rose froze mid-eyelash-investigation, and her whole body went rigid in a dangerous way. Without moving, and in less than a second, she'd gone from casual interest to a defensiveness that was ready for violence. I didn't want any violence, even if I was pretty certain of my capacity for coming out on top.

She said, "You're a cop, are you? Just a cop?"

"I beg your pardon?"

"I don't believe you. I don't believe you're a cop, and I want you out of here, right now. Sooner than now." She was standing again and looming, prepared to bully me if it came to that.

"I'm not here to make any trouble for you," I babbled. "I spoke to your parents last night."

"Get out."

I stood up, too, since I wasn't willing to be the only one with my butt that close to the floor, and I wanted to give her the impression that I wasn't the kind of girl who takes bullying lying down. "I won't get out, not until we have a chat about your sister," I said, running with my practically-totally-obvious theory that I was talking to the estranged brother.

She was visibly thrown, for all she tried to hide it. Her breathing was suspended for a pair of shocked seconds, and beneath a trowel's worth of cream shadow, her eyes widened, then contracted. "My sister?" she asked, committing to nothing, but not ordering me out of the dressing room, either.

"Your sister. Your little sister," I added, extrapolating from the approximate age of the person in front of me. Sister Rose was in her late twenties or early thirties, by my best approximation. "Isabelle deJesus, who went missing about ten years ago." I then parroted everything I knew from the closed and semi-sealed police report. "She never came home from school."

Rose went from discreetly shocked to stricken. She wanted to know, "Why now? Why *you*? I don't even know who you are. You say you're a cop, but I'm sorry, I still don't buy it, and I want to know what's really going on. What do you want from me?"

"I only want to talk about your sister. I know you've had a falling-out with your family; I went there first, and it was your father who finally gave me this place, and your . . . your stage name, as a lead."

"But why?" she demanded, more desperate than commanding. "Are there any new leads? Nobody cared a decade ago. Why now?"

I held out my hands and said, "Please, sit down. Let's both sit down, and just have a little talk. I'll tell you what I know, and you can tell me what you know, and maybe we'll have a productive conversation, okay?"

"Okay," she said, not certain that she meant it, I could tell. She descended slowly back onto her seat—a small, round vanity-style stool that didn't look large enough or strong enough to hold her. "Okay, but you have to tell me the truth."

I agreed and likewise backed down gingerly into my seat, being careful to keep eye contact. "Let me start over," I tried. "My name is Raylene, and yours is Adrian—yes or no?"

"Yes."

I was almost surprised. I almost expected a token denial, or at least an insistence that it *used* to be her name, and now it was Rose, et cetera. But no. All she said was, "Yes." So I said, as a gesture of good faith, "You're right, I'm not a cop. But I don't work for the government, either, and that's what you're afraid of, isn't it?"

She didn't really answer, except to flip her head in a disdainful shrug. She said, "Motherfucking meatheads."

"Right now, those are my sentiments exactly," I commiserated.

She countered loosely with, "Oh yeah? What have they done to you lately? Did they ever kidnap your little sister and refuse to give her back? Did they ever try to hunt you like a dog, and chase you into hiding?"

"The first part, no. The second part, actually *yes*." I was already out on a limb anyway; I figured I'd go in for a pound if I was in for a penny. "That's how I ended up here, in a roundabout way."

"Looking for my sister?"

"Sort of."

"Sort of?" It wasn't quite a question. It was more of an accusation. "Who are you really, besides some very pale woman named Raylene?"

"I'm not a cop, but I *am* an investigator," I said.

"What kind of investigator? And why won't you tell me what you know about my sister?" Something funny in her tone made me wish I was a stronger psychic; I wanted to surreptitiously poke around in her mind while we talked, but I'm not good enough to get away with it. It's not like walking and chewing gum at the same time. It's like patting your head and tying your shoes.

"You've already expressed some hate for the government. Was that because they had your sister's case closed?" The scowl I received wasn't a satisfying response, so I kept pushing. "Someone went to great lengths to seal your sister's case. Were you aware of this?" I asked, which pretty much exhausted my guesses and credible suspicions.

"Yes."

"And?"

"And what?" She drummed a set of flawless acrylic nails on the vanity table and pretended to adjust the dress around her knees.

"And you know more than that, don't you?" I only realized it as I said it. "It's more complicated than that, isn't it?" I had this moment of epiphany, and there was almost nothing I could do about it, because a knock on the door interrupted us. It wasn't the firm, secure knock of I Totally Belong Here; it was a knock of Jesus Christ Get Your Ass Out Here.

This was heartily confirmed by a bitchy tirade on the other side of the door. "Honey, all God's children need that goddamn dressing room, and Dave's screaming about the electric lemonade. You going to get out here and set the bar, or am I going to tell him you're holed up with a date?"

"Fuck off, Fanny," Rose growled—all man, all of a sudden.

Rose swiveled, stood, and leaned the two steps across the dressing room to the door. Whipping it open, the drag queen added, "I'm having a little conversation with the police right now, if you don't mind. I'll be done here when I'm done here, and until then, you can piss right off, do you understand me?"

Fanny got it, but Fanny made a scene about it. "Oh fine, *sir*. You big scary *bastard,* you. I'll pass it along, you giant fucking cock-up."

Rose slammed the door, and under the makeup I was having a hard time not seeing Adrian, who was big and angry, and rather startlingly masculine. I questioned my pronouns as well as my personal security, for all that this was silly, I was undead, and what was he going to do, scratch my eyes out?

This stupid thought made me think of Ian, and I almost thinked myself into a panic spiral.

Rose was still standing there, hand on the back of the door, either holding it shut or holding herself upright with it. The performer was pondering something, analyzing something. Evaluating something—me, I guessed—and I was worried about where the roulette ball was going to settle.

On Rose's left biceps I saw a shadow that had a funny shape to it, and it took me a second to figure out that I was looking at a tattoo covered in makeup. I wondered what it looked like when it was unhidden.

I wondered what Rose was going to say, and then she started talking.

"Fanny will be back in under a minute. I swear to God, I don't have time for this." There was no softness, feigned or otherwise in what Rose was saying. If I hadn't been staring at her, I would've assumed she was a thirty-year-old man who was royally pissed and ready to punch something.

"For what? For me?"

"For you. For this conversation. For right now. The doors open soon and I have to start the night working the bar, because our guy is out sick and there's no one else who can do it, and if I don't do it, I'll blow this gig. This cover," Rose added, almost as an after-thought.

Footsteps came clipping down the hall, and it was the sound of high heels on carpet that didn't have any padding under it.

Rose said quickly, "Here she comes now, fresh from tattling. Look, you have to leave."

"Not until—"

"No. *Right now,* but we can talk later. Not here. Not like this. I don't trust it, and I don't trust some of these people." She waved at the door, indicating the people on the other side of it in general, maybe Fanny in particular. "And I don't trust you, exactly, but I get why you're holding back, and maybe we can help each other. I don't know. But I'm willing to talk."

"Later?"

"Later," she said as the knocking on the dressing room door commenced afresh. "When I'm off tonight. Around the corner and down the street there's an all-night diner. Meet me there." The knocking grew louder and grouchier, and it was underscored by obscenities. "I won't talk here. I can't talk here, and you *shouldn't* talk here."

"Me? What do I have to do with anything?"

"Maybe plenty," she said, eyes narrowed. She grabbed the door's tiny hook fastener and slapped it into place, as if it could stand alone against the wrath of an impatient drag queen. She low-ered her voice to something wholly unladylike and menacing when she said, "My sister might've run away, but after that she was *taken*. And I know who took her, and I know *why* they took her. So you're no cop and Bella was no runaway, and neither one of you is alive."

Now it was my turn to be shocked into a slack-jawed drool-drip of confusion. "You think your sister's dead?" I asked, because it was the only thing I could think to stutter.

"I'm coming in there!" announced Fanny from the other side, and she shoved against the door. The hook-lock held for the first assault, buying just enough time for Rose to lean down into my personal space.

She said, "Oh, she's dead all right. I just want to know if she's any deader than *you*."

The door burst open and Fanny strolled inside with a glare and a sneer. "You're supposed to be in the bar, asshole, and it's my turn for the mirrors. Who the fuck is this? This the cop you're talking to? She doesn't look like a fucking cop. She looks like a fucking real estate agent."

I started to say, "And you look like—" but Rose cut me off with a very large hand, pushing Fanny aside so I had room to leave. It was just as well. I couldn't think of anything suitably catty anyway. I was in over my head in the catty department, I just knew it.

"Get out," Rose reiterated. "Tonight. After three. Around the corner. We'll talk."

7

Sister Rose turned back to Fanny and started swearing in Spanish, flinging her arms around like she was
guiding a very flamboyant airplane onto a very
bumpy runway. I squeezed out through the narrow
space where the door was half blocked by their bick-
ering bodies and shimmied out sideways into the corridor, which seemed unaccountably dark after the
brilliant face-painting-worthy glare of the dressing
room.

My eyes adjusted accordingly and I stumbled out
down the hall until I found my way back to the foyer.
There, the front doors had been opened (a few minutes early, I thought) and a couple of people had milled
inside, past a smallish man wearing ordinary man-
clothes. He was sitting on a bar stool that had been
dragged over to the entrance, in order to check IDs.

I scooted past him with an "Excuse me" and darted back into the street, where I felt like I could breathe again.

I stood on the sidewalk and oriented myself, scanning the blocks for a twenty-four-hour diner and spotting what looked like a sign for one down at the end of the street. I made a mental note of it and went back to my car.

You may recall that I tend to keep a change of clothes in my trunk. You may also recall that among these clothes are such diverse elements as a hot skirt and heels. I didn't intend to stick around the drag bar all night, but if I was going to hang out in this part of town, I wanted to look less like a fucking real estate agent. Because really, Fanny was right and I knew it.

I wished I had something more like party clothes handy, but there was no way in hell I was going to drive all the way back home, then all the way back out to the Poppycock Review. Not on a weekend night. I'd rather suck it up and wander around looking like . . . well . . . like a slutty real estate agent. But it was better than nothing.

Because I have literally no shame whatsoever, I changed clothes in the backseat. No one stopped to watch, which was not quite insulting and, technically, should be considered a mark in the win column. Then again, I was only changing into a skirt and swapping out shoes, so I guess I wasn't exactly putting on a show.

When I emerged from the vehicle I looked a little more like I belonged in the neighborhood, or at least I hoped so. If nothing else, I appeared young enough that—it was to be fervently prayed—I didn't look like a middle-aged swinger looking for a third.

And God, it was still early. I had five or six hours to kill before it'd be worth my time to stroll over to the diner. So it was a real good thing I have a secret soft spot for disco. I roamed from club to club, watching show after show, and pickup after pickup in bar after bar.

I only treated myself to one glass of wine, so I stayed plenty sober throughout the evening, even for me. And in that last hour before the end of Rose's shift, I wended to the Poppycock Review in order to hang out as a patron and—in all honesty—make sure my new lead didn't magically disappear in a poof of glitter and a hearty snap of her fingers. I didn't like being put off until later, and I didn't intend to be stood up.

By the time I returned, the Review was jumping and jam-packed.

Pre-menopausal Madonna chirped aggressively from every speaker, and the press of bodies was close, salty-smelling, and frankly delicious—so very delicious that I wondered if this was such a good idea after all. For the previous chunk of the evening I'd been crashing in bars and keeping to the edges of the social scenery as a matter of personal sanity, but this was invigorating and fun, if cramped. I hadn't been out dancing in longer than I could re-member (since disco was popular the first time around? Maybe), and although I wasn't dressed as appropriately as I would've pre-ferred, I couldn't keep my body from moving, bouncing, lunging along with the crowd as I made my way back to the stage area.

It wasn't really a stage, exactly. It was just a swath of the dance floor that was being forcibly cleared for the night's grand finale. A small dyke herded swaying, bopping dancers off to the edges, un-derneath the balcony overhangs and up the stairs so they could dan-gle off the banisters and lean over the rails. Those below were splashed periodically with beer, Long Island iced tea, or other con-tents from drunkenly handled pitchers up above. I picked the dri-est spot I could reach without hurting anyone and braced myself against a support pillar to watch the proceedings—hoping they'd include Sister Rose. If she came out to perform, I'd know she hadn't flown the coop while I was out.

I'm not sure why I was so confident she hadn't taken off, ex-

cept that she seemed to know something about me—and by exten-
sion, perhaps about her baby sister's condition before she vanished.
If I'd played my cards right, Rose would be dying to know what I
knew, just like I was dying to know what *she* knew. Maybe we'd both
come out of it disappointed, or maybe we wouldn't.

But my desire to see Rose perform *wasn't* disappointed. She
was announced as the next girl up, and all the late-night, drunk-as-
hell partiers retreated the last few feet out of the performance area
from respect or fear. I stayed where I was, except that I took a half
step back, up onto a short, low pedestal against which the pillar
was set. It gave me about three inches of height I wouldn't otherwise have, and that, coupled with my obscenely tall shoes, let me
see pretty much everything.

"Everything" consisted at first of "not much." The lights
dimmed, and then changed color before exploding afresh into vi-
brant shades of gold, blue, and scarlet. From the DJ booth a swift,
naughty beat began to blare, and with it came a deeply fey voice
that announced, "Ladies, and gentlemen, and everyone in between . . . we're saving the best for last here at the Poppycock Review, and you know what *that* means, don't you?"

The crowd announced in raucous stereo, "Pussy Party!"

And I wondered what the hell I'd gotten myself into, until the
spotlight appeared and the song began. Don't ask me why I recognized it; I'll only lie to you. But suffice it to say, it was "Pussy" by
an old band called the Lords of Acid. And then, oh yes—there was
Sister Rose in the spotlight. And running a little late, the DJ said,
"That's right! And leading tonight's Pussy Party, I give you, Sister
Rose!"

A brief and hearty cheer went up, and then was silenced as
Rose stepped into the clearing and began to lip-sync.

Rose wasn't wearing much, but the whole ensemble sparkled
from strap to strap. It looked like the skeleton of a beauty queen's

apparel in the swimsuit competition, done up in silver, with a tiny hint of beaded fringe down south, where it counted. But fringe or no fringe, I was impressed with the tuck-job. It was a tuck-job that made me feel less odd about calling a six-foot-plus man a "she" in my interior monologue. It reinforced the very shiny illusion, but so help me God, there was nothing to be done about her legs.

Don't get me wrong—they went for miles, and the muscle definition was absolutely to die for . . . but you'd never mistake them for belonging to a woman, unless we're talking the She Hulk. Still, this observation did not prevent me from feeling a touch of envy. If Mattel ever makes a Drag Queen Barbie, they damn well ought to pattern that doll's proportions after Sister Rose. Those were legs that could crack a horse's ribs, and they knew how to move.

They scissored and stretched, and banged apart, dropping Rose's crotch down to a floor-level split that *I* would've considered too painful to attempt, but she never dropped the beat or the verse. Rose grabbed the nearest rail and scaled it with the ease of the world's most glamorous chimpanzee, slinging herself easily and gloriously in time to the music—and all the while never flashing even a hint of anything incriminating.

If I seem fixated on this point, well, I'd never seen a drag show this up close and personal before, and it fascinated me. The pageantry, the artifice, the unapologetic pretense . . . It was effusive and charming, albeit loud as hell. By this point in the night, I was wishing for earplugs and wondering if my unnaturally sensitive ears would ever truly recover, but I couldn't muster any real concern about it.

Rose's big black wig was outfitted with big faux gemstones that caught the lights and hurled them around like lasers, and her darkly painted lips contorted themselves around lyrics that only barely pretended to be a double entendre. If there was any such thing as a single entendre, this was it.

But out of the corner of my eye, I saw something I didn't like—although it was gone as soon as it'd snagged my attention. I asked myself, "Self, what was that?" and nobody heard me, which was just as well, since it wasn't that funny and I was actually kind of serious. The subconscious is a strange thing, the way it sorts and settles what needs our attention and what doesn't, and mine was screaming at me that I was missing something—not that it would've surprised me. How could anybody take in the whole scene without missing half or it, or more? The spinning lights that changed color on the fly were enough to induce seizures all by themselves, and when added to the head-splitting volume of the music, and the spectacle of the show, and the crushing waves of inebriated late-night partiers, it was hard to think straight, much less evaluate anything.

Even danger.

And I didn't like that.

The thought was a land mine, setting off an explosion of sudden panic. "I shouldn't have come here," I said aloud since no one was listening. "This was a bad idea." The room was big, but too crowded to either get away or hide effectively. I scanned quickly for the exits and saw several lighted signs with arrows, but those weren't the exits I wanted. Those were the exits that *everyone* would be using.

Again, I saw something through the crowd—a snippet of suit, a swatch of hair. I struggled to fish it out again, to discern the man as he moved through the crowd because yes, I was pretty sure I'd seen a man. And then he was easy to see, or easy to track, because he wasn't moving like everyone else. He wasn't dancing. He wasn't even doing that sideways sway people do when they're trying to walk across a dance floor, moving along with the flow and yet trying to maintain some preservation of the rhythm.

I could see him moving like a snake through the grass, flat and sneaky, and utterly out of place at the Poppycock Review.

He was wearing a dark suit, maybe a black suit—I couldn't tell. But he was definitely dressed for business at a quarter till three in the morning, in a drag bar, in the less-than-awesome part of Atlanta. Which may or may not have meant a damn thing, or so I told myself. I had to tell myself that, and I had to *keep* telling myself that as I began to slide around the side of my pillar, keeping my shoulders pressed up against it. For no sooner had I almost convinced myself that he was somebody's dad or some random swinger than I saw that the man in the suit was not alone.

A second guy was worming his way from the other end of the room, gliding through the crowd like he'd just stepped out of the Matrix. Except that I was prepared to bet he'd freshly stepped out of a long black car instead.

I don't know how I knew, except that I always know bad news when I see it, and staring back and forth between these guys—while simultaneously trying to spot any others—I was damn near positive I'd spotted a problem. And the longer I stood there spotting it, the more obvious it was that they were working their way toward Rose, who was almost finished with her song.

On the one hand, this was a relief for me, personally. On the other, it was definitely Not Good for Rose, and oh God, what if I'd led them straight to her?

But that didn't make any sense. I'm neurotic and self-second-guessing about many things, but I was absolutely confident that I hadn't been followed since Seattle. So what did this mean? I was frantic for an answer, but nobody was going to give me one and the show was winding down.

I had no idea what to do.

A third man of the same suspicious tribe came slithering from another corner, and that only left one corner, which meant there was probably someone coming up behind me, too, and I'd just have to cross my fingers that nobody was looking for me—not on this trip. I held my breath and Rose pretended to hold that last note, and as the music died away the three men—yes, shortly joined by a fourth from over my left shoulder—converged on the dance floor.

The suited man nearest me was walking in front of me, with his back to me. He turned sideways to facilitate his passage, and I saw the distinct bulge of a gun. But surely they wouldn't just whip 'em out in a crowded room?

Frantic, I shifted my gaze back to Rose—whose face was covered with a dawning sort of horror because she, too, had seen them now.

The DJ was making his closing announcement, stating the hours the club was open, thanking everyone for coming out, and sending them on their way with the old bit about how "You don't have to go home, but you can't stay here."

The crowds were thinning, and thinning fast.

I closed my eyes and concentrated on building up a shout—not a vocal one, but a psychic one—in an attempt to draw Rose's attention. I gathered it up and sent it out, projecting it toward the drag queen and smacking her with it: *Over here!*

She blinked and recoiled, and spied me at my pillar. She gave me a scowl that implied very strongly that she believed I'd brought the suited men here, when of course I had *not*, but I'd be hard-pressed to prove it in a shouting match across a still-considerably-loud club floor covered in people.

So I sent it again—*Over here, goddammit! Now!*

For some reason, it took. She jolted into action, not pushing her way through to an exit, but grabbing the ironwork circular stairwell behind her and using it to climb the nearest banister. From that banister she skipped onto the rail, up above the people and with a far clearer path than anyone down on the floor could've managed. She moved so smoothly and with such strength, that within moments she was down to the other end of the floor and was forced to drop down in front of me. Her high heels crashed loud enough to be heard above the lingering exit music. She grabbed me by the shoulder and yanked me forward.

"What the fuck is going on?" she demanded in her man-voice.

"I have no idea! But we need out of here, *now*—" which was an understatement, because the floor was clear enough that, with a bit of shoving, the suited men were able to run toward us.

Still holding me by the shoulder, Rose shoved me forward and I let her. Nothing could be gained by fighting between ourselves, after all, and *she* knew where we were going. I didn't. I asked, "Is there another way out of here?"

"This way," she said, propelling me face-first into a very large woman (or man?) who didn't like getting hit, but who was too drunk to do anything about it. I ricocheted off her (him?) and almost into another support pillar under the balcony, but I steadied myself and wiggled out from Rose's grasp. I was going to need more mobility than her vise-like handhold would permit.

"Which way?" I asked, and this time she shoved me back, around a corner, down into a very dark place that, after one more turn, was all but pitch-black.

She stumbled and I heard a shuffling sound that indicated she'd decided to jettison the shoes, which—let's be fair—was a totally great call. I didn't know how she could walk in the things, and I say that as someone who was running in four-inch heels. "Where are we?" I wanted to know.

She said, "Storage. Move it." And she gestured with the shoes, which dangled from their straps in her hand.

"I can hear them behind us."

"Thanks. Like I need the motivation." She whipped back and

took my hand, but they were getting close—very close. Close enough to be scrambling for a light switch somewhere behind us, only a few yards back.

So I said, "No, let go."

"I'm not backing us into a corner—it opens back here, to an alley." And then she smashed against something hard, and it didn't move. I piled up behind her; I just couldn't stop in time, and I smacked my face into the back of her shoulder, earning me a mouthful of sequins and a moment of panic.

"It's locked!" I blurted.

"It shouldn't be," she complained. "From the outside, maybe?"

"They tend to be pretty well prepared," I said feebly. Then I added, "Work on it."

She sputtered, "What?"

"Work on it. Bash it down if you have to. I'll take care of these guys."

"What if there are guys outside?" she asked, which was a perfectly valid question.

I said, "We'll cross that bridge . . . oh, just work on the door." As I ran back into the corridor without any lights, I added over my shoulder, "We might not need it anyway."

The first suit never knew what hit him. The darkness meant nothing to me, or next to nothing, and I cut through it quickly. I jumped at the last second, grabbed him by the throat, and twisted his head until his skeleton snapped and everything inside the suit ground to a halt. The man went limp and I picked him up, held him low, right around knee level, and flung him down the darkness like I was bowling for feds.

But by then the other three guys suspected something was amiss. I heard whispers going back and forth between microphones and earpieces, but my ears were badly bludgeoned by six hours of too-loud music, and I didn't catch anything but a collection of ferocious hisses. They were spreading out, and crouching down— I could tell that much.

I took the opposite approach and reached up for a set of pipes that ran above my head. I could see them in the blackness, slick as eels along the ceiling, worming through the building like veins. I propped one foot up onto the nearest crate and it jingled faintly, revealing that it was filled with small decorative bells, damn it all to hell. Might as well have been packed with exploding whoopee cushions for all the noise it made. But with a shove and a jump I'd reached the overhead pipes and hauled myself flat up against them—just in time to dodge the blast of gunfire aimed at my great jangling fuckup.

One shot, and it could've been a nine-millimeter or a cannon in that dark, narrow storage room. But I was well out of its range, up there with the pipes clasped to my chest and my ankles interlocking to hold my full weight up above the floor.

Sister Rose barked, "Raylene!" but I couldn't answer without revealing myself, so I didn't. And when one of the feds began a grim charge down the narrow thoroughfare, I swooped down and picked him up Batman-style: one hand over his mouth, one arm around his neck. I held him up off the ground and let him struggle while the third fed came scooting onto the scene. But hey, since I was holding this big heavy lug of a bastard (and if I were to be honest, gradually losing my feet's grip on the pipe), I swung him around like a pendulum—breaking his neck with an almost-accidental snap—and I clocked the incoming suit with his buddy's corpse.

Then I dropped down; I had to, my ankles were giving way and my shoes were on the verge of slipping off. I clattered down to the narrow walkway, landing heavily on the freshest fed. He squirmed and shoved me away, drawing up his gun and getting ready to fire it in my general direction, or maybe Rose's.

I didn't let him. I wrenched it out of his hand before he could squeeze the trigger and I used it to bludgeon him into stillness. Something broke and his skin began to leak, but the tang of blood was only a faint distraction. I willed myself to ignore it, because I couldn't be hungry and be aware of my other pursuer at the same time. This last guy was smarter than the first wave; he was hanging back and patrolling the perimeter as best he could—lurking out by the lights in the hall, where the doorway was open, letting the glare of the cheap bulbs cut sharp shafts of light against the darkness.

I could hear him whispering back and forth into the tiny microphones that were tucked into his shirt collar, and I could even pick out most of the words. He was calling for backup and debating the best approach, which was good. It meant that whoever was after us didn't know where I was, or what I was.

I *hoped* they didn't know what I was.

Behind me, I heard Rose's shoulder slam against the back door and then there was a pop as the thing flapped open, sucking a little of the dark out of the storage room. "Raylene!" she cried out, and I still didn't answer but I was beside her in a flash, behind her and urging her outside, into the alleyway.

"Son of a *bitch*, you're fast," she observed. "I thought maybe they'd hit you."

"Me? Hell no," I assured her. "But they'll be on us in a minute, so come on."

"Where?"

Around us the alley was dark and nasty, cluttered with decomposing trash and pocked with puddles that were filled with something that was more *eau de bum piss* than rainwater. Overhead, the moon was rolling slowly across the night sky, ducking behind a few thin clouds and peeping back out the other side. "This way," I said.

She asked, "Why?" but she followed regardless, which I appreciated.

"My car."

"You found a parking place out here?"

I would've responded but the back door smacked behind us and the last fed had found a friend, and they were on our trail. I ushered her forward and jammed her around the nearest corner, praying we hadn't been spotted.

If it'd just been me, it wouldn't have bothered. I'd have taken to the rooftops and been a mile away before their eyes adjusted to this new level of light. But Adrian deJesus was only human, and we had too many common interests and enemies to part company now.

She was barefoot and I was wearing high heels, which was a strike against the pair of us, but she moved easily and, just like she'd climbed the rail indoors, she grabbed a rain gutter and hoisted herself up. The metal tube creaked and groaned but held, and she swung her body over onto the Poppycock Review's angled roof.

"Come on!" she breathed, reaching down a hand.

I took the hand because I didn't want to push our luck by relying on the gutter, and I was impressed by how easily she lifted me. Underneath that skimpy drag garb, Sister Rose was built like a brick shithouse, and she moved smoothly to draw me up beside her.

She flashed me a military-style hand gesture that I didn't really understand, but I nodded and followed along. We were on her turf after all, and this wasn't my corner of town. For all I knew she hung out on the roof and ziplined around the city easy as you please, just for shits and giggles.

I opened my mouth to ask, "Where are we going?" because she'd started leading me at a leaning pace around the edge. But she smacked me in the mouth—more roughly than strictly necessary—and hissed a *"shh!"* that could've cut tile. She pointed at my shoes and pretended to hold them by the heels. Who was I to argue? I played copycat and joined in the angled game of walking at a sideways lurch, heels dangling from one hand and bare feet sticking grittily to the shingles.

"My car," I whispered softer, at her back. Because I was confident that I could dodge her if she tried to smack my mouth shut again, now that I knew to expect it.

"Where?"

"Peachtree, a block that way." I pointed when she looked over her shoulder to see what nonsense I was going on about.

Down below us we could scarcely hear them, but we could see them.

They were splitting up, circling the building. If they knew we were up above them, they were careful to hide it, but one of them buzzed into his mouthpiece that they needed reinforcements and asked something about a satellite. Call me a pessimist, but I figured that whatever came back through his earpiece wasn't good for us, which was a bummer. I'd thought it might be worth my time to hop down, wreak a little havoc, and boom—two feds out of the way, and permanently off our trail. But if more were coming, it might be too much of a time sink to be worth the trouble.

"Do they know?"

"Know what?"

"About your car," she whistled quietly between her teeth.

"Not unless they're magically tracking me by the pixie dust that spills out of my ass. It's down *there,*" I said, as if I might've somehow parked it on the shingles where we stood. Lest that be the last idiotic thought ringing through Sister Rose's ears, I added, "We have to go down and get it." Because I didn't plan to carry the bulky queen anywhere. It'd scarcely be any faster than hobbling around in high heels. Behind the wheel, I could get us out and clear at eighty miles per hour, if it came down to it. "Besides, they're

looking for two . . . woman-shaped people on foot. Let's go get my
wheels and scramble their assumptions."

"Okay. We'll split up and do that."

"Are you crazy?" I demanded, a smidge too loud. "Don't you
ever watch any horror movies?"

"They can't chase us both."

"Yes they can. There's *two of them*."

"Look, they've called for backup," she said, indicating the two
men below. "They're going to hang together until backup arrives.
They won't divide to chase us."

She sounded pretty confident of this fact—confident enough
to risk her life. So I replied, "Fine. I'll go get the car." I jacked a
thumb to the west. "And I'll pick you up . . . ?"

"Down at the diner, as originally planned." I detected an accusatory scowl, and ignored it. "Give me five minutes."

"Five minutes?"

She reconsidered. "Three. And you'd better be there. What
kind of car?"

"Dark blue pseudo-cop-car. Crown Vic."

"Fantastic," she said, and I couldn't tell if she meant it or if
she was being bitchy.

"Three minutes," I repeated.

"Three minutes," she said back.

And on the count of three we each dove in a different direction
and went leaping, scattering, splashing down off the roof.

I shudder to note that I was the one doing the splashing.

Barefoot and now stinking of something homeless people do in
public, I hightailed it around the corner and down the block—
without bothering to pretend like I was just an ordinary lady,
dressed somewhat sluttily, barefoot, and running for her life from
a rapist or carjacker or something. No way.

I ran full-tilt, bumping into the late-night (or early-morning) clubgoers hard enough to send them reeling, and then wondering what on earth had just shoved them. I moved fast enough that I probably looked like a blur—a conspicuous blur, to be certain—but I didn't care. Whoever was on my tail already knew enough about me to cramp my night, and while I'm usually the very soul of discretion, every now and again a girl has to tear loose and run like the devil knows her name.

Because he does. And he has a serial number with which he'd like to replace it.

I reached the car approximately thirty seconds after I'd launched myself off the roof, and then I spent a rather fumbly, humiliating moment searching for my keys. I wasn't carrying a bag so they had to be in one of my pockets and yes, they were. I dug them out and my hands were shaking. No longer a blur on a sidewalk, I was now a disheveled hussy quaking her way home on a jittery, shoeless walk of shame. Or so I imagined. And so I hoped I projected, because it wouldn't draw a second glance in that neighborhood.

Finally I got the car open, and got myself inside it. I shoved the key into the ignition and started the thing with a sigh of relief. Then I wondered how much time had passed. Three minutes? Maybe? It wasn't like we'd stopped to synchronize our watches or anything. We'd just nodded at each other and taken off, as if by pure synchronicity we'd meet up 180 seconds later.

I pulled out into the street, cutting off some asshole in a low-riding car with a racing stripe. The driver swore and honked and flipped me the bird and I flipped it right back as I gunned the gas and heaved my big-ass car out into the street.

The diner wasn't far away. One block? Two blocks? A couple of blocks, yes—because I was parked on the other side of the Poppycock Review. But traffic was heavy and the only streetlight I hit between my starting point and my destination *surely* held me up longer than the three promised minutes. I tapped my bare, wet, grimy foot against the brake and muttered, "Come *on*," as if my irritation could somehow bend the universe to my whims.

If only.

And just when I was working myself up to a neurotic frenzy wherein Sister Rose had been captured, or had vanished, or was lying dead in one of those foul-smelling puddles, a knock on the passenger window gave me a shock that would've stopped my heart if I'd still been alive.

She was there, slapping her hands against the window and saying, "Come *on*," just like I'd been saying about the stoplight. Only I couldn't call her "she" anymore. In three minutes (or four, or five, or however long it'd taken me), Sister Rose had morphed into Adrian deJesus, brother of Isabelle and wearer of clothes that looked suspiciously like they might've come off a federal agent. It was the fastest identity swap I'd ever had the pleasure of witnessing.

I pressed the button to unlock the car, and with a swift yank of the handle and a sliding leap that landed him in the passenger's slot, he was inside. I locked the doors again.

The light turned green.

We rolled through it like the most ordinary of couples, doing the most ordinary drive home ever. I saw two long black cars pulling up to the block where the drag bar had all too recently been the scene of several murders (on my part), and the fleeing of one great drag queen (on Adrian's part).

I made a point to quit looking in the rearview mirror as I drove.

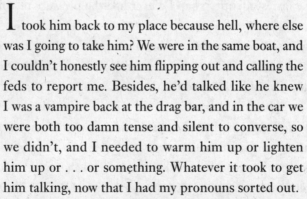

8

I took him back to my place because hell, where else was I going to take him? We were in the same boat, and I couldn't honestly see him flipping out and calling the feds to report me. Besides, he'd talked like he knew I was a vampire back at the drag bar, and in the car we were both too damn tense and silent to converse, so we didn't, and I needed to warm him up or lighten him up or . . . or something. Whatever it took to get him talking, now that I had my pronouns sorted out.

I'd sorted them thusly: When he was dressed as a man, talking like a man, and looking like a man, as far as I was concerned he was a man. In ladywear, with full lady persona, she was a woman. And if he/she had any issue with my designations, he/she could take it up with me later, when no one was trying to kill or capture us and stuff us into the trunk of a long black car.

So *he* stood in my kitchen, leaning over the bar, his neck glistening with sweat—and a dusting of leftover glitter. That stuff really *is* the gift that keeps on giving.

We were both sullen and uncertain of how to begin speaking, but he was downing a glass of scotch he'd found under the sink and I was wrestling with a bottle of nice red wine, on the very verge of smashing it against the counter just to get at the sweet, sweet goodness inside.

The cork sprang free just in time to stop me. I grabbed a goblet and filled it up—damn the torpedoes and all that.

When I had a full glass in hand, and he had a mostly empty one before him on the counter, I said, "So."

And he said, "So," right back.

I gave up and said, "This is ridiculous. You know I'm a vampire, I know you know I'm a vampire, and we both know your little sister was part of a government project. Feel free to stop me when and if I'm wrong."

He didn't stop me.

"All right, then," I continued. I was not exactly reassured by the illusion of control but I'd accept it in lieu of actual control, so I bullied the conversation forward. "She died, years ago. The military told you . . . they told you what? That she'd killed herself? That she'd merely passed away as part of some test or experiment?"

"Something like that."

"And you bought it?" I asked, incredulous only because half a glass of red was breaking down the barriers between my brain and my mouth. And let's be honest, those barriers aren't exactly reinforced concrete under the best of circumstances.

He didn't quite sneer, but the look he made wasn't pretty. "Of course I didn't buy it. But congratulations, you tracked me down. And while you were at it, you led them right to me, didn't you?"

"No!" I objected instantly. "I have no idea how they found

their way to you, but I've survived under the radar for nearly a century, thank you very much, and it was only when I stumbled over the trip wire of your sister's project that anybody in any black suit and any shiny car ever had any specific interest in me, personally."

"I find that difficult to believe," he said.

To which I replied, "Yeah? Well I don't give a shit. I don't have anything to prove to you." And I didn't tell him anything about Cheshire Red, or the half dozen international agencies that had wanted me for decades.

"Then what are you doing here?"

"What?"

"You," he said pointedly, picking up the glass again and aiming it at me. "What are you doing here, if you don't have anything to prove?"

"Oh, I've got work to do and things to prove, just not to *you,*" I insisted. "My investigation accidentally stumbled *across* you, which is not at all the same thing. I wandered into your circle by hunting down the military records for Project Bloodshot. In case you're unaware, those records effectively vanished, years ago. But I bet you aren't unaware. I bet you know *exactly* where they are, because I bet *you're* the one who took them."

His eyes simmered over the highball glass. He downed the last couple of drops and acted like he wanted more, but was too smart to ask for more—much less drink any more. He said, "Yeah. I took them."

"I knew it!" I said, and it sounded sloppy. Which somehow didn't stop me from finishing the glass of expensive old red. I was wound up tighter than an E-string, and I needed to get a grip on myself before dawn came up in a handful of hours. So I drank.

"I have no idea how you got so lucky," he said. I liked the Spanish roll to his vowels, and I liked the hateful simmering. I wanted to piss him off more, and keep him talking. I wanted to pin him down and demand that he say, "My name is Inigo Montoya—you killed my father, prepare to die." But I suspect that would've been deeply inappropriate in any number of ways. I told you, alcohol hits me hard and fast. I can't help it if my mind wanders.

And hell, yours would've wandered, too, if you'd seen that body of his attired in fishnets and spangles. He was a good-looking man—maybe even more so than he was a good-looking woman. Good bone structure, that shiny blue-black hair with a faint, pretty wave . . . I wondered if he was gay, but I didn't dare ask. Don't ask me why; all I can say is that it was on the tip of my tongue and it took every ounce of remaining self-control to keep that query to myself.

Instead I told him, "I'm not lucky, I'm persistent."

"And whose records do you want?"

"It wouldn't matter if I told you. He isn't mentioned by name, just a serial number."

"All right." He signaled to me that he wanted more scotch, twitching his finger my way as if I were a bartender. "Then what do you hope to find when you score those records?"

I serviced him anyway. I mean, you know. I topped off his drink, and let mine stay dry. And I figured that possibly, given the circumstances, honesty was the best policy. Veiled honesty, but honesty all the same. My inner choir girl sang.

"One of the other victims of the project is a client of mine. He needs his medical records."

"Medical records? Can we really call them that?"

"I don't see why not," I all but snapped at him. "His body was experimented upon, and there are records of it. What else would you call it?"

"I don't know. Necropsy?"

"Fuck you very much. Dead we may be, but still we bleed," I said, trying to quote something and bombing it. I cleaned up my fumble with a lazy, "You know what I mean. You wouldn't want someone cutting on your eyes either, I assume. Or"—I went for the heart of the matter as soon as I remembered where it was—"you wouldn't want anyone doing it to your *sister*."

"No, I wouldn't," he said with a flare of something hot and hateful.

"Then don't begrudge my client his humanity either. Asshole," I added.

He picked up his glass like he'd like to empty it further, or maybe whap me upside the head with it, but he did neither of these things. He sat it back down again and leaned against the counter, raising his hands to his face and rubbing his eyes. "It's been so damn long," he said. "She's been gone all this time, and I've been invisible. And then *you*." He shot me another napalm glare, but it surprised me by cooling into something more sorrowful. Mercurial, this one. I liked it. It was hot.

"I guess it doesn't matter. If you didn't lead them to me, someone else would have, eventually. Or I would've screwed up, or someone would've recognized me, somewhere."

"Does that mean you aren't mad at me?" I asked, just in case.

"I didn't say that. But it was probably a question of when, not if. Hey," he said suddenly, in a whole different tone. Then he began patting himself down, running his fingers inside the seams of his clothes. Only then I remembered—they weren't his clothes. He told me, "I nicked these off one of the guys who was chasing us."

"Like I didn't figure that out."

"I just wanted to make it clear that I didn't mug any innocent bystander." He grabbed his own ass and then, with a victorious flourish, produced a very slim wallet. It was not the world's most promising wallet. It almost looked like a pair of leather credit cards bound together, which led me to guess what it actually was. An ID folder.

I sidled up to him, sneaking in close to look around his arm and over his shoulder. "What does it say?"

"It says I mugged Peter Desarme." He brandished the badge so I could see it in all its glory. "CIA agent."

"Wait. What?"

"That's what it says," he noted redundantly.

He let me swipe it out of his hand. I examined it up close and personal. It looked real. "I don't get it."

"What's not to get?"

"I figured these were army guys. Or, high-ranking, suit-wearing . . . I don't know. Men in Black. In my head I'd been calling them feebs. But CIA? That's really out of left field."

"There's no good reason men in black can't be CIA agents. And besides, it's not *that* crazy," he objected. "Project Bloodshot was closed. Maybe it was reopened as a civilian operation."

"How do you know it's closed? I mean how do you *really* know? We're talking about the *military*. It's a whole organization of left hands dedicated to not knowing what the right hands are doing."

"You may be right, but I bet you're not. Some asshole with money might've picked up where the army left off. It happens sometimes."

"You can't be serious."

He said, "Think about it—all that money and research and effort, all dumped into something that winds up blacked out and shredded. It happens all the time. And every now and again, a private corporation will take an interest, and take another stab at it. They use whatever's left of the military documentation to seed the new experiments, picking up where they left off. Sometimes they even look up the former researchers, engineers, and scientists. Anyone who took part in it."

"Then where does the CIA come into it? Doesn't the very presence of CIA operatives mean it's not a civilian operation?

Or . . ." I reconsidered my words. "Or at least that it's a different *kind* of official operation?"

"Nah," he said. "CIA guys are wild cards. They're allowed to freelance, and a lot of them do."

"Like mercenaries?" I asked.

"More or less. People are always talking about setting guidelines for what they can and can't do, but nobody ever does. There's plenty of . . . let's say 'conflict of interest' going on where they're concerned. But . . ." He shrugged. "There's no regulation. So they moonlight wherever the money's good."

"Huh." I handed the ID back to him, but only after noting for the record that Adrian deJesus and Peter Desarme bore no resemblance whatsoever, and we wouldn't have any luck repurposing the official cards. "You learn something new every day."

He said, "Yeah. I'm learning a bunch of new things today, for example." Then he dropped his hands and slapped the wallet onto the counter. His gaze went back and forth between the floor and the scotch glass, respectively. Quietly he asked, "So let me see if I can learn one more thing, while we're talking. Did you know my sister? Is there any chance of that?"

"No," I said. "But there's a chance my client did. They were in the same program, anyway. Can you tell me a little about her? Something I can use to refresh his memory?" Or satisfy my own curiosity, as the case may be.

He sighed. "Isabelle ran away from home to go live with a boyfriend—a useless piece of shit she'd met someplace downtown. Our parents wouldn't have it; they threw her out."

"Can you throw somebody out who's already moved out?"

"It was the principle of the thing," he said. He tipped his finger at the glass and asked, "A little more? If you don't mind."

I didn't mind. It was expensive scotch, but I never drank much of it anyway. I think that the bottle was a gift from Horace, received ages previously. Adrian was welcome to it—and all the more so if it loosened his tongue.

While he sipped, I asked, "She was your younger sister, I assume? Did you try to talk her out of it? Being big brother, and all?"

"Of course I tried. But she wouldn't hear it, and I was already overseas by then—"

"Military," I said, remembering what the PDF had said about the thief.

"Navy SEAL," he specified. "I was wrapping up training far enough away from here that there was nothing I could do about it. Anyway, she started to dabble in drugs, and then the boyfriend died or disappeared—I'm not sure which. She tried to come home but our mother wasn't having it. Momma gave Bella the line about how if she wanted to go be an adult, she could stay out there and be an adult."

"Ouch. What'd she do then?" I was going for the sympathy play, and it wasn't entirely a ploy. I honestly wanted to know about his sister—how she'd been turned, how she'd been captured, and how she'd died.

"Lived on the streets, I guess. Bounced in and out of shelters."

"Dropped out of school?"

He nodded.

Well, that was one more paper trail I wouldn't bother chasing.

"By the time I had leave to come home, the household was a war zone between my mother and my father. And Isabelle was nowhere to be found."

"Your mother wanted her to stay gone, and your father wanted her to come home, is that right?"

"Yes." His eyes narrowed, watering with exhaustion or very old pain. "How did you know?"

"I told you, I went there and talked to them, remember? Your dad gave me your stage name. Your mom acted like she wanted to burn my face with a road flare."

"That's them." He waved one hand carelessly, then froze it in midair. His body language and his tone changed abruptly, to something sober and tense. "You spoke to them?"

"I told you I—"

"You went to visit them? At their house?"

"Yes," I told him, not sure where he was headed with this line of interrogation, but sensing that I wouldn't like the destination even a little bit. "But I told you that *before*."

"I wasn't thinking. We . . ." He dropped the glass and it stayed upright, but sloshed. "We have to go back there. What if you led the agents right to them?"

I held up my hands in a gesture that wouldn't have stopped an aggressive poodle, much less a frantic, tipsy drag queen. "Don't, Adrian. Don't go there, not like this. Your parents aren't in hiding, are they? I was inside their house, yes," I confessed, and then I grasped at straws. "And it looked to me like they'd been there for years. The government doesn't want your parents. It could've had them at any time—"

"Okay. Okay, yes. You're right," he said, and it was pitifully apparent that he was leaning on my words, trying to calm himself down. Hey, I know it when I see it. "You're right, they've been there since before I was born. Nobody wants anything from them. Everybody knows they don't know anything . . . except, my father gave you my stage name . . ."

"Well, he sort of scribbled it—"

"He told you where to find me. If he told you, he could've told anybody!"

"Goddammit, Adrian, settle down. He didn't tell just anybody, he told *me* and I was doing a very convincing cop impression, I'll have you know."

He glowered at me and then he growled, "You mean, you showed up in an official-looking car, in a suit?"

Oh. I got it. "Well, it wasn't . . . it wasn't a *black* suit, and it wasn't a *black* car. And I had a badge . . ." I looked back down at Peter Desarme's clothes on Adrian's back, and his badge on my kitchen counter, and I figured he, too, would've likely had an official-looking car to complete the package.

"You don't understand. My parents, they . . . They aren't very trusting of authority, but they fear it and they'll cave to it, if it comes on hard enough. Please, for the love of God, tell me you did not lead anybody to my parents."

"I couldn't have," I hoped, and I prayed. "Listen, I was *not* being followed. I'm smarter than that, and more careful than that. If I weren't, I never would've survived this long."

He was tapping his foot and tapping his wrist on the edge of the counter, trying to come to some kind of decision. "You would've noticed someone tailing you in a car."

"That's what I'm telling you, yes."

"But what if you were being followed some other way? Something less obvious?"

"Like what?" I wanted to know, but a word bubbled to the surface of my attention, and I didn't like it. "Like with some kind of . . . I don't know. Surveillance system."

"That's what I'm thinking," he mused, poking at the wallet. "Something like a satellite."

"A satellite?" My blood went colder than my drink. "That's not possible."

But Adrian didn't say anything to help slow the ramp-up of my paranoid frenzy. "The technology wasn't really live yet when I was still in the service, but you could see it coming. Satellites were the next thing that would save us—we'd be watching our enemies from space, in high definition."

"But . . . but can they do that *now*?" I demanded. "That's something that happens on TV, and in movies once in a while. But in real life? *Bullshit*. I call bullshit."

"Call it what you want. The gear these guys were wearing—it was advanced stuff. Those earpieces." He made a fiddly motion, as if he were holding one up. "Those microphones. A quarter the size of what we were using a decade ago."

The only satellites I knew about that didn't carry TV signals fed straight to the Internet, like Google Earth . . . and that was just a snapshot, right? Satellites—which is to say, powerful cameras out in orbit—only give you an image. They don't give you live video feeds.

Unless I was wrong. Unless there were other kinds of satellites.

I racked my brain, trying to dredge up memories of CNN coverage or other news organizations showing footage from Iraq or Afghanistan. Some of those military satellites were more advanced, weren't they?

Whoo *boy*. The implications made my head spin. I just might have stumbled across some whole new and exciting thing to be terrified of. I tried to catch up and calm down. I said, "Sure, fine. Tiny trackers, the size of pocket change, okay. But that's just radio contact, old-fashioned and reliable, right?"

"Probably," he acknowledged.

And then he started taking off his clothes.

"Not that I'm complaining, but what the hell are you doing?"

"Peter Desarme might've had a tracker on him. It could be anywhere, sewn into a seam or clipped into a pocket," he said as he kicked the pants off—revealing the hilarity-inducing fact that he was still wearing the silver spangled bikini in which he'd performed earlier. Apparently this didn't call for any comment on his part, and if he noticed I was looking, he didn't bring it up. "Here," he said, chucking the pants at me. "Feel around all the seams, turn the pockets inside out. Do you have a washer or dryer here?"

"Yeah."

"Okay, we're going to have to run all this stuff through them, on the highest heat settings."

"Even if we don't find anything?" I took the pants and began pinching around the bottom hem, feeling for . . . I didn't know what, exactly.

"*Especially* if we don't find anything. If we find something, we can rip it out and toss it into the microwave. If we don't, and we want to play it safe, we'll have to destroy the potential threat somehow or another. A good hot-water wash and an hour in the dryer ought to do it."

"I still don't know what I'm feeling for."

"Anything that doesn't belong. Something the size of a shirt button, or maybe as big as a dime. Just . . . keep looking." He was down to the spangled britches, and I was dying for him to turn around. Yes, I was still wondering about the tuck. It couldn't be very comfortable, could it?

"Do you, uh," I broached. "Want a robe or something?"

"If you've got one," he said without looking up or standing up.

I was about to tell him he could go grab one off the back of the bathroom door, thereby forcing him to get up off the floor and walk away from me . . . but that felt like too much calculation even for me. So instead I wandered over there and got it for him, and tossed it on his head.

He frowned at me, removed it from his skull, and slipped his arms into it. The fit was kind of tight around his shoulders, but oh well. I'm no burly man-shaped thing, and I didn't have any stray clothing that would fit such a body. He'd have to make do.

Without a word of thanks he tossed me the shirt he'd been wearing, a white button-up. "Give this a once-over, in case I missed anything. And give me those pants back."

We were double-checking each other. I got it.

I was happy to accommodate him because I didn't seriously think there was any kind of signaling device inside the clothing. Usually I can sense that stuff. I can't smell it exactly, though there is a faint metallic, ozone-y odor that goes along with such things. It's just a sense I get when I'm around cell phones, televisions, cameras, and the like. It might have something to do with my psychic sense, like it's tapping that same electromagnetic whatever-the-heck. I don't know. But I definitely wasn't getting any vibe off the duds.

Far be it from me to discourage anyone's paranoia, though.

We ended up sitting together on the floor, going over everything with a figurative fine-tooth comb before throwing everything in the wash to rinse out the very last of our phobias.

Following this act of domesticity, we adjourned once more to the kitchen bar and resumed drinking. We also resumed our original topic, because one thing had stuck in the back of my head.

"Hey, when was the last time you even talked to your parents?" I asked. "I got the distinct impression you weren't in touch." Maybe we weren't friends enough to pry about such matters, but we were well past coddling each other's feelings. Already.

"Years ago. They were finished with me when they found the feather boa in the back of my closet while I was overseas for the last time. But I try to look in on them once in a while. I want to make sure they're all right, or . . ." If he had anything left to say on the subject, he kept it to himself. "Come to think of it, I really *do* have to go check on them."

"*Now?*"

"Yes, now."

"Forget it," I told him, even though dawn was only a few hours off and once the sun came up, there was precious little I could do to stop him. "It's too dangerous. Worst-case scenario, they're getting interrogated right now, and there's nothing you could do except go barging in and get caught."

"They could be in danger. I should check—"

"Not right now you shouldn't." I put a hand on his arm—a risky prospect, but he didn't lash out or even do that thing guys do where they flex up the moment you touch them, lest you think they weren't total hard-bodies 100 percent of the time. He just sagged, drooping on the bar stool that serves as dining furniture in just about any home of mine.

"I'll wait until tomorrow night." It was a compromise between what he wanted and what he knew was most likely best for everyone involved. "It won't do any good for me to show up now. If they're being interviewed, I'll only make them look like liars who know more than they've said."

"Attaboy." I patted his arm and this time he flexed, but he might have only been pulling himself upright from his sad-man droop.

My phone chose that moment to ring, and ring loudly enough that we both jumped and damn near punched each other from the pure surprise of it.

I scrambled for it and didn't immediately recognize the number it displayed, which told me it was probably one of those tele-marketers who isn't supposed to have anybody's cell phone number, but somehow always *does*. But then I remembered that I'd called Cal, and I pressed the button to answer the call before I completely missed it.

"Hello," I said. Noncommittal. Blasé.

"Ms. Pendle?"

It was all I could do not to melt into a little puddle of relief, right there on the floor. For a moment I considered it; after all, isn't that what linoleum is for—easy cleanup? But I restrained myself and said, "Ian, thank God. I had no idea if you'd get my message or not."

Whoops. I'd let his name slip.

Adrian noticed, damn him right to hell. He raised an eyebrow in a perfect arch, like a child's drawing of a bird's wing.

I gave him a hand-flap that told him to stay quiet, and turned away from him, strolling into the living room. Ian was already talking.

"Yes, I got your message. And I was glad to hear from you. Considering the terms on which we parted—"

"I know, I know. And again, I'm sorry I buggered off like that, but I think the fact we're both free and able to chat implies it was the right thing to do."

"Have things gotten . . . hairier? Where you are?"

His use of the word *hairier* was more hilarious than it should've been, but my laugh was louder than it should've been, too. It was a relief laugh, and those things get boisterous. "Hell yes, they've gotten hairier, but I've also got a rather significant lead or two for my trouble." I eyeballed Adrian, who was no longer sitting on the stool, but standing in the archway that separated the kitchen from the living area, still wearing nothing but the spangly silver secret-agent underpants and my robe.

He eyeballed me back.

I returned my attention to the phone. Ian was saying, "Leads?"

"Yes, good ones. I think I might have a pretty fair idea of how to go about getting your paperwork. *Don't I?*" I asked the man in the archway.

Adrian crossed his arms, bracing for a defense . . . then he changed his mind. He shrugged and nodded.

"That's wonderful news!" quoth Ian.

"But let me ask, while I've got you: Is everything still all right where you are? Did you go where I told you? Have you remained there unmolested?"

"Yes on all three counts. Your excessive precaution has proved quite helpful. We've done as you suggested and we've been utterly left alone. Lovely waterfront out here, I must say."

"Yeah. It's a real delight." I shifted the phone to the other ear.

"In our . . . shall we say, 'unmoored' condition, I don't have a fax machine or computer handy, but I can change that if you can send me copies, or emails, or . . . or however you can most easily transmit the documents. Though, heavens. Pardon my manners— we still haven't had that money conversation yet."

"Don't worry about it. Not yet. I don't have the paperwork in my hot little hands, but that's about to change, *isn't it?*" Again, I addressed the last two words to Adrian, who nodded some more. I liked him. Cooperative gent, once you got through to him. "Will I be able to consistently reach you at this number?"

"Absolutely. I've commandeered the phone from Cal, who has been most gracious about the situation."

"You're awesome. And tell Cal I said that he's awesome, too," I said, even though I didn't really mean it. Ian was awesome, yes. Cal was respectably competent. But he had yet to earn any serious feelings of awe on my part.

"I'll do so," Ian said, and I could hear him smiling. "How long do you think it'll be before we can have a chat about this informa- tion?"

I said, "Hmm," and I held the phone down against my chest. "Adrian, how long will it take us to retrieve the paperwork you stole?"

"Depends on what you're planning to do with it."

Ooh, stubborn all of a sudden.

I gave him the answer I thought he'd swallow best. It was

mostly true, anyway. "I'm going to use it for two purposes—one, to help my client possibly repair some of the damage that was done to him; and two, I'm going to do my damndest to make sure that the program is utterly disbanded, unfunded, and burned down—and then I'm going to salt the earth where it stood. Will that work for you?"

He said, "That'll work for me."

I lifted the phone back to my ear. "Ian?" I returned my attention to my client.

"Still here."

"Excellent. I'm standing here with the . . . well, let's call him a gentleman. I'm standing here with the gentleman who pilfered the papers you require."

"A gentleman?"

"Well, a drag queen who's not in drag, so, yeah. The important bit is that he has your papers."

"Is that so?"

"A true fact." I bobbed my head. "And he's willing to assist with our little predicament. Adrian," I asked again, leaving the phone up near my ear so that Ian could presumably hear any response the sometimes-drag-queen might offer. "How long will it take us to recover the paperwork?"

"Not long."

"Could I trouble you to be more precise, darling?"

The shift of his eyebrows suggested he didn't really care to have me calling him "darling," but I didn't retract it. He sighed and said, "I stashed them years ago. They're on the other side of town, but it wouldn't take more than a couple of hours to get them."

I was right. Ian heard him. He said eagerly, "Then you can fax them, or email them?"

"Okay Ian, give us through tomorrow morning to retrieve

them. It's close enough to dawn that I don't want to give it a go tonight."

"Understood." Oh, he understood all right. But impatience simmered under that one word, making it tight enough to bounce a quarter. "Tomorrow?"

"Tomorrow. Absolutely. I'll call you when the files are secured, and we'll proceed from there. I don't want to put the cart in front of the horse or anything."

"Understood," he said again.

"Great. I'll be in touch. Hang tight," I added. Then I hung up before I could say anything dumber.

"Hey Adrian?" I called, suddenly noticing he wasn't standing there watching me anymore. He leaned his head out so he could see around the archway entrance.

"What?"

"You're not shitting me, are you? You really do know where these files are? Because let me be crystal clear—this client of mine, I'm rather fond of him and I honestly want to help him. If you give me any runaround, you're going to answer for it."

Somehow, that came out less menacing than I intended. Maybe it was the size of him, half a head taller than me and bulky as . . . well, as an old Navy SEAL. Or maybe it was the utter apathy on his face, in the cracks between the sadness.

He only said, "I'm not shitting you. I know exactly where they are. I buried them under the marker my parents put up for Isabelle, in the Memorial Lawn Cemetery."

9

When I rose at dusk, I could smell Adrian somewhere nearby, and for a moment it confused me. I'm easily confused when I first awaken—which probably sets me apart from very few people, I know—but it's always a strange moment, that first snapping open of the eyelids. Many nights I awaken on the verge of a panic attack, wondering what new and hideous situation I've gotten myself into *now*. So when I shuddered myself to consciousness and smelled the burly drag queen (and the leftover glitter, and a hint of somebody's body lotion. Mine? I guess he helped himself) . . . I spent a split second wondering where the hell he was and if he was trying to kill me.

The other half of that split second remembered that I'd brought him here and he was ostensibly cooperating with me, which took me down a notch back to "cautious alertness" instead of "barely lucid hysteria."

From lying in bed, in my shut and locked bedroom with the curtains that could stop a bullet, I could hear him puttering around in the living area. Things were banging softly, as if he were being careful not to make too much noise—which was either considerate, or worrisome.

As I dragged myself out from between the sheets I also smelled coffee and fast food—something with french fries—and that meant he'd left the apartment. I didn't like it. He didn't have a key, and if he'd left, it meant he'd left the place unlocked. While I slept! He may as well have hung out a shingle that said DISTURB, WITH PREJUDICE!

God. Waking up is hard.

I filed all my stupid, crazy thoughts into their appropriate drawer in my head, found some clothes to throw on, and followed them up with a pair of combat boots I'd nabbed from an army/navy surplus store years ago. Because irony is my friend, that's why—and because we were supposed to go digging in a graveyard. No need to break out anything expensive if it was only going to wind up covered in mud anyway.

I unlocked and opened my bedroom door to find the condo mostly dark, except for the lights in the kitchen. I wandered toward them like a moth, and found Adrian polishing off the french fries I'd smelled. Somewhere, he'd scored a couple of shovels and a black shirt. The shovels were tarnished with a thin layer of rust but appeared otherwise sound, if filthy. The shirt fit him like a paint job. I approved.

"Where'd you get this . . . stuff?" I asked in greeting. I didn't really want the shovels on my counters, even though I never ate off them or prepared food. Irrational, yes, but you should expect that by now.

All he said was, "I know a guy."

I grunted, stretched, and popped my neck and back in a couple of moves that weren't very graceful, but made me feel much better. "Well, I hope he's the kind of guy who can keep his mouth shut."

"He is."

"And I hope nobody saw you."

"Nobody did."

"Not even—"

"Look," he cut in. "You gave me the speech yesterday about flying under radars, right? Well, here's mine: I've been on the run from the military, the government, my family, and a neighborhood-ful of grabby frat boys trying to check my package for the last few years. So trust me, *I know how to lie low.* By the way, you didn't get my parents killed."

"Good to hear."

"Yeah, it is. Because if I'd found out you'd done anything to get them involved in this in any way, you wouldn't have awakened this morning . . . this evening. You know what I mean." He said it dead-pan, his mouth working around the gummy starch of a half-chewed fry.

A thousand comebacks came to mind, and great personal af-front welled up behind them—shoving them forward—but I swal-lowed them back down. For one thing, if I'd gotten his parents killed, he would've been right to be murderously pissed. For an-other, Navy SEAL or no, he'd have to be a supernatural goddamn ninja to take me while I slept. Some people drive defensively. Vam-pires sleep defensively. Violently so.

Mind you, he could've tossed a grenade into the room and that would've been the end of me. Or he could've started a fire. Or . . . oh shit. Well, I had reason to worry about his threat after all. But by the time my neuroses had calculated them, the moment had passed and it would've been silly to say anything blustery about it.

So I said, "Great." Because it meant nothing.

Note my careful restraint. I didn't breathe a syllable about how I'd practically saved his life the night before and how this was no way to treat somebody who'd pulled your ass out of the fire. Mostly I didn't say this because I didn't know if it was true or not. Usually, that doesn't stop me. But when dealing with a vengeful gendershifter with covert military training and the patience to hold a grudge for years at a time . . . I could let it slide. I had enemies enough. I'd rather not add another one to the tally, especially not one who knew I was a woman, and who knew at least one of my safe houses. And, as I reflected morosely, he also knew more about one of my clients than I ever should've exposed.

Goddamn, I was getting sloppy. I wanted to sit there and punch myself, but Adrian was watching me, and I felt like it would be inappropriate to have a nervous breakdown in front of a man who just casually mentioned that he was not going to have to kill me after all, at least not today.

But in the future, I needed to be more careful.

I'd been saying that a lot lately, but hey, it was true. If I had nothing else to thank Ian Stott for (apart from the inconveniences), I could thank him for the wake-up call. I needed to get my business back in gear, and my head back out of my ass.

As my mind had been wandering right up that rearward canal, Adrian had been pondering. He pointed at the gear and said, "Tonight, we can work together. As long as you understand that I don't trust you, and that I still believe that somehow, this is all your fault."

"This? What *this*?" I demanded to know. "Even if I blew your cover at the drag bar—which I most certainly did *not*—I'm not the one who stole sensitive government documents and buried them out in the open, where any damn fool could come along with a bulldozer and retrieve them!"

He gave me one of those shrugs that made his torso ripple. "No one's bothered it yet. And okay, you can have that one—that part wasn't your fault."

"Thank you," I spat, even though I didn't feel very thankful. But I had to say something, and it was either be polite or start fighting with him. I didn't want to fight with him. I wanted to get along with him long enough to get Ian's paperwork and get back to Seattle, or to wherever, and leave this jerk to whatever covert disco nightlife he best preferred.

Unflapped and cool, he said, "You're welcome. Are you ready to go? Let's get this over with."

"I'm ready. And I couldn't agree with you more." Even though I had a feeling I'd be doing most of the digging, purely by virtue of the fact that I'm faster and stronger. Ah, well. Hand me a shovel and call me a feminist.

We skulked out of the building together, trying to simultaneously act normal and be super-careful. I don't think we succeeded very well at either goal, but I had to give credit where it was due—Adrian could skulk like a motherfucker. That was a man with skulking in the blood . . . or maybe, it'd been trained into him. I didn't know much about Navy SEALS or what they do, but just from watching him navigate a corridor I could guess that they were pretty much total badasses. Or maybe just this one was. I'd need a broader sampling to really form an educated opinion.

He moved almost as silently as I did, though I think he put more effort into it. And when he moved, he looked like some kind of big cat—all long, lean muscles and poised tension. It was nice to watch.

We made our ninja way out to the parking garage and over to my mock-cop-car. For a split second he acted like he thought he'd be driving, but I disabused him of that notion immediately by jingling the keys and hip-checking him away from the driver's door.

"Sorry," he grumbled. "Force of habit."

"Yeah. Well by force of my personal habit—my car. I drive."

"Wait a minute."

"What?" I asked.

"Should we even take this car?"

"What?"

He said, "Just in case we're being watched. Satellites. You know."

I stood there with the keys hovering before the lock, suddenly torn. "Do you think? I mean, it's a big dark car. There have to be zillions of them in the Greater Atlanta metro area. I always pick the blandest vehicle possible."

"Easily jillions of them," he agreed amiably. "But this is the one you drove to the Review, right?"

"Right."

"And not long after you showed up, *they* showed up."

I pulled the keys up into my palm and frowned. "True. But they didn't follow us *here*."

"It's a busy part of town and, like you said, big dark car. Jillions of them. You might've lost them. It's hard to follow one car through a river of cars, especially when it looks like any other car."

"I like the way you think," I said, even though I hated what he was thinking. "But . . . if I lost them before we made it home—and God help us if we didn't, and they're only watching us, stalking us from afar—then they won't know to chase this car again. Will they? I mean, in case there are . . ." I had a new scariest word, something to usurp *reconnaissance*. I said it. "Satellites? Watching us?"

He shook his head and said, "Maybe we're overthinking it, but I'd rather overthink than underthink. If you were followed . . ." I began to object but he held up a hand and said quickly, "And I'm not saying that you were, but just in case . . . let's put one more piece of distance between what they might know and what we're really doing."

"Fine. What do you suggest?"

He looked around the parking garage. "No cameras in here?"

"None. And I like it that way."

"Then how about that car?" He pointed at the precise opposite of my mock-cop-mobile. A tiny white Prius.

"Are you shitting me? That's a *hybrid*. What if we have to run away from someone? Jesus. We'd have to get out and push. Or God help us if we have to pass somebody going up a hill. No way. Forget it. What about that one?" I indicated a gray Cherokee with a few years on it.

"That one?"

I said, "We could climb difficult terrain in it. Four-wheel drive, I bet."

"Control freak much?"

"You have no idea," I said. Though he'd spent nearly twenty-four hours in my company, and he probably could guess.

"Whatever makes you happy," he muttered, and *that* was an attitude I liked to hear. "Got a Slim Jim?"

His directions to the cemetery were precise and limited, doled out in monosyllables all the way to the other side of town, where we got caught in the midst of a three-car pileup and the subsequent cleanup. On the other side of that, we puttered down into a neighborhood with which I was unfamiliar. It was somewhere on the south side, at the edge of the sprawl that makes Atlanta look like a big ol' stain on any given map of Georgia.

We found the general location and parked a few blocks away— or at least, the general equivalent of blocks. There weren't many buildings and there weren't strict blocks; it looked like an abandoned quadrant of someplace that was never very well built up in the first place. I almost asked Adrian why his parents had put up a marker there, of all places, but then I remembered their modest home and I realized that the property out here in the boonies was probably pretty cheap.

The cemetery itself was surrounded by a low wooden fence that was too small and rotted to keep anybody out, and unlikely to keep anybody in, either. We found a particularly darkened corner, away from even the fuzzy white lights of a distant streetlamp that was probably a hundred yards away.

I heard a rumble, somewhere not too far off. I gave it a second of attention and called it a train, then recalled that we'd driven over tracks. This distant clatter of metal wheels on rattling rails, the soft shush of our feet pushing through the grass, and the salty puffs of my companion's breath were all I heard. We were all alone—blessedly alone, but almost unnervingly alone, there with the dead.

"This way," he whispered, despite the fact that (as I just now established) we were all by ourselves. It's something about graveyards, I guess. They make you quiet. Like libraries.

Hell, I'm mostly dead already and I whispered back, "Okay. Can you see all right? I've got a flashlight back in the car."

"I'm fine," he said.

I took him at his word and followed him along the unmowed rows and stepped sharply past fallen monuments and dismembered cherubs. The cemetery was old, but it wasn't that old. If you forced me to take a guess, I'd say that the oldest graves were dug right around the turn of the twentieth century, but some of the graves were newer. You could tell, because the monuments were flatter.

I tripped down into a pit created when someone's casket had collapsed, there under the sod. "Pardon me," I mumbled.

"What?"

Drat his hearing. I said, "Nothing."

But yes, I had begged the pardon of a corpse. Believe me when I tell you that I know how stupid this is, but people who've been dead a long time freak me out. Fresh corpses? No big thing. I've created more than a few of them in my time. But moldering old bodies, left in the ground to mulch themselves into dust? I shudder to consider it. And on those rare occasions that I traipse through graveyards (and believe me, they *are* rare), my obsessive compulsions become extra-ludicrous. I cannot bear the thought of walking over anybody's . . . well . . . *body*.

It feels so fucking impolite, you know? And worse than that, mostly these old folks are buried on a grid system of sorts, and once I know there's a grid I can't keep the OCD on a leash. Step on a crack and break your mother's back? Step on a grave and horrifying things might befall you, or maybe not, because, like, who's going to do the befalling? I know. It doesn't rhyme. But that's what it is, and that's how I roll—awkwardly, and mumbling like a lunatic past the cracked and crooked stones.

"Are you still apologizing to the dead people?"

"No," I told him.

"Because it sounds like that's what you're doing."

"Shut up. And where's—" I almost said, "your sister's fake grave?" but I thought that might annoy him. I tried to think of some nicer way to put it, since I was relying on him to find it, but he beat me to the punch.

"Almost there. See? Under that tree."

"Awesome," I grumbled.

"Why?"

I approached the stone and accepted one of the shovels. "Because it means tree roots. Harder to dig through. I assume." I had to assume it. I'd never tried to dig up a grave before, so this was new turf for me.

I suppose it bears mentioning that I *kind of* lied just now because I *have* dug up a real one. But that's a long story, and the grave was so old I justified my actions by calling it "archaeology." Which may or may not have been fair. And it was practically out in the desert. No tree roots.

Anyway.

The marker was simple, just the poor girl's name and the dates she was born and apparently died. Nothing but a little dash in the middle, marking the rest. And not even a body underneath— nothing to be commemorated. The whole thing felt achingly futile.

Adrian stared down at the little patch.

I stood on the other side of it, facing him, mirroring his posture with my shovel. One of us had to be the first to dig, but I decided that it shouldn't be me. So I waited for him. He didn't move.

He said, "The last time I saw her, she was like you."

I knew what he meant, even though he wasn't looking at me; he was looking at the ground with an expression I couldn't really read. It might have been as simple as sadness, or as complicated as nostalgia. He was still quiet, so I said, "That's how you knew, I guess. When we first met. You knew what I was, because you'd seen your sister."

He didn't nod, but he didn't have to. "She came to me for help. Showed up while I was home on leave, visiting with my mom and dad. I'd shut myself up in my bedroom, getting ready to call it a night. The window was open. I closed it. And when I turned around, there she was . . . looking like . . . looking wrong. Looking dead."

I assumed that anything I had to say would be unwelcome, so I kept my trap shut. But he looked at me suddenly, like there was something he wanted to hear from me. I didn't know what it was. I just said, "I'm sorry," because it seemed all-purpose.

He swallowed. "She looked like you, but not exactly. You look less . . . you look more . . . it's hard to say." Giving it some thought, he amended the sentiment to say, "If you were really, really *sick*, maybe."

"Um. Thanks?"

The hand that wasn't holding the shovel flapped with frustration. "I could tell, when you came into the dressing room. I knew what you were, but not right away. It took me a minute. It took your eyes—the way they're black like that, and the way you don't . . . you don't . . ." He derailed again.

"I don't move like somebody who's alive. I know what you mean." ·

My beating heart stirs cold, recycled blood around. My skin doesn't blush or flush unless I'm eating (or unless I've freshly eaten); you can't see my pulse at those little spots on my neck and my wrists. Other people have noticed it before, and been similarly unable to articulate it. Vampires . . . we move like dolls, all clockwork and hydraulics, but no soul.

"Yes," he said. "Yes, that's it. But she didn't look . . . *healthy* like you do. She looked like she was strung out on drugs, or starving to death."

I made a noise that implied I was thinking, and I was. "Did you ask her about it? Did she tell you anything? My kind—we heal up fast, and survive things with, shall we say, aplomb." I've seen hungry biters that looked like skin and bones, and that's not pretty. But most of us don't bother with drug abuse because our systems don't process it well.

"Do your kind . . . do they ever do drugs?"

"Not most of us. We don't have much reaction at all to those things."

Leaning on the shovel, driving it an inch down into the turf, he observed, "But you were drinking last night. It changed the way you looked, and the way you spoke."

"Did not," I argued.

"Did too. It definitely had an effect."

"Okay, fine. Alcohol does, yes. So does caffeine. Look, I can't give you a list of what does and doesn't work on us—I haven't tried much myself. Mostly I'm giving you hearsay. All I can really tell you is that, as far as I know, most young vamps don't shoot up or snort up. Maybe your sister was an exception." I cocked my head at her stone. "Or maybe she stumbled into something weirder or worse. I have no idea."

"I don't either, and she wouldn't say. Maybe she looked that bad when she was turned," he ventured, but it wasn't likely. Vampirism is like Photoshop for the flesh—it fills out, rounds off, smooths over, and brightens up everything. I've seen cancer patients turn into supermodels with a good undead infusion. So if his little sister looked like hell, it must've happened after her bite.

Adrian went on. "I asked what had happened and she wouldn't say. She was frantic, and she kept talking about how her House had turned her over, whatever that means. Then she told me that she needed a place to hide during the day, and she begged me. She begged me . . ." His voice trailed off.

"What was that about a House?"

"I don't know. She kept saying they were handing her in, or turning her over. But she didn't say more than that. What'd she mean by a House, anyway? Is that a vampire thing?"

"Yeah," I said. "It's a vampire thing. Kind of like a family, only the blood relations are a different sort. Some of them are pretty powerful; some are barely little clans, living out on their own in the middle of nowhere."

"Like hillbillies?"

"I wouldn't have thought to put it like that."

"But like hillbillies," he said again, more certain this time.

"Fine. Like hillbillies." Quite the mental image that scared up. I almost laughed.

"In cities I guess it's different," he mused. If I'd guessed where he was going in time, I would've changed the subject before he could go there, but I was slow, and I didn't see it coming until he asked, "Is there a House that runs Atlanta?"

Yeah, there was a House running Atlanta. A big one. The biggest in the South, and one of the biggest vampire Houses, period. I swallowed. "Sure."

"Only one House? Or several Houses?" He drummed his fingers on the shovel.

"Watch it, mister."

"I want to know," he said, and it was clear that he wanted to know before he planned to do any digging.

I flailed, throwing my hands up in a shrug and almost dropping my own digging implement before catching it quickly again. "You want to know what? That there's a House? I just told you that, and I'll tell you this, too: You don't want to go messing with it. That's a big fat bees' nest, right there. You poke it with a stick and you'll wish you'd never been born."

"Okay, I won't go poking with a stick," he said drolly, and I only assumed that this meant he'd poke it with a Glock, given half a chance.

"I'm *serious*," I stressed.

"You must be. You haven't said anything about having a House of your own. Do you?"

"What?" I stalled ineffectually.

"Do you belong to a House? You haven't mentioned one, and your . . . *home*"—he said it like he was using the word loosely—"is a lone-wolf bachelor pad if I ever saw one. You live alone, you work alone. You don't belong to a House. Am I right?"

"Fine, you're right. I don't. But I used to, and my reasons for jumping ship were many, varied, and valid. Houses work for plenty of vampires, but they don't work for me. I don't . . . um . . . play well with others."

"Are there rules?"

"Of course there are rules."

"Restrictions?"

"Those too."

"Oaths of loyalty?"

"Now you're just stabbing in the dark," I accused. "A House is all that shit and more. Under the best of circumstances, it's a family. It's your backup. On paper it's very Three Musketeers— one for all, all for one, blah blah *blah*. In real life, it's just like belonging to the mob. Sometimes it works for you, and sometimes it works against you. It depends on who's in charge and how willing you are to follow rules."

"So, the Atlanta House. Is it a bad one? Bad vampires in charge, bad rules?"

He didn't know the half of it. I told him the truth without telling him anything. "I've never been part of the Atlanta House. I'm not from around here, okay? I've never tangled with them, and I don't care to. Largely because, as you've so astutely noticed, I don't have any House of my own to back me up."

"But you must know *something* about it."

Well, yeah. I knew that the Barrington House of Atlanta was not the House with which you wanted to fuck—and if his little sister had been brought on board there, she should've been in pretty secure company. If the House had turned her over for . . . for what, medical experimentation? Like in that Monty Python movie? Then she'd probably done something to royally piss somebody off.

Vampires tend to take care of problem members "in House" you might say. They don't outsource their problem people. They find other ways to make examples out of them. Unless the times, they were a-changing.

So I decided to tell him, "Look, I know what you're thinking."

"You do?"

"I'm psychic. A little." May as well stick to the truth while it was convenient. The rest was easy to guess. "You're thinking that if there's some organizational structure in place, you can infiltrate it or at least learn enough to navigate it. And you're wrong. The Atlanta House"—I made a point not to tell him its name— "isn't just bulletproof. It's *nuke*-proof. You'll have better luck fighting Uncle Sam, and your corpse will be more readily identifiable when he's done with you."

"What about you?"

"Me? If you think I'm going to go around ringing doorbells, looking to find out what happened to your sister, you've got another think coming."

"What if I could pay you?"

"You can't," I said flatly.

He asked, "How do you know? Name a price."

"There isn't enough money."

"In a drag queen's stash?"

"*In the world,*" I specified. "Now are we going to dig up your sister here, or what?"

Adrian scowled, and shivered.

It was cold out there in Memorial Lawn. Not as cold as Minnesota, but cold enough that I was uncomfortable. They don't tell you that about Georgia. They tell you it's all peaches and sunshine, but it isn't. It's a sauna in the summer and, come winter, it's cold enough to freeze. Cold enough to snow, sometimes. But I'm pretty sure I've never seen that on any of their tourism brochures.

Adrian hoisted the shovel up high and straight, and drove it down into the grass in front of the headstone. I did likewise. Together in the near-perfect dark, we swung and shoved, grunting and flinging dirt over our shoulders, onto the graves nearby. Every now and again one of us would hit a rock or a particularly tough root, and the steel shovels would chime like church bells—pinging loud and clear in the emptiness.

The whole time we worked, no one drove by on the road where we'd left the Cherokee. And even though I kept one eye on that road the whole time, I never saw a single person come or go, as if the cemetery and all its surroundings were truly abandoned, and forgotten, or avoided.

Finally, after fully four feet of mud, worms, and rocks as big as frogs, my shovel scraped up against something decidedly un-dirt-like.

I stopped. I tapped at the something and Adrian did likewise, probing at the mass with the tip of the shovel and prying out a corner on his side of the corpseless grave.

With some wiggling, cursing, and further excavation, we were able to pop it up out of its spot and onto the grass. I looked for a place to sit that wasn't covered with loose dirt, but gave up and sat down on a little heap of it. Adrian came to sit beside me. He held the box on his lap and picked at the latches.

The box wasn't terribly interesting; it was just a metal jobbie that he'd put inside a very thick plastic bag to keep the rust and rot off. The bag had mostly held up and the box was mostly intact, though threads of rust ate the corners and the latches. One of them broke off in his hand. The other took only a small tug to release.

Adrian had thoughtfully wrapped the interior contents in plastic, too, so they looked pretty good. Some of the edges were curling, and some of the pages were turning the color of an old photograph, but everything appeared intact.

Impatiently, I took the lump out of the box and set it in my own lap, peeling the plastic away even more. "Is this everything?" I asked.

"It's everything I took. And if you want the truth, I don't even know what most of it means," he confessed. "It's coded, like most of the paperwork they filed on me, too."

And there was Ian's serial number.

Right there, in black and white, 636-44-895. I dragged my finger down the page and stopped on it, then kept skimming. "It's too dark to read much out here, right now," I observed. Technically I could see it well enough to read, but Adrian was right and everything was coded anyway. I wanted to take the docs back to my condo and examine them in the comfort of my own home, with the help of my own artificial lighting.

"You promised," Adrian said softly.

"What?"

"You promised you'll use these to help your friend, or your client, or whatever he is. And you'll try to shut the program down. That's what you promised. Did you mean it, or did you only say it so I'd take you here?"

"Oh, I *meant it*. This—" I said, indicating the paperwork, the program, and everything that was wrapped up with it. "It horrifies me. Do you know what they were doing, here? In these tallies?"

"Not really."

"They were classifying people like your sister, and my client, and *me* . . . as animals—and treating the documentation like this was all some experiment on apes. Some of the subjects didn't survive. One of the ones who *did* survive is maimed for life." I climbed to my feet, and used the plastic-wrapped papers to swat dirt off my pants. "Worse, really. He's maimed for afterlife. And whatever you believe and however you feel about what your sister became, she was a person, and she could still feel pain. She could still be *killed*. And she deserved better."

Adrian was still holding the empty box, at least until he gazed back down at the hole and tossed the container back inside it. He didn't respond to anything I'd said, which was maybe a little uncool, but he was having a moment there so I didn't disturb him. All he said was, "We should fill this in."

"Why?"

"Because a freshly dug grave in a graveyard is less suspicious than an empty one that somebody dug up. Are we trying to cover our tracks here, or what?"

He had me there. I sighed.

I put the bundle down on top of Isabelle's headstone and retrieved my shovel once more. A fresh grave in an effectively abandoned cemetery was, in my estimation, only marginally less interesting to any passerby than an empty one, but Adrian was right. In the grand scheme of things, anyone who noticed would be less likely to call the cops if there wasn't a gaping hole in the ground.

We weren't grave robbers, after all. There'd never been a grave.

There'd only been a package of incriminating documents, left in memory of a girl who wasn't even a girl anymore when she'd died.

Later that evening, back at the homestead and on the far side of a nice hot shower, I sat at the kitchen bar and busted out my laptop. I had a note from You-Know-Who.

Abigail,

You're going to be in D.C. next weekend, you said? Actually, that's pretty convenient. If you do a good job getting inside that Pioneer Square location, I'd like to talk to you about it. Assuming you pull it off, can I talk you into coming out on Friday afternoon or Monday morning?

Swing by the receptionist's desk on the way in. Give her my name, and she'll point you in the right direction.

While you're here, you might want to check out some of the local parkour groups. There's one that meets near my office called Presidential Parkour. You may find it interesting.

Below his name he'd added an address. I demanded that Google Maps give me the satellite view of the location, because two can play at that game, that's why.

Nothing interesting. A boring building in a respectable part of town. I'd file it away and do a better investigation on it later. I'd bought myself until next Monday, after all.

So I wrote a quick email back, pulling it right out of my ass. I hoped the offhanded nature of it came across as juvenile and enthusiastic, rather than floundering in the dark, trying to figure out what the asshole major wanted me to look for—and being careful not to give him anything to rouse his suspicions.

If I played this right, it could be perfect. I'd scored the assignment to investigate my own building. And who better than me to reassure him that there was nothing at all to see there?

Major,

Went poking around at the address you sent me. I'm not sure what you're looking for in there, but I didn't see anything too exciting. It looks like you're right, and there are squatters camping out, maybe. I saw some bedding and some emptied cans of food, and some soda bottles. One of the bathrooms works, and the place has electricity, but not much use for it. Just a couple of bare lightbulbs, one per floor. LOTS of old machinery, though. I think it used to be a factory or something. Everything looks rusted in place, and I don't know what it was ever used for. I couldn't tell. I don't think any of it works. I couldn't find anything that would turn on, anyway.

Is there anything you were looking for in particular? I could take another look.

~Abigail

Once that was sent off, I hung around and messed with the paperwork we'd dug out of Isabelle's fake grave, since Adrian was still in the shower. The water was gushing noisily and the steam smelled like a lavender-and-rose-scented soap that once again reminded me that my temporary roommate was exceptionally secure in his masculinity.

While he bathed, I felt as if I almost had a modicum of privacy.

I threw away the plastic wrapper and used paper towels to take the edge off the dusty, funky, musty flakes of dirt that had accumulated over however many years the documents had been stashed underground. The paper still smelled like mold and tree fungus, and it was itchily dry to the touch, but it was mostly clean and I separated the sheets into piles according to my instinctive sense of what was useful and what wasn't. Some of the cover sheets and filler pages could be discarded, for they were blank. Some of the rest were out of order, and needed rearranging.

Here and there I saw incriminating keywords. Jordan Roe. Holtzer Point. A fistful of serial numbers beginning with 636. Ian's stood out most prominently, but only because I'd seen it before. The others could've belonged to anybody. Adrian hadn't said which one indicated his sister. I skimmed for the kind of contextual information that could've pointed her out to me, but didn't see much. The medical notes seemed either imprecise to me or entirely too precise—and outside my field of expertise.

So I was hanging out, staring at the sheets while Adrian took his shower, when another keyword leaped out and smacked me between the eyes. Literally, for a moment, I could not breathe. I said it aloud, in a feeble attempt to break the spell.

"Bruner."

The man who'd sent a douchebag named Trevor into my storage facility. The man who wanted to hire *parcours* kids to perform "reconnaissance" on me, or my stuff—or other vampires, and their stuff. Major Bruner, misogynist pig on the phone and sneaky military official in the office.

The man I'd just emailed, lying through my teeth and crossing my fingers.

I am absolutely certain that my heart stopped.

Then the shower stopped, and I knew my alone-time was drawing to a close.

Reaching for a drawer, I yanked it open and rifled around through the dried-up pens and broken pencils that accumulate in every single place where I ever spend more than a week at a time. I hadn't been to my Atlanta condo in quite a while, as I admitted earlier. But still, the trappings of my neuroses were present—as distinctive as a fingerprint.

Finally I found a pencil that had enough lead to leave a mark. I used it to circle all instances of this Major Bruner and I even underlined a serial number—or a shorthand number, maybe—that seemed to be connected with either him or with this project. By the time Adrian exited the bathroom, wearing a fluffy crimson towel and trailing a billowing cloud of steam, I'd scribbled a stack of notes and drawn an army's worth of arrows.

"You okay?" Adrian asked, possibly noting my gritted teeth and manic attention to the musty papers.

"Oh, I'm just *ducky*," I assured him, but I assume that the frenetic triumph in my eyes told him there was more to the story, so I pointed the pencil down at the sheet and said, "You see this guy? You see his name?"

"Bruner? You know him?" he asked, slinging around behind me to get a better look. He smelled like my soap, my shampoo, and whatever I'd last used to clean the tub.

"We're not friends, but I've spoken to him. Once, on the phone." Suddenly he was suspicious. I wasn't explaining myself too well, so I added, "And several times by email. This asshole's been following me. Or looking into me. Something like that. And I don't like it."

I left the papers on the counter and turned around so I could face him while I offered something like an explanation. "See, I have this . . . this *place*. Let's call it a storage facility. And last week, some dude broke into it. I went through his clothes and his wallet and found—"

"You killed him?" I heard idle curiosity, but no judgment.

So I said, "Yeah, I killed him. He broke into my property, and his name was Trevor and . . . and he was menacing a couple of homeless kids who pretty much live there. I did the world a favor."

"No need to get defensive."

"Who's defensive?" I asked. "Point is, I went through the guy's stuff and I found a note with a phone number, which led me to *this* guy." I punctuated the last two words by jabbing the pencil at the sheet of marked-up paper. "We've been emailing back and forth. I've been trying to figure out what he knows, and why he's looking at me. He thinks he's talking to a teenager named Abigail."

He thought about this, took a closer look at the sheet, which brought his towel-only self up closer to me, but I wasn't complaining. Goddamn, he really was good looking. No wonder he made such a hot woman. I also noticed that the tattoo—which he usually kept covered with stage makeup—was on full display. It was typical military ink. Eagles and banners. The kind of thing guys get when they're in a group, drunk to the gills, and excited about the prospect of matching forever.

"That can't be a coincidence," he said.

"Coincidence? Are you shitting me? No *way*." Bruner was obviously in this up to his eyeballs, no doubt fancying himself a puppetmaster or something equally sinister. But how was he coordinating the operation from all these different angles?

Earlier, Adrian had brought up satellites, which was superlatively worrisome—because I'd been tailed, that much was clear. But I hadn't seen or heard or sensed any electronic equipment and I knew damn good and well it hadn't been as simple as sending a car after me.

I would've noticed that. I'm old and wily, and I'm not the kind of girl who fails to notice when she's being chased.

From a certain crazy, paranoid, conspiracy-theory slant, observation-from-space wasn't the dumbest conclusion I could draw. It was frankly terrifying, the idea that Ian and I—and maybe, once upon a time, Isabelle, too—could be watched by some radar or spy satellite, just because this dickhead Bruner thinks vampires make excellent experimental subjects.

The thought had me glaring down at the paper, in case I could channel all my rage through that signature upon it, sloppy and arrogant, and make the major's head explode.

"It's my own fault," I grumbled.

"What is?"

This time I shook my head, not sure how to tell him what I meant without telling him too much. "I've gotten into this guy's sights, somehow. Just like your sister did, and just like my client did, a long time ago."

"You said that already."

"I meant it, too. See," I said, putting on my teacher voice and refusing to notice that the towel was slipping, "most vampires conduct business through thralls or ghouls—in order to keep their own names and identities out of the social security office, or the DMV, or anywhere else. But I've spent a very long time conducting my own business, apart from any of the Houses. As you so astutely gathered."

"Why *do* you go it alone? If it's so much safer to work through other people, I mean."

"Habit, I guess. I left my House just a few years after I turned." And I wasn't sure why I was telling him all this, except that I so rarely had anyone to talk to, and once I got started talking I found it difficult to stop. Besides, I wasn't telling him anything important. All of this was ancient history as far as I was concerned. "I had a falling-out with the matriarch, a woman who thought I ought to wait on her hand and foot, and take the fall for her . . . indiscretions."

Talk about your euphemisms. She'd fucked and killed her husband's favorite ghoul, and then she tried to pin it on me. I was new to the family, and no one was willing to take my word over hers—even though everyone knew she was lying. It was bullshit politics, plain and simple. I never got over it. I never shook the idea that other vampires are exactly as horrible as regular people, except that they have a greater capacity to ruin lives and wreak havoc.

No thank you. Call me lone wolf and leave me the hell alone. Besides, I've already mentioned my deep-seated mistrust of ghouls. Houses almost always come with ghouls, often a whole consortium of them. If I don't like and don't trust *one* ghoul, you can imagine my comfort level with an entire slave class of them.

I went on, "I may have built up more of a paper trail than I thought. And I don't have anyone out there watching my back. Most of the other vampires I know I don't like much. Except Ian. He's okay."

"He's your client?"

"Yeah. He's the guy I'm working for." It could be argued that I never should've told him this, but he'd already overheard Ian's name and I decided it was all right . . . because I'd already come to a conclusion. "I think you're going to like him."

Adrian was taken aback. "Like him? When am I ever going to meet him?"

"Sooner rather than later. Bruner's office is in D.C., and I'm interested in paying the major a visit. A very quiet visit. The kind where I rifle through all his shit and maybe do him a little bodily harm while I'm at it."

"How do you know where his office is?"

"Because he told me in an email." Something else occurred to me. "And I told him I was going to be in D.C. come the weekend. What's today, Tuesday?"

"Tuesday, going on Wednesday," he said, glancing at the clock as if it were a calendar.

"Shit. Well, we still have a few days to get there and kick around before he expects me."

His eyes widened. "You told him to expect you? What kind of—"

"Look, I had my reasons. I needed to know where his office was, so I asked him if he'd tell me—on the grounds that I'd visit him when I'm in town. And he went for it. Sometimes it's exactly that easy, you know? The vast majority of people in this world are not even a *fraction* as careful and crazy as I am. So this is fine. It's no big deal, and nobody knows we're coming. We're free and clear, and we're going," I insisted stubbornly, even though I only half believed myself.

"What makes you think I'll come with you?" Adrian asked.

"I think you'll come with me because Ian might've known your sister. He might even know what happened to her—how she was turned, and what happened to her before the military caught up to her, and kept her. And you want to know about it."

He mulled this over, and then said, "No promises past meeting your client, just for a conversation. But okay. I'm in at least that far."

"Good," I said, as if that settled everything, but I was pretty sure it hadn't. I was pretty sure I had Adrian along until Major

Bruner was taken out of the picture in a permanent fashion, but maybe that was an unfair conclusion to draw.

Yet when I looked at this beautiful man with one hand holding up a towel, his jaw set firm, and his eyes staring down at the paper . . . I knew that this was a man who wanted answers. He wanted the vengeance he'd never had the opportunity to take.

And here I was, offering to draw him a map and give him a ride.

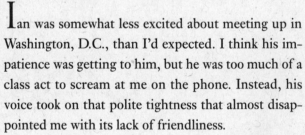

10

Ian was somewhat less excited about meeting up in Washington, D.C., than I'd expected. I think his impatience was getting to him, but he was too much of a class act to scream at me on the phone. Instead, his voice took on that polite tightness that almost disappointed me with its lack of friendliness.

Not that I should ever try to make friends with my clients, because obviously, I shouldn't. But still.

Eventually I conveyed the urgency to him—how I'd reconsidered, and we'd be running extra risks by scanning and copying and emailing the material, opening ourselves up to heaven knew what sort of tracking was tied to my email account, or my computer, or whatever. We knew I'd originally scored the feds' attention via the contact with Bad Hatter, may he rest in peace or live on in infamy wherever he was, but given our nervousness about potential satellite observation, we didn't know if I'd brought the net down on Adrian.

This final point did in Ian's resistance, and his voice turned from icy aggravation to unhappy acquiescence. "You're right," he told me with a sigh. "I know you are. It's only that I've waited so long, and Dr. Keene has been so patient."

"He's the guy who's trying to fix your eyes, in Canada?"

"That's right. And I hate to drag this out any longer than strictly necessary. I've been keeping him loosely informed regarding the situation, and I fear he's becoming tired of hearing that I *almost* have the paperwork in hand. So far, he's been kind enough to keep himself available—nearly on call—for me over the last year, but he's preparing to leave the country next month and I don't know when I'll next have the opportunity to consult with him."

"He's leaving the country?" I echoed.

Ian said, "He's a member of Doctors Without Borders. He'll be going away on a volunteer work sabbatical, to Southeast Asia I believe."

"Sounds like quite a saint. Can't you follow him there for treatment?"

"I could," he told me. "And I almost certainly will, if I have no other choice. But I'd rather engage him at his own facilities in Toronto. He's led me to believe that they're rather superior to where he'll be working *gratis*." He laughed nervously. "By now, he's almost as impatient as I am."

To soothe him, I said, "If you just swing down here and meet me, then we can sort all this out and have you on your way back to Toronto in a week or less. No problem."

"Are you sure?"

"Absolutely," I fibbed. But he was hard to fib to, so I amended my certainty to include, "Barring unforeseen catastrophe. And anyway, Adrian wants to meet you." Perhaps I exaggerated.

"He . . . he does? He's still with you?"

"Yeah, he's still with me. He's coming to D.C. on the off chance I turn up something thrilling about Major Bruner and his connection to the project, and unless I miss my guess"—I didn't bother to lower my voice; Adrian was watching TV in the other room and either he'd hear me, or he wouldn't—"he's plotting a little street vengeance."

"Really?"

"Uh-huh. Wait'll you meet him. He's a former Navy SEAL who's on the warpath."

"I thought you said he was a drag queen?"

"That too. He's a man of many mysteries." Again I remembered that silver spangle outfit and the tuck-job. "And maybe I'm wrong, but I bet I'm not. More to the point, however, he wants to talk to you about his sister. She was in the program with you."

"She was?"

"You knew you weren't alone," I said, trying to avoid the roundabout talk that he resorted to every time the subject of his imprisonment came up. "You've already told me that much. Well, she was one of the others."

"One like us?" he asked. It felt like his umpteenth question in a row. I heard fuzz and noise in the background. I assumed he was outdoors somewhere, and being careful with his language.

"Yes. A vampire. And I have no idea if you knew her or not, or if you ever spoke to her or not, but this guy is grieving for his sister and desperate for any scrap of information. If you don't want to talk to him, that's fine. But you can tell him so to his face."

My phone began to beep, and I glanced at the face. "Hey, Ian, I've got to go. Getting another call." We'd already exchanged all our connection information anyway; we'd picked a hotel and a date, and we'd talk again when we both got into D.C.

"Very well. See you soon."

I hung up on him and pressed the button to accept the other call. The number looked familiar, but I couldn't place it right away. The voice on the other end of the phone brought it all back in an instant.

"Raylene?" Soft. Whispered. I didn't like the whisper. I'd never heard him whisper before.

"Domino. Glad you got the phone. Is everything okay?"

I could hear him breathing softly into the receiver, and I couldn't hear his sister, which didn't necessarily mean anything. But his further silence probably did. He didn't say anything for another five seconds. "No."

I asked, "What's going on?"

The urgency in my voice snared Adrian's attention. He manifested in the doorway wearing a questioning look and a fresh smearing of my best avocado face mask. I waved him away. I wasn't prepared to explain, and I had a feeling I was about to have a full-body freak-out. My waving and dodging did not prevent him from following me, though. All I could do was turn my back on him as I said into the phone, "Domino, you little shit, you tell me what's going on right this second!"

"Shh!" he hissed.

I'm not ordinarily the kind to be shushed by anyone, much less that prepubescent cretin, but this was different, I could tell. And after a few more moments of silence, I realized he was holding up the phone and trying to let me hear something.

The television was still on in the other room. I snapped at Adrian, "Go turn that off. Now!" And the command was passed down to someone else who doesn't ordinarily obey random commands, but Adrian did it, and he did it swiftly.

I turned my back to the living room and jammed my eyes shut, as if that could make it even quieter in my condo. I strained to hear any scrap of static and I prayed that Domino wasn't pulling some crazy stunt. Because if he was, I'd have to beat him to death the next time I saw him. And that would be sad for his sister.

Pepper. I said her name aloud and then I breathed into the phone, "Where's your sister, Domino?"

His response made me go cold all the way down to my toes. "I don't know."

"What's going on?" I asked again, confused and alarmed, and conflicted, too. Obviously I was worried about my stuff. I have lots of stuff—easily millions of dollars' worth of stuff in that warehouse. And as I've implied before, I didn't really care if Domino vanished off the face of the earth at any given moment. But goddammit, that little girl didn't have anybody else looking after her and, okay, she wasn't exactly a ghoul or a pet person or anything like that, except that apparently she was all of those things almost, and very suddenly I felt like I was going to throw up.

It was frankly unexpected.

"Listen," the boy urged in his softest voice yet. He may as well have been shaping the word with his lips but holding his breath. If I hadn't been what I am, I would've never heard it.

But I heard him shift the phone in his hand, the scrabbling of his fingers almost slipping, almost dropping it, but holding fast and turning it face-out, I imagined—to better catch the sound of whatever he wanted me to hear.

I held out my hand toward Adrian, who'd come back to join me in the "dining area" (if any room in any home of mine can be dubbed such). He wasn't wearing the face mask anymore, though tiny threads of it showed around his hairline where he'd washed it off too quickly. I don't know what I was trying to do with the gesture—hold him at bay, keep him from talking, shoo him out of the condo. Any of those things. All of them. I was only trying to concentrate, and concentrate hard. I directed every ounce of my supernatural hearing to the scene back in Seattle, and I even tried to picture it: my warehouse, my things, my floors full of unsecured merchandise and two children who shouldn't be there, really, but where else could they go? I visualized Domino, doing one brave thing, perhaps—just this once. Because when it came to his sister, I didn't think he'd lie to me, and that vestigial psychic sense was bouncing up and down behind my tightly shut eyes, telling me that he was telling the truth, and trying to tell me more without making a sound.

At first, I didn't detect much. The scraping of dry hands on the phone's plastic shell. A shuffle and the rustle of clothing. An occasional breath that sounded like a ragged gasp, and sounded like Domino.

Then the rest began to come into focus. At least, it did whatever sound does when it phases from white noise to something more specific.

It must've looked to Adrian like I was in pain, hunkered over almost double with my eyes closed and my hand still held out, still keeping him away. I backed up slowly until I hit a wall, and then I sat down against it and listened, and listened, and listened.

And now I could catch static—not miscellaneous noise, but actual electronic static, in tiny fuzzes and blips. Footsteps. Carefully uttered words, spoken low and without any of the rambling stutters of ordinary conversation. I couldn't make them out, no matter how hard I tried.

"Domino," I whispered, trying to match his closeness to silence, yet trying to make sure he heard me, too.

"Raylene," he said back. "They're here."

"Who?" I asked, knowing he couldn't say. Even if it weren't blindingly obvious that the boy was hiding for his life, the odds were great that he wouldn't have any idea who was invading our turf. My turf.

Bless him, he tried anyway. I caught a scrambling of clothes and sneakers that sounded like a herd of elephants in my ear, but surely made nothing more than tiny scuffs and squeaks in the vast labyrinth of the old factory. Even so, I cringed with every rustle of cloth against the microphone. I tensed myself into an even tighter ball as the boy on the other end of the line adjusted himself, and I tried to remember if there was anything . . . anything at all . . . incriminating inside that building.

It was a ridiculous thing to wonder.

Everything inside it was incriminating. But try as I might, I couldn't think of any paperwork, or electronics, or anything like that. They'd already found my Seattle condo; I was virtually certain of this. Where else could the storehouse send them, except to Interpol? And baby, I'd rather face off with international crime fighters than mad-scientist military yahoos any damn day of the week.

Everything was unraveling. I could feel it, my whole world being teased open, like a thread of spaghetti pulled twisting onto a fork.

But I listened, and listened, and listened.

Somewhere in the distance of wherever Domino had secreted himself away, I heard a digital pop—the kind you hear when people are using walkie-talkies, or those phones that come with that same function. It was chased by a man's voice, confirming something.

"Affirmative."

The phone shifted again in the boy's grasp; I suppose he was bringing it back up to his face. "I can't find Pepper," he said. "I think maybe they got her." He was whispering as only a kid who's truly half afraid to death can whisper, but apparently he felt secure enough to do so. I thought maybe there was a metallic echo to the soft puffs of words, and I assumed he'd climbed up into one of Pep's favorite old hiding spots—inside the square aluminum tunnels of the ventilation system. They weren't original to the building, of course, but they'd been added by the man who'd owned it before me.

"Why do you think that?" When I spoke back to him, I was quiet, too. Didn't want to give him away. "Did you see them take her?"

"No. I got here, and she was gone, and *they* were here. But they were talking about her."

"Are you sure?"

"Yes," he asserted, but I thought he was only assuming the worst. Like I'd blame him for it. Like I wouldn't do exactly the same thing. "They found a dead guy in the basement."

"Bullshit," I said, too loud.

He replied, "No bullshit," and if there'd been any less peril to go around, I fully expect that he would've sounded smug about it. Awesome. So he knew, or he suspected. But what did that mean, anyway? He'd always known, and always suspected.

When in doubt, change the subject. "Domino, tell me. Who are they?" The answer was more pressing than what they were going to do with Trevor, anyway.

"I don't know."

"What do they look like?"

His hair or his neck, or maybe a scarf went dragging across the microphone. He was looking out, checking to see again if they were close, or if he could see anybody. He said, "They're all wearing black. They look like army guys. But some of them are in suits."

"Great."

"I don't think it's great. I think it fucking sucks!" His voice got a little too loud, just a squeak.

"I was being sarcastic. Stay cool, kid. Don't get loud or get mad. That's the most important thing, right now."

"No. Finding Pepper is."

Devoted little bastard. You had to give him that. "The two goals are one and the same. You can't find her if you get yourself caught."

"Maybe I can. At least if they catch me, they've caught us both and I'll know where she is. I'll know she's okay."

He was right. He'd also just revealed that he wasn't positive they had her; otherwise, he'd have already joined the fray. I was pretty secure on this point, so I ran with it. "Forget it. Keep your head low and keep watching. Your little sister, she's a damn good hider."

"But they were *talking about her.*"

"What were they saying?" I asked.

"They said they thought she might still be here. They said they know someone's inside. They've been watching."

"They could've meant anybody." I pointed out, "They could've meant *me.* I bet you a dollar she's stashed someplace where they haven't looked yet."

"Make it fifty," he said. Ah, greed and a sense of humor. Or grasping at straws.

"Very funny."

"Raylene?"

"Yeah?"

He said, "They're going to find us."

"Why would you say that?"

"They're looking everywhere. Floor by floor, moving things around. Taking pictures."

If I could've cringed myself into a tighter ball and still remained upright, I would've done so. Pictures. Perfect. It was all crashing down, wasn't it? All of it. Fifty years of accumulated wealth and work, right out the window. Was it my life savings? No, not by a long shot. But it was still an awful lot to lose. And Pepper was there, someplace. I knew better than anyone how well that kid could hide. I had to trust her now; I had no choice. It was either assume the best or have a nervous breakdown right there on the phone . . . which would only send Domino into a downward spiral.

I could sense it. The kid hated me, but he was clinging to me—or just the sound of me, someplace far away.

As if he'd heard my thoughts he asked, "Raylene, where are you? Can't you come help?"

"I'm a long way away," I told him. Old habit wouldn't let me say more, and it wouldn't help him anyway.

"How far?"

"Thousands of miles. I wish I were joking."

"Can you send anybody?" Ooh, I knew that pitch—that tone that lifts up the words at the corners and makes them into a nightmare scream in a bottle. He was frantic, and balancing on the edge of doing something very stupid.

And I had no idea what to do. "No," I gulped. "There's nobody."

This wasn't strictly true. There was Ian, and there was Cal—somewhere within ten miles or so. But a blind vampire and a hipster ghoul would be no good at all; truth be told, they'd only make the situation worse. Also, they'd get themselves caught, or so I was willing to bet.

So it might not've been strictly true, but it was functionally true.

There was no cavalry coming.

"Listen to me," I said, keeping my voice down but trying to keep it firm. I opened one eye and saw Adrian, silent in the doorway and not moving, but watching me. I didn't care. I couldn't care, there wasn't time. I just thanked God he knew when to stay silent. "Listen to me, and I'll tell you what to do."

"Okay." I hated the relief I heard in that word. The relief wasn't warranted. I didn't even know what I was going to say next; I only knew that he needed to *believe* I had something to say next.

"First, tell me where you are."

"I'm on . . ." More swishings of cheek and fabric into the phone. "I'm on the third floor, up in the ceiling. They're not up here now, but they were a few minutes ago, and I think they'll be back. They've been sweeping the place over and over again. Like they're looking for something."

They could've been looking for anything, but much like Domino assumed they'd already taken his sister, I assumed they were there hunting for me. It was small comfort, knowing they wouldn't find me. No matter what else they found, or *who* else they found, or what crates they opened, or what locked doors they kicked down . . . they wouldn't find *me*.

Small comfort indeed. And as sharp and cold as an icicle. Never mind meaningless to the boy on the phone.

"They're coming back!" he wheezed. He fumbled with the phone again.

"Domino!" I said, almost speaking loud enough to bring my voice out of the whisper that neither of us had yet dropped.

"What?" The word was thin, compressed, and shoved out from between his teeth.

"Stay with me. Which end of the third floor are you at?"

"They're popping open the vents! They're going to find me in here!" Not quite shrill, but you could see it from there.

"Your vent?"

"Not yet!"

"*Okay*. Okay. Which part of the ceiling are you in?"

He panted for a moment, then said, "I'm near the main staircase."

"And they didn't start there?"

"No. They came up the back way. I don't know why. Raylene, they're moving stuff around. They've got crowbars. They're taking this place apart. They're going to find me!"

"*They're not going to find you.* You're going to nut up and wiggle out of this, you hear me?"

"Where would I go?" he asked, and it almost hurt me, even though I didn't like him. The pain and the terror were almost too much to hear. "I can't leave Pepper!"

"These guys who came in, they must have cars, vans, something like that?"

"I . . . I don't know."

"You need to look. You need to get outside and make sure they don't have your sister stashed inside one of those cars yet, or one of those vans. If she's there, then we can talk about rescuing her."

"What if she's not?"

"If she's not," I relied upon past experience when I said, "I say let her stay wherever she's at. I heard you say they're taking the place apart, but even if they go brick by brick, they're never going to find your sister. She's tough and smart, and she's an Olympic-caliber hider—as she's proven to us both, on more than one occasion. So if she's not outside, and if they haven't caught her, then you and me, we're going to trust her. We're going to assume that she's holed up deep and she ain't coming out, and they aren't going to find her. Can you do that?"

"I don't know," he said for what must've been the thousandth time.

"Yes you do. Yes you can. But first, you have to get out of there and check. Come on, Domino. You're a sneaky motherfucker, I know it for a fact." And I did. He wasn't quite as good at sneaking as Pepper was at hiding, but I'd definitely give him a bronze in the sport.

"I'm a sneaky motherfucker," he repeated.

"That's right, and you keep saying it."

"I'm a sneaky motherfucker."

"There you go. Now—" And I did my damndest to recall and imagine the major airway workings of the factory. And yes, of course I was familiar with them. You do remember what I do for a living, right? It's basically my job to know all the ways in and out of a place, and this extends to my own places, too. "—now are you facing out, over the main shop floor?"

"Shop?"

"It used to be a shop. They made rubber boot soles or something. You're facing out over the floor, right?"

"Right. I can see these guys, Raylene—"

"Ignore them. Turn around and, quiet as you can, head back inside."

"Inside the vent?" More squeaking.

"Did I mumble? Yes, get back inside the vent. It ought to be big enough for you to turn around, but do it quietly."

"But it's dark back there!" he complained. "I can't see anything."

"Doesn't matter. I know which way the thing goes. I'll talk you through it, come on. Turn around and start crawling."

"I'm putting the phone in my shirt pocket," he told me. "Hang on."

So I hung on while he scraped, scooted, and dragged himself down the square metal track that wormed back deeper into the building. During this lull in the conversation, Adrian came to crouch beside me—moving without making even the slightest sound.

"Everything okay?" he asked.

I put my hand over the phone's "receiver" end. "Not so much. And thanks for being quiet. Do me a favor, please? Stay that way. Nothing personal, but this is bad."

"Are you talking to a kid?"

"Yes. It's a long story. I'll tell you soon. Please, please, *please* do me a favor and leave me alone for a few minutes. Just let me talk him through this, and I promise I'll tell you anything you want when this is sorted out."

"Raylene?" Domino called softly.

I waved Adrian away again. He nodded grimly and walked away, going back to my bedroom and closing himself in there. I couldn't complain. He'd slept on the couch after all, and my bedroom was definitely the most isolated part of the unit.

I returned my attention to Domino. "What?"

"Who are you talking to?"

"A . . . a friend. Don't worry about it. How's your progress?"

"I can't see anything!"

I said, "I know. And I'm sorry. But there's a fork up ahead."

"I already found it."

"You found it?" I pinched at the spot between my eyebrows and fought to remember the layout. "Then you'll need to take the right tunnel. And I'm sorry, but it's going to be blind. You just have to trust me that it's going to play out all right."

He said, "I trust you."

I didn't believe him. I didn't even think *he* believed him. But he didn't have a choice and I appreciated the vote of confidence, so I said, "Good. All you have to do is listen to me, and I'll have you out on the roof in a jiffy."

"The roof?"

"Yes, the roof. There are two old fire escapes up there, either one of which you can use to let yourself down. They aren't super-sturdy, but you don't weigh a hundred pounds and I've seen you scramble like a monkey. You'll be fine."

"It's raining. They'll be wet."

"It's always raining. It's always wet." In Seattle, if you let the weather keep you from going about your business, you'll never leave the house. He knew it as well as I did, though. I understood that he was only talking to hear his own voice, however quietly.

Domino was alone in the dark, in a space so narrow I would've thought twice about using it myself. He couldn't see his hand in front of his face, and I shuddered to consider the rats, roaches, and other assorted nasties he was pushing aside in order to follow my directions. All things being equal, he was probably better off without a light. Without a light, he couldn't see the spiderwebs he was breaching with his hands and his head; he couldn't see the riveted seams that were rusty around the rims, and always looked ready to split and break.

"How you doing in there?" I asked.

"Okay," he grunted. "Wait. I think I've hit the end."

"You have. Sort of. It's going to go up now. You're going to have to climb."

"What?"

"You heard me, monkey-boy. There are seams in those joints about a foot and a half apart. It'll take some learning and you're going to have to play it very, very cool—but there's no way around it. You're going to have to climb."

"I . . . I don't know."

"You can do it," I vowed. "You're lanky enough and strong enough, and you'll be fine."

"What's lanky got to do with it?" he asked.

I could hear him adjusting himself, sitting upright in the place where the vent took a sudden upward turn at a sharp, narrow joint. I said, "Keep your voice down. You're between the floors, but you're not in another dimension. Be careful or they'll hear you."

"Okay."

"Good boy. Now work your way into that shaft and brace your back up against one of the sides. Then stick your feet out and brace your knees and toes against the opposite side. You understand what I'm saying?"

"I think so."

I hoped I wasn't about to let him down, because in truth, I had no idea if he was capable of climbing this way. "This next part's going to get a little noisy, but you're going to be going up inside one of the walls and if anybody hears you, they might assume rats." And for very good reason, I thought, but I didn't say that part out loud. "As long as no one hears you talking."

"Got it."

"You said you'd stuck the phone in your shirt pocket before—can you do that again and still hear me?"

"Yeah."

The phone went through yet another shift, brushing up against his shirt and his hands and casting back that metallic echo from within the squared-off tube.

In a fairly soft whisper he asked, "Can you still hear me?"

"I can still hear you," I said back, in something closer to a normal tone of voice. It had to carry from his pocket to his ear after all. "Now this is what you do—"

"I think I got it," he cut in. "Use my butt and my feet to hold myself, and my arms to pull and push myself up."

I was silent, then I said, "That's pretty much it. You catch on quick."

"I'm not *stupid*," he assured me.

My instinct was to retort, "I never said you were." But I was pretty sure that somewhere, at some distant point in the past, I had almost certainly said precisely that. So I let him have his little victory, proving me wrong. "Let me know when you get to the top."

"Will . . . there . . . be . . . another split?" he asked, muffled groans and slipping mumbles interrupting his words.

"No. It'll veer off to the left, and then it's a straight shot to the ventilation hut on the roof. You'll have to kick your way out, but that thing is sixty years old if it's a day and I'm pretty sure you can handle it." I said all this glibly, as if I'd remembered all along that the ventilation system was capped outside. In fact, I'd completely forgotten—and I'd also forgotten that this was a fourteen-year-old boy, and not a vampire who could pop the thing off with a twist of his wrist.

"All right," he said. He sounded about as sure as I felt, but I went on faking it, because what else could I do?

"Seriously, don't worry about it. It's rusted all to hell, if it's even still in place. It's just one of those old spinny things that lets the air out and keeps the rain from getting in."

"Like a fan?" he asked, and the squeal of his shoe on the metal made my teeth hurt.

"No, not like a fan. It's not going to eat you alive or anything. It's just a little metal piece . . . more like a pinwheel, really."

"What's a pinwheel?"

"What's a . . . ? Jesus Christ, I'm not *that* old. A pinwheel— you know. You blow on it, and it spins around. Usually made of pretty colored paper or foil or something. Work with me, kid."

"Whatever you say."

I got the distinct impression he thought I was yanking his chain, but that was fine. Anything to keep him occupied while he scaled the entirety of a sixteen-foot story vertically, in a metal tube with not a shred of light.

"It's an old-fashioned toy."

"Never seen one." Another three-word response. It was probably all he could get in between heaves and hos.

After what felt like an interminable amount of time just waiting for him to reach the top, he did in fact reach it. He reached it with a fumble and a slip that came perilously close to dumping him straight back down the chute. He didn't tell me this, but I could hear it in the havoc of the phone turning and flipping in that pocket, and in the desperate scrabble of his feet on the metal, hunting for some purchase that wasn't compromised by dust and the decay of decades.

"You make it?" I asked, once I was pretty sure that he had, in fact, made it.

"Yeah," he said with a gasp.

"Good job. Now like I said, just go left."

He did, and before long he'd worked his way up to the vent with the spinner, and thank God I was right—he dislodged it with just a couple of shoves. I could hear rusty metal giving way and a clatter as the rooftop wonder burst up into the open sky and into a faceful of rain.

I had no way of knowing if he'd made enough noise to summon anybody, so I said to him, "No time to dawdle. Run around the rooftop edge and see where they're parked; then pick the farthest fire escape and let yourself down onto the ground."

"What?"

The phone had still been in his shirt. Out in the open, he couldn't hear me that way. I repeated myself, and he said, "Yeah, I'm way ahead of you. Hang on."

The whistling of wind and the occasional patter of rain on the microphone made a strange symphony while he darted from corner to corner, keeping low and staying light-footed if he knew what was good for him.

"They're parked out front, on the street. I don't see any cars in the back."

"Then go down the back, but be careful. Put the phone back in your shirt. Let me know when you've got your feet on the ground."

"Okay."

Again I waited—always this god-awful waiting, where there

was nothing I could do and I couldn't even say anything to be helpful, because the kid would never hear me, and anyway, I'd only distract him.

I detected the wet creak of old metal, and bolts that were rust-
ing into place.

A splash announced his landing, and shortly thereafter he had
the phone back up to his face again. "I'm down," he told me.

"Right. Now I want you to walk away from the building at a
swift but innocuous pace, all the way to the end of the street where
the frozen yogurt place is, next to that coffee shop."

"Away from the building? But Pepper—"

"Pepper is either in one of those cars outside the building, or
inside it very securely."

"And what does that word mean? Inno-something."

"*Innocuous.* It means try not to look like you're running away.
Listen, punk. When you get to the end of the street, I want you to
go into that coffee place and buy some hot chocolate."

"Are you crazy?" He was on the verge of losing his whisper.

"And stop whispering," it occurred to me to tell him. "It makes
you look guilty." Before he could interrupt me again I continued,
"Go get some hot chocolate and then, nice and lazy and slow, I want
you to stroll back down the street to where their cars are hanging
out."

"Oh. Okay."

Good, he was catching on. "They don't know what you look
like, do they?"

"I don't guess."

"Let's assume they don't. And let's also remind ourselves that
being a nosy kid isn't a crime. So go get yourself some hot chocolate and mosey back over to the vehicles. Hang around and listen,
if you can. See if you can overhear anything. But keep the phone up
to your ear. Pretend like you're talking to somebody."

Suddenly he sounded afraid again. "You're not going to hang up on me, are you?"

"I am, in a minute. But only for a minute, while you go get the hot chocolate. I didn't spring for an expensive phone, bucko. The battery on that thing isn't going to last all night."

"Oh yeah," he said, and the proximity of his voice to the mike told me he was checking the display.

"I haven't heard it beeping low battery, but still you want to conserve the thing. I'm going to go out on a limb and guess you didn't take the charger when you ran?"

"Shit," he complained. "I should've thought of it. I should've grabbed it."

"Don't worry about it," I said. "Only a crazy person would've thought that meticulously about evacuating a scene." By which I meant that I, personally, kept my chargers and all important electronics in my oversized purse-slash-messenger-bag. "It'll be fine for a little while. Now I'm going to hang up, and I want you to call me back when you're at the edge of the action, okay?"

"Got it. And Raylene?"

"What?"

"Thanks," he said before flipping the thing shut.

I'm not going to lie. It almost gave me a warm fuzzy.

I exhaled a huge breath—one that I hadn't even realized I'd been holding. As if this elongated gasp were a signal, Adrian came swanning back out of the bedroom (how could he have heard it in there?) and into the dining area, where I was sitting just shy of a fetal position upright. I began to uncurl, letting my legs straighten out on the floor and putting my head in my hands—leaving the cell phone beside me.

Adrian said, "Dare I ask?"

Without looking up I said, "Ask away."

"What was that about?"

So I told him. I didn't tell him everything; I mean, I'm not *stupid*. I didn't know him well enough to give him the address of the place or the finer particulars. But I filled him in on the kids, and I made my standard disclaimers regarding my place in their maintenance. I told him about the place that once was a factory, and now was my warehouse, and how it was at right that moment being swarmed over by federal agents—or special forces ops, or CIA dudes, or whatever those guys were. Guys like Peter Desarme.

Right around the time I'd finished explaining everything I felt like explaining, the phone rang again. I'd forgotten I was holding it, and when it began to yodel and vibrate I nearly had a heart attack, flipping the thing up into the air and catching it—miraculously without hanging up on Domino, who was calling me back.

"Kid," I answered, knowing it was him.

"Hey," he said in a casual voice that only trembled around the edges, a tiny bit. He was doing good.

"Where are you now?"

"Oh, I'm just on my way home, you know how it is," he told me, which also told me that there were other people within listening distance.

"Any sign of your sister?" I asked.

"No, not yet. I've checked all the obvious spots, but I can't find her. And near as I can tell, nobody else has, either." Still level and cool, and now tempered with hypothetical relief. In the background I heard car engines and men talking, and I detected the drizzling patter of rain—which only made it a night ending in *y*.

I did most of the important question-asking-type-talking, since he obviously couldn't, out there where all the action was. "Were you able to look inside their vehicles?"

"Pretty much. Nothing to see there."

"Good. That's good. Do you think they could've taken her away already?"

He slurped at something, the hot chocolate I assumed. Or maybe it was a latte with Irish whiskey in it. There really was no telling with that kid. "I doubt it. Man, there sure are a lot of people out here at this hour. And they keep arriving, too."

I nodded, as if he could see me or hear my head rattle. "They're still incoming, and not clearing the scene, that's what you're saying."

"You got it."

Somebody came close, with a gruff "Move along, kid."

I could imagine the look Domino gave the speaker, and I didn't have to imagine his response. "Hey, fuck you, asshole! It's a public street, I got a right to be here! What's going on, anyway?"

"None of your goddamned business, you little shit," the somebody growled at him.

I almost laughed. One of these days, Domino may as well change his name to "Little Shit." But I said to him, "Don't antagonize anybody, dumb-ass."

"Ooh, asshole's got a baaadge," he said in a singsong voice.

"Asshole's got a pair of handcuffs, too, and a big car over there. You wanna take a ride?"

"Fuck you," Domino said again.

But I had an idea. I said, "Ask him what kind of badge it is."

The boy said, "For all I know that badge is a fake, anyway. Doesn't look like any badge I ever saw."

"Good boy," I whispered.

"I don't have to tell you anything. What are you, fifteen? You got any ID?"

"I don't need any ID. I'm fifteen," he lied. He was fourteen, but he could run with it either way. "And my parents don't care that I'm out, so don't bother asking to call them."

"Maybe I'll just throw you into the car."

"Maybe you can just suck your own dick and flash your fake

badge at somebody else, and see if it gets you anywhere. You're not even a *real* cop."

"I'm worse than a real cop."

"What is he—like, a rent-a-cop?" I asked.

Domino read off the badge, answering both me and his interrogator, "CIA? Like I'd know what a real CIA badge looks like. For all I know you got that thing at Party City."

"Are you still talking on that cell phone?" asked the man with the badge.

"Yes, motherfucker. What are you gonna do about it anyway? You big-ass knob-gobbling donkey-raping—"

There was a clatter and a crunch, and the phone went dead.

I sat there, stupidly holding my own phone up to my ear and listening to a whole lot of nothing. As soon as I realized I was doing this, I folded it up and let my hand drop to the floor. I said, "Wow."

Adrian was still there, unobtrusive in the arched doorway that led to the living area. "Is that good or bad?"

"Not sure," I confessed. "Probably . . . well. It's probably okay," I told him, thereby telling myself.

"What happened?"

"The little shit with the big mouth got his phone taken away."

"While he was talking to you?" He sounded worried. "Could they trace the call back to you?"

"I doubt it." I should've been worried, but I wasn't. "Domino was doing a good job of acting like a low-life street punk. It wasn't much of a stretch, I'll grant you, but he was working it. I don't think anybody suspected anything except that he was an adolescent douchebag, and I don't think the officer—or whatever he was— actually took the phone. I think he broke it. Sounded like he smashed it against a wall, or stepped on it."

Adrian considered this, and then said, "I don't know the little shit, but I'll take your word for it. I guess I have to."

Setting the phone down, I said, "There's no reason for anyone to pick it up and try to put it back together except Domino. It won't do him any good, but that's all right."

"Don't you need some means of contacting these kids?"

I put my head in my hands and rubbed at my temples. "Yes, but I'll just express them another phone. I keep a PO box down the street; the kids have a key and they know to check it." The only thing that really worried me was Pepper, but if Domino didn't see her captured anyplace, it was like I'd said—we might as well just assume that she'd holed up tighter than a turtle's asshole. She'd come out when the trouble was gone, and she'd calm her brother down, and maybe keep him from doing anything stupid.

Credit where it was due, the boy had handled things downright admirably.

I hate to revisit my assumptions; I prefer to let them lie and fester, but one of these days—when I have nothing better to think about—I might get thinking about it and decide there's an off chance he's not wholly irredeemable.

Adrian said, "Okay. Well, whatever. Now what do we do?"

I picked up the phone and opened it again. "Now we arrange for another disposable phone, call the airline to confirm our tickets, and start packing for Washington, D.C."

"Still? You're sure about that?"

"Absolutely. And the sooner the better. They're watching my place, man. They're watching for *me*, which means they think there's a chance that I'm still in Seattle, and they don't know for certain that I've skipped town. We need to hit this guy fast, before he figures out that I made a run for it."

11

Twenty-four hours later we were at the Lincoln Memorial, me and Adrian. Not the most inconspicuous place to gather, no, and we sure as hell weren't alone. Tourists peppered the big white stairs and tried to make shadow puppets in the spotlights that lit the old guy, seated up there in all his stony glory. Security guards ambled fatly about. Children who really should've been in bed by now shrieked and shoved at one another, leading to at least one little girl's headcrack on the stairs and subsequently to two fighting parents, debating who should've been watching her.

We made a point to dress blandly and refrain from skulking, pretending to take in the sights and occasionally check the walking map of the lawn, as if we really gave a shit. Nobody looked at us twice, not that I noticed.

Not until I heard the soft clearing of a throat. It could've been any throat, cleared for any reason at all, but it wasn't. It was a signal from Cal, projected from the bottom of the steps—where he stood beside Ian. I'd known it as surely as if he'd sent a text message. You can write that off to my middling psychic abilities or to my expectation that he'd arrive any minute, or you can assume I'm lying, and that's fine, too.

I gave them a friendly wave—acting so aggressively normal that it must've looked weird, but I couldn't stop myself. I gestured them up to join us, and within a few seconds they stood before us while the thin nighttime crowds milled around us.

Ian was as tastefully dressed as always, in expensive and well-fitting clothes plus a slim black cane and the ever-present glasses. Cal could've been wearing the exact same thing he'd worn the last time I'd seen him. I couldn't tell and didn't care.

"Ian," I said, beginning the introductions. "This is Adrian. Adrian, this is Ian and . . . um . . . Cal."

"A pleasure," said Ian through lips that were a little too tight to have meant the sentiment, but he did not seem frightened or even angry. Just uncomfortable.

"Cal is Ian's assistant," I explained with a hand-wave indicating that yes, I knew I was being vague, but no, I didn't intend to be any more precise.

Adrian said, "Nice to meet you both." He was every bit as stiff as Ian and even more nervous.

Everyone stared back and forth awkwardly, except Ian, of course—but I'm pretty sure he would've been right there staring awkwardly along with us, if he'd only been able. So I said, "Well!" with too much forced cheer, and then I went on to suggest, "There's a bar a couple of blocks away—not far, and it's still a nice part of town, with a fireplace and everything. Let's adjourn there, shall we?"

Anything to get the conversation moving along, even if that meant moving us along, too.

We walked in relative silence except for my vain attempts to get people chatting, which mostly fell on deaf ears. The winter air was cold anyway, and it froze my throat when I tried to breathe or cough sociably, so I gave up and instead of being the conversation instigator, I settled for shepherd. Together, in an unfriendly clot, we found our way to the Revolutionary—a joint that was hopping with posh-looking tourists and overworked civil servants, with a smattering of lobbyists on cell phones.

I ushered everyone over to a table near the fireplace because I liked the warmth and glow of it, and the blend of orange shadows with flickering yellow light made Ian and I look more alive and less suspicious than usual. Not that we usually looked dead and suspicious, but you know what I mean. Firelight is like Photoshop for the flesh.

Wait. I already said that about vampirism.

So I'm redundant. Sue me.

We all sat down, though Cal looked as if he'd love nothing better than to resume a spot somewhere out of sight rather than hang out with this group of loonies. If by force of habit he usually lurked in the background, tough noogies. He could stay quiet if he wanted, but for the moment, he was stuck with us.

Wine arrived for me and Ian, and a double whiskey neat for the ghoul. Adrian had a Guinness because I guess he felt like drinking a loaf of bread or something. That's what it smelled like, anyway.

Finally we were all settled, served, and left alone, and there was no further excuse to keep us from talking. I broke the ice, since nobody else would.

"All right, guys," I opened. "I know this is awkward, but we're going to have to have a civilized conversation about some uncivilized stuff. Speak in euphemisms if you feel the need, since we're in public, but there are some things that have to come out into the open."

Ian bobbed his head gently, and asked, "Did you bring the paperwork? Do you really have my files?"

Adrian answered for me. "We have them. I've been sitting on them for years."

The vampire's head continued to bob as he took this in. He said, "I understand you had a sister in the program." It came out with difficulty, and I almost felt bad about having pushed this. But I thought it couldn't hurt, and maybe it'd even help him to have someone to tell . . . and it'd definitely help Adrian, hearing about his sister, even if what he heard wasn't very nice. Without even thinking about it very hard, I trusted Ian not to share anything too jarring.

Adrian said, "Yes. Her name was Isabelle. Did you know her?"

"I knew no one by name. And after the first few weeks, I likewise did not know anyone . . . on sight," he finished softly.

"She was . . . she was quite young," Adrian tried a different approach. "Sixteen or seventeen, or at least that's how she would've seemed. Since she had become . . . like you. She would've sounded like a girl, still. With an accent," he said suddenly, as if it'd just occurred to him. "Like mine. But hers was stronger."

If I were to guess, I'd say he'd spent some time deliberately uncultivating his own, in order to better hide himself. But I didn't accuse him of it, in case it was a sensitive subject. And anyway, it was none of my business.

"Spanish," Ian murmured.

"Cuban," Adrian clarified. "Our mother came over on a raft before we were born."

"Such strange stories we have. All of us." Ian sipped at his wine. He grimaced faintly, but not at the vintage, I didn't think. And he said, "Please understand, Adrian—I am a vulnerable man in a dangerous position, even now. It is not in my nature to discuss my past and my infirmities with anyone apart from my doctor."

Adrian almost cut him off. "But—"

"But in a case like this," he carried on, "I suppose I must make an exception. Though I'm not entirely sure what you'd like to know, or what I could possibly tell you."

"Anything. Everything."

"I can't tell you much; I saw almost nothing. And I never saw *her*. But I heard her, as you said. And her scent . . ." His nostrils flared so barely that I could hardly see them move. "It was something like yours. I believe you, when you call her kin."

Eager and desperate, and reining it in with some difficulty, Adrian asked, "She was there, with you?"

"Yes."

"What did they do to her?"

"I . . ." Ian hesitated. "I could not say. Most of us there, we were *different*, as you can guess. Someone, somewhere, had the idea that our abilities could be tapped—and taken. Or at least designed for use in a less . . . conspicuous person. For example, they wanted my night vision. There was talk of developing a bio-hack that could be introduced to soldiers, to special forces. To men like you once were," he added quietly.

Adrian glared at me.

I shrugged. "Yeah, I told him. We're operating on a need-to-know basis here, and he needed to know. But don't worry. I'm pretty sure he's not going to lord the information over you. Or . . . I don't know. Use it to get you into trouble. I mean more trouble than you're already in."

Ian said, "Now, now, Raylene. Do you mind if I call you Raylene? I feel like surely we've endured enough together at this point that first names shouldn't be so far out of bounds."

"Go for it."

"Raylene," he said again, and I kind of liked hearing it. "I have not at any point used any of my information to bring you harm, have I?"

I said, "No, and I'm trusting you to stay that course. Adrian, it's okay, really. He's covering his ass, that's all."

"You can explain the politics to him later," Ian said toward me. Then to Adrian, "I do not know what they wanted from your sister, I only know that she was there, and that sometimes she was in the same holding area as me. There were two others like us, also. I never saw them, either."

"Where were you kept?" he asked, and I thought it was a strange question until I remembered that yes, he was a special-forces-type guy himself and maybe he had more than a tangential interest in the particulars.

Ian shuffled his shoulders in a move that was halfway between a shrug and a hand-wave. "Underground? Someplace without windows, I assume. It was dark and quiet, with . . . with . . ." He struggled to recall. "Fluorescent lighting. I could hear the hum and buzz of it, all night, and all day when I tried to sleep."

"And this compound was called 'Jordon Roe'?" Adrian asked.

"That's what they called it, yes. It was on an island off the coast of Florida—a tiny, vegetation-covered sandbar with no bridges to the mainland. Everyone who came or went came or went by helicopter, or by boat."

"Did you ever talk to my sister?" Adrian wanted to know. "Did she ever say anything? About me, or about anybody? About anything?"

Ian's eyes were all but hidden behind the tinted lenses, but I think I saw them tense, and soften. He said, "I heard her crying, sometimes. And I tried to talk to her, once. I asked her who she was—I was only trying to distract her. We were all lined up in these cells, you see, with walls between us. We couldn't have seen one another even if I hadn't been blind by then. But I heard her, yes. And I tried to engage her, but she only told me to go perform anatomically improbable acts on myself. I didn't take it personally," he added. "We were under so much stress and uncertainty. She was terrified, that much was obvious. I felt sorry for her. She gave me someone to pity other than myself."

Cal, who hadn't yet said a word to anyone, lifted his hand like he wanted to pat Ian's shoulder in a show of sympathy, but he restrained himself.

Ian sighed, took a mouthful of wine too large to call a sip, and swallowed. "I heard her talking to other people, mostly begging to be told what was happening, or arguing, or screaming to be let out—before she figured out that no one was listening, and that help was not coming from anyone, inside or out."

"Did you leave her there? When you escaped?" Adrian asked, his hands gripping hard on his glass, leaving a fog halo around his fingers even though the beverage inside wasn't very cold.

The vampire shook his head. "I escaped after . . . a storm destroyed the premises. I was in no position to look for her, or anyone else. But I called out to her, and to everyone else who remained— and if she heard me, she did not respond. If she survived, she must have been injured. Or perhaps she escaped, but was recaptured. I wish I could tell you more, but that's all I know. She didn't answer me. No one answered me."

He tapped one fingernail against the base of the wineglass, considering something else. I was about to ask him what it was, but he spared me the effort. "Once I heard her talking in Spanish, very quickly, to one of the guards—or scientists, or soldiers, or whatever they were there. She might've overheard a Spanish name, or heard him speaking, or perhaps she only guessed by looking at him that he might understand her. Regardless, she attempted to sway him—she was pleading with him, one morning when most of the residents were already turned in for the day, and trying to rest. Even when we can't see the sun we can feel when it's up, you see, and when we can feel it, up there or out there for very long, it makes us want to sleep—though we can delay it if we're motivated to do so."

"Do you speak any Spanish?" Adrian asked.

"I'm afraid not. She was whispering, pleading. I couldn't pick out a single bit, except *por favor,* and I know that means 'please.' She said it several times. But whoever she was talking to, I could tell by his tone that he was telling her no."

Adrian exhaled and leaned back, taking his drink with him and downing the last of it. He held the empty glass against his chest. "Thank you," he said. "I know you didn't have to tell me any of this."

"I wish I could be more help."

The part-time drag queen shook his head. "There's no help to be had, not anymore. She's gone, and I'm still here. And I've done everything I could to keep her death from being swept under a rug, but until Raylene here stumbled across me—"

"Hey—" I objected. There hadn't been any "stumbling" about it.

"I'd run out of ideas. I didn't know what to do with what I had. The government allegedly closed the program some time ago, but I suspect it's been reopened—maybe as a civilian operation."

"There's no *suspecting* to it," I sulked. "Someone's up to something again, and I've got a name—Ed Bruner. I even have a half-assed idea of how he's trying to drum up new subjects."

Ian asked with a hint of worry, "What do you mean?"

"One of my properties was broken into the night you and I met. I caught the breaker-inner, and he had a number on him that lead back to a guy named Ed Bruner. The same name turned up in Adrian's folders. You'll see it when you read through it—or when

Cal does. I don't believe in coincidences. I think he's fishing around for more test subjects, and he's using a group of urban explorers as cover."

"Urban explorers?" Cal asked. "What, like people who take pictures in abandoned buildings?"

"Yes, but worse. These guys—like the guy I caught on my property—they aren't looking around abandoned buildings. Bruner is using them to try and flush out people like me, or chase down leads that might lead him to people like me. I can't prove it yet, but I don't really have to. I know he's tied up in Project Blood-shot, and that makes him interesting enough to chase down, re-gardless of what his involvement in the burglary might have been."

Ian said, "Indeed," and he brought the subject back around to its primary purpose, from his point of view. "And for now, I'd like to ask if you'd let me have those files. I've come a very long way to see them. Or rather"—he made a self-deprecating gesture—"to have Cal see them."

The ghoul took his hands off his whiskey long enough to re-trieve the blue folder stuffed full of that enigmatic paperwork and place it in front of Ian—and halfway in front of himself, so he could see it.

Ian couldn't read it, but he seemed eager to touch it, if only to know for certain that he'd finally found it. He asked Cal, "Is it . . . ?"

And Cal said, "Looks like it. I think so, yes." He flipped through the pages, licking his thumb for traction, and gave every-thing a cursory examination in the dim light of the Revolutionary. "It appears to be rather comprehensive," he muttered. "But coded, like everything else we've found so far."

"I've also included the paperwork regarding two of the other subjects who were featured in the Holtzer Point file cabinets. Your stuff is in there, but it's not much you don't already have. As for the other dossiers, they're coded, too. It's almost impossible to tell any personal details about any of them, except Isabelle." I'd given her paperwork to Adrian, in case it meant anything to him. I theorized, "And that might be because they knew she'd been reported as a missing person, and they figured out that someday, they might have to account for what happened to her . . . to someone."

Adrian agreed, saying, "Maybe. I made a big stink for a few years there, until I tracked her down and went after her documents. Then I had to knock it off, obviously. But everything I ever found on Bloodshot was coded—and that's not so unusual, really. The military loves nothing more than muddling things that ought to be clear. Maybe you'll find something useful in it. I hope you do. It hasn't been doing much for me these past few years." He said it with irritation, but not directed at anyone at the table. I think he was irritated with himself for hanging on to it all this time and not knowing what to do with it.

"Thank you," Ian told him again. He dragged his fingertips across the pages as if he could osmose the text. "Cal, would you stash these, please?"

"Of course," replied the hipster, gathering everything together and tapping it on the table to straighten the pages. Then he stuffed the lot of it into a satchel he'd left at his feet. "I can fax them to Dr. Keene in the morning."

"And then tomorrow night, barring unforeseen catastrophe," I said, tempting fate, "you and I can finally have that money talk."

"You'd rather not do so now?" Ian asked.

"No. Not while there's still work to be done."

"I'm not sure I understand."

So I made him understand. I brought him up to speed on everything that had happened since I'd left Seattle, including de- tails on the initial breach by Trevor and the subsequent full-scale *official* raid on my storehouse at Pioneer Square in Seattle. Then I told him about the Poppycock Review, and how I'd possibly been tracked by satellite.

"And you're certain Bruner's behind all this?" Ian asked, worried lines crinkling around the edges of his eyes, just beyond the frames of his glasses.

"More certain than I'd like to be. I'll grant you, half of it's hunch. But I haven't lived this long by ignoring my hunches, and I think the coincidence is simply too much to ignore. What's the old adage? I may be paranoid, but that doesn't mean they aren't after me. Anyway, moving right along, I'd like to bring another issue to the table of this little . . . meeting, or committee, or whatever we are. A little digging brought me to a couple of pieces of information that might be of use to us."

Adrian already knew about them, so he kept his mouth shut, leaned back, and signaled the server for another beverage. But Ian hadn't heard yet, so he took the bait. "What kind of information?"

"For starters, Ed Bruner's not in the phone book, but I know where his office is located. It's here in D.C., less than two miles from where we're sitting right this second."

Cal murmured, "You can't be serious."

"Oh, I'm serious. I guess he thinks he has nothing to hide, or maybe he's just that arrogant. From what I know of him—which admittedly isn't much, but none of it's flattering—it could go either way. Regardless, he's easy to find. At least his official offices are easy to find. How much time he spends there, I couldn't say and haven't the foggiest. But tomorrow night we're going to go take a look around and see if there's been any movement or revival of Project Bloodshot—under that name, or any other."

"Wait. We?" Ian asked.

"*We* meaning me and Adrian. He's got training and I've got moves. We're just going to take a quick poke around the premises, bust open a safe or two, rifle through some filing cabinets, you know. Stuff like that. Depending on what we find, I might need to borrow your expertise."

"My expertise on the project is rather regrettably limited," Ian said wryly.

"Oh, don't be so modest." I waved at him without looking at him, because I was reaching for my bag and digging around in it for a piece of paper. "You're a living witness to what went on there, and as you've demonstrated admirably, your ears and nose observed much."

"What are you doing?" Cal asked curiously.

I said, "I'm looking for something. Ah. Here it is."

I withdrew the computer printout of a website advertisement and slapped it down on the table. "I give you the District of Columbia's premier organization for parkour enthusiasts of all ages and skill levels."

Cal picked up the paper and read aloud, "Presidential Parkour?"

"Silly name, yes I agree." I then said to Ian, "It's not related to Northwest *Parcours* Addicts in Seattle, not in any concrete sister-organization way or anything. They don't even spell *parcours* the same way—the D.C. group does away with that sissy French spelling and gives it a good old Anglo-Saxon *k* instead of a *c*. In fact, the two groups only have two things in common: one, they're both chock-full of military wannabes who like to run around and climb on stuff; and two, they both have a surreptitious connection to the army."

"Bruner's affiliated with this group, too?" Ian asked.

"Yup. And he uses similar groups in Seattle to recruit. This one advertises that it comes with soldier oversight in the form of Tyler Bolton, a lieutenant with somebody or another—they aren't too clear on the website as to who, precisely, he lieutenants."

Adrian made a harrumphing noise and said, "Tyler Bolton. What a name."

"I know, right? It's almost worse than Trevor," I mused aloud. "Regardless, we're going."

"We?" Ian asked. "You and Adrian, again?"

"Actually . . ." I gave Cal an appraising look. "Adrian's a poor choice for this particular mission, since he's been AWOL for quite some time."

Ian was frowning, anticipating where I was headed. He asked Adrian, "Do you know this Tyler Bolton?"

Adrian shook his head. "No. But army guys are like cop cars— you never see one by itself. And if this is a front for only marginally legal activities, or for a resurgence of Project Bloodshot, that's all the more reason I should stay away. They know I took the original paperwork, so there might be a file on me that gets passed around to interested parties. It may sound paranoid, but . . ."

But I'd already used the line about how they might still be out to get us, so he stopped himself there. Instead he said, "It's best that I stay away for now, that's the short version. Until we know if there's any connection to the program, anyway." He was understating for effect, of course.

Ian frowned harder and said to me, "I can't imagine it's too much safer for someone like *you*, given the circumstances. I hope you don't mind me saying so, but this whole thing sounds like a trap."

"You may be right, but I'm the only one who's had any experience with these yahoos, and it was *my* building they raided."

"All the more reason it sounds like a terrible idea, in my opinion." He did *not* sound happy. "They're luring you out, Raylene. This whole thing looks like a setup."

"But they don't even know that I'm not in Seattle," I insisted. "Somebody knew I made it to Atlanta, but the fact that they were checking out my home turf in the Northwest proves they think I might've hightailed it home. They aren't looking for me *here*." It was a gamble, and I knew it. But I put on a brave face and swore to the contrary. "Worst-case scenario, they're scouring the gayborhood in Atlanta and wondering where the hell I'm holed up."

"Worst-case scenario," he muttered. "I suppose I'll pass your worst-case scenario on to Dr. Keene and tell him to stand by. The poor man must think I'm sponsoring someone to take a vacation across the nation."

I tried to sound sympathetic, warm, and downright motherly when I took one of his cold hands in mine and patted it with authoritative gentleness. "Ian, if this program isn't shut down for good, it can only come back to haunt you. To haunt *us,* even. They caught you once and you got away, so they know *you're* out here someplace. And we already know they've got an eye on *me.* Better to shut it down now while we're so close, and while they think they have us on the run."

He sighed and withdrew his hand. "It's not that I disagree with you . . ."

"Great!" I said, deliberately interrupting before he could give me the rest. "Then it's settled. Me and your buddy Cal here will swing by tomorrow night's field club meeting for the D.C. parkour program."

Cal gave a wet little gasp, and Ian lifted a finger as if he had something to contribute before I went any further, but I ignored it and kept talking.

"Because obviously, that's the only way this is going to work. I can't take Adrian, because there's too much risk of him being spotted, recognized, and outed. I can't take you, because, well, bless you darling, but you can't see, and we don't have any trustworthy third parties we can bribe or bully into reconnaissance, so that leaves me and your ghoul."

"Why don't you just go alone?" Cal asked.

"Oh, I plan to. We're going alone together, which is to say, we're arriving separately and pretending we don't know each other—because if they figure me out and make a play to bring me in, somebody has to tell Ian and Adrian what's gone down. If you're right, and this is a setup, and they're on to me . . . you can bet they're on to you, too. And you can bet this program is going to be up your ass again, sooner as likely as later. Cal is the party least likely to be identified as one of us. It has to be him."

Ian said, "I don't like it," but he didn't sound like he was going to put up a fight.

Cal also said, "I don't like it," which surprised no one.

I turned to Cal, trying to stare him down and take him seriously—or possibly gauge how seriously I could expect to take him. He looked worried and a little nerdy in that contrived way, like he got bad haircuts on purpose and deliberately chose aggressively retro clothes that were only marginally flattering. But he didn't look stupid, and he didn't look particularly fragile. He wasn't a big man, no. Nor a fat man, either. Underneath that slacker uniform he had slim arms and square shoulders that were thin but didn't look like bird bones. The more and the harder I looked at him, the more I could've guessed him for a runner, or a cyclist maybe.

Now it was Cal's turn to be on the receiving end of my best persuasive voice. "Buddy, I know this is weird and uncomfortable, but if you like working for this guy"—I jerked a thumb at Ian— "it might be in everyone's best interest if you just pretend for an evening that you wouldn't crawl backward away from me screaming, given half a chance."

"I wouldn't . . . I wouldn't *crawl*," he vowed weakly.

"Hyperbole, man. Hyperbole. But you don't want to hang out with me and I don't have any burning desire to hang out with you—not that there's anything wrong with you or anything, just that you're kind of an unknown quantity to me in this arrangement, and I'm not in a super-comfortable position here myself."

"How's that?" he asked, trying to copy Ian's wry face.

"You think I always get this up close and personal with clients? I didn't know how thoroughly your case would tie up my life in such an elaborate, choking fashion." I wrapped up by asking, "But it did, and here we are. So Ian, Cal, what do you say?"

I honestly didn't know what they'd say. Didn't have a clue if they'd be down with my plan or if they'd tell me to go jump in a lake and blow bubbles. They glanced back and forth; or Cal glanced, and Ian went through the motions. Nobody said anything, so I picked up my flag again and waved it.

"It won't be such a big deal, and it'll be over in one night. At six thirty PM me and Cal will mosey into the parkour class, and when it's over we'll part company. Then Adrian and I will throw on some black clothes, don a little warpaint, and storm the major's office, sabotaging everything we can get our hands on in our wake."

"This is a terrible idea," Cal said with sincerity, but no conviction.

"You may be right," I conceded, putting on my best grave-and-sincere face. "But right now it's the only plan we have, unless you're offering something bigger, better, smarter, or safer. And don't get me wrong—I'm willing to listen. But I'm not willing to wait a few days and see how this pans out. For just this moment, we have the closest thing to an advantage we're likely to get. And if we don't use it, we're gonna lose it." Look at me, busting out all the tired old metaphors. Like I'd been saving them all winter just waiting for an opportunity to trot them out.

After a pause, Ian said slowly, "How do we know they aren't on to us? Raylene, you've been in contact with this man. You said he invited you to come to D.C. and told you where his office was."

"Yeah, but he didn't know he was talking to *me*."

"So far as you know. They must know we're coming, that's all. They probably already know we're here."

"No way," I said.

"How can you be so sure?" Cal asked.

"Because if they knew where we were, they would've come down on us by now. Like the fist of God, unless I'm mistaken."

"No," Ian argued, but the resistance was leaving him. I was winning him over or wearing him down. "They want us to come to them."

It was then that Cal surprised me, in the wake of a long, drawn-out pause that hung over the table like a funnel cloud. He said to his boss, "I think you're right. They want us to come to them." Then he said to me, "So I'll do it. I'll come with you."

"Cal, you don't have to—" Ian started to say.

"Yes, I do. I'll go to them, if it keeps them from coming to you."

12

Cal sat nervously on the couch while I got ready for our evening out. Either by way of making conversation or just being fretful, he asked, "Does it always take you this long to leave the house?"

I said, "No," as I examined the contents of my go-bag. Lock picks, glass cutters, one small firearm (the .22, more for show than for firepower) and extra ammo, an envelope full of cash, my most recent disposable cell phone, handcuff keys, and some duct tape because hey, you never know. I've used that stuff as getaway rope, as restraints, and much more. Once I used it to strap a diamond necklace to my thigh like a garter, because I didn't have a better way of carrying it. As an old acquaintance of mine used to say, "If you can't duck it, fuck it." I'm pretty sure he knew it was *duct* and not *duck*, but I'll forgive him for the sake of the rhyme.

I also begged a baggie of A-negative off Ian, who traveled with a supply kept on ice in an Igloo chest. Usually, tracking down a butcher or blood bank is a vampire's first priority when relocating, but neither Ian nor I had gotten a spare moment to scope for an in-town supplier, so the old stuff would have to suffice.

"Is this a special occasion, or what?" Cal asked, still looking nervous, and a little bit prim.

"Special only in the sense that it's going to be dangerous— though more for me than for you," I added, because why give him something else to fret about? I already had the feeling I was going to have to watch him like a hawk and maybe save his ass later on. But I wasn't sure I'd mind saving his ass, if it came to that. He'd gone all Prince Valiant on me there, back at the Revolutionary— stepping forward in order to save his patron's hide. Truly selfless, or so it appeared on the surface.

Still, my innate mistrust of ghouls did not let me give him any more credit than a baseline assumption that he would play along and not go out of his way to fuck it up for us both. And I didn't like extending myself so far as to make that assumption. For all I knew, I could be wrong.

Except . . . if Cal wanted to bring Ian to real harm, there were easier ways to go about it. And he'd had ample opportunity over the . . . years? I had to assume they'd been a pair at least that long. More assumptions. I hate those things.

I added a cigarette lighter and a bottle of lighter fluid to my arsenal, then a small thin saw with a pointed tip, some waterproof matches, a second cell phone for good measure, and went ahead and zipped up the canvas bag. I said to Cal, "You ready?"

He said, "Yeah." Then he watered it down by adding, "I guess."

Apart from a ludicrous level of personal loyalty, I couldn't figure out what Ian saw in him.

He continued, "You're not going to need half of that. Probably not any of it."

"I hope you're right." In fact, I knew he was right, but I wasn't about to tell him that. I never needed even a fraction of what I packed, but this was just one more parachute designed to cushion my neurotic topple into madness. And sometimes my obsessive emergency preparedness actually worked, so I didn't feel compelled to stand around and defend myself.

I bet I wouldn't need to defend myself to Pepper or Domino. Especially not after I'd already expressed them another phone, which ought to be waiting in the post office box within another night or two. Overprepared my ass.

No such thing.

Cal was driving because we were moving around in his rental car, the one he'd picked up at the airport as soon as they'd arrived. I'd been taxiing about and hadn't had a chance to do my usual buy-something-secondhand-off-a-lot thing yet, so I let him fiddle with the keys to the white 2008 Malibu (which would not have been a first choice of mine, but whatever).

Once inside, he checked all his mirrors and the dashboard as if he hadn't been the only person driving it for the last day or two. It wasn't like Ian was tootling around town in it. "Um," he said. "Put your seat belt on."

"Way ahead of you," I said, snapping at the belt with my fingertips.

"Oh. Okay. You're going to have to tell me how to get there," he added.

"No problem." I'd printed out map directions to and from the parkour meeting joint, as well as a larger map of the neighborhood in case we had to improvise an escape. Or in case we felt like going for gelato afterward.

You never know.

The field club meeting went down in a building that hosted a dive bar, a Christian Scientist bookstore, and empty restoration lofts. Upon parking a block or two away, paying for a sticker (you never know when those bastards are watching the lots), and poking around the building a bit, we realized that the empty and restored segment of the old building was populated after all. On the second floor a light was on and I could hear voices, and down by the stairwell was a handwritten sign that said, FIELD CLUB USE CODE #3314, COME TO ROOM 212.

Cal went to input the digits but I put out a hand and caught him by the arm.

I said, "Remember. You and me, we just showed up for this shindig around the same time. We don't know each other."

"I remember," he said.

"And you should probably be aware, I'm going to let myself be a little . . . uh . . . conspicuous. I want to see if these guys would know a vampire if she—I mean, you know. If she walked up and bit them."

His eyes widened. "You're not going to—"

"No, I'm not planning to *bite* anybody." It'd only been a week or two since I'd nibbled on the unfortunate Trevor, and I'd be set for another week or two, no problem. The extra blood I had in the bag was a backup just in case. Or to be more precise, just in case I got hurt and needed a quick hit to heal myself up enough to run. The blood would taste like ass and lose efficiency after a few hours, but I was crossing my fingers that "a few hours" would be plenty of time to get in and out of this joint.

I said, "I'm not going to sashay up there in a cape and you're not going to behave like Renfield. I only want to see if they're looking for some of the telltale signs that mark me as something else. I want to know if they're trained to spot us, or if they have experience dealing with us. Do you understand?"

He scratched nervously at the back of his neck. "Yeah, I guess." Oh, we were back on *that* again. "Just . . . I'm. I don't know. Be careful, is all. Ian wouldn't like it if you got yourself captured, or anything."

"That'd make a pair of us," I said curtly, but I was somewhat warmed.

"I mean, he'd want to come after you, you know? He'd want to try and rescue you, but with his eyes . . . like they are . . . I don't know. I don't know what he'd do. He's a capable man, but . . . I don't know what he'd do."

I didn't know either, so I said, "Let's not get ahead of ourselves," as if that wasn't something I did all the damn time. "This could turn out to be the most boring night out any two people ever had."

"I'll hold my breath," he muttered.

I pressed the suggested digits into the keypad and a buzzing noise announced that the "security door" was more than willing to buzz itself aside and let us through. Cal let himself inside, and I stayed outside to wait for a slow, steady count of one hundred— then I buzzed myself up and stepped inside a narrow corridor that smelled like newly cut wood and drying cement.

Even before I opened the door to suite 212 I heard a man's voice and the echo of people sitting unquietly in chairs and milling about on a hardwood floor. There's a timbre to it, the sound of people not doing much in a big empty space.

From my vantage point at the bottom of the stairs a couple of floors down, I heard Cal say, "Hello?" in a voice that was firmer than I expected. "Is this the parkour field club?"

"Yes!" said a man inside. He sounded young but authoritative, which is rarely a good combination, in my experience. "Come on in, have a seat. We're just giving an overview to the newbies. Do you count as a newbie?"

"Probably." I could almost hear him shrug.

I took my time, walking up slowly to the correct suite. The door was propped open just a sliver with a plastic wedge. I pushed it, and poked my head around it.

"Hey there!" said someone less authoritative and decidedly younger than the original speaker. The kid was a teenager, maybe a couple of years older than Domino. In the back of my head I had an idea that this was an activity for the eighteen-and-older crowd, but I wasn't about to start quoting chapter and verse from fictional guide manuals within five seconds of entering the room.

So instead I just said "Hey there" back.

The room had quieted considerably, merely by virtue of— I realized almost immediately—the presence of a woman. I was the center of attention, and conspicuous without even trying any fangy little tricks. Almost parroting Cal, I said, "This where the parkour people meet up?"

A large grunt of a man stood arms folded, dressed and posed like a GI Joe action figure. He said, "This is it."

He was maybe in his early thirties. Hard to say. Narrow face with few lines, but deep ones. Crew cut that had his sandy brown hair as tidy as a low-shag velour. He looked to be in charge and I assumed he was the lieutenant, but I didn't accuse him of it.

I let myself shrink, doing that shy thing where you make yourself look smaller and talk somewhat softer, as if gosh darn it, you're only a girl, and lookit all these big strong men. Because I have no shame, that's why.

"Wow, okay. Cool," I said, hoping I was approximating the speech of kids these days, in case I might pass for a teenager myself. I probably didn't, but I knew I looked young and I made myself sound young. "I'm here to learn about it. Is that what this is for?"

"That's what this is for," he said. "Come on in, find yourself a seat. We're just getting started."

"Great," I said, picking a spot toward the back and on the end. There were only four rows of metal folding chairs, each row about six chairs long. Most of the chairs were empty, but half a dozen were occupied—and three or four other guys, the veterans of the group, I guessed, were lurking in the background. They sat up against a folding table like the kind you see at church potlucks, and they fiddled with a coffeemaker or with cigarettes they weren't supposed to be smoking indoors.

Or were they?

In Seattle, there are all these laws about where you can and can't smoke, and mostly the laws amount to "you can't smoke anywhere indoors, and only a few places outdoors." So I might've only been surprised to see it because I'd been in the Northwest so long. Or there was always the chance that D.C. was every bit as strict, and the young bucks over there were demonstrating their powers of rebellion.

I settled into the chair, which creaked under my weight and stank faintly of rust, and I checked out my surroundings in the usual way—scanning for exits (two: the way I'd come in, and a second door on the far side of the room), counting my fellow occupants (ten, including GI Bolton up there), and calculating whether or not I could fight my way out if push came to shove (totally).

No one was sitting on either side of me; my nearest seatmate was three chairs down. He too looked young, and he was looking at me when he thought I wasn't looking. Apparently a girl in the midst is a real treat at a sausage-fest like this.

Even if I hadn't appeared supernaturally young, and if I'd only been the early-twenty-something I'd been at death—I still would've been the oldest person present except for Cal and the cross-armed boy-doll up front.

He glanced at his watch, decided that we were it for the night, and started talking.

"All right, guys . . . and, uh, lady. Welcome to the District's first and premiere parkour field group and urban exploration society. I'm Tyler Bolton and this is my clubhouse, and you can take it or leave it if you like—but I'm here to make sure that everyone knows the rules, knows what to expect, and stays out of trouble. So if you don't want to listen to me, then fuck off and get yourself arrested on somebody else's time."

Nods of agreement went bobbing around the largely unfinished space, echoing off the drywall, the ceiling timbers, and the incongruously shiny wood floors.

I did not nod. I did not move.

Like any other vampire, I can do the spooky no-motion thing, the one Adrian had already called me out over. If I'm paying attention, I can hide it fairly well, though not perfectly. If I'm *not* paying attention, or if I'm perfectly happy to have it noticed, I stick out like a dead squirrel in a pile of puppies.

So I did my best to stick out. And although I got the intermittent side-eye glance or outright leer, at no point did I feel that I was making anyone nervous, or interested in any fashion beyond the prurient.

GI Bolton continued. "After this general introduction, we'll be adjourning to Rock Creek Park for some low-level introductory parkour—by which I mean, the kind that isn't likely to get you killed, but ought to be fun."

More nods. More murmurs. Not from me.

But I caught the lieutenant's eye. Or he caught mine, as the case may be. Regardless, I saw him looking just a smidge too long, and something about the gaze felt intensely curious beyond the expected. I wanted to close my eyes—they were getting dry, pried open corpse-like as I sat there—but I didn't. I held my unblinking ground and tried to use my psychic feelers, even though they were kind of shit in this sort of situation.

Too many people. Hard to single out just one. Too many shit-head boys thinking inappropriate (yet immensely flattering) thoughts about me.

Mostly I made them uncertain, it seemed. They didn't know girls were invited into this clubhouse, and at least one asshole in the front row was hoping that I wasn't any good at this parkour thing. I swear, some men just can't stand the thought of being beaten by a woman. At anything. Funny. In my experience, and as a matter of irony, they're the men who most desperately need a good ass-kicking.

I was aware of Cal's . . . well, not his *thoughts* exactly. More like the presence of thoughts, or the presence of *him*—sitting ramrod-straight in his chair, displaying better posture than I'd seen him use yet. He was antsy, and fighting the impulse to look over his shoulder at me. For reassurance? For confirmation that I was present? I couldn't tell. His motives were too tangled for me to do more than scan him. I wished for a second that I had Ian's link with him, and I could pass along a tiny nudge of encouragement. But I didn't have that link, so when I concentrated hard and thought, right at the back of his head, *You're doing a good job. Keep your eyes on the beefy grunt up front.* I had no way of knowing whether or not he'd heard me.

"We have a van outside to take us to the park," the grunt up front announced, and I realized I'd probably missed a few key phrases while I was doing my amateur-hour psychic spelunking. "Though the park is open to the public, we have special permission from the park service to cordon off one acre for use with our activities. Some of you guys who've been doing this longer can go ahead and get your pissing and moaning out of the way now, but the newbies have to start somewhere, and this is a safe place to test your physical capacity and your commitment to the sport. Any questions?"

I raised my hand so swiftly that it would've shocked anyone who'd watched me do it. But no one was watching, much to my chagrin. The hand successfully drew Bolton's attention, though, and he pointed at me. The finger-point was accompanied by that gaze, the same one that I'd felt earlier. It was not exactly a knowing gaze, but a suspicious one.

I had the floor, so I asked, "I know what parkour is and I'm pretty sure I'll be fine, but I want to know what that other thing is."

"What other thing?"

"The other thing you said, at the beginning. Urban exploring. What's that?" As if I didn't know. I thought of my storehouse, and of Domino and Pepper, and it was all I could do to keep from seething.

I felt it more intensely, when he looked at me now. His interest was less a vague fog in a room full of mist, and more like a flashlight beam. "We'll get to that later."

"Well, before we get to it, I want to know what it is." Really, I wanted to get his attention and get him talking. I wanted him to look at me and know that something was wrong.

I lucked out and a couple of the other guys in front of me were ignorant on the matter, and they mumbled that they, too, would like some information. I was half afraid Cal would chime in, but he didn't.

Good ghoul, Cal. Don't agree with me too much. Don't even notice me. Don't forget, you're mostly here in case something goes horribly, horribly wrong.

"All right," Bolton relented. The irritated twitch to one eyebrow told me that this was considered jumping some gun, somewhere, and that I'd derailed his evening's lesson plans. But he was game, and so he said, "Urban exploration is, at its core, a propensity toward trespassing in abandoned buildings. It doesn't always go hand in hand with parkour, but you could . . . I don't know. You could think of it as a master's class in parkour, if you wanted to."

"A master's class with night-vision goggles and burglary gear?"

I followed up, knowing I was pushing my luck and wondering if it wasn't too much—if he didn't have some secret panic button hidden in his uniform, or a lackey at the table behind me. Any moment, the doors could burst in and armed maniacs from Project Bloodshot (or whatever it'd morphed into) would take me away and drop me in a basement on an island, never to be seen again.

Or I could needle the fucker a little more and trust my powers of bullshit and escape to see me through. I squeezed the handles of my go-bag and it gave me confidence. Maybe undue confidence. It didn't matter.

"No," he barked. "We don't do that kind of thing."

Everybody in the room instantly thought he was lying.

He stuck to his guns anyway. "It's not a master's class because anybody's burglarizing anything. It's a master's class because there's a lot of legal legwork to untangle, making sure that the abandoned buildings are actually abandoned, and that they don't belong to anybody who'll prosecute if you get caught. Working your way up to urban exploration also means you go out there with a good working knowledge of the distinctions between breaking-and-entering and merely trespassing, and the legal hairsplitting that can mean the difference between jail time and a slap on the wrist. But since that's the master's class and this is the bunny slope, we're going to save that for later, Miss . . ."

He was clearly cueing me to give him a name, so I said, "Raylene. Raylene Spade."

"Spade, very nice," he said, and I felt a stab of condescension that said he knew for a fact that I was lying. I didn't like the condescension because it had come radiating off him, flaring through my psychic radar like a laser beam, not a flashlight. Oh yes. He knew something now, or he suspected it so positively that the semantics wouldn't mean the difference between saving my ass and becoming a pain in his.

"Something funny about that?" I played it cool.

"Not at all, Miss Spade. But we'll save the UE talk for later and for now, if you don't mind, we'll talk brass tacks instead."

What a stupid expression. There were no tacks involved, and not much that any idiot who'd ever seen a cop show on television couldn't have sussed out. That which followed was a miniature thesis on how to fall without breaking an ankle, how to roll without bashing your head in, and how to climb without tearing all the skin off your knees. It was basically a twenty-minute starter class on stunt falls, and I could see how it might be useful to some of the pasty-faced high-schoolers present, but I had to pretend to give it my rapt attention while my real attention wandered elsewhere.

Near as I could gather—a qualifier that was in no way authoritative—Bolton seemed to be alone, insomuch as he seemed to be the only military representative present. If anyone else was there on Uncle Sam's dime, he was out of uniform and keeping his allegiances to himself. But as I'd previously speculated, that didn't mean Bolton didn't have an easy means of summoning more of his camo-uniformed buddies at a moment's notice.

I didn't really know anything. I had nothing but suspicion and a crappy psychic sense urging me to play my cards carefully. I kept an eagle eye on Bolton as he pranced back and forth up front, lacking only a long wooden pointer and a blackboard to be a junior caricature of Patton himself. Wait. Did Patton have either of those things? Or just a big American flag behind him? Maybe I'm confusing him with John Madden.

Things eventually wound down and Bolton quit pacing up front, announcing that this was the time for people to finish up coffee and use the restroom before getting into the van and heading out to the park. And just this once, the line for the men's room was the slow-moving one.

Actually, I think there was only one bathroom, one small

single-seater with a naked yellow bulb and a box of matches for air freshener. Thank Christ I didn't need to go. No woman anywhere wants to follow that filthy man-funk parade to a potty. I may have been functionally dead for a few decades, but some things never change. And trust me, that's one of 'em.

While the boys lined up to do their duty, at least the ones who had to go, I considered sidling up to the lieutenant but he sidled up to me first, giving me quite a start. "Why hello there," I said, shooting for *casual but idly interested, and ooh, aren't you kind of cute?* This was a stretch, since his sudden appearance had in no way charmed me and frankly made me a little worried, but this had been the plan, hadn't it? Figure out if he—or anyone else affiliated with the club—knew about my kind.

I hadn't thought past the point where he might. If he were utterly clueless, that'd be one thing. I'd write it off and continue exploring the exciting and aerobic world of parkour for fun and fitness (as the awkward marketing text suggested). But if he knew? About me? I hadn't considered that far in advance. Because it's always the one thing I don't think about that turns around to bite me in the ass.

He said, "Hey. You new in town?" Only it didn't sound like a line. It sounded like he actually wanted to know, in a calculating fashion.

"Sort of."

"I can't place your accent."

"Oh. I wasn't aware that I had one," I said coyly. I knew I didn't have one. I'd been in the Northwest long enough to have matched the bland diction that's so common there. Unless you want to argue that the absence of an accent is an accent in itself, in which case I'd have to kick you in the shins. And I can kick very hard.

"Where'd you move here from?"

"I haven't moved here from anywhere. Just visiting. Saw your flyer. Thought I'd check this out on my free night. It was either this or wander around on the lawn with a map of the big white monuments, trying to tell the difference and deciding whether or not to care."

He grunted like a man from a tourist town who'd already seen all the tourist bits himself. "Okay. Welcome, then."

Standing so close like that, almost right up against me in a fashion that might be considered harassment under different circumstances, he was a whole goddamn cluster of laser beams, projecting his intentions like a searchlight on a river. He'd locked on to me, and I didn't like it. I didn't like his welcome. I didn't want it. And suddenly I didn't want to be anywhere near him, and I considered bolting on the spot except that a flash of panic kept me standing there, not quite touching this guy and not quite running away.

"Thanks," I said. My mouth was dry. His was predatory. I lowered my voice, thinking it might be best to barrel forward, rather than play patty-cake politics until he could rouse the cavalry and have me carted off. So I said, "Maybe we could take a moment to talk in private, eh, Lieutenant?"

"Why would we do that?" Ah. Not stupid. Not wanting to be alone with me, even though a casual observer might've assumed that was all he wanted. The body language is not so different, when you watch it from afar.

"Because I want to ask you some questions. And you want to ask me some, too, or maybe you don't want to ask me anything. Maybe you just want to get the hell away from me and get on with your Cub Scout activities."

"You're quite a—"

I turned to face him full-on, letting him get a good and nasty look at my too-black eyes and my too-white skin with the fragile blue veins crawling spider-like beneath it. I wasn't wearing any makeup and that, too, had been deliberate. "Look buddy," I growled, still keeping it quiet. "I know about your program, and I know what you're doing here, rounding up these assholes for re-connaissance." I used Major Bruner's word. The one that gave me the shakes if I thought about it too hard.

"You don't know *dick*," he argued.

Trying to lure him now, trying to draw him outside, I turned my back to him halfway and began to ooze toward the rearward door where the back stairs appeared to be. "Dick? Oh, I know him. But I think his name is actually Bruner," I sneered, keeping close watch on his face as I retreated.

"Boss?" somebody said. One of the young grunts, the parkour acolytes.

"Not now!" he hissed, reaching out to take me by the arm.

I moved it out of his grasp fast enough to make his eyebrows shoot skyward. And still it looked like I hadn't moved at all. Cat-like, I lingered a step beyond him, but I did not run. "We should talk," I told him.

And I practically slithered toward the stairs.

He shuffled behind me, too heavy and loud for a man who taught a class on how to sneak around and run away, but maybe he was just that nervous. He was young after all, and maybe he'd heard lots about my kind but hadn't encountered many of us.

Or, as I considered with scorn, it might be that he'd only ever encountered us while we were restrained, or blinded, or crippled, or dead. The very thought made me want to turn around and rip his head off but I didn't, not yet. Self-restraint is not one of my chief virtues, but self-preservation is—and I still had my uncertainties to anchor me to nonviolence.

We slipped together into the stairwell and let the door ease shut behind us. It was dark in there, and would've been romantic or, like, totally hot under different circumstances. He started to talk, but I wasn't listening yet. I was looking upstairs and down-stairs, and opening my psychic sense to feel around for other peo-ple in either direction. I was wondering about the bare lightbulbs screwed into the wall fixtures at the platforms where the stairs lev-eled, and turned.

"What are you doing here—what are you *really* doing here? I know what you are, yes, if that's what you want to know. I know, and I'm not going to sit here and bring you along on one of these game nights, just to have you toy with the kids who—"

I caught up to his rambling and chose this point to interrupt. "Toy?" I blurted. "You accuse me of planning to toy with your Boy Scouts? A fine attitude, you motherfucker, given what you've been known to do to *my* breed."

"I don't know what you're talking about."

"Project Bloodshot, and Major Bruner and his sick Nazi ex-periments."

He paled. "Bloodshot's a closed program," he insisted.

"That's what I heard, but that's not what I'm seeing. Bruner's still at it, and you're in it with him."

"No. You have no idea!"

"Then what's this for? These junior paramilitary enthusiasts? Don't try to tell me you're not using them for recon; don't lie to me and say that this is some stupid extracurricular activity. You're sending them after us, using them as disposable pawns to track down safe spots and homes, and then raid them and turn them in-side out."

"No one said they were disposable," he objected. I couldn't gauge his sincerity. He was too rattled by being so close to me, which told me I was probably a novelty. A known novelty, but a novelty all the same.

"You send them into facilities that are owned and maintained by vampires, unarmed," I added, remembering Trevor's utter lack of defensive weaponry. "If you don't expect them to get killed, you're stupider than you look."

"Fuck you," he said, resorting to that last argument of vice presidents.

"I know you're working with Bruner," I added. "I know he's been using parkour clubs like this to scout, and I know he recommends this one in particular."

"Then what do you want?" he asked, hands in the air in a shrug that might've been reaching for a weapon for all I could see. I had an image in mind of Bruce Willis in *Die Hard,* with the guns duct-taped to his back (see? A thousand and one uses). So rather than take any Hollywood-inspired chances I kicked him backward against the stairs, hard enough to take his breath away and keep it away for a few seconds.

I used this interlude to stand over him. "I want to know what it'll take to close the program. For good this time."

"You're . . . out of . . . your mind," he wheezed, clutching at his chest.

I jammed my foot down on top of his fingers, pressing harder against the place where I'd kicked, and where I suspected a rib or two had cracked, and must surely be jabbing against his lungs. He grimaced and grabbed at my calf, trying to force me off. If I gave him time, he'd do it. I'm crazy strong but I don't weigh much, and he probably had me beat by eighty pounds.

I said, "His funding was pulled years ago, and he's retired. So he's gone civilian. Using mercenaries and someone else's money."

"Is that what you think?"

"Yeah, that's what I think." I jerked backward, clipping his jaw with the toe of my boot as I retreated. "And I'm not alone. Not like you are," I said, trying to make it menacing and cruel.

"Oh yeah, that's me. Lone gunman, grassy knoll. You already know it's Bruner's pet project. So go after him, for fuck's sake!"

He was getting scared, and I liked it. I could also smell a little blood. Maybe he'd bitten his tongue? "But Bruner isn't acting alone. Someone's signing his checks."

"I don't know anything about that," he said, and the words came out with a whistle. His right hand was sneaking toward his boot, so I kicked that, too—and a flash of metal flicked out of his hand to clatter on the stairs below.

"Pathetic," I said. "Big man like you, trying to take a tiny vamp like me. Cheating, and still not getting anywhere. That ought to tell you something, dickwad. It ought to give you some idea of what we're capable of—and if it scares you, well, it ought to. You know what?" I blathered on, oblivious to the events on the other side of the door, whatever they were. "I'm not even the oldest or strongest of my kind. Not by a long shot. I'm just the little lady who twigged to your schemes first. I've already pulled a few friends onto this . . . onto this *case*," I called it the only thing that fit. "And we're going to put a stop to it. All of it."

"And how do you think you're going to do that? You can't just delete a few files, kill a few people, and it'll all be over!"

I knew that already, so I asked: "Where's the money coming from, then?" Because shutting off the money was the one surefire way to shut down the program—and that was the one big puzzle piece I was missing.

"Private backer. Nobody knows who he is."

"Give me something I can work with," I ordered, "and I might let you walk out of here in one piece."

"All I do is . . . I just herd the volunteers, that's all."

"Kids like these, I get it. And just a few minutes ago you were telling me how they weren't disposable."

He shook his head. "Most of these kids never go near anything interesting. Only the A-grade gets recommended up the food chain. That's all I do. Send them up the food chain."

"Fine choice of words," I said.

"You know what I mean!"

"Yeah, I know what you mean." And it didn't make him a choir-boy, even if I thought he was telling the whole truth, and I didn't.

While I stood there deciding what else to ask, if anything, he wanted to know, "Then what about me?" He was wobbly, trying to sit up. I thought I heard something scrape and slide—definitely a rib.

"What about you? Oh, darling," I said with a purr, having concluded that really, there was no way out for Mr. Bolton. Not now. Not unless I wanted him to go running to his boss and let the whole world know I was in town ahead of schedule. "You're going to give Bruner a message for me. That's what you're going to do."

"A message?"

"That's right." I reached back quickly to the spot on the stairs where the knife had fallen. It was a good one, gator-edged and curved. Probably a climber's knife, made to slice through bungee cables and ropes. I didn't want it. But I picked it up anyway, and I chucked it hard up at the nearest gleaming yellow bulb, smashing it with a clatter and plunging the stairwell into total darkness.

In a flash I turned to the stairwell door and found the sliding bolt I'd spotted as we'd exited. I slipped it into the locked position and then I turned to Lieutenant Bolton, who was attempting a backward scramble up, as if it'd take him away from me.

And then I fell on him, shoving his head to the side and baring his neck for optimum heavy nibbling. Yes, I remembered what I'd told Cal about nobody getting bitten, but come on.

I'm a big fat liar.

13

Cal swore under his breath, copiously and repeat-edly, all the way back from the parkour meeting. He knew what I'd done. He wasn't psychic or anything; I'd told him, quietly, right before we made a hasty exit back to the rental car and out of the neighborhood.

"You *said* you weren't going to bite anybody."

"I wasn't *planning* to." But I'd been leaving it on the table because sometimes you just have to play these things by ear. Sometimes you get a good eyeful of a man-sized action figure—and he knows what you are, and what you can do . . . and you know what he is, and what he's done before, or what he's helping other people do. And you just can't stand it because for all his bluster and bullshit he's weak and horrible, and cowardly, and if he caught you, he'd do terrible things to you—the kinds of things that were done to Ian and Isabelle.

Adrian wouldn't have any pissy moral qualms about what I'd done. Ian probably wouldn't, either.

"I can't believe you're being such a bitch about this," I said to Cal, whose lips were jammed together in a grouch-face scowl.

"I don't care that he's dead. I don't even care that you killed him," he insisted, lips still drawn tighter than a clothesline. "I care that you deliberately endangered yourself—and me, let's not forget *me*—after all your careful planning, and all your . . . all your crazy, self-righteous talk about being prepared for anything!"

"Who's self-righteous?" I demanded. I'd own up to crazy any day of the week, but self-righteous I was prepared to fight.

"*You*—you act like you've got everything under control, like nothing that happens will surprise or inconvenience you, and everything is covered all the time because you've made all these preparations. These *crazy* fucking preparations. Did you even use anything at all in that bag of yours?"

"No, but I might use some of it later." And I almost certainly would, once I got rid of this crybaby and picked up my drag queen.

His nostrils flared but he kept his eyes on the road. Deliberately, I assumed. Not wanting to look at me. "We were only supposed to be there looking around. And you didn't *just* look around. You didn't *just* ask questions. You could've gotten us both rounded up and . . . and *wrangled*."

Wrangled. Stupid word.

"Wrangled, mangled. Lots of things could've happened, but didn't. And yes, I said I was there to look around, and hey—I looked around. I came to some conclusions and acted on new information. You know what, Cal? That's called *flexibility*. You're one rigid son of a bitch, and someday it'll get you killed."

"I'm more careful than you are."

"You're . . . ?" I was flabbergasted. "Do you seriously want to play *Who's More Careful* with me? Because I'll wipe the floor with you, junior. I've been around longer than your great-grandparents and I've had plenty of time to become the carefulest person you'll ever meet!"

He shook his head, eyes still locked on the road, to the traffic light and to the rear bumper of the car in front of us. "I'm more careful. Ian's more careful. Lots of people are more careful than you. You're reckless as hell, but you're lucky. That's all."

"Fuck you," I said.

"No, you know what? I take that back. You're *not* lucky. You *are* prepared, just like you like to go on and on and on about. Your ridiculous plans for things that never happen, okay—it's your coping mechanism, I get that. And it's a damn good thing you have it. Otherwise you'd have never made it to thirty behaving the way you do. Sometimes, I guess, you save your own ass. But you're always the one putting your own ass in danger first. And I don't want to be any part of it." His nostrils rippled and billowed like peep-show curtains. "And I don't like Ian being any part of it."

Ah, the meat of the matter. "Don't worry, *ghoul*. In another night or two I'll be out of your hair and you and Ian can go back to your little love nest or whatever—and you'll never have to hear from me again."

"Yeah, well, I thought that would be the case once we got his records, but it wasn't. Here we are, still hanging around. Here I am, driving the getaway car from the scene of a murder—"

"Scene of a snack."

"—and Ian won't leave yet, not while he thinks you've got more to learn or more to tell him. But you don't fool *me*."

"Oh I don't?" I asked rhetorically. Previously I'd had him fooled on a number of points, but this was not the time to rub it in.

"No, you don't. You're just a selfish brat with a big bank account, and there's nothing you can tell us that will do us any more good. Ian's already sent the records up to his doctor in Canada, and there's no damn reason—" He swatted the steering wheel in a tepid display of anger. "—none at all for us to be hanging around D.C. waiting for you to expose everything, and everybody. Waiting for you to get us all killed, or worse."

"Oh ye of little faith," I said, watching the breathless thrall squeeze and unsqueeze the finger notches on the wheel. "And for your information I *like* Ian, and I have no intention of putting him into any danger. Or you either, you little shit." I went immediately for Domino's pet name and suddenly felt unfaithful for it. At the moment, I was actually feeling kindly disposed toward the quasi-homeless kid, but this fucking hipster was jumping rope on my last nerve.

"I didn't put you in any danger," I went on, "and I didn't leave you there stranded, like I could have. I didn't even leave the body anywhere that someone would stumble over it anytime soon. We're in the clear. They'll wonder where he went, wait around for a while, and then start looking. We have plenty of getaway time and nothing to tie us to him, or to what happened to him."

"Except a room full of people."

"Less than a dozen people," I said. "Maybe they'll describe me in more detail than 'uh, some girl' and maybe they won't. But nobody knows we arrived together, and I don't think anyone noticed we left together. I'm telling you, we're in the clear. Everything's fine."

"Where'd you put him?"

"I took him upstairs and stuffed him in the bathroom. Renovation hasn't reached that far yet, and the whole floor looks like nobody's gone up there in a hundred years."

"You stuck him in a bathroom and figured that'd cover it?"

I gritted my teeth and said slowly, "I stuck him . . . in an *unusable* bathroom . . . on a *disused* floor . . . of a building that's more abandoned than occupied. I had to almost pull a door off its hinges because it'd rusted shut. Nobody's going to look there for ages. Not until he starts to smell, and maybe not even then."

I had no idea if I was telling him the truth or not, but the general fact of the matter stood: We had plenty of time to leave the scene, and we were unlikely to be connected to it. We'd be thousands of miles away before anyone even thought to ask the parkour kids what had happened the night that GI Jackass went missing.

"Maybe that's your problem," I mused aloud.

"What? What's my problem?" he asked with the kind of scorn that told me he'd like to give a dissertation on *my* problems (as he perceived them), but he was good enough to let me finish.

"You're not good enough at getting away."

"What's that supposed to mean?"

"It means that fleeing the scene is an art, and I've damn well mastered it. You can get away with a tiny bit of sloppiness so long as the getaway is clean."

"But it *isn't*," he sulked. "We're still here, in town. And it's too late for any of us to leave tonight."

"You could leave," I noted. "Adrian could leave."

"I won't leave Ian, and Adrian won't leave until he's burned down the whole world, or at least the part of it that killed his sister. I don't know what you think is going to happen with that lunatic, but you can't give him what he wants."

"You may be right," I muttered.

"What?" I heard his honest disbelief, and nearly smiled but didn't.

"You heard me. I said, you might be right. I can't give him his sister back, and he's just going to run around breaking things until he figures out that she isn't coming home, and nothing he can do is going to change that."

"So you're using him."

A little too astute for his own good. See? Ghouls. Bad news, the lot of them. "Sure, I'm using him. But he's using me, too. He spent years sitting on the evidence that covered up his sister's death, not having a clue what to do with it until I came along."

"How very gallant of you."

"He needs me more than I need him, and at least he's not a useless Seeing Eye ghoul."

"Then why didn't *he* come on this errand with you?"

I growled, "We've been over this. You were the only warm body we could trust, and Ian agreed that I could use some backup—if only to spread the word that I'd made a wreck of things, brought down the parkour school in a blaze of glory, and gone home to Jesus."

"It's a shame I won't be bringing that message back," he said, which was needlessly mean, in my opinion.

"Is that so?"

"Sure it's so. If you'd crashed and burned, at least the rest of us would be headed home."

"Tough shit. You're not headed home, you're headed back to the hotel with me, and if you don't like it you can stuff it up your ass and let it melt." I leaned back in the car's cheap fabric seats and crossed my arms, tired of fighting with him. All it did was make me angry, and all I did was make him accusatory.

The fact was, I didn't give a damn what he thought. I liked Ian—hell, maybe I liked him more than was strictly smart, given the circumstances—but when all was said and done he was a client, and I'd come through on the assignment, and all that remained was for him to pay me. Then we could move on with our lives, never seeing one another again.

Literally, and figuratively.

That'd be best for everyone. We'd sort it out when Adrian and

I returned from doing our own little reconnaissance on Major Bruner's office. We'd make our arrangements, write our checks, see one another off, and that'd be the end of it.

When we reached the curb, Cal dropped me off on the sidewalk and went to park the Malibu under the building. I left him to it, and went upstairs to the rooms—adjoining suites—wherein I'd find two guys whose company I could actually stand.

Adrian answered the door when I knocked, and his hand was behind his back. "Oh. It's you."

"You were expecting . . . ?" I fed him the straight line, but he didn't bite. He only withdrew that hand and revealed the big carbon steel blade that looked obnoxiously familiar. "Hey, that's mine!"

"I know," he said with a shrug. "But you can't be too careful."

"Hardy har *har*."

"What's that supposed to mean?" he asked.

"Who's More Careful," I muttered, pushing past him into the room. "Stupid Cal."

"What?"

"Never mind."

Ian was sitting on the couch, facing the television, which was broadcasting a PBS special about submarine disasters of the thirties. Listening, I assumed, since he obviously couldn't watch it. But he asked, "Where's Cal?"

"He's parking the car. I had him drop me off."

"Ah. Should I assume that things went reasonably well, since you seem to be in one piece?"

"You should absolutely assume that," I said. "Though you should be aware that I might have sort of, hypothetically, killed Lieutenant Bolton."

"Hypothetically?" Adrian asked.

"Okay, so I totally killed him. And I figured I'd bring that up before Cal came upstairs being all morally superior and trying to call me out about it."

Ian's mouth turned up in a faint smile, but stopped in a pose of bemusement. "I don't suppose he would've approved of that."

"No. I heard about it all the way back," I complained.

"Did you draw any undue attention to yourself, or to him?" he asked.

"No. Except that I drew out GI Jerk-face for a private conversation. I don't think anyone saw me do it, and we'll be long gone from D.C. before anybody goes looking for him," I concluded with more confidence than I felt.

Maybe Cal's admonitions had worn me down more than I thought.

"I'm prepared to trust you on that matter," said Ian. "Did you learn anything important from the man, before you made him into supper?"

"Yes and no. He confirmed some suspicions, and tried to point all the blame at Bruner—which may or may not be fair. He insisted that Project Bloodshot was closed, and that any further activities related thereunto were squarely on the major's now-civilian shoulders. Except that it's being funded by someone else. He claimed not to know who."

"Do you believe him?"

"More or less. And I was right about Bruner using parkour clubs to scout for trespassers."

"Trespassers?"

"Pawns. Disposable ones." I sat down on the end of the love seat and drew up one leg so I could face Ian. Then I admitted, "I think Bolton might have actually seen it differently. He took umbrage at my suggestion that he was rounding up these kids for the slaughter. Maybe he assumed it was just a covert recruitment pro-gram. Maybe he didn't know exactly what they'd be called upon to do, or how dangerous it would be."

Adrian folded his arms and leaned, as he was prone to doing. "Maybe?"

"Maybe. And he's too dead to ask for clarification now. So," I tried, changing the subject. "What about you two? What'd you do while we were out wreaking havoc and killing people?"

"Watched TV," said Adrian.

Ian smiled graciously and nodded. "I kept an ear on it. Ah. Here comes Cal."

My joy overfloweth.

Sure enough, as predicted, he skulked into the room, shot me a disparaging look, and greeted his master. "Did she tell you she killed a guy?" he asked without any preamble.

"She told us," Ian confirmed. "I'm sure she had her reasons."

"I bet she did. So does this mean you two—" He made windshield-wiper finger gestures back and forth between me and Adrian. "—will be heading out now? I'm tired, and I'd like to set-tle in."

"Enough adventuring for one evening, eh?" Ian asked, casual and not at all curious, probably knowing that Cal would be happy to settle down anyplace away from me. His loathing reeked off him like cheap cologne.

"Plenty," he said.

"Great. Give me the keys," I said.

"Give you my keys?" he parroted so high it was almost a squeal.

"You heard me," I told him. "We don't have a car yet, and there's no such thing as a getaway bus. Remember what I was telling you?"

"I remember," he grumbled as he forked over the keys with a

slap. "Here. Take them. But it's under my name, you know. So take care of it."

I thought surely he must be joking, even though it didn't sound like it. Who used real names anymore? Sometimes people are a mystery to me.

I let Cal off the hook by giving a *let's go* head-nod to Adrian and saying, "Don't worry, Cal, I'm done with you for now. You two have a lovely rest-of-your-evening, and we'll be back in a few hours."

Cal practically shoved us out the door and locked it behind us with what I felt was unnecessary, insulting speed. But the clack of the lock and the flip of the deadbolt made me feel like they were safe and secure, or at least staying put for now.

Adrian said, "You sure know how to win friends and influence people."

"That's why they call me Raylene. It's Greek for 'charming.'"

"You're so full of shit," he observed.

"You're not the first to suggest it. You ready to hit the town?"

"Ready as I'll ever be."

He was tense. Really tense. It looked good on him; made all his manly muscles and lumps stand out, even though they were squeezed in close by the black ribbed sweater that fit him like everything else he owned: perfectly. I knew it was new. I knew he'd gone through my bag and taken money while I was asleep. So long as he didn't go nuts with it, I didn't mind. It was only money, after all. It's not like I didn't have more of it stashed all over the place, and what was I going to do? Lecture him on the evils of petty thievery?

When we'd bolted from the Poppycock Review he'd been wearing not much more than some glitter and a smile. His next set of duds came off Peter Desarme, but I didn't assume he'd pulled the rest of his wardrobe out of his ass . . . or from wherever he tucked his—

Never mind. I retrieved my wandering thoughts from the gutter.

We reached the car, and I adjusted all the mirrors and seat so I could drive without feeling Cal's butt-print beneath me. Even if I was only imagining it.

On the other side of the neighborhood we found office buildings of a bland and utilitarian nature, though here and there were older structures in brick or stone. We parked Cal's rental two blocks away in a lot between two office buildings that were almost fully dark—save a few pinpoints of light where the last unfortunate souls were chained to their desks, working late. We liked that particular lot because it was almost entirely devoid of light, and running low on other cars, too. These two details were possibly related, or possibly not. There's no telling in D.C.

Murder capital of the nation. Or so I've heard.

And, I supposed, I'd already done my part to contribute to the beastly reputation of the place. One new murder so far, but the night was still young.

I closed up the car, took my go-bag and slung it around my chest, and watched Adrian feel himself up—checking for equipment, supplies, structural stability, whatever. It was worth watching.

Between him and Ian, I was getting more eye candy in a week than I'd enjoyed in years. Different brands of candy to be sure, but you didn't hear me complaining about it.

I hadn't been able to scare up much in the line of building schematics when it came to Major Bruner's office, which was kind of surprising. Government buildings are often their own little forts, but private industry structures—like the one where this guy's office was located—tended to be a little easier to crack. But all I could find out indicated that it was owned by some California company registered to someone named Jeffery Sykes. I could hardly turn up a damn thing about the offices, conference rooms, storage facilities, or shit—even the vending machines. Nine times out of ten, the vending-machine companies are an easy back door to places like that. Somebody from Coke or Pepsi has to restock the soda machines, and usually a rep from Starbucks or Folgers is keeping tabs on the coffeemakers.

Almost every actively used building everywhere has a thousand and one ways inside.

I wished I had more time to research and familiarize myself with a few of them, but it was like I'd told everyone earlier: They already knew we were coming. We needed to act before they knew we'd arrived.

I filed the name Jeffery Sykes away for future investigation. Anyone who makes a building that airtight is up to something. You mark my words.

Anyway, without a good mental layout of the building, Adrian and I paced around the block once or twice, quietly discussing our next move. It didn't look complicated, but looks could be deceiving. We agreed that the route of least resistance and most discretion would probably be the roof, and I left him for a few minutes to scout for cameras. I found three, which meant there were probably twice that number.

But the funny thing about cameras is that, half the time, at least a few of them aren't working. This time, only one of the cameras was totally dead, but hey, I'd take it. Two of the others I adjusted very, very slightly—so slightly that whoever monitored them (if in fact anyone anywhere was doing any monitoring) probably wouldn't notice the change . . . but my tweakings created a blind spot at the back north corner.

I retrieved my partner-in-crime and trusted him to scale the corner without a whole lot of whining about it.

He wasn't quite as swift and effortless about it as I was, but that couldn't be helped. He was only human, after all. But for being only human, he did a damn fine job. We were even able to skip the creaky gutters and fire escapes, because Adrian took the corner rock-climber-style.

I approved.

And in a moment, I was beside him on the roof—crouching down to hide behind the topmost ledge. Before we left the hotel we'd had a conversation about hand signals and keeping quiet, and God bless the man, I didn't have to reinforce or reiterate a bit of it. He was a professional from toes to top, all business. All ready to work in silence.

I loved it. Even though, if you'd asked me a month earlier if I'd enjoy working with a partner, I would've laughed in your face. But I liked this guy. He knew how to behave and he knew how to keep his head down.

It flicked through my mind that he might make a formidable vampire.

But it only flicked. I shook my head to loosen the thought and let it go.

While I was wrestling with my distracting thoughts, he was finding an entrance and taking a small prybar to it. That kind of can-do attitude was just what I wanted to see, so I joined him and gave the low, half-sized door a nudge that flipped it quietly open.

It wasn't a stairwell. That would've been too obvious. This was a maintenance chute that allowed electricians and roofing workers to go down below the surface for repairs and renovations. I wasn't 100 percent positive there would be an outlet down into the main body of the building, but I assumed that should we hit a dead end, we'd find a thin spot where we could cut our way down through the drywall.

Sometimes you have to wing it.

I knew for a pretty safe fact that Adrian would be happy to

wing it with a flamethrower if he could've snuck one inside. As it was, I didn't know how far I could really trust him once we reached the office. I didn't believe he'd do anything dumb, but I had every confidence that he planned to wreak some havoc . . . if those two things can be mutually exclusive.

Like I said, I wasn't sure.

But he knew how to move and he didn't mind getting dirty. That much was clear when we ducked down through the maintenance chute and found ourselves stomping in old mold-smelling insulation that may once have been pink, but was now only some pale, ghastly shade in the dim ambient light from the sky outside.

My feet sank into it and I shuddered at the texture—like cotton candy spun out of glass—but I extricated my boots and found some support beams to stand on instead. I had a feeling I'd be picking that shit off my clothes for days.

Adrian was rustling through his satchel and retrieving a pair of night-vision goggles, which he'd also acquired on my dime and without my official commendation. God knows I didn't need them, but I was glad he had them. We both needed to be able to see if we were going to rely on each other at all.

We hunted, pecked, tiptoed, and ducked our way through the ceiling crawl space—a narrow band between the top floor and the roof. It was just about high enough to allow a midsized dog to walk upright; Adrian and I, being somewhat taller, either went down on all fours or crouched painfully along, hunkering through the near pitch blackness.

I took the lead, and I led by instinct . . . and by virtue of my copious experience.

I headed east, toward the place where I'd perceived a main stairwell while we were outside checking the place out. If there was going to be a hatch of any kind, dumping into the building's main corridors, it would probably be somewhere over the stairs. I had no idea why this tended to be the case, but there you have it. I'm sure an architect or an engineer could lay it out for me, but I can honestly say I don't much care. As long as the generality would hold true, just tonight. Just this once.

It did. Sort of.

Before long we found ourselves atop a promising trapdoor that flat refused to open. So I pulled the long, slim saw out of my bag and went to town, cutting through whatever was keeping the thing from dropping and letting us out. I ended up cutting all the way around, in a full square; and when we finally got the thing to open, I understood why. Someone had plastered over it.

No matter. It was open, and we dropped down—me first, landing light on my toes, then bracing myself to catch Adrian or at least lend him a hand. It was a solid twelve-foot drop to the steps below, and while it didn't bother me in the slightest, I didn't want Adrian to break an ankle.

Much to my delight, he didn't make a manly show of refusing the assistance. He lowered himself through the hole, hanging by his hands, and allowed me to support his feet and knees, then his thighs and his midsection, as he slipped down onto the landing between the sixth floor and the fifth.

I'm not saying I didn't cop a feel, but I *will* cry plausible deniability.

And furthermore, I will add that he was a goddamn magician to get that whole package tucked. I suspect a space–time portal. Or at least I *would* suspect it, if I weren't denying everything. Which I am.

He flashed me a look that said at the same time, *Hey, I felt that . . .* and *I choose to believe it was accidental. For now.*

But no time to dwell on the pleasantries. Soon we were inside.

We had no way of knowing how well the building's interior was being watched, but I'd given him a crash course on how to avoid and disable cameras, and he knew to stay back and let me go first. Not because he wasn't awesome, but because I was smaller and faster, and when I turned on the vampire speed I could even kick up a pace so mighty that most cameras wouldn't detect me at all— or if they did, I'd only turn up as a blur. I can't move that fast for very long, but I'm deadly at a sprint and I had some serious sprinting to do.

We didn't know where Bruner's office was.

So it was Adrian's job to scan for guards and neutralize them in whatever fashion he found most satisfying, and mine to dash from hall to hall in the six-story building, looking for a nameplate or some other indicator that we'd found the bastard's headquarters. When I found it, I'd send a psychic call over to Adrian—who could apparently hear them all right if I focused hard enough, though he couldn't reply. (We'd tested it out a little, since it worked that one time in the Poppycock Review.)

We'd meet back at the stairwell, near our entrance hole, in ten minutes.

He headed down. I stayed up top and worked my way from wing to wing, then went down to the next floor and so forth. I kept myself low and thanked heaven that the lights were all turned down or turned off altogether, with the exception of a few safety lights in the stairwells. I ducked from corner to corner, sweeping the rows of doors with my eyes and trying like hell to read as fast as I could run.

I wasn't finding it, and it was making me mad.

I was down to the third floor and I had about five minutes left on the clock when Adrian hissed at me from somewhere below. He waved to gesture me into the stairwell (where we'd already established that there were no cameras), and then he pissed me right off.

"His office is on the fourth floor. Room four fifty-one," he whispered.

"I've already checked the fourth floor and I didn't see his name anywhere," I insisted. "How do you know that's where his stuff is?"

"Because," he said with a flap of his hand that meant he'd found it somewhere over there, "there's a receptionist desk near the elevator on every floor. Receptionists keep directory sheets."

"Oh. I should've thought of that," I said. "Nice work."

"Thanks. But I'm sure you would've found it eventually."

"How very kind of you to say so," I told him, with an undercurrent of irritation that told him I suspected sarcasm on his part. He didn't disabuse me of the notion. He only started climbing up to the fourth-floor entry door.

I said, "Let me," in order to reestablish my dominance.

I gave the door a careful yank and dashed down the corridor to the camera at the far end. With a twist of my wrist, I re-aimed it to record a corner of wallpaper. It wasn't a permanent solution or even a very good one, but it'd do for the moment. If we were lucky, no one was watching and no one would notice for a few minutes. Anyone who saw the viewing area change might've assumed that a screw or a bolt had given way, and the camera had merely dropped off its mooring. Because he (or she) sure as hell wouldn't have seen me charging toward it.

Unfortunately, the moment I moved the camera I felt like I'd turned over an hourglass. Whereas before we were only being sneaky and taking our time, now we'd done something that could reasonably draw attention.

Now we had to work fast.

"Let's find this office and get the fuck out of here," Adrian suggested.

I didn't have any other plans, so I agreed. I looked at the nearest door and saw the number 443, then said, "Okay, so it's on that side of the hall, evens, odds. It must be down there."

I pointed. He nodded.

And then we heard it. Not a footstep, not a creaking door. Something worse. That goddamn static of a communication device. Faint, but not very distant.

Adrian and I looked at each other. We looked at room 443, which was the wrong room, but the nearest room.

My partner froze beside me, only for an instant. His second instant was devoted to blocking me, like he was tougher than me and could protect me or something. Must've been years of ingrained training, I guess, because there was no way he was tougher than me. One of us could take a couple of bullets and keep on ticking. One of us couldn't.

I shoved back, almost smashing my shoulder through that little window on the door. The whole thing whapped open and we toppled inward just in time to dodge the first wave of fire from the north end of the hallway.

They tore around the corner—suited men, at least. Not commandos, in case that mattered. Their guns were shiny and blazing, and their aim was none too bad. I felt a bullet's hot breath graze my leg as I flew half backward, half sideways, totally dragged by Adrian, into the office.

He swung a leg around and kicked the door shut behind us, as if that'd slow them down longer than a big old sheet of construction paper might. "They're on to us!" he declared.

"No shit, Sherlock!" Though to his credit, he didn't ask anything dumb like "What do we do?" I was the one who blurted out that particular question, even as I was looking around for something big and heavy to block the door.

God bless him forever, he was already bringing down a floor-to-ceiling filing cabinet like a lion on a wildebeest. It toppled down in front of the door, but not so fast that I didn't see a swarm of shadows through the frosted glass. The glass broke. Either the cabinet nicked it or the sheer weight and shake of its falling rattled the thing apart in its frame.

I followed his lead and nabbed the other big-ass cabinet and yanked it down, then shoved it into place. It was huge and sturdy; the pair of them would've done the French Revolution proud so far as improvised barricades went. But there were two main problems in our cute little plan.

One, they wouldn't hold forever. Two, we'd shut ourselves inside. And we weren't even in the right office, so it wasn't like I could pull a repeat performance of the Holtzer Point smash-and-grab.

We were locked in, several offices over from the one we needed, and armed men were outside trying to extract us. And they were prepared to do it the hard way. The harder the better, I suspected.

"We have to get out of here," I said.

"And into room four fifty-one" he said, amending the obvious.

"At this point, I'd settle for just 'out.' We can try again, come back later. Maybe—"

"Maybe what?" He almost shouted it at me, which was totally unnecessary. "Come back sometime when they don't expect us? Because it's pretty fucking obvious they expected us, Raylene!"

"Fine!" I shouted back at him. The guys outside were trying to ram the door, but since they didn't have much room to back up in the narrow hallway, they weren't getting a lot of leverage out of it. Mostly they were making a whole lot of noise. "Fine, they were expecting us! Nothing I can do about it *now*, okay?"

He was already ignoring me, which was fine. I wasn't saying anything important anyway. His eyes scanned the ceiling hard, and my eyes joined them. "What are our options?" he asked, but he wasn't really asking. He was preparing to catalog.

"Window," I pointed out. Smallish, but the only obvious way

outside. It was also a way *in*side, but I wasn't prepared to worry about that yet. One thing at a time. "Two vents."

"I can't fit through those," he said, and in saying that, he said plenty. He looked at me evenly.

"I'm not sure I can, either . . . ," I began, but I was already doing the mental calculations.

"You can. You have to. Give me your gun, and go for it."

"What?" Damn. I was getting good at asking stupid, time-stalling questions when I already knew the answers. "You want to stay holed up in here alone?" I whispered it fiercely, despite the ruckus of the men trying to force aside the cabinets. Lucky for us, the barriers had almost interlocked in their falling—and it'd take something pretty significant to move them . . . at least it'd take real work to move them quickly. Still, we didn't have long. It wouldn't take more than a few minutes for them to figure out they could get at us from another angle. Or, God help us, it wouldn't be much trouble to phone someone for explosives. They could take out half the floor if they wanted us that badly, and I had a feeling we were pretty badly wanted.

"I'll hold them off. You go over to four fifty-one and take every-thing you can."

"And then what?" I demanded. "*I* can jump out a window. As far as I know, you can't!"

"I'll figure out something. Go! We don't have all night."

I jammed a hand into my Useful Things Bag and pulled out the .22, which was all I had on me since I tend not to rely on these things. He looked at it like I'd handed him a straw and a spitball, rolled his eyes, and shooed me over to the vent while he took up a defensive position to the left of the door.

Wasting more time wouldn't get us anywhere. I crammed my-self between the big office desk and the wall, and used my weight to shove it under the larger of the two vents. It was only larger by a marginal value, but it'd have to be larger enough to hold my big ass, so that's what I went for. Forget the screwdriver; we were well past discretion here. I punched my hand through the slim metal grille and ripped the whole thing out of the wall, then without even looking—without even hanging out, calculating my width of ass versus the opening now before me, or anything that might await inside that filthy space—I lunged up and over and squeezed myself up into the metal chute.

I did some quick, thoughtful fiddling and realized with relief that I'd entered facing the right direction, because there was no fucking way I was turning around.

Down in 443, things were hot in a bad way. Behind me as I wriggled I heard all the commotion as the men in the hall rallied, smashed, and shoved. I could also hear someone squawking into a mouthpiece or a walkie-talkie. I caught the words "exterior window" and "demo team" and I didn't like any of it. Backup never bodes well.

There was nothing I could do but squirm faster and try to trust Adrian, who was surely one of the most competent mere mortals I'd met in years. He had a (small, girlie) gun, he had his wits, and he had . . . I don't know. Maybe a silver bikini under his commando-wear, for all I knew.

I counted, dividing by two and guessing at which office would be the right one. My first pick was clearly wrong; I almost let myself down into an empty room that was in the process of being remodeled.

So I went with my next hunch and elbowed my way out of the vent, then caught it before it could hit the ground with a clatter. I'd have to be quiet. The action in the hall was escalating. More people had been called in, and people were shooting again—though I couldn't tell what or whom they were trying to hit.

A set of burly, dark shadows went hustling past the office door with its frosted-glass window inset. No one even glanced inside. Everyone was focused on the maniac holed up in room 443.

I wished that maniac well and dropped myself down quietly . . . onto a rolly-wheeled office chair that nearly sent me skating smack into a wall, but didn't quite.

Recovering with haste but precious little dignity, I took a look around.

Room 451 didn't have Bruner's name affixed to it anyplace that I could see—even in the reverse letters on the other side of the glass—so I felt somewhat better about having missed it the first time around. Instead, upon the pane had been painted the legend OFFICE OF EXPERIMENTAL BIOENGINEERING RESEARCH, which I thought was tacky, if more or less correct. It took me a few precious seconds to parse it because hey, I don't read backward very well, okay?

But I knew I was in the right place.

The office was nothing to write home about. In the center squatted a desk covered with two large phones, a beige desktop computer, and one of those big paper calendars that you treat like a place mat, and behind the desk was a wall of dull gray filing cabinets, two of which had their handles either broken off or rusted off. On the floor beside the desk was a wastepaper basket that had, alas, been freshly emptied. And stuck between the far right filing cabinet and the wall was a duffel bag that turned out to be full of clothes . . . the kind of clothes a man keeps around when he occasionally spends the night at the office—socks, underwear, a clean shirt, and a shoe-polishing kit. The polishing kit struck me as a little anal-retentive, but who am I to judge?

Something kept me rooted to the spot, staring at the certificates of commendation that were framed on the walls and wondering what kind of man could do the kinds of things he'd done.

Did he not understand that the undead were people, too? Or did he disagree? Had a vampire bitten someone he cared about? Was he just a psychotic fucker who would destroy anyone he fancied?

Nothing gave me an answer. Not the cup full of mismatched pens and pencils, or the brown coffee mug without so much as a logo on it.

I went to the wall of cabinets and started with the one farthest from the door. With one ear on the commotion in the hallway (certain that at any second someone would hear me and come busting in), I began to pull them open—locked, all of them, but they all came loose with a twist of my pick, which was quieter than the yank-and-break method—and I started to dig.

Most of what I found, I didn't understand. Code names, project names, and numbers . . . all of it swam together. I forced my eyes open and concentrated hard. In the fifth drawer I found a file labeled PBS. And as I knew, it probably didn't stand for Public Broadcast Service.

But it didn't stand for Project Bloodshot, either. "Project Bandersnatch," I whispered to myself. I poked through it anyway, and swiftly realized that even *ex*-military asshats are positively stupid for continuity. One fast glance down the first few sheets told me that I'd found the right project—or one frighteningly similar to it. And a second fast glance told me these weren't all old records. Some of this paperwork was dated within the last year.

"Officers." I swallowed. "Subjects. Contacts . . ." All with Bruner on top of the letterhead. "Wait a second," I said, momentarily forgetting that Adrian was several offices over, and not in immediate hearing range. I remembered flashing past a cabinet drawer labeled FUNDING, so I went back to my side of the cabinetry and located the folder corresponding to Bandersnatch.

I pulled it out and opened it. "Millions," I said, again wishing

I had someone handy to exclaim to. And all of it was going to the same set of numbers, same set of contacts, as Bloodshot. I didn't have time to get too hung up on the tiny details; I could steal all this stuff and read it later at my leisure. But I couldn't take my eyes off it.

Same officers, same numbers, same contacts. Same program, just lacking government oversight this time.

"Wait. Same contacts," I mumbled, because once you've started talking to yourself, it's hard to stop. I felt like an invisible pop-up ad had leaped off the page and was trying to flag me down.

Harvey Feist, James Ellison, David Keene, Richard Wing.

I singled out the name "David Keene." I shook my head, feeling a flush creep up from the pit of my stomach. They were physicians, affiliated with Bloodshot previously, and Bandersnatch now. It looked like they might've been investors, too, or maybe researchers who did some of the work themselves.

David Keene. Ian's Canadian doctor.

My throat was so pinched and dry that I almost reached for that awful little half pint of blood. "Goddamn," I whispered, taking the papers and stuffing them into my Useful Things Bag.

I reached for a cell phone as I began climbing for the vent again.

We'd left Cal and Ian alone—and there was an excellent chance that Ian had been making some phone calls, asking about those records and trying to figure out if the doc was going to give him back his eyesight.

The phone wasn't getting me anywhere. It gave me nothing but unending rings. No one was picking up.

"Shit," I declared, slammed the cell phone shut, and popped myself back into the vent.

About halfway back I reconsidered. I could leave Adrian. I

could get along just fine without him, couldn't I? Ian and Cal were likely in danger—real and serious danger, perhaps every bit as bad as what was going down over at room 443.

I considered it. I really did, even knowing what a douchebag that would make me.

Then something exploded over near my destination, and I was shocked out of my ambivalence and right into terror. I squeezed and shook, with hardly enough clearance to hold my head up off the dust-smeared interior of the nasty metal tunnel, and I clamored back the way I'd come.

It felt like it took longer, coming back. It felt like I had more like miles to travel than mere yards, but that only made me shimmy faster.

I smelled smoke. It wafted up and inside. I'd only just registered it when I heard gunshots responding from inside room 443. I knew the sound of my piddly .22, and it was up against the kind of firepower I should've brought along, but hadn't.

Something splintered and shattered. The window?

Shouts and protests and bullets, and the prickly static of electronic signals, and I reached 443 with a vengeance—exploding out of the vent and landing smack on the back of the man closing in on Adrian, who was backed up against the far wall. Two bodies were collapsed at his feet, but he was wrestling with a third and now I was on top of the fourth.

Shards of glass glittered on his clothes and yes, the window was completely blasted inward. That's how they got in; I could've figured it out by noticing the filing cabinets were holding their ground (for the time being), but I wasn't thinking that fast. I wasn't thinking past *break this fucker's neck*—which I did—and then a second explosion sent the heavily laden cabinets buckling and scooting into the interior of the room.

One of them stopped right at my feet. My ears were ringing

from the detonation but I was mad now, and I wasn't going to stand there and rub my ears while the Men in Black swarmed inside like ants.

Hell no.

The cabinet had split in two. I picked up the smaller half, torn, smoking, burning-hot metal surface and all, and I swung it as hard as I could—releasing it at the doorway and probably killing the first two guys who were trying to spill inside. Or maybe it just made them a whole lot less pretty.

Adrian was out of bullets. He used the gun to pistol-whip the last window-breaching attacker and then went to the empty hole in the wall to look outside.

I'd moved on to the desk. I upended it and shoved it—hoping it'd work like a cork to buy us time—more time, any time!—and it mostly just succeeded in flattening another couple of black-clad dudes who were too fucking eager. It wasn't going to plug the door. It wasn't quite big enough.

"More outside," Adrian said. For the first time I heard real fear in his voice. Well, now was as good a time as any to be really afraid. We were cornered, outnumbered, and outgunned. "How many in the hall?"

"A dozen?" I estimated. Most of them down toward the north end; only a scattered couple were coming in from the other angle. "How many out there?"

"That many and change. Coming down from the roof and—" He ducked back inside as a spray of fire strafed up from the ground. "—and more waiting below."

"I've got an idea," I exaggerated. It was barely half an idea, but we were going to have to wing this, goddammit, and we couldn't sit around all night with our thumbs up our asses.

"Let's hear it."

I didn't spell it out. I just acted, trusting him to play along.

I seized the upended desk just as someone's arm went reaching around it—and I shoved it hard enough to break the offending arm. I heard a shout of dismay and a groan of pain but I didn't hang around to dwell on it. With a hearty shove I pushed the desk out the door; it squealed along the floor in jerky fits, and it was heavy as hell but I'm pretty damn strong and I kicked it around—using it as cover for the both of us.

Adrian got the drift. I let go of the desk and let him hold it up with his shoulder, and I set to the fast, messy work of disposing of the guys standing between us and the stairwell. There were more than a couple (four by my vicious, bloody count) and they had guns.

They opened fire. I leaped forward, taking down the first one so fast he probably never saw me coming at him. I broke his neck and used him to catch a few bullets from the remaining assholes, then I flung him aside and went after the other three.

One slug caught me just under the collarbone and another went zipping through my side. They both burned like crazy but there was nothing I could do about it right that moment. I worked through the pain and I worked fast, bringing the other guys down one after another while Adrian used that carbon steel blade he'd adopted to hack, slash, and slice any body parts that came jabbing around the desk.

In less time than it takes to write a paragraph about it, the path to the stairwell was clear . . . but probably not for long. I couldn't hear much over the din of close-quarters fighting and gunfire, but when I took an instant to stretch my psychic sense—listening with it, for lack of a better way to put it—I detected people crashing around downstairs, maybe on the first floor. And outside there were cop cars, fire trucks, and other official sorts of vehicles wending their way toward us with the speed of the righteous.

But we didn't have to make it all the way back down. We only had to make it to our hole over the stairs, and then we'd pray that no one who'd rappelled down from the roof had noticed our point of entry. Or was hanging around waiting for us.

I was back at Adrian's side in a flash. He was busy acting like a tiger around the edges of the desk. I hissed into Adrian's ear, "Can you hold it?"

"Alone? Not for long."

"I don't need long," I said and I gave the desk's underside a shove that concussed at least two skulls on the other side. We didn't have the advantage of numbers, but the defensive position was ours and two were far more maneuverable than however many were on the other side.

I was bleeding. Not bad. It was slowing to a trickle even as I trickled it all over Berber carpeting. Had to ignore it. Had to keep pushing. We were in deep shit. Ian and Cal might be in deep shit. First things first.

Out.

And that meant using whatever was at hand, up to and in-cluding whatever the dead guys behind us were toting. I rummaged through their clothes, pulled off two guns, stepped back, and began firing two-fisted badass-style—which chased a few of the more ad-venturesome bastards away from the corners.

One corpse left, the farthest one. By the stairwell.

He was carrying bulky loot; I could see it under his zipped-up sweater. And when I unzipped it with a one-handed rip, I saw that he was wearing a bandolier loaded with grenades.

I have no doubt that a wide, manic smile spread across my pretty little face.

I unbuckled the bandolier because the canvas was hard to tear and anyway, I wanted to bring the whole bunch, not just one or two goodies for chucking. I returned to Adrian's side.

His eyes bugged out when he saw the grenades. Then he made a smile just like the one I'd made when I first saw them. "On the count of three, okay?" I said, and I jutted my head toward the stairs.

He got it. He nodded.

And on the count of three we each grabbed a leg of the rocking, battered desk which was increasingly full of holes . . . and we withdrew with it. It scrabbled across the carpet with a nasty wail and whine, bumping unevenly behind us as we retreated to the stairwell.

When we were as close to the stairwell as we could reasonably get without dropping the desk and running, we held them off a few seconds longer while he and I each took a fistful of boom and bit the pins, pulling them out with our teeth.

Simultaneously we pitched them around the desk. I gave it a final shove, causing a tangle and a stumble on the other side—and then a whole lot of panic followed it once our small, bumpy offerings had been discovered.

Together we turned and ran.

The whole hallway went up behind us like a lode-bearing boss in a video game. Fire curled around the desk, which I saw out of the corner of my eye as I ran. The desk split into gold-veined fragments that went in every direction; the last I saw of it, huge slivers were wedged into the walls and up in the ceiling.

But I didn't dwell on it. I had Adrian in front of me and I pushed him—because I could run faster than he could, even with a couple of holes in me, though the stress and effort were starting to drag me down. I'd lost blood. That's never helpful.

Up we went anyway. We didn't have a choice. People were coming up the stairwell below us, shouting and dodging and brandishing weapons. They were still a couple of floors down, but I didn't like it and neither did Adrian.

He reached around my arm and swiped another grenade out of

the bandolier, then pulled the pin and aimed down. A fortuitous bounce and a good throw sent the thing down a full floor and some change. When it went off I heard small bits of metal whistling in every direction.

Somewhere beneath us a fire had started. I suspected the fourth floor. I don't know what they'd been stashing up there or what the Men in Black had been toting, but something smelled like chemicals and flame when the first grenades went off—and I didn't think it was just the expected shrapnel.

We reached the hole we'd cut above the stairs and boosted each other up, over, and inside it without even checking to make sure it was free and clear. If it wasn't, we were screwed anyway—so we went for it and hoped for the best.

The shaft was filling with smoke. I didn't want to say anything or point it out as we fled on hands and knees in the dark, but I was pretty sure that the building was actually aflame. I wondered why I hadn't heard any sprinkler systems right around the time I heard the fire alarm finally go off. Useless device. If their building was so hideously unprepared for invasion, firefights, and subsequent collateral damage, then it damn well deserved to burn to the ground.

Adrian coughed and my eyes were watering, but the roof was blessedly close and the fresh air tasted great. No one was up there waiting for us, which was a relief, but the guys who'd broken into 443 through the window had left their rappelling gear and a pair of very convenient ropes still hanging over the side.

We pulled them up slowly, because we didn't need the attention from the guys who were milling about on the ground, speaking into cell phones and waving new support troops into position. They were still concentrating on that window. As if we were still hanging out in that room or something.

Eventually we were able to let ourselves down quietly on the far side of the building, where it almost smashed right up against another building in a very narrow alley. We dropped down into something wet and disgusting, but we had hit street level in almost perfect darkness and it was only a short, side-cramping run back to the car.

I looked over my shoulder to see the fire spread and gnaw hungrily, and I would've smiled if I hadn't suddenly been so afraid.

We'd made it out, yes. But I was afraid for myself and Adrian; I was afraid for Ian and even Cal, a little bit, insomuch as Cal looked after Ian and that made him important whether I liked it or not. And I was afraid for a basement full of monsters like me, imprisoned and tortured, cut and sliced and prodded—wherever they were, if they were still alive or if they hadn't been alive in years. I watched the fire and I wanted it to take everything—not just the paper goods and the horrible records, but everything. The project, the building. The crimes—mine and theirs. I wanted it all to go up in smoke.

I let Adrian drive back to the hotel.

I was shaking too badly to do it myself; I was too wound up and frenetic, and too flustered and wounded to be any use—not right then. He was driving fast and hard, but not running into anybody and not causing any wrecks in his wake, which was better than I would've done. For a flash I had a small worry about running the red lights, and about getting caught on one of those stupid traffic cameras, but I forgot it almost as soon as I thought of it.

We had bigger problems. Worse problems. Real problems.

Behind us, the Office of Experimental Bioengineering Research burned itself to ashes, and as we fled the scene fire trucks and cop cars barreled toward it.

14

Not for a minute did I believe we'd burned the whole building down. They'd catch it before it got that far, in a big old stone place like that. Best I could hope for, it'd take the whole office and maybe the whole hall, leaving it a graveyard of charcoal and bones.

I said out loud, "There must be backups."

"Of what?" Adrian asked through tight lips. Never taking his eyes off the road. Considering his path, and snapping the Malibu's wheel around to take us a new way, closer and closer to the hotel. Christ Almighty, I probably could've run faster.

"Backups of the paper trail. Nobody . . ." My mind wandered briefly. I led it back. "Nobody just *files* things anymore. It's all scanned and stored on disks. Or on someone's computer, somewhere. Or a thumb drive," I rambled on.

"Bruner probably has it."

"Yeah," I agreed. "But I bet he doesn't have *all* of it." Then I said, right as we pulled around to the hotel's valet parking, "I'm going to kill that motherfucker, and I'm going to enjoy it."

We leaped out of the car, and Adrian tossed the keys to the nearest uniformed dude. As we started to run he said, "I thought I had dibs."

"Fuck your dibs," I said, and I bypassed the elevator altogether, heading instead for the stairs. If Adrian wanted to wait he was welcome to, but I was going to fly like an eagle without him.

The emergency exit door banged shut behind me and I didn't hear Adrian follow; but then again, I wasn't listening for him. I was concentrating on the stairs, two or three at a time, pumping for all I was worth and simultaneously wishing I had a beverage to refresh my strength . . . and forgetting I had one. It was just as well. There wasn't time. There was only the unending staircase, crooking ever-upward.

I burst onto the floor where our suites were conjoined, and before I rounded the corner I knew something was wrong. Before I'd staggered, panting, upon the scene I could smell it—a wet mess of metal and plasma. Before I'd opened the door—and before I'd even seen that it'd been forced—I knew that something was horribly, horribly incorrect, and that nothing was going to be the same, ever again.

Sometimes I overreact.

This was not one of those times.

Without even thinking to draw my gun (just as well, since it was empty and back at the office), I shoved myself against the door and forced it inward, flapping with a crash against the closet door and shattering the mirror there.

My entrance startled two men who were busying themselves by going through Ian and Cal's things. They jerked to attention at the sight of me, but they didn't stay that way long. I flung myself at them, faster than they could've processed—and I broke one's neck before he had time to lift the Taser he'd been holding in his free hand. I tasted the crackle of electricity and smelled the sizzling ozone as the thing deployed, even as he died. It fired straight into the wall and the two little prongs stuck, vibrating and shining, humming and harming nothing.

The second guy—Christ, both of them dressed like Trevor, only with a little more precision—had the presence of mind to duck out of my way and break for the door, but I caught him by the feet and brought him down like an antelope. I was so outraged by his mere existence that it was all I could do not to tear off his arms and beat him with them. I settled for stomping on his throat and taking his gun—a very nice Glock that reminded me of mine back home in Seattle.

This reminded me in turn of Domino and Pepper and the storehouse, and how I didn't know if any of that was okay, due entirely to asswipes like the ones in that room, dead now, both of them, and me running from the room without knowing where to go next.

Cal hadn't been there. Ian hadn't been there.

But there'd been blood before I arrived. Plenty of blood. I didn't know whose; I hadn't even had the clarity of thought to notice if it was vampire or mortal blood, and I sure as hell didn't have the cognitive felicity to consider it as I fled next door. Where else could I check but my own room? Where else might either of them have escaped to?

It didn't make perfect sense and I knew it, but it was all I could think of so I burst inside, where the lock had also been forced. Brutally, I had to gather, since it fell away under my shoulder as easily as a doggy door.

The room had been trashed with prejudice. All available

drawers had been ripped off their rails and emptied onto the floor; the bed had been unmade and the space beneath it violated. Slash marks defaced the cushions of the settee and the love seat, on the off chance I'd been hiding anything good inside them, I supposed.

I knew Adrian's footsteps, even running. I'd learned the weight of him and the rhythm of his pace. He was coming up fast.

"Raylene!" he gasped, stopping when he saw me standing in the middle of the destroyed room.

I don't know what kind of look I gave him, but it was enough to send him back out and around the corner. I heard him checking in at Ian and Cal's room, seeing the carnage, making some assumptions, and exiting—shutting the door behind him, which was something I hadn't thought to do.

By the time he'd rejoined me, I'd found Cal.

Cal was sprawled out on his face between my bed and the window, half covered by a curtain that had been brought down in what must have been a struggle. I could tell by the way his head was bent, and by the way his arms and legs were all uncomfortably akimbo, never mind the pool of blood that spread beneath him.

I could tell he was dead.

I crouched down beside him and moved his face so I could see it, but it told me nothing. There was no revelation waiting in his eyes, or a clue to what had happened clutched in his fist. He was just . . . gone. That was all.

"Cal?" Adrian asked. It sounded like a guess, and I thought it was a stupid thing to say except that he was still in the doorway, and could only see Cal's feet.

So I said, "Yeah. It's him."

"Shit," he said, but I hardly heard it for the sound of men tramping up the stairs, clicking their walkie-talkie buttons and organizing a response to whatever danger the building's security had

diagnosed. Or maybe they were more Trevors, party to whoever
had done this.

Either way, Adrian was right when he took my arm and said,
"We have to get out of here."

"No," I said reflexively. "We have to find Ian."

"Ian isn't here," Adrian pointed out, so infuriatingly reasonable. "So we have to go somewhere *else*. This is about to get sticky.
Come on," he urged me again, being gentle, almost. But firm.

"Where would he go?" I asked, and I hated myself for how
much it sounded like crying.

"We'll figure it out on the way."

"Do you think they took him?"

"No," he said, I assume in order to humor me.

I settled for it. Hell, I clung to it. And I clung to Adrian's hand
as he shoved open the sliding balcony door and pushed me outside,
shutting the thing behind us both and beginning the long, cold
crawl down over the edge.

15

We were halfway down when I caught a whiff . . . but that's the wrong word. Not a "whiff" exactly—it was more like a sweeping impression, some sense that I was going the wrong way and that I was required elsewhere. It was the impression of tugging, not as subtle as a psychic whisper, and not quite as hard as a punch in the gut.

I stopped, dangling by my hands perhaps half a dozen floors above the ground. When I stopped, Adrian stopped, too.

"What?" he asked in a quiet hiss.

I looked up and saw nothing but the underside of the balcony. In the distance I heard police cars and fire engines; someone with a walkie-talkie had made it out in one piece.

Someone had found Cal, I assumed. Someone was looking for us.

My companion was straining to hold himself in position, balancing on the edge of a rail that looked too thin to hold him. "Raylene?" he asked, more urgently this time.

I told him, "Up."

"You can't be fucking serious!"

I looked down and over to where he was perched—not ten feet away. I said, "Yeah, I think I am. I think Ian's up there. I think he's on the roof," I added, even though I had virtually nothing to back up that hunch. Just that warm, strange pull that leaned against me and made me want to climb.

"What is it with your kind and rooftops?" he muttered, not really expecting an answer.

I gave him one anyway. "Rooftops are a way inside," I said, pulling myself up now, instead of lowering myself down. "They're someplace where people tend not to go, and once you're up there, especially at night, it's easy to hide. And sometimes, if you need a way out, it's the last stop and only way to run."

Up, lift, and over the balcony.

Half a floor down and . . . I looked up, craning my neck around. We'd started from the fifteenth. We'd descended maybe seven. I thought there were twenty floors in total, so maybe twelve floors to the top from where we were camped out.

Adrian was struggling, and I wasn't so far away from exhaustion myself. I looked back at him, teetering on that rail, trying hard just to make it to the ground. He'd never be able to take himself up another however-many-floors.

I told him, "Go down without me."

He said, "No."

"Yeah, seriously. You won't make it to the top, and I promise,"

I said, turning around and getting a better grip, "I won't think less of you as a man or anything." I tried to give it a wink and a grin.

Say one thing for him, say he wasn't crazy. The sweat was shining on his forehead, dripping down his temples, and his arms were shaking. "Okay." He nodded. "Okay, you're right."

"Meet me back by Lincoln, in . . . I don't know. Another hour or two. I'll meet you over there, soon as I can."

"Got it," he told me, and he gave me a head-bob that said *goodbye* and *I'll see you there,* or possibly just *whatever.* Regardless, he began to descend again, a little more jerkily than before, but I was pretty sure he'd be all right. It'd been a long night for everyone, and he needed a break worse than I did.

But not much worse.

I scrabbled, clawed, and heaved myself up another few floors until I thought I couldn't go even another foot, and all the while that pulse, or that warning, or that summons . . . whatever it was . . . it was still drawing me along.

With a sigh and an upturned nose, I reached into my satchel and drew out that god-awful little pouch of blood.

I gave it a disdainful squish, noting that although it was cold, it didn't appear to be chunky with ice—which believe you me is fucking *disgusting.* And it's not like my body heat would warm it up or keep it nice and gooey. Best I can hope for (unless I want to tote a hot-water bottle around with me) is Not Frozen and Totally Preservative-Laden Dribble of Sustenance.

God. Half a pint. Barely enough to bother with, and if I hadn't been so busted and worn out by the evening's activities I wouldn't have done it. I would've sucked up my pride, wandered down to skid row, and taken a nibble off a bum like a civilized woman.

But I didn't have such a homeless meat-sack handy, so it was just me and my pouch of goo. I scrunched up my nose and bit down on a corner, puncturing it and spilling a bit down my chin. Ladylike, yes. Also ladylike was the way I guzzled it as if I were dying of thirst in the goddamn desert. It was revolting, but it was exactly what I needed, and my body demanded it with such a vicious insistence that I came close to sucking the plastic bag down, too. Then, I guess, I would've starved to death like one of those sea turtles that swallows a baggie, thinking it's a jellyfish. Man. What a way to go.

I wadded up the empty baggie and tossed it off the balcony.

Thus somewhat invigorated, I resumed my climb. It wasn't the shot in the arm I wanted, but it was enough to let me man-haul myself up and over the balconies, one after another, straight up into the sky—well beyond the point at which I would've collapsed and given up if I hadn't had any refreshments.

Finally my fingertips crossed over the very tippy-top of the building's edge. I grunted, heaved, crawled, and hauled until I'd slung one leg up over the side and could flop onto the tar-covered surface.

But even through my exhaustion, I had to look. I had to see.

The sky above was swirling, very faintly but very distinctly—pitching to and fro as if it were being stirred. All the clouds swished like they'd been flushed, doing that lazy, sliding spin. My head was spinning, too. My eyes were closing from the pressure of it . . . not just the crushing psychic fog but from pure weariness the likes of which I wasn't sure I'd ever felt before.

I dragged myself to my knees, and then staggered up to my feet. It was dark there, darker than it should've been. I rubbed at my eyes in case that would clear them.

It didn't.

Stepping forward, I immediately tripped and fell on my face—or rather, onto one cheek and one hand. The other hand got caught in the strap of my go-bag and the short version is, I tumbled over the obstacle with every bit as much dainty precision as I'd dropped myself onto the roof in the first place.

It was not an auspicious beginning.

As I pushed myself up I patted the obstacle. It was wearing wool pants and some kind of uniform. Something with a badge clipped onto a pocket. Didn't matter. The obstacle was dead and posed no threat to yours truly, so I tried to ignore it and keep moving.

If only I could see . . . What was wrong with my eyes? What had happened to my superlative night vision and my winning stealth?

I could only see clearly when I looked at the sky, so I tipped my chin up and gazed at the immense funnel, hoping it could tell me something.

Hands out, I stumbled forward, feeling my way around.

I tripped again, dropped to my knees this time, and cried out because, hot damn, that hurt! The impact split my favorite black burgling pants and jammed my knees clear down to the bone.

My feeble whimper was answered by a shudder in the fog, something I couldn't describe but could feel up and down my spine.

At this point, I figured I was screwed coming or going, so I hunkered beside what turned out to be yet another corpse and I whispered, because I couldn't bring myself to shout. "Ian?" It came out in a squeak that hardly sounded like me at all. I wished I wasn't so worn out; I wished I had fresh blood handy, and lots of it—but all the blood at my immediate disposal was cooling and pooling in the corpses, and corpses are notoriously bad bleeders. I'm not saying it can't be done, but drinking from the already-dead requires a lot more patience and leisure time than I had right then.

The fog shuddered again and I shuddered with it.

"Ian, is that you? Are you up here?" I tried again.

The fog remained, but it thinned.

"Ian, I know you're up here," I lied. I only *prayed* he was up there. Because if this wasn't his doing, I had no idea what I was dealing with and I was genuinely afraid. Hell, I was genuinely afraid regardless. I'd never seen anything like this before—from a vampire or any other immortal. "It's me, Raylene."

The story Ian had told me—his vague, reluctantly shared story about how he'd escaped Jordan Roe, and the weird power he'd somehow developed—was this what he'd meant?

Then I heard Ian's voice, thick and wet. "They killed Cal." He was somewhere in front of me, and to my left. I tried to scoot toward the sound of him, and kicked some dead bastard's hand.

"Jesus," I said, wondering how many people had followed him up there, and how many people he'd killed. What was he doing up here? Was this the result of some weird new sense, developed to make up for the lack of his eyesight, as he believed? It was a tantalizing thought; it made me wonder if I could develop it, too—or if any other vampire could, given the right set of circumstances. Not that I wanted to go blind in order to find out.

"I couldn't save him," he said.

I'd almost caught my breath. Almost found my footing. "I saw him, downstairs. There were two other guys hanging out in your room, but I took care of them."

"Violently, I hope." His voice was so cold it was brittle, and ready to snap.

I followed it, drawing myself through the shaded dark, hoping to reach him. Any minute. Any second. He was only a few feet in front of me—he couldn't be any farther than that. Any moment my fingers would graze his shoulder, or maybe his knee. From the sound of the echo, I thought he might be sitting down on something.

"Ian?" I said, hoping I sounded sweet, innocent, harmless, and interested. "What's going on?"

"They shouldn't have taken Cal. He had nothing to do with

this—not any of it. He was only a helper, not a conspirator. But there was nothing I could do. They surprised us. And I don't understand . . . there's so much I don't understand."

"Maybe I can help."

"They took everything," he told me, as if I hadn't said a thing. "They destroyed everything."

"Ian, Adrian, and I made it to Major Bruner's office. We found more paperwork—more files. Much more than what I was able to give you from Adrian's stash."

The black fog held its breath. "Is that true?"

"Of course it's true! I've got it in my bag. Let's get downstairs and get the hell out of here. I'll read it to you, start to finish. We'll find someplace calm to sort this out."

Dream-like, he said, "We can't go downstairs. We can never go back there. They'll try to take us away."

"Not downstairs in the room. Downstairs *outside*. We're meeting up at the Lincoln Memorial—"

"When?"

"As soon as I can talk you down off this ledge," I said, though it seemed like an appalling choice of words and it no doubt was. "Please, Ian. Come with me. Let's get out of here. Let's go, and we can sort everything out somewhere else."

"I should've left when Cal wanted me to leave. He'd been begging, insisting. But I stayed, because you wanted me to. You convinced me to." The swirling above became more aggressive—more like a hurricane than a mere storm front.

"That's true." I still held out my hands, hoping to find him. Where the hell was he? I felt like an idiot, sweeping around in the dark, hoping to knock up against him. "But I didn't know it would come to this—you have to believe me. I was only trying to help, and now I know why they came after us. I know how they kept finding us."

"It was my fault. I could've packed up and returned home at any time, but I did not. The fault lies with me."

Yes and no, but this wasn't the time to emphasize the "yes." "Ian, the Canadian doctor you've been feeding information to—his name's David, isn't it? David Keene?"

Time ground to a halt. The barometric pressure changed, and the fog pulsed with something like rage, something like horror.

"David, yes." His words were choked now.

"Ian, he was one of the original contacts for Project Bloodshot. He was either an investor or a researcher—we didn't have time to read everything on the spot."

"That . . . it can't be!"

"Did you ever meet him in person?" I asked.

"No. We corresponded by phone and email."

"You've been talking to him, since I've been on your case?"

A pause. A swallow. Then a protest. "Only a bit. Only to keep him abreast of progress, since he would be leaving the country soon."

"You told him I was in Atlanta. Did you tell him I was looking for someone who'd stolen the files you wanted?"

More silence. Finally he said, "Not . . . not in so many words. But yes. I think. I certainly didn't tell him our address, though—or give him any names!"

"He didn't need addresses, and he already had enough information on hand to put the names together." If he knew I'd gone to Atlanta, and he knew one of the program's subjects came from Atlanta, the math was fairly easy. All Keene had to do was have somebody watch the deJesus household and wait for me to appear. "Ian." I wanted to change the subject. He couldn't have known. I couldn't hold it against him. "I think he was trying to lure you back for more. The program started again as a civilian enterprise; it's run out of Bruner's office, in a building owned by a guy named

Sykes. I don't know the whole picture yet, Ian. But I've learned a lot, and I'll tell you everything. All of it. You can help me put the pieces together. And . . . and . . . Bruner is still out there. We'll hunt him down and ask him the rest. There's a lot I don't know, but I do know this—it's not your fault Cal's dead. It's Bruner, and that lying bastard Keene. Please." I was reduced to begging. "Please, stop this. Let's get out of here. I'll help you . . . or . . ." It might've only been my imagination, but I felt like the fog was thinning. I saw two more bodies, for a total tally of six, I thought. "Or I'll just keep you company. And you and me and Adrian, we'll put an end to this. We'll dig it up the rest of the way, and tear it out by the root. Whatever it takes."

"I can't ask you to do that."

"I'm offering—on the house! You've lost your ghoul, Ian. Listen, I'm not much of a guide-vampire, but I'll do my best. I promise you, among the three of us, we'll put a total, complete, and *apocalyptic* end to this." And then I said something I'm pretty sure I'd never said to anyone else before, ever.

I said, "I won't leave you."

Whatever was holding the sky in that amazing pattern of swirls and stars . . . it shattered . . . and the motion came to an abrupt sloshing halt. As if a carousel had stopped spinning, everything drawled back into focus, and into stillness.

The darkness quivered, and in a blink it was gone.

Ian Stott was right in front of me, seated on an overturned box or crate of some sort. Blood had splashed and dripped down his chin, over his hands. Red meat hung in globs under his fingernails. His beautiful, impeccable clothes were dirty and torn. He was missing a shoe. He leaned forward so that he rested his elbows atop his thighs, and folded his hands loosely between them.

Without looking up he said, "Don't promise me anything."

"We're in this together now, me and you. And I *won't* leave you to the mercy of . . . of . . ." I eyed the broken, torn bodies that lay around him in a circle as if he'd been a bomb that exploded. "Yourself."

"It's my fault," he said, one more time.

One more time I said, "It isn't."

He put his head in his hands, but I wouldn't have it. I lifted his chin and I looked right into those empty gray eyes of his—their glasses long gone—and I kissed him because I didn't quite know what else to do.

It took him a minute to kiss back, but he did, and the taste of other people's blood mingled in our mouths. He put one hand on the back of my neck and drew me closer; I leaned into it, into him. His hand slipped down to the small of my back, then his other hand joined it—clasping me there, holding me in place in case I hadn't meant it.

We stayed that way until the crackling static of radios buzzed up to our ears, and we knew the moment was passing, as all moments must.

I reached down for his arm and lifted him up, like I'd carry his ass all the way down to the ground if he made me. "Ian, pull yourself together. I think I see your other shoe."

"I don't know where it went."

"I've got it. Come on. Sweetheart, come *on*. Adrian's waiting for us."

16

I waited perhaps two hours for David Keene to come home. During that time I made myself comfortable; he didn't have any security system to speak of—just a cheesy keypad unit that five seconds with a scrambler took down. Inside everything was unguarded and even unhidden. It was the home of a man who believed he had nothing to fear.

Of course, he was wrong.

I'd found him. And soon, he would fear *me*.

I'd see to it.

But first I saw to his records—to his laptop, his desktop machine, and the drawerful of tiny thumb drives and CDs labeled with a Sharpie. I took them all, everything I could find.

Because the universe likes to tell stories in circles, I was willing to bet I'd accidentally scored myself some porn in this catch all sweep of the premises. That's how this began, after all—with me complaining about having too much other-people's-pornography in my life. Yet here I was, emptying drawers and confiscating everything in sight.

Based on what I'd gathered about the man who lived in the sprawling mid-century ranch, I went out on a limb and guessed I was going to find some Japanaporn. Probably something with schoolgirls and tentacles.

When I was finished gathering everything and my trap was sufficiently laid, I set my go-bag down on the couch and dropped myself beside it. I thought about turning on the television, but that seemed like an unnecessary risk, so I didn't. I just sat there in the dark and I didn't move a muscle until I heard a car pull up into the driveway, and then footsteps on the paved walk outside, then a fumbling of keys and a turning of the tumblers in the lock.

I faced the door, leaning against the couch's arm, with my go-bag serving as lumbar support. I'd like to imagine that my eyes were glittering cruelly, or that I glowed and leered like some otherworldly beast. But I knew that when the man flipped on the living room light, all he saw was a petite brunette in black, with a face that meant business.

It was still enough to startle him.

I could've smiled at the wide-eyed confusion, or laughed out-right at the way he froze—a prey animal caught in the gaze of something hungry.

I didn't. I only said, "Hello, Dr. Keene. Please, come inside. And shut the door."

If the doc had possessed a lick of sense, he would've run back outside and made for his car. Not that it would've saved him, mind you—I'm just saying that's what a sane man would've done. Or maybe that kind of action is only for men who aren't accustomed to taking orders.

Dr. Keene did as he was told.

He stood there with his back to the door, keys in hand, unmoving. "Who are you?" he asked.

"My name is Raylene. And I'm just your kind of girl," I purred, striving for sinister and going for the gold.

"I don't know what you're talking about."

Ah, that was a misstep on his part. He should've saved that grand denial until I'd asked him some questions. This guy was a total failure at ass-covering, in every way possible. An innocent man would've demanded to know what I was doing in his living room. Guilty men open with excuses.

"Sure you do. You've spent a decade and change rounding up people like me, throwing us in basements and leaving us there, or cutting us up for curiosity's sake, or for the sake of a government contract or two. This is a nice house," I said. "Can't imagine how you've paid for it."

All the blood drained from his face. He'd been white before, when he'd first spotted me on the couch. But now he looked like death itself, chalky and slack-jawed, with a shock of reddish brown hair sticking up in surprise. Under his lab coat he was wearing the dullest kind of business-casual, brown shoes and belt, blue polo shirt.

To his credit, he nodded—a tense, terrified bobbing of his chin. "I know what you are."

"Good. But it may or may not interest you to hear that I'm not visiting on my own behalf." I chose this moment to stand, and to glide across the low-shag beige the poor bastard had picked for flooring. "You don't know me, but you've nearly had me killed— or worse—several times over in the last few weeks. I've been trying to help one of your victims."

He sputtered, "Help? You . . . your kind. They don't help *anybody.*"

"Really? You know that for a fact, do you? Then answer me this: What am I doing, hanging out in your living room, having ransacked your home, if I don't want to help Ian Stott by giving him a little closure—or a little proxy vengeance?"

"Ian?"

"Don't act like you don't know the name."

It wouldn't have done him any good. His face was a mask of guilt, but also confusion. "You're the one he hired?"

"Not sure what you were expecting," I said, even though I knew good and well he'd assumed I was a man. My greatest secret—an accidental secret, born of masculine assumptions and simply never corrected.

"I expected someone . . ." He hesitated. "Taller."

I said, "I get that a lot."

"But why . . . ? Why are you here?" he asked, so plaintively I could've almost felt sorry for him if I hadn't known what he was, and what he did in his spare time. It was plain from the question that he'd already figured what I was doing. He was only stalling, or wondering if he could change my mind. In other words, he was wasting everyone's time.

This didn't stop me from doing a little rambling.

"Do you have any idea what you've put Ian through? Never mind the personal hassle you've caused me. I can take it. I've been on the receiving end of worse, sent by better than the likes of *you*. But Ian? All he wanted was to get his sight back. And all you had to do was help him, and he would've been eternally in your debt— a debt you can *bet* he would've honored. Since you've chosen to wad up all that trust and throw it in his face, I'm going to go ahead and assume that you have no idea exactly how valuable a vampire's debt can be." It could've meant anything—up to and including eternal life—but I let him do that math on his own.

"You figured he was weak, and that you had nothing to fear

from him. You strung him along with promises of help; you gave him hope, and then you betrayed him. So make no mistake—I'm not here on my own behalf. I'm here for *him*. I'm here because you aren't allowed to hurt him anymore, and you're not allowed to inconvenience *me* anymore, either."

"You're here to kill me?"

"Bingo, Sunshine."

"But, but . . ." And here came the bargaining. "But if you think you can avenge your client just by killing me, you're wrong. I was only a pawn in this whole thing! I was just doing my job."

"The last excuse of cowards," I said. I drew up much, much closer. So close I could feel his breath on my face, and the warmth of his feverish terror radiating from his body.

"But it wasn't me!"

"Are you about to blame Bruner? Because buddy, that ship has *sailed*."

"No—" He was frantic now, flailing. Throwing out anything he thought would slow me down, as if anything could. "Not Bruner. Not *just* Bruner, anyway—it's that other guy. He's the one who's been dumping money into it. He paid for the offices, for the CIA thugs, for everything. He's the one who wanted the old experiment documentation, bad enough to kill for it. Then when he found out a vampire was going after it, I . . . I don't know. I guess he wanted the vampire, too."

"Are we talking about Sykes?" It'd been the only loose name I'd ever turned up, connected with the offices. I was glad I'd filed it away because look—here it was again.

"He made his money in Department of Defense contracts," Keene babbled. "Doing high-definition satellite surveillance programming and camera systems. Real long-range stuff."

I actually stopped. I held him out at arm's length and narrowed my eyes. "Keep talking. I'm listening."

"That's . . . that's all I know. He's the one who turned the program back on; he's the one who's paying for it. The guy's loaded. Uncle Sam's made him a billionaire."

Okay. Something had slipped between the cracks here. Jeffery Sykes. I'd figured the name was a front, or just a figurehead on a corporation. Apparently I needed to look closer. He sounded like an actual man. He sounded like an actual problem . . . maybe even the root of an actual problem.

I asked, "What does he want with people like me? What does he want with Ian?"

His desperation hit a fever pitch. "I don't know! Why don't you go and ask him, and leave me alone?"

"Oh, I'm going to ask him all right." Viciously, once I caught up to him. "But leave you alone?" I gave a little laugh, and let the hunger I was feeling in my gut go all the way to my eyes. "That was never going to happen."

David Keene was cooling on the couch, and I was feeling good.

In the grand scheme of things, I didn't know how much his death would affect a program like Bloodshot, or Bandersnatch, or whatever they were calling it these days. Maybe a little. Maybe not at all. But I felt good for having killed him all the same.

I fully planned to burn the place down behind me on general principle. I was getting the hang of arson. It really sends a message, you know? Not only will I kill your dudes and steal your shit, but I will burn your place down behind me. Yes, I will.

But before that, I had something I wanted to do.

Okay, I didn't *want* to do it. But I feel like I *needed* to do it.

So I sat there inside the dead doctor's house and I reached for his phone. It was a cordless jobbie with more buttons than any phone ever needs, but it'd work all right. All I needed was something that no one could trace back to me—not under any circumstances. Making a call from a line in a house that was about to burn down . . . yeah. That'd just about cover it.

I called information and asked for a number in DeKalb County, Georgia. Family name Barrington. I had some questions about Isabelle deJesus, and maybe no one at the Atlanta House would talk, but even denials could tell me plenty if I asked the right way.

It was a shot in the dark, that was for damn sure. But I was pretty sure Adrian would agree that it was a shot worth taking.

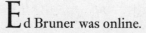

17

Ed Bruner was online.

So was I. I'd given him a Yahoo Chat handle and told him to ping me at a certain time, on a certain date. It had been a week since his office had gone up in flames, so he and I were doing this whole song-and-dance thing.

It was a game, probably to both of us.

We had this back-and-forth going on.

I knew about him. He knew about me. But we both kept pretending . . . just in case we were wrong.

In a way, we had plenty in common. We were both too paranoid to give up and play it straight. Too set in our ways to take the chance. Both of us convinced we were coming from a place of power, and both of us terrified we were wrong.

He typed: "We've had some setbacks over here, in the last week or two."

I replied: "That sucks. I'm sorry to hear it. I really want to come on board with you guys. This whole thing sounds like a blast."

EBrun1956: You could put it that way.

AbbieGFTW: So when are we going to make this happen, Ed?
AbbieGFTW: I'm chomping at the bit over here.
AbbieGFTW: Want to learn cool new stuff. Find more interesting abandoned buildings and raid them in case of cool shit.
AbbieGFTW: Ed? You there?

EBrun1956: I'm here.

Something was bothering him. Good. The silence of his blinking cursor was louder than any all-caps debate between two teenagers. I decided to prompt him.

AbbieGFTW: Hey, did you ever find out what happened to Trevor?

EBrun1956: Yeah. It turns out, he died.

AbbieGFTW: Seriously? How?
AbbieGFTW: What happened?

EBrun1956: Somebody killed him. Buried him in a basement.

AbbieGFTW: Wow. Crazy!
AbbieGFTW: No wonder we hadn't heard from him.

EBrun1956: Yeah, no wonder.

AbbieGFTW: Anyone expecting to hear from you?

AbbieGFTW: Anytime soon?

. . .

AbbieGFTW: Ed?
AbbieGFTW: Ed? You there?

EBrun1956: What kind of question is that?
EBrun1956: Is anyone expecting to hear from me? Lots of people are. More people than you know. Why the fuck would you ask me that?

I quit typing. I crept up behind him and shut the silenced
smartphone from which I'd been IMing him. The tiny click of its
closing made his whole body go tense, and rightly so.

But to answer his question, I said, "Just curious."

And to give the old fart credit where credit was due, he
swiveled around with some pretty impressive reflexes. He reached
for the .38 he kept strapped under the desk, but he didn't find it.
Adrian and I had liberated it hours ago.

Ed Bruner, formerly Major Bruner, now retired . . . was pretty
much exactly what I'd expected. An average-sized man, probably
buff once, but age and inactivity had made him soft. His hair was
starting to gray, and it was cut fairly close to his scalp. Not quite the
buzz of an army drone, though. He'd let it get a smidge of length
on top. I liked to think it indicated a rebellious spirit buried somewhere deep down in that middle-aged schlub.

I already knew he didn't like to play by the rules. Maybe the
military hadn't been such a good fit for him after all.

"You," he said. One word. All he needed, really. Until he saw
Adrian, at which point he said, "You?"

My partner in crime answered. "Us."

"That was a hell of a trick," the major conceded.

"It's kind of you to say so," I said, "but it wasn't a trick. We were starting to bore each other with all the pretending. It was time to throw down before you lost interest."

"Or before I forced your hand," he said, his eyes narrowing, trying to follow us both.

He didn't move, which was smart. I wasn't visibly armed, but Adrian was holding the major's own .38, aimed steadily at its owner.

The old man's eyes darted back and forth between us. Me immediately in front of him. Adrian off to the right, holding point by the hallway. "Forced my hand?" I said, sitting down slowly on the edge of his mahogany coffee table. It put me about ten feet away from him. This is to say, I was outside *his* immediate lunging distance . . . but he was well within *mine.* "I don't know what, precisely, you think you forced. I just got tired of it, that's all."

"Bullshit."

"Think whatever you want. I'm not afraid of you," I said in all honesty. "Even though I know what you've done. What you're trying to do again."

"You don't have any idea what we were about—what we were doing," he objected.

I shook my head. "I'll admit we don't know all the ins and outs, but we've read enough of your paper trail to have a pretty damn good idea."

"If that were true, you wouldn't be here."

I sat up straighter. Then I leaned back on my hands—like he'd surprised me, but I was prepared to roll with it. "Wow. It's all or nothing with you, isn't it? Meet me in the middle ground for a minute, will you? I have some follow-up questions."

He snorted. "And you think I might answer them?"

"It depends on how badly you want to survive this little meeting."

His eyes slipped over to a bookcase off to my left. That's because he kept a big knife there, a cousin to the carbon steel foot-long that I gave up and let Adrian keep. I let Bruner look, and didn't call attention to it. Why bother? I'd already swiped it, to replace the aforementioned carbon steel foot-long. It was the only piece of weaponry I was carrying at that particular moment, but it didn't matter. We all knew I didn't need it in order to bring him a whole lot of discomfort.

"You don't have any intention of letting me out of here."

I told him, "It's smart of you to suspect that. But it's all going to come down to how useful we think you are, and how good your information is. If we'd seriously wanted you dead and nothing else, your B-positive would be all over that screen right now. And you can take that to the bank."

He swallowed. "What do you want to know?"

"That's the spirit! Let's begin at the beginning," I suggested. "Project Bloodshot."

"What about it?" he asked. Working hard to stay cool as a cucumber. Neither completely succeeding nor utterly failing.

Adrian chimed in, "It closed, but it didn't die. Just like you retired, but you didn't go away."

"Sounds like you already know all about it," Bruner snapped.

But Adrian said, "No, not all about it. I don't know what really happened to Isabelle deJesus."

"Who?"

"My sister. Subject 636-40-150. Her name was Isabelle. She was a vampire. You kidnapped her—"

"No," he interrupted, but Adrian didn't let him get any other words in edgewise.

"You experimented on her. You took her hearing, like you took Ian Stott's vision. Why?"

Bruner snorted. "What do you mean, why? It was just a job, same as any other except that it was so damn interesting. The combat applications of their . . . of your"—he nodded at me— "*abilities.* They were epic. They were paradigm-shifting if we could harness them for the military. And anyway, who gives a shit? *You're* the monsters, and you'd do worse to us, given half a chance. I've known some of your kind. I've seen what you do, to yourselves and people like us."

"Monsters? Is that what you think? We're none of us more monstrous than we were before we turned. If you don't want to believe that, then I won't make you, but you ought to be kicking yourself, you know. It's a hell of an opportunity you've squandered. You should've just recruited some of us on the up-and-up, but now that's never going to happen. There's not a vamp on earth who'd have anything to do with you, now."

One corner of his mouth lifted in a sneer of irony—the worst kind of sneer, in my opinion. "Is that what you think?"

Well, *yeah* . . . but I refused to show him that I knew I might be wrong. I asked, "After Bloodshot went belly-up, why'd you start it again?"

"That's a complicated answer."

"Break it down for me," I said, hoping I injected the command with a hearty dose of menace.

"I, personally, didn't reopen the damn thing. Surely you can understand that, can't you? I was just a guy collecting a paycheck. I didn't have the authority or the resources to take it elsewhere."

It almost made me sad, how calm and cool he was. This was a guy who'd been under fire before—literally, I imagined—and he'd come out the other side as a guy I could almost *like,* if he weren't a total fucking maniac. My initial impressions held true. We were more alike than either of us would've admitted. I cast a glance at Adrian, still keeping his distance, and still just as tense but calm as the rest of us. I wondered if he was thinking along those same lines, or if he was too angry with the major to identify with him in any way.

As if my glance had given Adrian a nudge, he asked the next question. "Then who *did* pull the trigger? Who paid to launch it as a civilian operation?"

He smirked. The son of a bitch actually *smirked.* "I don't know the whole answer to that," he flat-out lied. Then he said, directly to me, "But what I do know, *you* won't like."

"There's not much about you or your program I *do* like, so whatever you want to spill, I think I can take it," I replied.

His hands waved casually, idly . . . like he was trying to remember a recipe for soup. "I never heard the whole story, but I do know he's one of *yours.*"

"One of . . . what?"

"He's like you. Undead, or whatever."

"Why would a vampire fund something as bizarre and fucked up as Bloodshot?" I demanded to know. "That doesn't make any sense—"

"He's a real self-hater. Didn't want to become like you. It was forced on him, as a punishment for something—and don't ask. Because I don't know *what.*"

"No." I shook my head, taking my eyes off him for an instant, then remembering myself and locking down his gaze again. "No, that's not true. That's not how it works with my kind. The Houses don't turn people to punish them. It's a gift. A reward."

"It's not much of a reward if they mutilate you first. Eternal life is pretty shitty if you can't see, or hear—or taste or smell. Really, honey. That's my idea of hell."

He had my interest now and he knew it, but he'd told me more than he meant to—and he didn't know *that.* His story had a note of truth.

I only know of that punishment being doled out once every hundred years or so. It isn't common. And on the rare occasion this terrible sentence *is* handed down, it's always given to a ghoul. Vampires consider it a form of high irony, and fitting of only the severest betrayals. It's used as a bedtime story to keep other ghouls in line. It adds the necessary element of threat to a relationship that's entirely too important to be left at the mercy of love, or other friendly sentiments.

I said, "You've got a point there. It must be a miserable way to spend eternity." And it *would* be eternity, too. Other vampires are forbidden from killing such a punished ghoul. Usually, he was kept in a cellar or something—watched like a hawk, to make sure he (or she, there I go again) doesn't run out into the dawn to end it all.

It's a serious punishment, intended to last. Vampires are vindictive. And they have very long memories, with plenty of room to hold very long grudges.

"What's his name?" I asked.

"It doesn't matter. He's holed up so tight even the bloodsuckers can't get him."

"What's his name?"

He was getting worried. I could tell it in the way he licked at the corner of his lip, and his eyelids kept twitching as his gaze jerked back and forth between us. "Sykes," he finally said.

I knew it. "And how'd he get so tightly holed up?"

"I don't know," he said, and the fear that was just now starting to waft off his skin implied he was telling the truth. Why was he getting scared now? Probably because he couldn't see the Glock he kept taped under a bookshelf. It ought to be at his eye level, and it wasn't. He was coming to suspect the truth—that we'd been here awhile, and we'd taken away all his toys.

"Take a guess," I ordered.

"Money. Money's my guess. He's loaded. Richer than God."

"How'd he get that way?"

"Department of Defense stuff. Designing . . . designing long-range, high-definition satellite surveillance systems. He sold everything to the government, cashed it all out. He still has his own grid, but he made his money on the patent."

"So that's how you followed me." A statement of fact, not a question. It was a relief to know for certain. One more thing to be afraid of, yes. But one more thing I could take precautions to avoid.

Again he swallowed. "You didn't make it easy. Driving those generic piece-of-shit cars. They're hard to tail, even from the sky. We only picked you up by keeping an eye on the deJesus house, then we lost you again once you'd picked up that faggot in the high heels. Goddamn Atlanta and its goddamn traffic," he muttered, but he was looking at Adrian funny—like it'd just now dawned on him that the faggot in high heels had a .38 pointed at his head.

Well, the state of Atlanta's transportation infrastructure was one thing we agreed on. "So the most common-looking cars are harder to follow, eh? Good to know."

"Any idiot could figure that out. Zebras on the Serengeti know *that*."

Adrian interrupted with a loud, "Ha! So you *did* lead them to me!"

"Fine. But only *technically*, dear," I said.

Bruner kept talking, like he was impatient with the both of us. "You know, if you hadn't been crazy enough to take me up on the invitation to visit my office, we'd have never caught up to you again. I still can't believe that worked."

It was my turn to squint with suspicion. "How did you know it was me?"

"I played a hunch. We were watching your warehouse, *Abigail*. You obviously knew what was inside it, but I know for a fact you didn't come or go when you said you did. You gave yourself away."

I wasn't sure how to respond. That'd been one hell of a slick play on his part, but I didn't want to give him any credit, so I didn't. I lied through my teeth instead. "So we played each other. Nice."

"You? You played me? *How?*"

"I didn't know where you kept your base of operations. You told me right where it was, and trap or no, me and him"—I cocked a thumb at Adrian—"still got inside, got what we needed, and got out in one piece. So the joke's on *you.*"

Then I remembered how Cal had died, and how hard it'd been on Ian, and I thought it wasn't a very funny joke.

"Wait a minute," Adrian said, frowning. "Back up just a second. You said you picked her up in Atlanta, watching my parents' place."

"How else would we have found her? Or *you?*"

Ah. I saw where he was going. Good point. I noted, "But you'd already found me in Seattle."

"Found you?" The major looked genuinely confused. "We had your warehouse on a list of suspicious places, yes, but nobody from our crew *found* you there. The place was empty when we checked it. We didn't even see your squatters. Look, if anyone chased you down, that wasn't us."

"Then who?" I challenged him.

"The military, I guess. Bloodshot was closed, but it was top secret and the army doesn't want anybody looking too closely. You were the idiot who played with a tainted file."

He was right, of course. And as the big picture dawned on me, I was flabbergasted. "You're telling me . . . that I shook Uncle Sam's tail in Seattle only to pick up yours in Atlanta?"

"Sounds like it," he grunted. "We're all using the same tech, you know. And listen, we weren't trawling for you in Atlanta, not really. We were looking for *him*." He nodded at Adrian. "All we wanted was the shit he stole from Holtzer in the first place, and when you got in the way, Sykes put you on his wish list, too. So it looks to me like if it weren't for bad luck, you'd have no luck at all, honey."

"Look who's talking," Adrian murmured.

Something about the tone of my wayward SEAL's voice actually penetrated the major's smug reserves. He said, more softly now, "You're going to kill me, aren't you?"

"Tell me what happened to my sister. We know she escaped when Jordan Roe was destroyed."

"No. I don't know."

Adrian said, "You sure do say that a lot for someone who wants to survive until dawn."

"I don't know!" he insisted. "She was just one more thing we lost in the storm. The roof came off, the walls fell in, and the subjects who didn't die, disappeared."

"You didn't kill her?"

"No! We just told her family she'd died so you'd lay the fuck off! You were keeping her name in the papers, enlisting missing persons organizations, and drawing too much attention to her! We didn't need the scrutiny!" He was talking in exclamation points now. I noticed it, and I liked it.

"So she's still out there."

"As far as I know, yes!"

As far as he knew. But there was a lot he didn't know, like maybe the House had gotten hold of her—though my phone call to Atlanta implied she hadn't gone home to roost. But they still knew of her, and they knew more than they were willing to tell me, which was going around a lot lately. The entry-level ghoul whom I'd finally badgered into talking . . . he was the one who told me she'd gone deaf, but that's all he could be persuaded to say. If he knew where she was or what she was doing these days, I couldn't pry it out of him over the phone.

Of course, it was always possible she'd been caught and killed by something or someone else. Or she might've ended it all herself—which was a distinct possibility. Not every young vamp is cut out to go it alone, much less with a significant disability and a House that had turned on her. With all that stacked against her . . . some people would give up.

"Well?" Bruner asked, since I'd been quiet while pondering these things.

"Well what?"

"Well, are you going to leave me alone now, and get the fuck out of my house?" Ooh. Fake bravado. Almost as obnoxious as real bravado.

"Well, I'll tell you what," I said slowly.

Then, faster than he could blink (no, literally), my hands were on his throat and my knee was on his chest. He'd leaned back so far that the chair nearly buckled under both our weight—and he was gasping, more with surprise than the pressure I was not yet applying.

In the next moment Adrian was at my side. He reached into the back of my belt, where I'd stashed the major's knife. He did it fast, but not so fast that I couldn't have stopped him if I wanted to.

I didn't want to. I let him slash at Bruner's throat just beneath the place where I held him, and together we let him bleed. Bruner's eyes bulged, and he struggled to speak.

But he didn't say anything. And we didn't, either.

When we were sure he was dead, and that no one would reasonably expect a vampire to have done it (yes, I know how that sounds), we torched the place and left. Bruner wasn't the beginning and end of the program, no. But he was a big, nasty part of it; and without him, it wouldn't be half so effective.

And there was one more thing I hoped Bruner's death might accomplish.

I hoped it might force the mysterious Jeffery Sykes to emerge from whatever hole he was hiding in. After all, we'd now killed two of his lead researchers and one of his parkour recruiters. He'd need more people. He obviously needed more vampires, too—because he'd put me on the shopping list. Oh, sure, first he'd wanted to help me find that paperwork, because he needed it, too—but once I had it in hand, he didn't just want the files. He wanted *me*. So he came after me. And I believe the record will reflect, that was a *huge* fucking mistake.

But I had time, and now I knew what to watch for. I also knew to drive less, and change cars more frequently. I knew to plant a few false leads in a few other cities, to beware of men in black suits, and to watch for urban explorers.

And I knew to start looking for Jeffery Sykes.

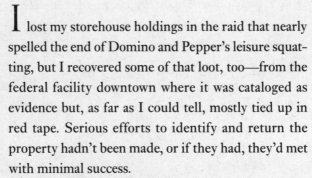

18

I lost my storehouse holdings in the raid that nearly
spelled the end of Domino and Pepper's leisure squatting, but I recovered some of that loot, too—from the
federal facility downtown where it was cataloged as
evidence but, as far as I could tell, mostly tied up in
red tape. Serious efforts to identify and return the
property hadn't been made, or if they had, they'd met
with minimal success.

It was difficult to say how much the authorities
knew about what they'd found.

Bruner had staged the initial raid, but he didn't
have any real interest in the building's contents, since
I, personally, was not among them. The stash had just
been dumped off at a precinct storage facility where
cold-case miscellany and stray evidential bits were sent
to be forgotten.

I didn't bust down the door and throw everything into the back of a U-Haul, even though I probably could have. Instead I let myself inside the quiet way, and after deciding what I could and couldn't live without, I removed the choicer pieces an item at a time, over a period of weeks.

The history of international crime is the history of official agencies fighting for dominance, and failing to communicate. I might never know exactly how much of this had occurred. I could only proceed as if everyone knew everything about me—worst-case scenario—and act with appropriate caution.

But I'm good at caution.

I bought a new building, since my old one was formally condemned and taped off. The "new" building was 110 years old, and it was only a couple of miles from my original hiding place.

Because I'm nothing if not a creature of habit.

The new location had some perks over the old one. For one thing, it was almost fully restored inside. Much like the parkour parlor in D.C., it had been gutted and refitted for office space . . . but the economy had tanked, and the offices had never come. So I picked it up for pennies on the dollar, turned the top floor into perfectly serviceable housing in less than five weeks, and furnished three separate lofts.

One was for Pepper and Domino, because it was time to quit deluding myself. One was for Ian, who had no place else to go . . . and I didn't want him to leave yet anyway. I'd made him a promise and I didn't intend to break it. Or maybe that was only the excuse I used in order to keep him close. Because I definitely wanted him close, and he wasn't exactly running away from me, either.

The kiss on the roof of Bruner's office . . . it'd meant something. And given time, given space—and given a little distance from the events that had upended both our lives—I think we both hoped it'd turn into something more.

But for the moment, we were both on edge and both trying to find our equilibrium. We didn't talk about the kiss, and for a while we didn't repeat it. I think we were too afraid of chasing each other away, when all we wanted to do was cling together like a couple of baby monkeys. Yeah, we're pretty goddamn stupid. And broken, and lonely, and needy in very different ways, but those differences weren't enough to pry us apart or let us really come together. If you know what I mean.

So one of the lofts was for me, because (a) I wasn't ready to share absolutely everything with Ian; and (b) my Capitol Hill condo was contaminated by filthy feeb fingers. I'd never returned to it.

Instead, I'd faked my death for the fourth time since I'd actually died in 1924.

This time, by all reports I had been Helene Marks, who sadly passed away of cancer in Canada, where I'd gone to seek treatment— lacking sufficient health insurance to seek treatment in the United States. The death before, I was Amelia Westerfeld, and I perished in 1978—in a car crash in Mexico. Before I became Amelia, I was Christine Johnson, who expired of an allergy to shellfish in Singapore in 1951; and before I masqueraded as Christine I was Ruth Chesters, who vanished in the Andes in 1933.

Before that, of course, I was just Raylene Pendle.

I never die at home in California. It's a matter of paperwork.

I let the state of Washington auction off my condo and all the property therein, what little there was. I then activated one of the other half a dozen potential identities I keep on tap, and started over as Emily Benton.

Say one thing for me, I'm prepared.

Say two things for me, and I've got a soft spot for drag queens.

A couple of months after the very fucking timely demise of Ed Bruner, I found myself up on Capitol Hill overlooking downtown Seattle, seated in a coffee shop because I like the smell of the stuff. It was a lazy night, which was good. I needed one. I had a copy of *The Stranger* and my laptop. And in the background, a guy who didn't completely suck was ensconced on the corner stage, strumming his guitar and treating us all to an evening of boring shoegazer tunes.

The coffeehouse's door opened with a jingle of the Tibetan bells that were strung along its handle. I wouldn't have looked up except that with the opening of the door a familiar scent was carried by the night air right up into my nostrils. I knew that scent. It was hair spray and self-tanner, mixed with Nair and glitter gel.

Sister Rose sauntered up to the counter, ordered a double shot of something that'd keep her awake all night, and came to sit across from me at the two-person table I was hogging.

I should've been embarrassed by my big stupid grin, but I wasn't. I only said, "Hey there, beautiful. Long time no see."

"Back at you, hot stuff." I was pleased to note that she was grinning, too, so at least I wasn't alone in my dorky delight. "I've been looking all over town for you."

"Really?"

"No, not really. I know you're back down on the Square someplace. I just hadn't pinned it down yet. Then I was walking home from work, and I saw you here in the window."

"Work?"

She cocked her head toward the door. *"Neighbors,"* she said, naming a drag bar a few blocks away. "I picked up a place over on First Hill—but, you know. Not the ghetto part. Thanks for the seed money, by the way."

I'd given Adrian fifty grand and a kiss on the cheek before we'd last parted company. "You're more than welcome."

The barista called out "Rose?" meaning that the double shot was ready. She left my company to pick it up and returned with a to-go cup. When she sat back down, she asked, "Any news on the mysterious Mr. Sykes?"

I filled her in on what I'd learned since then, mostly with risky legwork conducted through the vampire grapevine. "He was a high-ranking ghoul, so far as these things go, for the biggest House in San Diego. Apparently, all the money he made from selling his soul to the Department of Defense didn't make him happy. He figured out one day that he couldn't take it with him . . . so he fell in with the Castors. I don't know what he did to piss them off—nobody's talking, but I'm still digging—but it was enough for them to give him an overhaul the likes of which he'd never recover from."

"Yikes."

"Yeah. Somehow, he got away from them. I guess when you have more money than God"—I borrowed Bruner's phrase—"you can do things like that. Anyway, he heard about Project Bloodshot, and I guess he thought there was a chance he could learn from the research—maybe get some of his vision or hearing or whatever back. That's why he wanted the paperwork on Ian and your sister. Whatever experimentation had been conducted on them might help him fix his own problems. So he restarted the program, hiring everyone back in a civilian capacity; and then he went looking for the former participants, if any of them were still alive. It took him a while, but he eventually lured Ian out of hiding by using David Keene. Keene had been in on the program back at the beginning, but Ian had never been anywhere near him, so he wouldn't have known that. Ian thought he'd found someone who could help him. In fact, all he'd found was someone who was trying to help Jeffery Sykes."

Rose blew at the foam on top of her drink, and said, "Devious."

I sighed. "Rationally, I know we haven't seen the end of this yet, and we won't until I can track down Sykes and put a nail in his coffin for good. But he's going to be hard to find. I know this, because the Castors haven't found him yet—and they have damn fine resources at their disposal."

"You think maybe he'll lie low for a while? Since you kind of fucked up his plans?"

"*We* kind of fucked up his plans." I smiled evilly. "And to answer your question, for now he'll go quiet if he knows what's good for him. The tables have turned, my friend. It's his turn to hide from us."

"I hope you're right. I don't know about you, but I could use a break."

"Agreed. I don't need that kind of excitement anymore. I'm getting too old for all this action and adventure shit."

"Preach it," she said.

I lifted the cup of cooling java in a toast. "To boring lives of total anonymity."

"To boring lives," she echoed wryly. "Filled with bitch-techno, too-high heels, and hefty tips in a lady's thong."

I laughed and set the cup down. "Or to new friends, and pet people, and shiny new storehouses for hot goods."

She lifted an eyebrow so sharp it could've poked a hole in a tire. "Pet people? Oh yes. The kids."

"One big happy family." I sighed.

"And that's why you're out here alone, on a Saturday night? Reading the paper and surfing the 'Net for . . . what, porn?"

Of course. Always the porn. It has a way of finding me. "Yes, you've pretty much got it. Last I saw them, Domino had stomped off in a huff over some perceived insult on my part—"

"Merely perceived, I'm sure."

"—and Ian was arguing with Pepper over whether or not she

needed to submit to his tutoring process, since she refuses to go to school, and I just didn't feel like listening to it."

The other eyebrow came up. "Ian and the kids both? Under one roof? You're serious?"

"Seriously insane, I think. I'm trying to sort out a new condo . . . or maybe one of those cool old houses back around Nineteenth Street up on Capitol Hill. I don't know. But for now, it just made sense to keep everyone together. Just until . . ." I wasn't sure that there was an end point in mind, come to think of it.

Rose took a dainty sip and agreed, saying only, "Just until."

In my bag, my phone began to buzz.

"Hang on a second," I said, and fished it out. I saw the display and said, "Oh dear."

"Trouble back at the homestead?"

"Nope. Trouble in New York. It's Horace's area code, and he's no doubt in full-on diva mode. I can tell by the ring." The phone quit vibrating, then immediately began anew as Horace proved to be his permanently impatient self. I said, "If I don't answer this, he'll just keep calling all night."

"By all means," Rose said with a smile. "Momma's gotta pay the bills, after all."

"Shut up, you."

"Not likely."

"Hey, when I'm done with this asshole, you want to come back to the *homestead*—as you put it—and have a drink?"

She said, "If you hadn't offered, I would've had to stalk you."

"Stalking is such an ugly word," I said as I fidgeted with the phone. "Goddamn, he's going to tear me a new one. I totally missed that last case he wanted to give me, and he'll accuse me of blowing him off."

"Did you?"

"I was otherwise occupied at the time. As you may recall."

Out of desperation, I almost pressed the button to silence the ringer and leave us all in peace for the night, but upon the third cycle of ringing I changed my mind and pressed the green button instead.

"I'm here, Horace, and I humbly accept your recriminations." I felt like I was stepping into a confessional. "Forgive me, you filthy crook. It's been over three months since last we spoke, and I know that I missed that big job you wanted to foist upon me."

It shouldn't have surprised me when he said, "Oh, fuck that bitch. I pawned her off on someone else, and the whole thing turned out to be an orgy of disaster. Consider yourself lucky. You dodged a bullet on that one, and let's call the whole thing water under the bridge."

"Uh-oh."

"What's that supposed to mean?" he demanded.

"You've got something worse lined up, don't you?" I asked, leaning back in the seat and giving Rose a wink.

"Worse?" He drew out the word like a salesman. "Or more *interesting*? Okay, Ray-baby, check this shit out. You are going to *love* this one."

"God help me."

"Oh, my beloved princess of pilfering. I wouldn't count on it . . ."

I couldn't help but smile. Life was getting back to normal again . . . God help us *all*.

ABOUT THE AUTHOR

CHERIE PRIEST is the author of eight novels, including *Boneshaker*. *Boneshaker* was nominated for both the Hugo Award and the Nebula Award, and it won the Locus Award for Best Science Fiction Novel. Cherie's other books include *Four and Twenty Blackbirds, Fathom, Wings to the Kingdom,* and the Endeavour-nominated book *Not Flesh Nor Feathers* from Tor (Macmillan). Her short novels *Dreadful Skin, Clementine,* and *Those Who Went Remain There Still* are published by Subterranean Press. *Bloodshot* is her first book from Bantam. She lives in Seattle, Washington, with her husband and a fat black cat.